I0787976

legacy and LOVERS

Untouchable

Legacy and Lovers
Untouchable #11
Copyright © 2022 by Heather Long
Editing: Kira of Leavens Editing
Cover: Crimson Phoenix Designs

Legacy and Lovers/Heather Long – 1st ed.
ISBN-13- 978-1-956264-23-4

To every person who ever stressed me the fuck out
about needing a damn plan for the future.

Bite me.

Foreword

Dear Reader,

Welcome to book eleven , the penultimate book of the Untouchable series. I thought finishing book ten was a heady experience. Yet, here we are. You are holding in your hands the final "cliffhanger" as it were to the series. The next book will be the last.

With everything that has happened in these characters' lives, they have become so damn personal to me. They are my kids, my friends, the people across the street that I have to watch through the blinds in a totally non-creepy, non-stalkerish way because the drama is so delicious.

Saying goodbye will be hard.

I've been saying goodbye though since *Songs and Sweethearts.* I legit have no idea if I said that in the last book, but there was a moment when I was writing it that everything just—settled. When I added two books to the series, I knew I needed them and that the story needed those two extra books.

At the same time, I had to take a deep breath cause that was almost another quarter of a million words that had to be written. Despite life delays,

I savored, delighted, and thrilled to every single word you're about to read.

I had the absolute best time with this book. I love these characters. They will probably live rent-free in my head forever. Thank you so damn much for being on this journey with me. Thank you for loving them too.

Just thank you. Don't forget to check out the afterword, join my group, leave a review, and in general, just keep being awesome. We have one more book to go.

One more.

Whew.

Please be aware there is a content warning located at the bottom of the letter following the housekeeping notes. This is there so you can make the right decisions for you.

Without further ado, I'll cover that bit of housekeeping and then we'll dive in. See you on the flip side.

This is the eleventh book in a series. If you haven't read the first ten, I encourage you to pause here and go grab them. While there may be no specific happy endings at the end of each of these books, there will be one to the whole series, that I promise you. Some of these books will have cliffhangers, largely due to the size of the story, but the happy ending has to be earned as part of the journey.

xoxo

Heather

TW: Miscarriage, Grief

Chapter One

IT WAS ME AN YOU, SINCE WAY BACK WHEN

Frankie

It was a beautiful day to take the subway out to Queens. Well, it had started out a beautiful day. The rain rolled in like it had just been waiting for me to appreciate the cooler temperatures. Granted, we were only two weeks into the new semester and it was barely past Labor Day, but it had been positively chilly. With the sun shining, the temps would have been perfect.

The rain definitely made it dreary. Blegh. Then again, it had taken me three trains to get out to Flushing, where Coop was volunteering this week. They'd been short staffed, so he offered to work his weekly hours out here rather than in Manhattan at the Middle School Community Center, where he worked with grades six through eight kids. Something he adored.

Before walking down the steps, I pulled out the compact umbrella Jeremy had given me the first autumn we were in New York, two years prior. That seemed so long ago and like yesterday. Weird. I opened it when I stepped outside. The rain came down steadily, but at least it wasn't in sheets.

Could have been better, I was in sandals. But I ignored the water hitting my feet as I checked the directions on my phone. Two blocks. Yeah, that was doable. There were messages from Ian and Jake. They were heading to the gym, but they'd be home before dinner. Did I want to do movies tonight?

I liked that idea. So, I fired back a text that said sure and I'd let them know if Coop and I were going to be late. Archie didn't say anything, but it was a group text, which meant he and Coop could get caught up when they checked.

At Jake's dinner question, I sent back a shrug emoji. I was good with pretty much all food groups. He just responded with a thumbs up and a kiss. Ian was typing something but the phone rang before he finished. Hank's name flashed on the screen and I shoved the phone in my pocket before tapping the Bluetooth earpiece.

I was practically a professional, look at me with all the toys. "Hey Dad," I said as I answered and he huffed out a laugh.

"That is never not going to make me smile, Frankie," Hank told me and I grinned wider. Part of the reason I did it. It wasn't always easy to think of him as Dad. But my dad? Yeah, that was actually becoming very familiar.

"Good. What's up?"

"You sound like you're on the move."

"Cause I'm walking. But I have a few minutes before I get there." I wasn't exactly racing. Course, my toes were getting cold.

"I just called to check in. First couple of weeks of a new semester is always an adjustment."

"Spoken with all the experience of a professor."

"Exactly," he said with a chuckle, a knock echoed over the phone. "One sec." While he didn't mute the phone, it sounded like he lowered it. "Hey there, no," he said to someone I couldn't hear as more than a mumble.

"Office hours are nine to twelve on Tuesdays and Thursdays. Two to Four on Mondays and Wednesdays."

It was a Friday.

"Not a problem, send me an email and if I have time, I'll look at it over the weekend. Right then." The door closed and he was back on the phone. "Sorry about that. Like I said, first couple of weeks take some adjusting."

"Aww, and you were just the big bad professor telling that kid they had to follow the rules. Where's the rebel in you?"

His laughter just made me grin wider. "The rebel has a mortgage, four kids, one of which is *in* college. No time for shenanigans."

"The way I hear it, shenanigans are the best."

"But the way you do it?"

"Yeah, yeah. You forget, I'm almost a bona fide rock star."

"I forget nothing," he said as if suddenly doing a bad Monty Python impression. "You are also a bona fide student." His accent dropped and there was a squeak of a chair. "So, give it to me straight, kiddo. How are you doing?"

The rain seemed to be lightening up thankfully, and I had half a block to go. "I'm good," I said. "Really good. I like my classes. It's a heavy load, but I'm okay with it. A couple of the classes are independent study, so other than checking in with my advisor and the teachers, I don't have to add more physical in class time. That leaves me with time to do the rest."

"Still interning with Standish?"

"Sorta? I mean, Eddie has been pretty great about keeping the position open with no time requirements, but it's more like we get together at the offices every couple of weeks, we have lunch, then I spend about half the day shadowing him while he gives me an overview of the business."

"You're enjoying it." It wasn't a question.

"Yeah, I am. It's weird. I never really knew him before—mostly because I didn't want to—and now?" I shrugged. Hank would get it. He and Eddie had been building a friendship of their own over the last year and a half.

Year and a half.

It kind of sucker punched me. Almost eighteen months since Maddy died. All the air whooshed out of me.

"Dad, I'm here, so I have to let you go." Thankfully, my voice didn't waiver. "I'll call on Sunday?"

"Sounds good, love you."

"Love you." He hung up which saved me the trouble of doing it. I could see the community center's front doors but I slowed and stepped out of the middle of the sidewalk. It had actually been fairly light foot traffic from the subway to here, but there were more people around and it was getting closer to four, so people would be heading home from work and school.

I needed a moment. Just one.

Breathe. It was easier said than done sometimes, but it was an important reminder. Stop. Take a breath. It was okay to feel the grief and the pain, even the surprise that it had been so long. The first anniversary had been on my past birthday. The two year anniversary was my next. Thanks for that Maddy. Still... it was okay to feel the way I felt. I was okay.

The world didn't stop turning and I didn't fall apart. Ever since that breakdown in Los Angeles, I had worked really hard to not bottle it all up again. It wasn't always easy. But when it got too difficult, I could and *did* ask for help.

Another breath, then the tight fist in my chest began to uncurl. A quick glance around said, no one was staring at me and I hadn't had some kind of freakout on the street. Go me! I pressed on through the still drizzling rain. I made it just in time for the door to open and I caught it and stepped back to let out a pair of kids and their father.

Well, I guess he was their dad. They nodded their thanks. Snapping the umbrella closed, I shook it off then went inside. A receptionist looked up from the desk, but she was talking on the phone and held up a finger.

I nodded as she continued her conversation and walked over to look at the cork board. There were all kinds of local announcements, including one about a band playing in a local park, some advertised needing a roommate while others offered handyman services and more. There were even some offering babysitting, tutoring, and a drama class.

Ian used to teach music to kids. He hadn't had as much time this year. Maybe I should ask him if it was something he wanted to get back into doing.

"Thank you for waiting," the woman said and I turned to find her looking at me expectantly. "How can I help you?"

"I'm here to pick up Coop Brennen," I told her. "If he's not done yet, I can wait."

She smiled. "I'll call back and let him know you're here. They should be wrapping up for the day if they haven't already."

"Thank you."

I stepped back and left her to work as I went back to skimming the board. A beep in my ear, accompanied by my phone vibrating in my pocket, had me tugging it out to read. Archie sent a message. Not to the group chat. Just to me.

I made a face.

The workshop was in Brooklyn, it would mean more trains, or I could just call for a car. Whatever he needed. I almost didn't add the last part because I didn't want to smother him. But he'd fallen asleep at the workshop twice the week before.

I got it. He needed space and he was working through things. I understood that. But I also needed him to take care of himself or let me do it.

Okay, so I was definitely smothering him. Dammit.

The kiss emoji made me smile. I sent one back.

"Miss?" The woman at the desk called me and I glanced back at her. "Mr. Brennen just called up. He said it would be ten more minutes."

"Thank you."

She nodded and I settled into a chair to wait. More to get out of the way of the parents coming in. They would talk to the lady at the desk, she called someone, and a few minutes later a kid would come out with their backpack. Their expressions often turned warm and smiling as they greeted their parent, or a grandparent as it was in one case.

It was kind of sweet. God, they looked so young. Coop was working with mostly middle schoolers. In Texas, that had been fifth and sixth grade for us. Seventh and eighth had been junior high. So what age was it here?

Fifth grade?

When did fifth grade look so far away?

Weird.

About a dozen kids were picked up before a familiar sandy blond head appeared in the open doorway. He wasn't looking out here, but talking to someone inside before he smiled at them, waved, and then headed out. I stood up as he crossed the room in three easy strides, grinning.

"Beautiful, you are a sight for sore eyes." The simple joy in his voice lifted the tired some, but there was no mistaking the tired. Even with his smile, there was a tension around his eyes. When he dipped his head, I gave into the impulse and just wrapped my arms around him. The brush of his lips to mine was gentle, there and gone again before he squeezed me tight.

Yeah, he was tired and very happy to see me.

"You really didn't have to come all this way to take three trains back with me."

"Yes, I did," I told him as I leaned back. More parents were coming in, so I clasped Coop's hand and he tugged me to him again as we headed to the door. My feet were still damp, but I'd kind of forgotten all about that. It had started raining again, so I reopened the umbrella and Coop let out a laugh.

Like me, he had on a backpack, so he just took the umbrella and wrapped an arm around my shoulders as we began the walk to the subway. When he swung his foot out a little to walk goofily, I matched him without even thinking about it. He chuckled and when we approached a puddle, we both jumped it.

More than one person hurrying past gave us a brief look, but that was another fun thing about New York. You wanted to be a little crazy, most people didn't notice.

"I'm glad you came," Coop admitted when we got to the steps leading down and I grinned up at him.

"I know." I'd missed him too. He'd been out here all week long which meant leaving earlier, coming home later and he had one evening class this semester. No way around it, not with the work he'd been doing. So, Tuesdays and Thursdays he got home *really* late.

Once on the train and squished together in a seat, he bumped my shoulder. "Okay, why did you come all the way out here to ride home with me?"

"Can't I just have missed you?"

"You could," he said. "I mean, I missed you. But seriously, what's up? You doing okay? I know I've been kind of absent this week. Everything is still good with your classes…" Actual worry crept into his voice and I squeezed his hand. Just the act of holding it had already made me feel a thousand percent better.

"I'm fine," I promised. "Really. Classes are great. I spent the day with Eddie yesterday after my morning classes. That was fine. I just—missed you, so I decided to come out and ride home with you because it gives me a whole extra hour. And—it's kind of cool to see you at work. You're so serious."

He snorted softly but some of the tension eased out of him.

"So, my turn," I continued. "What's up with you? You good?" I wasn't going to point out how tightly he'd hugged me or the fact that he was gripping my hand with equal force.

"I'm good," he said. At my raised eyebrows, he crossed his heart with his free hand. "Promise, Beautiful. I am. Not going to lie, this week was a little packed. They needed me more hours here than when I'm at the Laymont Center and you add the commute and new classes…"

"And you're tired. You didn't come to bed last night." Coop had more or less moved into my room after Rachel moved in with us the summer before last, but even after she moved back out this June, he hadn't really gone back to his room. So, the guys all made accommodations for that. When Jake and I went to bed, there was no Coop, and when I woke up, also no Coop.

He winced. "Crap, sorry, I hoped you wouldn't notice."

"Right. Clearly, I'm not observant enough to realize when you're not there so that's an excellent idea to hope that." I wasn't annoyed, but the idea I *wouldn't* notice his absence grated just a little. So, a little scold never hurt anyone.

Another grimace. "Fair point, bad choice of phrasing. I was hoping you'd just think I woke up before you and now that I think about that—I get why that's a terrible plan. I'd never leave a bed with you in it." He grinned.

It was funny because it was true.

"Exactly. So, promise me everything is all right and I'll get off your ass about it."

"You don't have to ever get off my ass," Coop said, his voice dipping a little. "In fact, I rather prefer having you chastise me when I've been bad and smack me around when I deserve it. I know you do it because you love me."

"I do love you."

"See…"

"And you're changing the subject. A lot. If you don't want to talk about it, you can just say that, you know." Three years of regular therapy seemed to be working out for me at this point. "I just wanted to make sure you were okay and if you weren't, then to do what I could to help."

He dipped his chin and his smile softened a little before it faded away. "I promise, Beautiful. I'm okay. It's really just me being tired."

"Okay."

"And Trina's been blowing up my phone this week."

Ahh. She was gonna be seventeen on her next birthday. She was a junior in high school. That was a lot.

She was also dating, but so far no sex and I was under sister swears to not say a word. Though the one time she had thought about it over the summer, she'd called me. Called me while *she* was at a party because the boy she'd been dating then had wandering hands.

It took no time to get her in an Uber and out of there. She'd let the guy drive her and then she was second guessing herself for taking off, but when she said, "I was just uncomfortable with the whole thing. There was a lot of alcohol and he was being really, really affectionate…"

"Trina," I interrupted her. "You made the right choice for you. Nothing else matters. You said it yourself, you were uncomfortable."

"Don't tell Coop…please? You know he'll just want to beat him up and really, that's done. I don't think he and I are gonna be going out anymore."

I didn't like lying to Coop. But, if he didn't ask me directly, then I wouldn't tell him. "Unless," I'd said very clearly. "I think he needs to know. If and when that happens, I will tell him. Understood?"

"You're the best Frankie."

Right.

"Is she okay?"

"She's fine, she's Trina." He shook his head. "She's just freaking out cause Mom went on a date."

Carly had a date? My eyes widened. "Really?"

He frowned. "Okay, don't get all excited. You did that about Trina and I still think her dating before thirty is a bad idea."

I rolled my eyes. "What's your excuse for your mom?" Cause she was definitely over thirty.

"She's my mom, it's excuse enough." He sounded positively grumpy and it just filled in all the missing pieces. His distraction this week, the tired, and even the overcompensating with school and volunteering out here.

"Well, would you like me to call her for some girl talk and see what I can find out about the potential walking dead man who wants to date your mom?"

He considered me for a moment then nodded. "I would like that very much. I need to know what I'm working with and if I need to fly back, and if Jake needs to go with me."

I did not roll my eyes. "Coop?"

"Don't say it."

I sighed.

"Fine, I won't beat the guy up." But I could see his crossed fingers and I didn't miss the "yet" he mouthed. I chuckled and leaned my head on his shoulder. It would be fine.

"I'll talk to her."

"Thank you, Beautiful."

"Someone should be happy for her. I think it's great."

He made a noncommittal grunting noise and it literally took everything I had not to giggle. Surly Coop was adorable.

"You didn't have a problem with Alicia dating."

He snorted. "She's dating Klara, and Jake's dad. You know, the guy she used to be married to."

"So, you wouldn't mind if your mom dated your dad again?" Talk about baiting a bear.

"Okay, so this guy has one point in his favor." Grudging admission or not, it was a point. I squeezed his hand and smiled. Coop kissed the top of my head.

"Feel better?"

"Yes, I do." The smile was back in his voice. "Thank you, Beautiful."

I grinned, then my stomach grumbled. Loudly.

It sounded like an alien on the hunt. I had to bite my lip to keep my laughter contained.

"The train needs to go faster, before we all start looking like steaks."

I snort-laughed and Coop started laughing. Then the giggles struck. We made it home, but we were soaking wet from splashing in the puddles and laughing all the way.

Worth it.

Chapter Two
MY BABY GIRL AND ME

Jake

Cutting across the ice, I slapped the puck away from the offense. Clearing the puck from our goal, I raced with it toward our opponent's net. The pre-season game was all about warming up, getting us back into the swing before we actively began competing.

Pivoting on my skates as their forward came for me and the puck, I sent the disc toward my right winger and he swept it away before serving it to the left winger. The cold of the rink burned my cheeks. Sucking in a breath as I shot into pursuit, I was right where I needed to be when the puck was free. I snagged it before the opposing team could and with a slice, sent it right into the net.

Yes!

Exhilaration flooded me as the others laughed. Even our opponents grinned. We were already moving to set up for the next play. I should have taken up hockey a whole lot sooner. I'd always enjoyed watching the game, but being back in Texas made finding a rec league a little harder, at least for my age group.

I was never going pro. Hell, I'd played a damn good game of football and I had zero intention of going pro there. It was about playing the game. I fucking loved pitting myself against others. Skill, endurance, and physicality—I loved it all. Taking this up last year had saved my fucking mind, particularly when Frankie and Bubba were on the road. It helped keep my temper in check and my focus on where I was.

Speaking of my heart and soul, I cut my gaze over to where she sat, all bundled up and sipping her coffee. She caught me looking and grinned. It was September and decentish outside, she did not need a heavy coat or woolen hat out there.

It was considerably cooler in the rink.

She also looked adorable.

She looked…

"Benton." The snap of my name yanked my attention back to the game and I chuckled as I moved to face off with the other team's forward. Randy Smith was about ten years older than me, with a wife and three kids. He grinned. Apparently, the ref wasn't the only one who caught my distraction.

Whatever.

Frankie loved me. She was watching me play a practice game, hanging out to spend time with me after, and we were all doing pretty goddamn well after a tumultuous few years.

I didn't care who noticed I was crazy for my girl.

Probably better for them that they did.

Though, I had to admit, I hadn't slugged someone for her lately.

Might need to work on that.

The puck hit the ice between us, then the whistle and we were off.

Ninety minutes later, I waved to Derek and Jenson as they followed me out. They'd invited us to get drinks with them and maybe grab dinner.

Great offer, but I wanted to spend time alone with Frankie. Next time, I suggested, and they called out greetings to Frankie who grinned at them as they passed her.

Her attention, however, did not stay on them but on me. The coffee cup she'd had earlier was nowhere in evidence. "Have fun?" she asked all the while wrapping her arms around my neck. I dipped my head and kissed that beautiful mouth with its beautiful smile. It wasn't an especially deep or lingering kiss, but more of a tease and a reminder.

Mine. I got to kiss her whenever the hell I wanted.

Life was good.

"I did," I said, hooking my arm around her shoulders. "Did you bring a backpack?" We'd come separately. She'd come up after class, so she'd missed about fifteen minutes of the practice.

"Yep, let me grab it." She gave me a quick side squeeze and darted up the steps to where her stuff waited. A flush pinkened her cheeks when I followed and snagged one of her books for her as she repacked.

"How much homework did you get done?" I was only half-teasing. Frankie taking a two hour chunk out of her day to come and watch me practice couldn't be high on her list of priorities, but she made time for me often and not just to come to our various games.

"Most of the assignments I have due this week." Her grin in no way diminished the flush to her cheeks or the fact she wrinkled her nose at me. "You know me."

"I do, Baby Girl," I commented before snagging her now closed backpack and slinging it on. I had my duffel in one hand. We stored most of our equipment with the manager, but I took my skates with me. I liked looking after my blades myself.

Once we were outside, she stripped off the jacket and the hat, before running her fingers through the wild mass of hair. At one point over the summer, in a fit of pique, she'd actually said she wanted to cut it off, because it had gotten so long. Talk about a red flag in front of a bull, we all began a campaign to prevent the cutting of her hair.

Then she went one afternoon with Rachel and her message had only said they were stopping off somewhere to get their hair done. I'd spent my whole afternoon bracing myself for what it would look like when she got back. Frankie would always be beautiful, but I also fucking loved her hair. I loved how it would spill over me like a curtain when she rode me.

I loved how it spread over the pillows when she slept. I loved how it felt when I fisted it, whether I was just kissing her or fucking her into the mattress. I just fucking loved her hair. Braiding it, brushing it, helping her wash it. Everything we could do with her hair, I loved it.

Archie had looked kind of ill and Coop said it would be fine. Did he *not* remember when she cut her hair at the beginning of junior high? Seriously? Bubba was the only one who didn't seem to be struggling with a reaction. Then again, maybe she'd discussed it with him? No matter how braced I'd been for it, when she came up the stairs after arriving home, the air had whooshed out of me.

She still had all her beautiful hair. Coop summed it up when he peered at her. "What happened to the haircut, or does that mean something different to you than it does to us?"

Laughter filled her eyes. "I was this close…" She held her thumb and forefinger together. "But then I remembered junior high." But the twitching of her lips gave her away. "That, and I did have them take off a full inch, it's much better behaved now."

Brat.

Archie cracked first. Then Coop, but I caught Bubba's half-hidden smirk and when he saw me looking at him, he just shrugged. Yeah, he'd known. Then he watched us all turn ourselves inside out.

Dick.

Though admittedly, it was kind of funny.

"Subway or want me to call a car?" Frankie asked as we paused while she pulled her hair back up into a scrunchie so the wind wouldn't whip it everywhere. She did it without losing hold of her jacket, which she'd tucked under her arm.

I scanned the skies. It was partly cloudy, but no rain. It wasn't late, but it was after seven and the sun had gone down. "How much of a hurry are you in to get home?"

"No big hurry," she answered, giving me a curious look before folding the jacket over her arm. I could stuff it in my bag with my gear, but she tended to not like it when we got our sweaty man smell on her clothes. On her was fine, not her clothes. "What's up?"

"Feel like a spontaneous date?"

Her smile was all the answer I needed. "It has been a while, hasn't it?"

"Yeah, but we've both had a lot going on. Your family. Mine. The guys." The last equaled out to our family.

"He's working at the shop late again." I didn't have to ask who, wrapping an arm around her, I headed away from the rink. There was a nice little Irish pub a couple of blocks down and while we weren't old enough—yet—to order the alcohol, they actually had good food on the menu. "Has he said anything to you?"

"No, Baby Girl, I think he's still trying to work through what it all means to him. I don't have to tell you how close they were."

"No," she agreed, leaning into me as I guided her down the sidewalk. We kept to our side of it and when anyone got too close to her, they got a look until they moved the hell away. Most people, though, were in a hurry to get where they were going and ignored us.

I preferred it that way.

"I'm worried about him," she admitted and I pressed a kiss to the top of her hair. Yeah, I knew that too. "I want to be there for him, like you guys were for me. But it's like he just—pulls away more and more and he's isolating himself at the shop."

True. "He's throwing himself into the projects we've got going. A part of him is just—putting all his energy there right now." Not that I didn't see her point. "You want me to kick his ass for you?"

Her snort of laughter and the not-so-gentle elbow she jabbed into my side made me grin. While not fully distracted, she wasn't quite so pensive. "No, I don't want you to kick his ass for me."

"Damn," I said, exaggerating it a little. "Been a while since I got to kick someone's ass for you."

"Oh please." She rolled her eyes. "I'm glad you haven't had to get in any fights for me."

"Well, yeah, it means guys aren't being stupid at you. That's a win." I was a big enough guy, I could admit that. "But at the same time, it means I don't get to take my aggression out on idiots."

The sound of her amusement was a magical thing. "It could also be that I'm getting better at looking after myself."

"Accepted," I teased. "Have I mentioned how sexy it is that you're a little bad ass?" Opening the door to the pub for her, I added, "Or how hard I get just remembering the sweet ways you've learned to break a hand?"

Giggling, she shook her head. "Not recently, no, but I'm liking the sound of this."

"Good."

The place was busy, but not packed. We were seated in a booth in no time. Frankie's stomach was already growling so stopping for food was a good plan.

"Did you text the guys?" I asked her as I skimmed over the menu.

"Shit." She wiggled in the seat and then pulled her phone out of her pocket. "I was thinking about it before you stole me away for a date."

"Stole?" I slid a glance at her sideways and she grinned at me. "Yeah, I can live with that."

"I thought so."

Frankie typed out a quick message into our group chat. She hit send. Bubba and Coop responded pretty quickly. Archie was a beat behind them. My phone buzzed with their messages to the group chat. Then a few extra pings that were probably varying levels of a middle finger and giving me shit. Those could wait.

"And done," she said, before taking a sip of her soda. "We've eaten here before, right?" She glanced around the Tipperary Inn. "I feel like we've been here before."

"Similar place, but over in the village. We went there last February. I think it was last February." It was another Irish place and they'd had an open mic night. While it hadn't been Valentine's Day specifically, we'd gone ahead and celebrated it.

"Oh, that's right." When she glanced around, I chuckled.

"They do live bands on the weekend, Baby Girl, no karaoke."

"Damn." Her mock disappointment, and snapped fingers amused me, then she settled back and leaned into me as I slid an arm around her. "Guess you're stuck just talking to me."

"Oh, whatever will I do," I teased. "Oh, wait, we have our phones, we can watch YouTube."

I was braced for the elbow this time. After the waitress took our order, she tilted her head back to study me.

"What?"

"Nothing, just—I like being here with you. This is nice."

"This is nice," I agreed. When I dipped my head to kiss her, she sighed at the first brush of my lips. The first stroke of my tongue had her lips parting and then I sank into the kiss. Frankie kissed with everything she had. The guys gave us shit about being noisy kissers sometimes, but fuck them. The whole world could listen to us for all I cared.

As much as I wanted to stay there, teasing her tongue and losing myself in her taste, I had to lift my head. My dick was already all in, but we couldn't do anything about it—right here.

"Tell me about your classes, I know you said over the weekend, you liked *most* of them." I hadn't missed that part.

She wrinkled her nose. "They're not bad. I don't like that you guys are in *none* of them this semester." Then again, we were juniors and most of our general education credits were done. "That said, I kind of like some of the classes more than others. Mostly, I think it's the teachers that I like. The professor in International Economics is *killing* me."

Snoring, she dropped her chin and I chuckled. "That bad? You could have swapped or dropped. I mean, there's still time to withdraw."

"No," she said with a grimace. "I'll manage. I just—the reading is interesting. But when he lectures, he drones on and on. I swear it's a test in torture. If you can stay awake while he's talking, you might actually get something out of the class."

I curled a lock of her hair around my finger and gave it a gentle tug. She tilted her head back to look up at me. "You really doing okay with the class load?" Instead of taking May off, she'd taken two May-mester classes to make up for the lighter course load the fall before. Then two summer classes, albeit one had been distance learning, so she could work on it during our June away.

Not that we'd gone too far in June this time. It had still just been the five of us and we'd gone hiking, escaping civilization to visit national parks from Rocky Mountain National Park in Colorado to the Cascades National Park in Washington. Different from previous summers, it had also been quieter and just given us a lot of time together.

Frankie didn't want to graduate behind us so, she'd been making up her extra credits. She had also engaged in full on overachiever mode. She didn't need all the credits she'd been taking. They made her happy though, so we didn't argue—much.

"I'm good," she promised me. "It always takes me a couple of weeks to kind of balance it out. This is the first time in like—ever—that I have *none* of you in my classes. Not even Rachel. It's a little weird."

"Just means we need to make the most of our time in between and around classes. We've got an hour between one of my classes and yours. Plenty of time to do a quickie in a study room if we time it right."

The fact she didn't snort her drink out of her nose almost disappointed me. I liked being able to tease her right up to the edge. Still, the flash of her grin and the playful gleam in her eyes was a far more desirable result.

"Tempting."

Well, all right then. "Tempting enough to give it a shot tomorrow?"

"We don't have classes tomorrow."

"Well, then we can hook up in my room for practice."

"Sounds like a date to me," she teased.

It did, didn't it?

All told, we didn't linger in the pub long after dinner. It was just nice to be the two of us, hanging out, and talking—about everything. Twice we circled back to the guys and plans. She was worried about Archie and Coop. Yep, I knew that. Me and Bubba were both doing okay, or at least she thought so. Then she studied me as I was paying for the meal. I swore, I could almost feel her trying to check if I was holding anything back that she needed to worry about.

"We're fine," I insisted. "Totally fine. I'm not even worried about Mom and Dad dating anymore."

At her raised eyebrows, I shrugged. Once I signed the credit card receipt, I tucked the rest back into the little book and then stood to gather our things.

"I *was* worried," I reminded her. "As I recall, you told me it was cute and that Mom was more than old enough to make her own decisions."

"Hmm-hmm." Frankie followed me out the door and I checked my phone. We could take the subway, but I'd rather enjoy the kind of sleepy satisfaction that came from a good meal.

"They're also taking their time. Dad's terminal leave is finished and he's officially out. Klara's got another three months?" I thought that was right. "And then they've all been discussing where they want to go. The girls are both thrilled and annoyed."

The car was five minutes away, so we found a spot near the restaurant but out of the way to wait. Frankie perched on the bench and I dropped down to sit next to her.

"The girls don't want to switch schools. I can't imagine Blake's thrilled at the idea of moving right before her senior year."

We shared a grimace at that. Cause, no, that would not have been ideal. "It was one thing when we did it all the time—you know, we moved where the military sent us. But the girls have had a lot more stability the last few years."

"So, maybe your dad and Klara move to Texas, they settle there at least until the girls are done with school—that's only four more years until Louisa graduates right?" She was a freshman this year. Blake a junior and Becca a sophomore.

Fuck, they were all probably dating. The soft touch of her hand on my arm pulled me back to the present.

"Stop plotting the deaths of boys you haven't even met," she advised and I made a face.

"Fine, maybe that would be a good reason for them to move. Break up all those potential boy crushes." It seemed like a fine goal.

"Would it have stopped us?" At her question, I scowled. "As I recall, I promised you I would have found you, whether you came back to school or not."

"Stop using your logic on me. That's you and me. The girls never need to date. Or at least, they shouldn't date high school boys."

"'Cause college boys are so much more experienced." The dry tone killed me.

"Sometimes… you're a brat."

She laughed. "Well, that's better than all the time. Come on big boy, we can plan your parents' lives for them some more on the way home."

I groaned. Even though she'd teased me, we didn't talk about that. We talked about my flight lessons. I needed a few more aviation hours to qualify for my full pilot's license. Frankie wanted to go up with me, and I promised

I would take her—eventually. When I was certain it would be safe for her.

The car was a good idea. It only took about twenty-five minutes to make it through traffic and back to the brownstone. We'd have been on the subway forty minutes or more. It was also later, so traffic wasn't as heavy.

Not-So-Little Miss Abigail greeted us as soon as we came in the door. She was all wiggling body and thumping tail. Damn thing was a threat to life and limb. The number of times she'd nailed me or one of the guys in the nuts in the last three months had stopped being funny. Now, I shielded my nuts when she came to greet us so enthusiastically.

"Hello, beautiful girl," Frankie crooned as she went to her knees and got a face full of slobbery kisses. Abby had gotten a lot bigger the last few months and she wasn't even full grown yet.

"Sit," Jeremy commanded from the hall as he approached and Abigail sat immediately. "Manners always, Miss Abigail." Then he glanced at us. "Miss Frankie, we've had this discussion."

Yes, he wanted Abby to sit before we greeted her so she could be calmer about it.

"I know, Jeremy," Frankie said, not a bit contrite. "But look at her face! How can I not give her hugs and get kisses?"

He gave her a patient look. "I didn't say you couldn't give her hugs and kisses. She has to sit first, she needs to show her manners, then you may shower her with all the affection you want."

I had to hide my own smile as Jeremy took Frankie's jacket from where it had fallen while she was greeting Abigail.

"Fine," Frankie said, then looked at the enthusiastic pup who was still sitting there good as gold, tail thumping. "Look at you, pretty girl, sitting all good. Come here and get hugs."

I didn't laugh.

I swear. But Jeremy almost rolled his eyes. Pretty sure he would have if he hadn't caught me looking. As it was, he shut me up with a haughty look. Yeah, he had about as much luck telling Frankie no as we did.

Chapter Three

SEXUAL HEALING

Frankie

"You think I'm kidding," Rachel said as she swapped lenses on her camera. The breeze had picked up, making me glad I'd braided my hair before setting off to meet her in the park. "My brain turned to sewage. Absolute pure sewage." Irritation rifled every single word she released, but she never slowed a step in getting the camera put together and then checking the light meter laying on the blanket we'd spread out when we got here. "She was so radioactively dumb, that—you know that thing in Altered States where he gets into the sensory deprivation chamber and he reverts to an earlier form of mankind? Like three generations back?"

I raised my eyebrows. "Um—yeah?" I didn't want to laugh even if my lips twitched violently and my face had to be going through any number of contortions to keep the laughter inside.

"*That* was how I felt," Rachel finished, lifting her camera to focus on me. She fiddled with the lens, then snapped a couple of images. On the third snap, however, I lifted my middle finger and her lips curved. "Perfect." Then lowering the camera, she said on a long, long sigh. "I mean it, I felt like I'd reverted three evolutionary leaps by the time the date was over. I was walking on all fours."

"Could it have been a fluke?"

The scoff she released made me snicker. I raised both my palms as she glared at me. The problem with that glare was the laughter in her eyes. She had trouble containing her amusement and the facial contortions proved it

"So, gonna go out on a limb here and say you won't be swinging for a second date?" I couldn't help it. Her groan segued into a laugh and she shook her head.

"I hate you."

"No, you don't."

"I could," she argued but she was still laughing as she pulled a notebook over to her and flipped the binder open.

"Maybe before the date," I suggested. "Hating someone takes a lot of energy and mental effort."

Yes, she flipped me off. "You want to know the truly sad part?" She asked, settling on her knees with her camera in her lap. "She was gorgeous. Absolutely gorgeous. And I couldn't even bring myself to appreciate it."

I gave up on trying to contain my laughter. She sounded so damn forlorn. "Poor Rachel," I gasped. "You can't even go for the meaningless one-night stand anymore."

"Yes, poor me!" Scowling through her laughter took talent, but Rachel somehow managed. "Ugh, I don't know why I tell you anything."

"You know, you don't tell me much—" Then I reached over and pinched her leg and she made a face. "So, you just have to live with my reactions to what you do share with me."

She stuck her tongue out at me, then glanced at her binder before picking up her camera. "Maybe this is why I don't tell you."

"Nah." I didn't believe that. "You never talk about the stuff that really scares you. Just the stuff you know I'll laugh about, and the stuff that you can twist to make it super funny so I don't look too closely at why it might be sad."

That hit a little too close to home and her smile faded. "I'm not lying to you."

"Never said you were." Never would either. "Just sometimes, I don't know if it's better for you to let you get away with the little fibs here and there or if I should push you harder."

It wasn't a question, precisely. There were a lot of areas where Rachel and I let each other get away with things. That said, not a shadow of a doubt existed within me that if I needed her, she would be there. She had been, over and over. I wanted her to understand the same was true for me.

"You can push," Rachel said after a minute. "I'll probably push back though."

That was the point. "I care."

"I know you do," she said, glancing down at her camera and not at me. "I keep saying I'm going to swear off dating, then…"

I waited her out.

"Then *he* comes over and it's like, we're horny teenagers." The sheer misery in her expression jerked at my heart.

"Do I need to kick his ass?" Cause I would. If I couldn't, Jake would.

Pretty sure I could do it though.

"No." A faint smile reappeared as if she were considering it, but then she met my gaze with a little more directness in her eyes. "No. I'm a grown ass woman, I can tell him to fuck off on my own."

"Then why didn't you?"

Rachel made another face. "He's terrible for me."

"Not from what I've seen," I said, keeping my gaze on her. "You like him."

"Except, I don't." The response came out more a snapped correction than anything else. Something more than anger inhabited those words. "I really don't. He's arrogant. He hears what he wants to hear. He's pushy as hell. And he damn well knows exactly how attractive he is. Smart. Fuck me, he's so damn smart, I swear, he is undercutting or destroying my arguments before I can even think them through."

She practically panted at the end of that, a flush in her cheeks and her eyes sparking with real fire. That was a lot of words for not being crazy about someone. With visible restraint, she got her breathing under control.

Finally, she said, "I don't want to talk about him anymore."

"Okay."

"I know you want what's best for me and I know if I need you, you'll be there."

Without hesitation or doubt. "Any damn time."

Opening her eyes, she glanced at me. "I'm going to be alright."

"I know you are. You're gonna be better than that. You're going to be amazing. Because you already are."

"Compliments will get you everywhere. Sadly, we're in public and the last time I checked, you weren't an exhibitionist."

I wasn't? Lips pursed, I considered my response to that. Technically, she was right. But technically, I also enjoyed some—we could be caught activities—so was that exhibitionist or not?

Rachel jerked her whole attention to me. "Oh, you've been holding out on me."

I chuckled. "Tit for tat," I answered, then raised my middle finger when she made a face. "Now, what are we doing for your assignment today? Am I here to be the subject, the helper, or just your partner-in-crime?"

"Why not all three?"

What she needed, it turned out, was both a model and a helper. "Want to do a series of shots. Some posed. Some organic. Also, you ever see those articles about photographers getting strangers to take photographs together?"

"Yeah," I answered slowly. "You want me to get strangers to take pictures with me?"

"Maybe, we'll see how organic it is. So we can start here, eat and I'll do some shots, then we'll pack up and roam around the park. Sound good?"

"You've got me all day." Rachel had asked for the time. "And I even brought a change of clothes." I motioned to my bag. This wasn't the first time Rachel asked me to pose for her. She'd done plenty of shots for me too. We'd even talked about the idea that if Ian and I ever did another album, Rachel would take the album cover shots for us.

If we did another album.

That was later Frankie's problem. Ian and I had a lot of juggling to do before we did another album.

"Yes," Rachel said, twirling an imaginary mustache. "Kick back and relax, it's just another day in the park…"

Some posed and natural, got it. I was no one's model, but I could do this with Rachel. Even if I felt absolutely ridiculous. Course, she almost loved any shot where I made a face at her. She even had one of me sticking my tongue out framed at her place.

I looked like such a dork in it, but she loved the picture. Coop had a similar one on his phone. Love me, love my weirdness I guessed.

We ended up giving Rachel's shots with a stranger a chance. We roamed around the park, approaching various people from a mounted police officer, to another NYU student cutting through the park on her way somewhere, to a pair of mothers with their kids, to a sociology professor—of all things—who seemed intrigued by the prospect.

All Rachel asked me to do was talk to them while she took the pictures. I had to admit, it was kind of fun. One of the guys we ended up approaching was actually trying to plan how he was going to propose to his guy. It was so sweet. When he asked me about it, I told him the truth—simple and straightforward was better. Yes, it was a memory, but it should be about the person you're proposing to and not some huge splashy thing—unless of course they were into that.

Another woman we found was feeding ducks and I sat with her on the bench. She was in her eighties and she'd been coming to Central Park once a day to feed the ducks since she was five years old and she would steal the crusts from the bakery where her mother worked. It was like a fascinating look back in time.

I could have sat there for hours. Rachel had no qualms about approaching people. Even those who gave us the brush off or refused, it didn't slow her down. We were almost to the edge of the park and there was a street vendor selling hot pretzels. My stomach growled.

"Starving," I told Rachel. She could follow or not. She had a bag with most of our stuff, but I also had a backpack with a couple of things in it. I had to wait in line, the guy in front of me shot a look toward Rachel who was snapping pictures. "She's working on a project," I told him.

"Yeah?"

"Yep. Don't mind her. If you don't want your picture taken, I can tell her to just get rid of those shots."

The guy chuckled and shook his head. "No, it's fine. I'm Patrick, by the way." He offered his hand and I shook it. I'd talked to so many different strangers it was almost becoming natural at this point.

"Frankie," I said.

"Is the project to take pictures of you too?"

I laughed. "Some of them, yep."

Patrick nodded, shifting so we were standing more together than one after another in the line. "What do you do?"

"Student at NYU. You?"

"Nothing quite so interesting. Starving artist."

"Hey," I said, motioning to the cart. "Me too."

At that, he laughed. "Fair enough. I actually work for my uncle two or three times a week. He does construction and local repairs and makeovers for places. If he has a lot of painting, he has me come in and do it."

That was kind of cool.

"So that's what you do? You're a painter?"

"Yes and no?" He gave a shrug. "I like working with a lot of different mediums. Wish they all paid the bills, but I like what I do so I'll keep doing it."

"That's cool. I've never been good with painting or pictures—that's Rachel's thing. She's got an amazing eye."

He glanced over at her then back at me. "I can see that. I mean, she picked you as her subject."

I laughed. "I'm a friend. I'm also free and available."

"Really?"

"No," Rachel said abruptly as she joined us. "She's not remotely available, Patrick. She's got a full dance card, so no flirting."

"Rachel, he wasn't—"

"He was," Rachel retorted and Patrick actually flushed.

"She's right. I was." He raised his hands. "Sorry. Didn't mean to presume anything. Didn't know you ladies were together."

I would have opened my mouth to deny it but Rachel's smirk was downright adorable. Instead, I just shrugged. "Totally my fault, apparently."

"Oh, without a doubt," Rachel said. She gave me a little pinch. When it was Patrick's turn he hurried through the buying of his pretzel then gave us a wave before he left.

"That was mean," I told Rachel, then again, I was chuckling.

"Mean? Me?" She snorted. "Girl, you'd think after all this time, you'd notice when someone was flirting."

"He was being nice. How is talking to me flirting?"

"Visual cues, the fact he turned his whole body toward you, even his *feet* were pointed at you and the way he was checking you out." She stared at me and then shook her head. "God, I love you, but you really just don't get how attractive you are."

I rolled my eyes. "Not everyone who sees me wants me. I swear, according to you and Jake I'm a walking sex magnet."

"We're not wrong," she said then glanced at the pretzel vendor as he handed over four huge, hot, fresh pretzels. I'd gotten a regular and a cinnamon. Rachel had gotten two regular, she paid. Then we wandered until we found an empty bench.

"Rach, I wasn't flirting with him."

"I know you weren't," she said. "He was flirting with you. You remain blissfully oblivious. Just keep an eye on them if they get that little secretive smile and face you like all the way, their feet pointed at you."

"What the hell is with the feet?"

She gave me a droll look. "You can tell a lot about a person's interest based on where their feet are pointed."

I groaned. "Yeah, I know the psychology. It's just—weird. I don't look at people's feet." At least she seemed to let it go after that. I devoured my pretzels in short order. We'd completely skipped lunch and it was heading toward dinner. But I'd promised her the whole day and she was gonna get it.

"I'm thinking about going to Europe."

That sentence caught me off-guard. "What?"

"Europe. You know France, Belgium, the Netherlands…"

"I know what Europe is, smart ass." I twisted to sit sideways on the bench. "When? Why?"

"Next semester," she said. "If not then, then definitely next year."

Next year was our senior year. "You're dropping out of college? Or doing an exchange program?"

"I don't know yet. I just—" Rachel wasn't looking at me anymore. She was staring out into the park. "I just need a change. I need—to be somewhere else for a while."

My whole heart ached at that sentiment. "I love the idea of you getting what you want, but I hate the idea that you have to go."

That was selfish, I guessed.

"I hate the idea of leaving you," she echoed the sentiment. "But I need to not be here I think. It's—hard to explain."

"Is it because of Dominic?"

"Yes and no," she said. "He's part of it, but it's also—" She glanced at me. "If you'd asked me in high school where would I be by the time I turned twenty-one, I'd have known exactly what the answer was."

Weirdly. "Me too. But—"

"That answer has changed." She lifted her shoulders. "We've both changed. We've both got—other things going on. But I need more. I don't think I'm going to get it here."

"More how?"

Her laugh held a hint of tears and I reached over to grip her hand. When she squeezed mine, I held on. "I don't know, and sometimes I think that's the scariest part of it all. I've been pretending for a long time, Frankie. Pretending I have it all together, that I know exactly what I want to do and how I'm going to do it."

"I don't think any of us know exactly how we're going to make it work. Being an adult kind of sucks."

Her chuckle this time was genuine. "Yeah, it kind of does."

But she leaned her head on my shoulder and I tilted mine so I could rest against hers. "I got your back," I promised. "Whatever you need."

"Well, first things first, I need to get this grant and acceptance into the program I'm shooting for. That will cover my expenses."

"Or I can just give you the money." I could afford it. "I believe in your art and your eye. I'll fund anything you want to do."

"Damn," she exhaled the word. "You sound like Rich Boy."

"I do, don't I?" How many times had Archie wanted to fix things for me? Just make it easier? "Doesn't mean it's not a good idea."

"I can't ask you—"

"You didn't ask," I promised, then pressed a kiss to the top of her head before I rested my cheek against it. "That's what friends are for. You go after the grant and the program you want. I'll be there as a backup. You want to go to Europe, you can do it. You want to study somewhere else, we'll make that happen too."

Even if I'd hate having her so far away.

"I'll miss you every damn day though, so you better call."

She chuckled. "I promise." Releasing my hand, she lifted hers to hold up her pinky. I locked my pinky around hers. "Pinky swear."

"Pinky swear."

We sat there for another few minutes.

Finally, she said, "We need to do some more shots."

"Ready when you are."

"Okay. Couple more minutes."

I smiled. I was okay with that too.

"Hey Rach?"

"Hmm?"

"Can our next shots involve food carts or a restaurant?"

My stomach growled its pitiful agreement and she shook with laughter.

"Done."

Chapter Four
TURN UP THE MUSIC

Ian

There were four messages from Boone waiting for me on my phone as I headed out of class. Screen scoring took every ounce of my concentration and energy. The class itself proved a challenge. In all honesty, I'd never really considered all the intricate layers that went into writing, developing, then directing a musical score to accompany a film. Getting into the class itself required two faculty recommendations and the approval of the professor teaching it.

The class was a three and a half hour chunk every Wednesday, but totally worth it. Boone's calls weren't the only ones I missed. There were two from Andrea, our social media director, one from my mom, two from a number I didn't know and one from Wittaker.

What the fuck had happened in the last three hours? I headed for the stairs and waited until I was outside and a little distance from the school.

Scoring was my only class on Wednesdays and Frankie would be finishing up her class in about thirty minutes. We usually met for coffee and to go home together, so I headed toward one of our preferred coffee spots.

Once I had my drink and paid for hers, so that she just had to pick it up when she came in—routines were great—I found a table outside where it was quiet and called Wittaker first. The attorney had been a fantastic ally to us and while he didn't handle as much of our business as he once did—he served as a great advisor.

When it sent me to voicemail, I left him a message that I was returning his call, then checked to see if he'd emailed or left a message. No voicemail from him, but there was an email. I flipped it open and blinked.

Mr. Rhys,

I'm reaching out to you directly as Roll City Records has reached out with an offer for both Bound Hearts as a musical group, and then a second one for you directly as a writer. I've attached the correspondence for your review. Your manager will likely be in touch regarding the potential second album, but I wanted to reach out to you specifically on the song writing.

This would not be covered under your current contract with Roll City Records. Prior to any agreements, we would need to review the contracts and make amendments. This is with regard to the creative work and how it would affect Bound Hearts and any future music you were to write for yourselves.

I'm aware of your heavy class schedule. After you've reviewed the materials, we can set up a conference call between us and Ms. Sippel. She'll be handling any business negotiations for you on the West Coast in coordination with myself and your New York attorneys.

I almost laughed. Our "attorneys." We had so many. Private. Corporate. Entertainment. At some point, it had stopped being strange. Huh. I was still debating that when another email popped into my box and this was from Elisabeth Sippel. She was fun and direct. She'd also taken over our contract negotiations and handled any royalty and rights discussions from the original attorney who was a partner at the firm.

Personally, I liked Elisabeth a lot better. The first guy had been all business, blunt to the point of painful—which had its perks—but also indifferent. Lis made Frankie laugh, talked to her without prompting and took both of our thoughts into account before she laid it out.

After all, it was still business, but Lis at least acted like she cared. Her email was pretty much exactly what Wittaker said, only this had a few more details.

A couple of inquiries had been made prior to Roll City Records reaching out about me writing music for some other labels—well, specifically other singers and bands. Our first album had done decently, we hadn't broken any records or anything. But the reviews on the music had been kind and I'd written almost all of the original material.

The last few lines of her email jumped out at me.

Avoid any calls with the label right now. They are likely trying to button you up into a contract so they can profit off any music you write that isn't for Bound Hearts. That's literally them just cutting into your bottom line. We also need to establish how much of the writing credit goes to you and to Frankie. Either way, we'll negotiate the best deal that allows you the most creative control and best return for your work. That is, if you are actually interested in it. If you're not, let me know and I'll shut them all down.

Attached was a PDF that included snaps of email inquiries they'd received. Holy shit, people really did want me to write music for them. That was—wild.

"Hey." Awareness rippled over me as the soft rasp of her voice preceded her. Shit, I'd totally missed her arrival. I glanced up when her hand settled on my shoulder. The sunlight lit her up from behind, adding a haloed effect. Not that my angel needed any enhancement to look amazing.

"Hey," I greeted her, meeting her kiss as I stood. She chuckled against my lips, tilting her head to accommodate the change in our height difference.

"Did you get your coffee?" I cupped her cheek, not looking away from her eyes as she smiled. The sunglasses didn't hide them, not at this range.

"I did, thank you." Another brush of her lips against mine, like the fluttering kiss of a butterfly's wings, had me shifting my grip to tease my fingertips over the tattoo behind her ear. "Everything alright?"

I let her go only to pull out her chair and she shifted her sunglasses up to rest on her head. She set her coffee down and I caught her backpack as she tugged it off, then sat it on the ground between our chairs.

"It's fine, did Wittaker or Boone reach out to you?"

"Yes, but Lis got to me first," she said, grinning before she saluted me with her coffee cup. "Congratulations, I told you everyone would want you."

I snorted. Then again, she had. "That's a little weird," I admitted. Only she shook her head. "You don't think it's weird?"

"I think that me being able to sing is weird. I think that me recording an album is weird." She raised her coffee cup and grinned at me. Her cheeks were flushed with a hint of pink. Even with the sun out, it was a cooler day. That said, Frankie was a lot like me, we'd rather be outside than in. While I didn't miss the insufferable heat waves in Texas, I did miss the warmer winters—sometimes. But we were heading into October and the cooler days would soon outnumber the warm ones. "People loving what you write and wanting you to write for them is not even remotely weird."

Amused, but adoring her nonetheless, I chuckled. "You're biased."

"I am," she said and spread her arms. "It doesn't mean I'm wrong. Ian, you're a talented musician. You sing, you play—and you *write* music. Not just music music, but also the lyrics."

I laughed. "Music music as opposed to…?"

The humor lighting up her eyes just made me grin. When she flicked her fingers at me, I chuckled all over again. "You know what I mean."

"I do," I agreed as I caught her fingers and gave them a squeeze. "Still, I never thought of writing for other people. I like writing for us." That hadn't changed. The tour last year had been both exhilarating and exhausting. Even then, I was glad we'd already elected to stay here or only tour when we could all go—that or shorter stints. Particularly after Archie's grandfather died.

It had been a cold, harsh way to start the year. Yeah, that sucked.

Still sucked.

"What do you think of the idea now?" Curiosity filled her eyes. "I mean—you do love writing music. This could be fun."

"Maybe." I agreed, enjoying the way she curled her fingers into mine. The table was kind of small and our knees touched. Frankie also leaned forward, all of her focus on me. The trust in her gaze, in her touch, hell—just the trust in her—it let me breathe easier. "I don't know."

"What is it?"

My frown deepened and I shook my head. "It's not the same—the idea of writing for other people."

"Well, no, I think it's not the same when we sing for other people either."

That was true.

"But…" She tipped her head, studying me. My angel had developed an acute sense of when I needed to be prodded. Maybe it was the time on the road or maybe *we* had just gotten closer. There were times when it was about what she needed. Other times, though, it was very much about me and my needs to take care of her.

"But…this is personal." I didn't have to explain it. The way her eyes softened and her smile deepened, she knew. Of course, she did. This was *us*. "It's really personal. Not sure I want to share that part of us with anyone else. The songs—when we sing them—they still mean something."

"But writing them means something far more to you," she finished for me. "And to me." Good girl. "I don't think they can have that part, even if you write the songs for someone else."

"No?" I wasn't so certain about that.

"Nope." She took a long drink of the coffee before continuing. "Ian, when you write music and add lyrics—that's all happening in your heart and your mind. When you put them together, that's a fusion in your soul. No one else gets to share that."

"Except you."

"To be fair," she said in a considering tone, as if asking me to listen to the whole statement even as she squeezed my hand. "I get to witness it. I get to bask in it. But I don't share it exactly."

Now my frown really did deepen. "Angel…"

"It's not a bad thing," she rushed to add. "Seriously, it's not a bad thing at all. Ian, I *love* watching you write music. I love how sometimes, you're sitting there just playing your guitar and the refrains begin to form and the bridges, then you're writing it down. It spills out of you like water through a magical fountain."

That was a hell of a description.

"Other times, you spend a week agonizing over a chord change." A half-snort, half-scoff of disbelief escaped her, but she was still smiling. "Then you have those moments where it suddenly all gels together and you have to reach for paper, any paper, and just get it all down."

The indulgence in her smile and the warmth in her eyes made me want to write a damn song right now, but I shuffled that away. "The question is, do I lose that if I'm not writing for us?" I'd literally *never* written for anyone else. It had always been for Frankie. Even when I was the one recording the songs and singing them.

She was my muse.

"Then don't write them for anyone else."

"What?"

"Don't write for anyone else." That sounded simple enough, except… "Look, I'm not the expert." She traced her thumb along the heel of my palm. "Clearly, not the expert. But it seems to me writing the songs is what you already do. So, you write the songs you want to write, you write them the way you've always written them and then if someone else records them— that doesn't take anything from you that you wouldn't have shared when you recorded it."

"Or you," I reminded her and she made a little face.

"Or me. But I stand by the idea that writing the music is very much you—how you write it and who you write it for is also your call. Who records it?" Now she lifted her shoulders in a careless shrug. "That's for whoever recognizes just how fantastic and amazing your work is and how privileged they would be to perform it."

"You are way too good for my ego, Angel."

The flash of her tongue as she stuck it out at me in no way affected my statement. She was far too good to and *for* me.

"What do you think?" So far, she hadn't *answered* that question herself. She'd asked me and offered encouragement, but I wanted to know what she thought.

"I think it's amazing that your talent is being recognized. I think I'm really very proud of you." She tilted her head to the side, smiling with simple joy and real affection. It was a smile impossible to not answer with one of my own. "I think I can't wait to hear what you write. I also pretty much think you're awesome and hot and I'm a very, very lucky woman."

"Well," I exhaled that sound slowly. Delight and love twisted together inside of me like a band of a Celtic knot, never ending and infinitely complex.

Amusement filled her expression. "Getting compliments takes some getting used to, doesn't it?"

"Yes, it does. Don't be a brat." I swore there was no depth of affection or love that I didn't feel for her. Just when I thought I might have found the limits, she filled me up again. It was like falling in love over and over. That was the kind of ride I never wanted to get off. "But thank you."

"You're welcome. I can tell you every damn day how amazing I think you are. I probably should anyway, but the truth is—whatever you decide to do Ian, I'm going to support it one hundred and ten percent."

Really? That was way too tempting to let slide. "Does that support mean you'll write some of the music with me?"

I'd seen her suck a lemon with a more pleasant expression as she grimaced. "Ian, they want you to write the songs…"

"I like writing with you," I reminded her. "We worked out more than a couple of those lyric sheets together. You also wrote a song on your own."

A flush touched her cheeks.

"Yes, that was you purging heartbreak, but the heart in those lyrics? The promise in them? I loved every single word. You can applaud my talent all you want, Angel, but don't think for an instant, I'm not going to be cheering you on for yours. If you don't *want* to do it, that's entirely different."

"I'm never going to not want to work with you," she said without an ounce of hesitation. "Even if all I do is sit there and listen—in between rounds of being tied to the piano bench or the wall or you know—wherever you need to get inspiration from."

Need vibrated through me. We'd made a couple of small changes to the studio downstairs. Changes that I made sure were completely tidied before I left it unlocked. Jeremy took care of the house, which meant he did go in the studio and as aware of all of us as he might be, there were some things that were just private.

Frankie's absolute trust in me and the scenes we played out when I needed to take care of her, or when she in turn needed to get out of her head—those were for us. Even the guys weren't always invited. We never deliberately excluded them, but we all wanted our time with Frankie alone, even if sharing had become as natural as breathing.

"I'll think about it," I said after considering it.

"I hope you will. I enjoy our inspirational get-togethers." There it was, an impish light in her eyes and she bumped my foot with hers.

"You really are cruising to get on the board," I said with a tsk. "We're up to three or four, already." It was five, but that'd been a bonus post-birthday gift to me after we'd cleared her tab and then some. What a blissful damn weekend that had been.

"Oh, Sir Ian—challenge accepted."

Yeah, the pressure in my groin seemed to double. I still cradled her hand, but I was already picturing her bent over my knee, soaking wet with her ass shiny and red from the spanking. That would just be getting us started.

I might just add one for doing this right here, where I could only savor the idea for later. Then again, I had started it. "We'll talk to them, read the offers, see exactly what is being discussed before we decide anything."

"That sounds like a plan." She drained her coffee before she pulled her phone out of her pocket. "I have to go see one of my teachers during office hours. You gonna be here for a bit? Or heading home?"

"I can walk back with you and hang out."

"It won't take me long," she assured me, as if that was a concern. I pushed back from the table and she claimed my empty cup with her own to toss while I grabbed her backpack.

"I'm done with the classes for the day," I reminded her as I waited for her to rejoin me. She paused for a beat looking at where I'd already shouldered her backpack and I met her gaze evenly. I had mine on and hers slung over one shoulder.

Rolling her eyes, she didn't complain and just let me tuck her under my arm. Good girl. The walk back was kind of nice. Even if it was chilly, there was enough sunshine to make it pretty. She wasn't kidding about not being long. She was in the professor's office for roughly seven minutes as they went over a project.

The door was cracked open and it let me listen, I couldn't help my grin. Especially as she double-checked the parameters, ran down a list of examples, and clarifications. The overachiever in her never wanted to do less than her best. The project wasn't due for another two months, but she wanted to get everything squared away before she started.

One more week. One more week to finish acclimating to the new class schedules, then I was carving out a night for the two of us. I needed it and from her playful teasing earlier, coupled with the stress of balancing the new class load, so did she.

Time to make some plans.

Chapter Five

NEVER GONNA BE ALONE

Frankie

The basket Jeremy put together was a little fancier than what I had in mind, but he had put in the Tuxedo Opera Cake I'd made, along with a meal for dinner, and sodas. He'd even insulated it with cooler packs to keep the hot food hot and the cold food cold. Based on the size of the basket, that wasn't all that was in there, but I didn't want to go through it all here.

"I took the liberty of adding wipes for hand cleaning, as well as mints for breath freshening, and I thought I'd pack a clean set of clothes for Mr. Archie to keep there if he is going to insist on spending so much time at the shop and not coming home in between."

It was a lot, but to be honest, I didn't disagree with Jeremy. "I'll take care of him," I promised and Jeremy gave me a solemn look, then threaded a blanket through the top of the basket. It was thicker than the one I'd picked out and had an insulated bottom, probably to make it more comfortable on the concrete floors.

Granted, my original idea was to take him leftovers. Jeremy had made the most amazing prime rib the night before and Archie missed dinner. He'd barely made it in after ten and I only knew that because I'd still been awake. The exhaustion lining his face had broken my heart. The last thing he needed was me yelling at him.

But that said… I wasn't leaving him to do this on his own. He'd been steadily pushing away for the last few months. I wanted to give him space, but enough was enough. If the mountain wanted to stay in Brooklyn working, then I would just have to go to him. Luckily, I could do homework anywhere and I was going to bring him a taste of home while I was there.

It had been bad enough over the summer, but since school started up again? It seemed so much worse. Or maybe I was just being too sensitive. After Maddy… Nope. I shoved that thought aside for the moment. Two totally different situations. Grandpa Ted had meant the world to Archie and his world was darker without him in it. The thing with Maddy was a hell of a lot murkier and far more complicated.

"I also took the liberty of arranging a car for you," Jeremy said as he checked his watch. "Is there anything else you need?"

"You are the master of getting things done," I said, then leaned up to press a kiss to his cheek before I took charge of the basket. I already had the backpack on and I'd changed into comfortable clothes with layers, cause it could sometimes be chilly in the shop—though it had been hotter than Hell at one point over the summer too. "Thank you."

"Thank you for looking after Mr. Archie," Jeremy said with a nod. "That young man thinks he has to carry the weight for everyone and refuses to lean on others. But you have always seemed to have a gift for getting through to him."

"Well, who knew being stubborn had perks?" Despite the lightness of my tone, Jeremy's smile remained solemn. Right, time to go. Jake was at hockey practice and Coop was going to be late at the community center. I'd already said bye to Ian before he settled into his studio to work. I felt bad about leaving him, but he'd only given me a swat and pointed to the door.

Turned out, he was worried about Archie too. So maybe it wasn't just me.

"See you later," I promised. "And if you're in bed before we get back, I'll see you in the morning." Before *we* got back. If he didn't come home with me, I was going to end up sleeping in the shop. Jeremy and Miss Abigail walked me to the door. She was so well-behaved, pausing at the edge of the tile to sit and wait. Jeremy nodded to her before he opened the door for me.

He checked first that the car was waiting before he let me out. One of the weirder parts of moving to New York had been Jeremy living with all of us full time. I thought it might get claustrophobic. Well, worried it would. I mean, I'd always adored him. But in the little over two years since we'd all relocated to New York and the brownstone, it had grown almost impossible to imagine being here without him.

The man was a gift. We needed to do more to appreciate him. The late afternoon drive took just over an hour. I checked in with KC and the girls, and on Rachel. KC didn't answer my texts immediately, but I owed her a few so it was fine. It was Friday afternoon, so if Rachel didn't have a date, she was probably out working on her portfolio.

I had the gate code to get into the area where the shop was housed, but I just had the car drop me off there. Basket and blanket in hand, I walked across the broken pavement lot toward the low-slung warehouse-like buildings. Jake and Archie had taken over one of them so far, but they were planning to expand to the other buildings as they grew their projects.

For now, it was more a place for them to experiment and test without worrying about what they blew up. Not my favorite description, but I got it. The code to get into the building was my birthday. The buzzer sounded as the locks released. Music washed out as I let myself in. Loud enough to carry, but not so loud it deafened me. Course, it probably masked the sound of the door.

Inside, it smelled of motor oil, engine fumes, and something pretty astringent. There was also a kind of damp scent that showed up in every single garage I'd ever entered. There were three cars parked by the entrance, two sports cars and an SUV. All of them had their hoods open. Three metal steps led from where I stood down to the floor.

Along the far wall were a series of offices, all abandoned, except for the two Jake and Archie had claimed, cleaned out and then furnished including computers so they could work on all areas of their "projects" out here. Whether it was adding velocity output to an engine or building a better breadbasket, they had all the toys they needed here.

I passed what looked like a completely disassembled vehicle. It had been sorted out by its parts—kind of like how Archie took things apart at home. Everything in its place so he could put it back together exactly as he'd taken it apart. The fact this looked like a full car, including its doors, gave me pause.

While I'd been to the shop a few times, this hadn't been here the last time I came out—a week earlier. Following the strains of music, I passed Jake's darkened office and continued down to the one with light spilling out of it. Only a section of the overhead fluorescents were on. Enough to see and make my way, but not terrifically bright. Both sides of the building had huge doors that could be rolled up. There were also fans lining the ceiling. In the summer, they opened the doors and turned the fans on.

Queen segued into The Who as I got to the open door. Archie sat in a chair behind a cluttered desk, with his feet up, his hands behind his head and his attention focused on the monitor, where something was being rendered. Leaning against the door jamb, I just studied him while his attention was elsewhere.

Shadows darkened the underside of his eyes. He had at least a three-day growth of whiskers on his face. If he kept it up, he was going to have a beard to compete with Jake's. His hair was disheveled, sticking up haphazardly in a few places, like he'd been raking his hands through it.

The muscles on his biceps stood out, almost hyperextended like he was flexing even if he looked relaxed. He was so wholly invested in whatever was rendering, his tension seemed almost palpable. I cut my gaze between him and the screen. It was at forty-eight percent and I had no idea how long it would take.

And, as much as I loved this quiet glimpse at him, I was a little more selfish than that. I wanted to talk to him. Shifting the blanket, I knocked on the door frame. His feet hit the floor and his whole body jerked just before Archie spun to face me. His expression went from shock to startled to genuine delight.

All at once, some of the tension in me eased. I wasn't entirely certain he would be thrilled at me coming to look after him. But the way he pushed out of the chair and crossed to me chased those concerns away.

"Babe," Archie said, a real smile softening his face as he circled the desk. I met him halfway and hugged him. It was a juggle with the picnic basket, but he snagged it out of my hand, then shoved some items out of the way to set it on the desk. He ignored the scattered pencils and paperwork before wrapping his arms around me again—only to pause at my backpack.

Amused grimace in place, he stepped back and twirled his finger for me to turn around. Chuckling, I pivoted and let him slide my backpack off. As soon as it was on the floor, he had his arms wrapped around me again and pulled me right to him.

"Hey, Babe," he said softly right at my ear and I lifted my right arm to curl it back around his head. As long as he held my back to his chest, I couldn't hug him properly. Still, this was damn nice. Even if he did smell like some kind of engine oil, the coconut scented heavy soap they used to get the grease off their fingers. There was a hint of soap from home and that underlying hint of *him*.

"Hey," I whispered, rubbing my left hand against the back of his hands where they were locked over my stomach. I swore his arms flexed as he tightened his grip. "Sorry if I surprised you."

"Best surprise ever," he declared, his breath a heated whisper against my throat. The rasp of his whiskers leaving a hint of a sting in their wake. Then he had me turning. The rough warmth of his hands cupped my face as he tilted my head back slightly and then his mouth was on mine.

I snaked my arms up and around his neck. The ache of missing him expanded as he nipped and sucked my lips like a starving man. He backed me right up to the wall, then his hands were under my shirt and somehow my bra vanished and I barely had time to gasp for air in between kisses while he got my jeans unbuttoned.

"Fuck," he whispered lifting his head, then dragging my shirt up. Dazed heat and delight curved through me at his ragged breathing echoing my own. The cool air hit my breasts and my nipples tightened almost painfully. The calluses on his fingers added to the teasing when he cupped one breast then stroked his thumb over the peaked tip.

My pussy clenched at emptiness but I didn't really have time to process that sensation before his hot mouth latched onto my other breast. He had to release me to tug at my jeans. It was a weird scramble to toe my sneakers off while he peeled the jeans down.

There was a brief pause as he lifted his head and I fought to steady my breathing.

"Red lace," he whispered, a genuine surprise in his voice and then he glanced to the desk where my bra now hung off the basket. Also red lace. A set he'd given me at Christmas. I just hadn't really found a good time to wear them for him so far this year. He dipped his fingers beneath the lace hem then looked at me. The heat in his eyes scorched me. "You're soaking wet," he whispered, then licked his lips.

"I've missed you." The intensity of that emotion couldn't compete with the need to just be close to him though.

"Fuck me, Babe, I've missed you too. Missed that beautiful smile. Those gorgeous eyes. These perfect tits and this delicious, wet as fuck pussy." Indecision seemed to hold him captive for a moment, as he glanced at his office then at me and then his gaze snagged on the blanket. "Oh, Babe, I fucking love you."

The chill in the air didn't do a damn thing against my overheated skin as he gave me one hard, furious kiss before he grabbed the blanket and the basket, then shoved everything off the desk. It was a shocking amount of papers, plans, and designs—as well as a couple of his books that went flying. Then he spread the blanket out and I'd barely gotten my jeans the rest of the way off before he picked me up and set me on the desk. He dropped into his chair with a wicked grin and set my feet on the arms of it as he rolled forward.

Resting on my elbows, I'd never been so glad for the thickness of the blanket or the naked want on Archie's face. He stroked his fingers up and down over the lace covering my pussy still and he grinned. "I'm pretty sure the basket is dinner, but I'm going for dessert first."

A laugh skated through me, only to break off into a gasp as he hooked his fingers into the panties and tugged them off. I pushed up to lift my ass so he could slide them down my legs. It took a little jockeying—thankfully I didn't kick him in the face—for him to get them off and then he planted my feet and spread my legs again.

"You comfortable, Babe?" The innocuous question held an element of pure mischief. "We might be here a while. I need to lick and kiss and suck my way through a few orgasms of this beautiful pussy of yours."

Liquid heat rolled through me and my face warmed. Locking my gaze on Archie's, I lifted one foot and curved my leg over his shoulder. "Put that dirty, sinful mouth on me, Archie, and make me scream."

I might not be quite up to his level, but the wicked grin on his lips promised he got the message. The heat of his hands slid under my ass as he gripped it and then lifted me a bit more. I was still on my elbows, but I tilted my head back to stare up at the white foam, faux ceiling that absolutely faded away when he plunged his tongue against my pussy.

Asked for his dirty, sinful mouth, Archie fucking delivered in spades. The hot suction of his lips on my clit demanded all of my attention and then he thrummed it with his tongue. Man was better than a vibrator. Fuck, I squirmed, but his fingers tightened on my ass and kept me still as he alternated thrusting his tongue and teasing my clit. The burn of his whiskers left a path against my skin, but who fucking cared?

The first orgasm split through me like a shocking splash of cold, leaving me shaking. Only he didn't let up, if anything, he intensified the pressure on my clit as the cries clawing out of my throat gained volume.

I couldn't fucking see anything. Heat kissed my skin with the same fervor his mouth delivered to my pussy. It was too much. Too fucking much, and I couldn't take it. Then I was coming again and he laughed against me before he began to lick and nip.

When he bit down against the inside of my thigh where it joined to my body, I groaned. He sucked a hickey into place, but the edge of pain barely touched the pleasure pounding through me with every beat of my heart. His lips were damp and shiny when he lifted his head to look at me.

"That tasted like more…"

Oh fuck.

I barely had time to catch my breath before he dipped his head again, this time, he used one hand to pump his fingers into me. It wasn't enough. I wanted his dick, but I couldn't even form coherent sentences as he edged me closer and closer, only to back off again.

"Fuck," I swore, the third time he did it, dragging that orgasm just out of reach and I wrapped my thighs tighter against his head. He laughed softly.

"Gonna have to let my face go for that, Babe." The deep timbre and throatiness of those words sent another wave of heat over me, my face was on fire.

"I need you," I managed to push out. It wasn't quite the demand or even a command, but more a plea.

The sound of his zipper was the most welcome noise ever. He pushed my legs apart carefully so he could stand. I rose to help him as he got his jeans undone, then his dick was out. I wrapped my fingers around the heated length, I knew every inch of him. All of them, really. I knew them all, it was like I both memorized the lines of his body and needed to re-familiarize myself each and every time.

I loved the way his dick had a curve in it and how it pulsed against my palm. I adored the way his gaze riveted on me and how he licked his lips like he could still taste me. Fuck, he probably could. As if reading my mind he grasped my hair and pulled me toward him as I rubbed his dick against my soaked pussy.

He was right about that, I was so fucking wet for him. His kiss swallowed my breath and I groaned as I angled him and then he thrust forward, sinking into me in one hard jerk of his hips. It was too much and not enough. I had my legs tight against his hips but I had nothing to push against as he began to pound into me, even as he devoured my lips.

The pace he set was a furious one and it was perfect. The rub of his jeans, the jangle of his zipper hitting the desk, even the rocking of the desk itself, added to the experience. The third orgasm detonated with unexpected force. He swallowed my screams along with my breath and the stutter of his hips seemed triggered by how tight I clamped down on him. Tearing his mouth from mine, he buried his face against my hair. He came in a rush and then it was me holding him up, as he shook and trembled.

Gradually, the trembling eased. Archie hadn't even taken off his shirt and his jeans were still on, just yanked down enough to let his dick out. His dick which still rested inside of me, semi-soft and drained. The little spasms quaking through me had me clench now and then and he'd give another little jerk. I wasn't in a hurry to let him go though, and he seemed to have no interest in moving.

Slowly, my breath deepened from panting gasps and my hammering heart slowed from a gallop. A little ding dragged my attention to the side and I glanced at the screen. The words "render complete" gleamed back at me.

"I think your thing is done," I murmured, pressing a kiss against his throat. Archie dragged his head up and looked at me, a puzzled expression on his face. Yeah, I'd done that. Shaken him out of his hyper-focus and utterly distracted him. I kind of wanted to pull a Coop and do an achievement unlocked. I settled for just saying, "Your render is complete."

He glanced over his shoulder at the screen, his puzzled look didn't vanish totally. It actually seemed to take him a minute to process what he was looking at. Then he glanced back at me and I grinned.

"You don't care about that?"

"Not right now, Babe. Give me a minute and I'll be ready for round two…"

That seemed ambitious, but his dick was already stiffening again and I had to laugh as he nipped a kiss at my throat.

"You're here for the evening right?" he asked. "No other plans?"

"Nope," I promised. "All yours."

"Thank fuck."

"But Archie?" I said as he began kissing a path down my collarbone and heading toward my breast.

"Yeah, Babe?"

"Get naked this time."

He paused.

"Yes, ma'am. Right away, ma'am."

Laughter swelled up through me as he pulled away and I got to delight in how fast he kicked off his shoes and tossed his own clothes. Only when he'd finished did he spread his arms and give me a good look at him, including his already erect once more cock, gleaming with moisture.

"I'll give it a nine point five," I teased and his eyebrows raised. "I mean, it took you a while to get them off and…"

Then he was kissing me and I forgot all about why it mattered that it took him a while. He was quite determined to wring a ten out of me.

Chapter Six

OH, SHE

Archie

We'd dragged the blanket off the desk and set it up on the sofa I'd added to my office over the last few weeks. We'd gotten a pair of them, one for Jake's and one for mine. If Coop or Bubba took us up on our offer of converting the other offices for them for whatever—or Frankie for that matter, we were gonna get sofas for them too. Mine proved comfortable enough the handful of nights I'd just passed out here. A habit I had zero intentions of continuing.

Sprawling next to Frankie as I drained a bottle of ice-cold water, I grinned at her flushed face and the way her hair curled against her damp skin. The sight of her standing there in the doorway had hit me like a bolt of lightning. One minute, I'd been spiraling and then she'd been there, exactly when I needed her.

I trailed the empty bottle up her arm and she gave me a drowsy smile.

Before tilting her own bottle up to drink. Yeah, my dick and I were debating round four, or was it five? But first, we needed to hydrate and she needed food. The basket sat there all stately and elegant, declaring she'd brought me some tender loving care and romance—while I'd basically gone for full body contact lust and love.

There was a hint of red rash on her cheeks and more on her breasts. The ones on her thighs were a bit more of an accusation, but before I could say anything, she pressed a finger to my lips. Meeting her gaze, I read the understanding there. "Sorry, Babe," I murmured, then pressed a kiss to her finger before I caught her hand.

The lack of shaving over the last few days had left me with harsh stubble and a lot of growth. I usually took better care to keep everything smooth for her. Particularly since she'd gotten into the habit of waxing, and now laser. I'd never thought of myself as a bare pussy man, but I was totally a Frankie pussy guy so—hey.

"I like it," she told me with a little laugh. "It reminds me that I can make you lose control too."

Well, when she put it like that. Turning her hand over, I pressed a kiss to her palm. "Babe, I promise, you shred pretty much every ounce of my control." My control. My focus. My loss. Frankie took it all apart and filled in all those bleak little corners. "I just need to take better care of you."

"You take fantastic care of me," she scolded. "And it's my turn anyway." With some effort, she stretched her leg and then hooked the basket with her foot and pulled it over to us. I chuckled and she gave me an impudent look. "Hey, it's not my fault my legs are spaghetti right now."

"No," I agreed with her, squeezing her hand and rescuing the basket so she could go back to relaxing. "I'll totally take the blame for that."

She giggled. Fuck, I loved that sound. Rising on slightly unsteady legs of my own, I set the basket down on the sofa next to her and made my way over to the tiny fridge. I liberated more water bottles from it and dropped our empties into the recycle bin before I walked back.

My muscles protested a little, but the desk in here needed to be replaced. I was already debating it, but it was just off being the right height to fuck her properly. Grinning, I settled back on the sofa without collapsing. "At some point, I need to pick up a new desk, care to go shopping with me?"

She snorted. "I thought this one was just fine."

"Oh, I could definitely work with it." I cracked open the water bottle before I handed it to her, then opened my own. "But I'm thinking I could do better."

She laughed again. "Archie, I think you killed it, but if you want to get a new desk and test it out—I'm all in."

And that was just another reason why I loved her. Even though we were the only two in the building, I'd actually closed the door and the blinds to my office. Not that I care if Jake walked in—but he had a game tonight. No, practice. Wait—was it a game or… "Jake didn't have a game tonight, did he?"

"No," she said and the air whooshed out of me. Fuck, if she'd missed his game because of me. Hell, if I'd missed his game. "He had practice. Games don't start for another couple of weeks. Or something. I don't always get the way his league does things, but since most of them didn't play over the summer, they wanted to get in as much ice time as possible before they started actively competing."

Her careless shrug pulled a real chuckle out of me. "You don't get hockey any more than you did football, do you?"

"Well," she said, frowning. "I know Jake doesn't get to beat up people on the ice and no one can beat up on him. Cause—of their league rules." The little wrinkle of disgust at the last left me uncertain of whether she was happy about that rule or not. "Jake enjoys it though and he's pretty good, so I know I like seeing him happy."

"And you're going to as many games as you can." It wasn't a question. Last winter… Fuck. Last winter. I cleared my throat and then turned to the basket. I'd already slipped a little and Frankie didn't need the burden of my grief or anything else.

It was bad enough she had to come all the way out here because I hadn't been home as often. "Do me a favor," I said, catching her about to reach out to me and I summoned up a grin for her. "Keep me in the loop on when the games are. I want to go with you."

Her eyes softened and she wiggled to sit up. I'd found some wipes to help clean up my mess earlier, but the fact there was still some of my cum on her thighs just did something to me. Helped push back the grief and it definitely made my dick consider getting back up. "I promise," she told me. "Hungry?"

"Nope, just opening the basket cause I'm curious about what you brought me."

A flash of a smile curved her lips. "Well, probably not the time to tell you the basket was just a ruse to get in here and have my wicked way with you."

Oh, I adored it when she would play with me. I mock-gasped. "You came here intending to steal my virtue?"

Her absolute snort made me grin. "Pretty sure you flung your virtue right at me."

I gave that all due consideration and then nodded with a grin. "Accurate." Inside the basket, however, despite her claims to the contrary, was a treasure trove of goodies. Sodas in cold packs. I pulled those out and then removed covered plates from the hot pack. The scent of roasted potatoes and steak hit me like a ton of bricks. If I hadn't already been hungry, I would have been starving now.

It didn't help that the scent of fresh hot bread came out of the hot pack too. Crap, we needed a table. No way was she balancing this warm of a plate on her bare thighs. I rose again.

"Gimme a sec, Babe." I moved the hot plates over to my cleared off desk then headed out into the shop.

We had all kinds of shit here. Somewhere—there it was… I hastened over to the trunk we'd grabbed to haul tools out here. We'd emptied it, but we hadn't taken it back. For now, I dragged it into the office. It would work as a makeshift table. Frankie rose to help me and I waved her back to the sofa.

"I got it." It wasn't remotely heavy, but it was sturdy. In fact, after I got it in front of the sofa I checked it for sturdiness and then eyed her. The red flush which had been in retreat as she cooled deepened to pink. "Later," I promised with a wink and she laughed.

"You'll do it, too."

"Yes, yes I will." But for now, food. So, I got the plates set up with the drinks, then pulled out silverware wrapped in cloth napkins. I chuckled. This had Jeremy written all over it. There was another cold bag and it had cake in it. Oh, that looked amazing. "You made me a cake."

"How do you know Jeremy didn't?" The teasing comment pulled a grin, but I peeled off the note from the side of it.

Miss Frankie prepared the cake. Do be a well-mannered young man and thank her for caring so much.

Real laughter escaped her and me, for that matter. I could *hear* Jeremy's tone in that note. Moving to sit next to her again, I brushed a kiss to her lips. "Thank you, Babe."

It was nearly midnight before I got her home, but after dinner and the incredibly delicious opera cake—which I was a fucking super hero and saved slices for the guys—we just flopped in my office and talked. I told her about the project I was working on and then we christened the sofa. In fact, that had to be a new rule. All new furniture needed to be christened with hot Frankie screaming on my dick.

Yep. That was my plan. Still, it was late when we got dressed and I called for a car. Inside, I re-armed the alarm. "Go on up," I told Frankie. "I'll put this stuff in the kitchen and the leftover cake in the fridge."

"You're coming up?" The house was dark except for the single light in the foyer and another down the hall near the kitchen. She paused at the base of the stairs and the worry she'd kept in check all evening seemed to be right there.

"Promise," I said, dropping a kiss on her lips. "Gonna put this up and come straight up. Want to shower with me?"

That was the right thing to say because her expression relaxed again. "I'll be the naked one under the hot water."

"I will be there *really* fast."

She chuckled then headed up the steps. It took me no time to unpack the basket in the kitchen. I put up the cake slices, then set the dirty dishes and the silverware in the sink *after* I rinsed them. The basket I left on the counter, cause I had no idea where it went, but I wrote on the white board attached to the fridge a quick thank you to Jere.

He'd see it in the morning. Upstairs, Coop sprawled on one half of Frankie's bed, there was a movie on and I cut a look at it as he said hello. "Why are you watching this?" It was the old He-Man movie from the 80s. Bad, but good in a bad movie kind of way.

"It was on," Coop said with a chuckle. "And I wanted to be awake when you brought her home."

"Fair." I jerked a thumb toward the shower. "I'm—"

"Yep," he said with an easy grin. "She already told me. Go have some fun. My make-up date with her is Sunday."

Make-up date? "You know, I'm not going to ask."

"Good plan." He switched his attention back to the movie and I slipped in to strip down and join Frankie in the shower. I also decided to shave while I was in there. Frankie offered to do it for me, and it was not a situation I'd ever have imagined as erotic, but it certainly encouraged me for a final round for the evening and the hot water was running a little cooler by the time we rinsed off.

"Y'all were trying to kill me, right?" Coop asked as we emerged. Fortunately, we all kept clothes in and around Frankie's room along with hers. I'd dragged on a pair of black pajama bottoms she had waiting for me in the bathroom.

Frankie just hadn't bothered to pull anything on, instead, she crawled onto the bed and gave me a lovely view before she nuzzled a kiss to Coop. "No," she teased. "That was just a perk."

His little scoff of outrage had me chuckling, even more when Frankie looked at the television and wrinkled her nose.

"Why are you watching this?" It was such a marvelous echo of what I'd said that I grinned. Coop flipped me off.

"Was waiting for you to bring that gorgeous ass home, because I am here and I wanted to say goodnight to you before we went to sleep."

Suck. Up. I mouthed at Coop over her shoulder as I set my phone on the charger along with hers. Coop's was on a charger on the other side of the bed. Frankie grinned as I slid into the bed and she curled up between the two of us. She stole a glance at the television and then at me. Coop held up three fingers, then counted it down.

"Want to watch a movie?" she asked just as he curled that last finger.

"It's late," I reminded her.

"It's Friday," she said. "We don't have to get up early—" She paused and eyed both of us. I raised my hands and so did Coop. "Excellent. Then we can sleep in and fuck off together tomorrow." There was a real note of pleasure in her voice at that. I didn't care what plans I might have had, I'd have canceled them in a heartbeat because she sounded so happy. "So, we can watch a movie."

Of course, that led to a debate about what movie to watch and it was almost one-thirty before we started a murder mystery that was also a comedy. Frankie was asleep after the first thirty minutes, but then we'd seen this one a few times. Coop fell asleep not long after her, but I lay there, my hand over hers where it rested against my chest and watched the movie.

Sleep hadn't been the easiest thing the last few months. I needed to do a better job of dealing with it, cause worrying Frankie wasn't something I liked doing. The rest of the movie, I tried to figure out the best way to fix it and I was still turning it over in my head when the credits rolled. I shut it off and then lay there in the dark.

"It's going to be okay," Frankie whispered and I turned my head to look. It was dark, and I wasn't sure if she was awake or talking in her sleep.

"Yeah?" I whispered.

"Yes," she said, and she pressed a kiss to my shoulder before settling back against the pillows. "It's going to be okay."

Right now, I could hold onto those words, so I did. Keeping my hand over hers, I closed my eyes and repeated them over and over until sleep finally swallowed me.

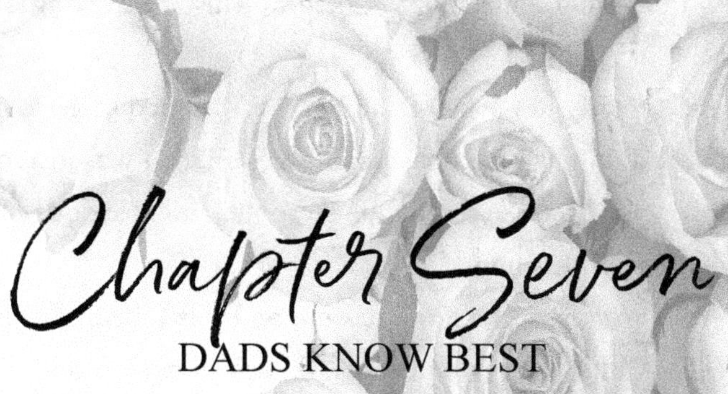

Chapter Seven

DADS KNOW BEST

Frankie

It was raining again. Seriously, rainiest autumn since we moved here. Definitely rainier than when we were in Texas. It was cool enough that I'd opted for a jacket. If someone had told me a couple of years earlier, I might actually be missing Texas in the autumn—well, I'd have laughed in their face. I'd probably laugh right now, despite the fact I'd gotten just damp enough on the mad dash from the subway to the restaurant that the breeze hitting me chilled me.

I did not miss sweltering summer temps in October. Nope. No, I did not. Though this chilly rain could go away too. Under the canopy, I closed my umbrella and shook it out before I made my way in the front doors. Jameson's was more of an upscale bar than a restaurant, but it was a favorite of Hank's so when he called to say he'd taken the train down for a couple of meetings today, I didn't hesitate to come and meet him.

"I'm meeting someone," I told the hostess as she gave me a sympathetic look and a small plastic slip bag to put over my umbrella so it wouldn't drip everywhere. At least I didn't look like a drowned rat. Fingers crossed anyway. "Jackson, party of two, I think."

"Three," she said with a smile. "If you'll follow me."

I shrugged out of my jacket, trying not to leave a trail of water droplets through the place. One would think after plenty of practice, I'd be more comfortable in these situations. But nope, I still felt like the girl who didn't get asked to the spring dance and worked at Mason's serving out Big and Thicks.

Except, I totally got asked to any dance I wanted to go to and I could ask them if they didn't ask me. The rest of it? Well, that was just me. I caught sight of Hank right about the same time he spotted me. He slid out of his seat and welcomed me with a hug.

"There's my girl." He squeezed me and I laughed as I hugged him just as fiercely. A little over two years he'd been in my life and his hugs had the power of promising me everything would be okay. Maybe it was a little hokey, but I'd take it.

"Hey, Dad," I teased. "You talked to me two days ago."

He chuckled, pulling back to give me a firm look, even as he rubbed my chilly arms. "But it's been almost a month since I saw you and we're going to miss this month's dinner. And you're cold."

I made a face. We'd already discussed that. Commitments at the university and Kelly's volunteer work just pre-empted this month. "If I could steal away up there, I would." But it was Coop's birthday, then Archie's, then Halloween… yeah, I couldn't get away either. It was fine. "I'll be up next month."

Thanksgiving was not a discussion I was getting into right now. There were feelings on all sides from various family members. Christmas was strictly us. We liked it that way. "I know, but when Eddie invited me down to the city—"

Ah. Eddie. I cut a glance to the *third* member of our lunch and he gave me an almost apologetic smile. The element of sadness clinging to him made my heart ache. I draped my jacket over the back of the chair and then leaned over to press a kiss to Eddie's cheek. Surprise rippled across his face.

"I didn't realize he was inviting you to lunch or I wouldn't have invited myself along," Eddie said as I slid into my chair. Hank just shook his head and I actually laughed.

"If he minded, I'm sure he would have said something." One of the things I liked about Hank, he was straightforward. "And I don't mind at all, as long as we don't turn this into a mentoring session, my brain still hurts from the other day's discussions of fiscal quarters net gains and losses."

A real smile touched his lips at that, as he raised a hand. "I solemnly swear. I appreciate the fact you didn't just snore all the way through it."

"I was tempted." The teasing was both weird and familiar. Thankfully, the arrival of the waiter kept me from getting awkward. Well, any more awkward. I already knew what I wanted, they made the best roast beef and au jus sandwich with thick steak fries. Just the thought had my mouth watering.

Hank and Eddie placed their orders after mine, and the waiter collected the menus while promising to bring me my soda. Once we were alone, I glanced between the men but they weren't saying anything.

"Okay, at the risk of sounding paranoid, this is beginning to feel a bit like an ambush." While I didn't think they'd done anything like that, I didn't like the way they seemed to be gauging what they should say.

"That's my fault," Hank said. "Apologies, Frankie. This is more spur of the moment so don't think of it as being some grand scheme."

"Okay," I dragged the word out. Somehow, that didn't make me feel better. "Spill it, Daddy-o."

Hank opened his mouth, but instead of words he let out a laugh. The corners of his eyes crinkled and he shook his head. Even Eddie laughed. I was a freaking comedian, who knew. "Daddy-o, remind me never to let you watch any sixties television."

I snorted. "Too late."

"Damn." He snapped his fingers, before taking a sip of coffee. Laughter still twinkled in his eyes. "I—we—wanted to talk to you about possibly arranging a family Thanksgiving, and before you say anything—I meant all of us. Me, Eddie, Kelly, the kids—Jake's parents, Coop's, and Ian's." He was the only other person I knew who called Ian, Ian outside of Sara and Joe, but they were Ian's parents.

That was a *lot* of people.

"And…depending how you feel about it…we could invite Eugene and Patience as well."

Ugh. Since Maddy's funeral, I'd only seen Patience twice. Neither time had gone well. The second time had been at Grandpa Ted's funeral. I'd actually spoken to Eugene a bit more.

"Hear him out," Eddie said in a gentle tone and I shot him a look. He didn't back down though. "I understand how you feel, but Hank has actually thought quite a bit about all of this."

And I owed it to Hank to at least listen. Yeah, I really didn't need Eddie to tell me that, but I appreciated the effort. The waiter returned with my soda and I peeled off the paper from the straw and slotted it in the drink. After a long swallow, I focused on Hank again.

He'd waited me out. The gentle smile was almost a chastisement of its own. Hank had been fantastic from beginning to end, listening to me, really listening, and respecting me. At my nod, he continued, "We don't want to put any one person on the spot, so we wouldn't all go to someone's house. We thought we'd rent a place, maybe out in Connecticut or down here in the city. The point is, we'd fly everyone in…"

"My treat," Eddie said and I glanced at him, he seemed a little less comfortable than Hank on this. "I don't want to create a financial burden for anyone and it's important to both of us that you have as much family around all of you as possible."

All of you…

Meaning me and Archie, but they were including Jake, Coop, and Ian. That was what was going on. The dads had been talking. Okay, that was really fucking weird and putting that aside for the moment. Maybe not so weird, I guessed. They had sorta known each other in college.

Oh, that was going to give me a headache. Right, not the important part here.

"You don't like it," Hank said, concern tightening his brow. "We're not trying to interfere."

"Well," Eddie countered. "Technically, we are, but we are trying to do it in a way that's helpful. It's also why we wanted to talk to you first…"

Because if I wanted to do it, the chances were the guys would be more likely to play along.

"Technically," Hank said with a frown at Eddie before he focused on me. "But only on a minor technicality. You have a big, noisy family. All of you do. While you may not have the most conventional—" He paused when our waiter returned with our meals. It gave me a moment to get my shit together.

No, this wasn't what I expected when I came to meet him for lunch, but this wasn't an ambush in a bad way. This was the pair of them *trying* to be inclusive and reaching out. The sandwich smelled divine and my stomach rumbled in appreciation.

"While you and the boys don't have the most conventional of relationships," Hank continued once we were alone again. I sectioned my sandwich into halves to keep from interrupting. "What you do have, works. I can tell you from experience that even conventional relationships run into hiccups at the holidays. Kelly and I often have to swap who we spend Christmas with versus Thanksgiving, so that the kids get to spend time with their various grandparents."

He paused again as I glanced down at my food. That was not an issue I was familiar with, though I'd certainly seen it with Coop and Trina after their parents separated. Jake too.

Eddie let out a long sigh. "It's definitely a common problem, unless, like me, you alienate everyone involved."

"Self-pity doesn't look good on you," Hank told him bluntly and I froze, with my mouth full of food. "You can't change the past. You can only learn and move forward. You and Ted were in a good place there and you're working on building that with Archie."

The brisk, no-nonsense tone resonated with me, and frankly, I agreed with Hank. However, beyond Archie and Ted, I'd never seen anyone take that kind of a tone with Eddie. Instead of a sardonic expression, Eddie stared at his food like he'd taken a bite of something quite sour.

"You know," he said slowly. "You have a real talent with words."

"I just don't shine on the self-pity or the bullshit," Hank retorted with a shrug.

"You don't say." Eddie's tone was both self-deprecating and faintly sarcastic, but he was smiling.

I almost choked before remembering I needed to chew my food. The pair of them both glanced at me and Hank snorted.

"Sorry, kiddo, this is just a conversation we've been having for the last few months."

"He's not wrong," Eddie said as he shook his head. "On any count there. So yes, it's conversations like these that brought us around to the holidays. Christmas is a no go. Archie has made that perfectly clear."

Hank nodded. Because so had I.

"That leaves Thanksgiving." Hank picked up the conversational baton smoothly. "The last couple of years have been tough, you're halfway through college, you've got a recording deal, Coop's studying and volunteering, Jake's flying planes, Archie's gonna build something amazing and Ian's writing music."

I managed to wash down that bite with a long drink. I loved that Hank had paid attention to our updates.

"Essentially, we know where everyone is this year and maybe next,"

Eddie added. "Once you five graduate…"

"What? We fall off the face of the planet?" The question was the right one because both men chuckled. "I get it," I continued before either of them could jump in again. "Really, and I really appreciate the effort you're both making here. I love the idea of a huge, noisy Thanksgiving."

"No, you don't." The smile on Hank's face was almost pure entertainment but there was no denying the affection in his voice. "You're already wondering what could go wrong—but you'll indulge us because you're you."

"Yeah, you don't get to know me that well yet," I retorted, but my face heated at the truth in his words. He just laughed. "Look," I said with a sigh. "I like the idea—in theory—but I need to run it past the guys, and we don't know if their parents…"

No sooner had I begun that thought then I realized, yes, they did know if their parents were free.

"You already talked to everyone."

"Just sound planning to make sure it's an option," Eddie suggested. "We were very clear that this wasn't going ahead until you kids were all on board."

Shaking my head, I stared from one to the other. "You do realize if we end up saying no, this makes *us* the bad guys."

"Honestly? It occurred to us, which is when Eddie decided to call everyone to mea culpa the plan and then said that if you kids said no, it would be on us and not you."

I didn't know whether to be exasperated or amused. "Did you pick out where you wanted to have this fine Thanksgiving with everyone and their brother?"

"Now that you mention it…" Eddie's grin was so damn Archie right there I knew they'd done more than come up with some ideas. I was being herded along to make the decision they really wanted. The damnedest thing was, I kind of wanted to say yes.

"Okay, Dads," I said, ignoring the brighter looks they both sported. "I'll talk to the guys, but I'm not promising anything. I'd also appreciate a heads up the next time *before* you make all the plans to show us how easy it can be and how little we have to worry." Because I did get it and it was kind of sweet.

Lunch ran a little long and it was fun. Afterwards, Hank walked me to the subway, even though I told him he didn't have to. He had to catch a cab to get back to the train station. He really had only come down for the day.

"You're not really angry at us, are you?" he asked.

"No, but I do want to know what Kelly said when you came up with this idea."

He chuckled. "She said you'd indulge me, but that it was not fair to spring this on all of you. Especially after you all volunteered to keep the kids for a week last summer."

I really did like her. "I loved having the kids here, it was fun."

"And that we should give you the option of declining, quietly and privately."

Yep. I laughed.

He kissed the top of my head when we got to the stairs leading down. "Thank you for considering it. I know we got a little pushy there and maybe a bit too enthusiastic."

"It's all right, it's kind of nice to be wanted." I could even say that without more than a bittersweet twinge. "Though, I think you and Eddie being friends is kind of weird? And cute?" Did that sound insulting?

"It is definitely weird," Hank agreed. "The guy kind of grows on you though. And I think he needs a friend. So—happy to step up."

"You're adorable."

"Right back at you, kid. Now, get home, study hard, get good grades and get more sleep. You look a little tired…"

I rolled my eyes but hugged him. "Let me know you got home safe?"

"I promise. Love you, Frankie."

"Love you too… Dad."

Before we could drag this out any longer, I headed down the steps to catch the train. Once on board, I sent a text off to let the guys know I was on my way home. I added a couple of lines about Thanksgiving and the invitation issued by the dads.

Their responses weren't immediate and I really hadn't expected them to be. They were in class or workshop—I checked the time—yeah, most of them were. Coop might be done, but he could already be on his way to volunteer.

At home, I paused just inside the door to get rid of the wet shoes and jacket before I hung the umbrella to dry. Miss Abigail waited for me at the edge of the tile, practically vibrating as she sat. I hesitated and then glanced past her to Jeremy.

"Has she been out for her afternoon walk?"

"No, with the rain, I was waiting to see if it would pass, but it does not appear to be."

"I'll take her."

He gave me a firm look and I raised my right hand.

"I solemnly swear to make her sit at each corner before we cross the street and that she will not be rewarded for going crazy and jumping at anyone. If, by chance, someone wants to pet her, I will make her sit to greet them and I will praise her copiously when she poops and pees."

It was killing me not to go over and pet her right now.

"Please?"

Jeremy chuckled. "Very well, I'll get something warm started for both of you, as I imagine you're going to get very wet."

Probably, but I just smiled.

"Come along, Miss Abigail." With only one quick look back at me, she trotted right after Jeremy but the tail didn't stop wagging. I glanced up the stairs where Tiddles sat giving me a baleful look.

"Oh, don't you start," I informed him. "I saw you cleaning her ears yesterday." If he could have harrumphed, I was pretty sure he would have. I pulled my shoes and jacket back on and then pulled my hair back into a ponytail with a scrunchie. By the time Jeremy returned with Miss Abigail in her harness, she was damn near prancing.

"Be careful," he informed me sternly as I took her leash and then gave her a good scritch. "You have your phone?"

Man, the desire to tease him with a 'yes, Dad' was right on the tip of my tongue, but I didn't. I patted my pocket. "Right here. If she's good, I'm going to take her by the dog park. It's raining, yes, but it's not too bad." Then because Jeremy did *care*, I added, "I'll text when we're on the way back."

"Very good," he said, then glanced at our avid audience. "You behave as well, Miss Abigail, you look after Miss Frankie."

He opened the outer door for us and Abby and I were off. She was so good on a leash and her manners were impeccable. She didn't seem to object to the rain any more than I did. The best part about taking her on these walks, she was good company and an excellent listener.

She also freaking adored playing fetch and I'd smuggled a ball into my pocket while Jeremy got her leash. We were probably gonna get dirty.

But I had a feeling Jeremy knew that.

Besides, I needed to think about this Thanksgiving plan with all of us. Right, that was kind of future planning. If we didn't, it would be a mess. We'd be rotating so often it would be once every five or six years with each family.

Huh.

Okay, maybe that was thinking just a little far ahead. Right. Get through *this* Thanksgiving then worry about the rest.

Chapter Eight

IT'S MY BIRTHDAY TOO

Coop

"It doesn't seem real that you're twenty-one," Mom said with a little sigh over the phone. She didn't typically get weepy at me, but today seemed to be an exception. "Half the time, I can't believe you're living in New York and I only get to see you a couple of times a year."

There it was. I chuckled as I weaved around the other students. "Well, you were all about getting me out the door."

"Pfft, you were already out the door." The cluck of her tongue elicited another grin from me. I could picture her expression, an exasperated smile, half-rolling her eyes as she shook her head. "But at least then it was only a couple of doors down."

"You and Trina are coming up for Thanksgiving, right? Trin wants to look at a couple of colleges while you're up here." That was gonna be fun. Was I a terrible brother because I didn't necessarily want her this close? But at the same time, I would like her to be close enough for me to get to if she needed me.

I made it to the doors to head out to the street. Thank fuck it had stopped raining. Honestly, wettest autumn ever. The air smelled damp though, hints of rain and the promise of more. Overhead, the gray skies weren't helpful.

"Yes, though I was a little overwhelmed by Eddie's offer. I think we could afford it on our own."

I debated my next words. "You know what, Mom, let him do it. I know it seems extravagant, but the man is really trying. This is his love language, in a way. A huge Thanksgiving so he can give his son something Archie didn't have growing up."

It was also looking after Frankie and by extension the rest of us. But it was about Archie, and while I still had my issues with my own father, I liked the idea that we *could* make things work, repair some of the damage and build a better relationship going forward.

Archie damn well deserved it.

Mom sighed. "I thought as much. Has the invitation been extended to your father?"

"Far as I know, but I don't know if he can take the time off or not." We didn't talk about Dad's struggles. The guy made some epically bad choices. "I'll call him next week if I haven't heard from him. I don't want you to feel ambushed."

"Well, I'm less concerned about that. Thomas and I are never going to be friends, but we can be civil." Fair enough. "I was considering bringing Peter though."

I barely managed to dodge a couple and a street lamp at that declaration. Shit... "The boyfriend?"

"Don't say it like that." Reprimand echoed in every syllable.

"Well, I'm not going to refer to him as your gentleman caller." I snorted and she laughed.

"Fine, just call him Peter and maybe I won't bring him. That seems like a huge step and we're probably not there."

I paused at the corner to shift over and stand closer to the building. "Mom, if you want to invite him, I promise to behave. I get being uncertain and scared. It's been a while since you even dated or were willing to date."

She sighed. "And you shouldn't have to bear this burden."

"Right, you're my mom. I love you. This isn't a burden. If you aren't comfortable inviting him yet, then don't. I don't have to meet him until you're ready." I hated everything about the idea of her dating when I was so far away. At the same time, I didn't like the idea of her being lonely. She deserved good things. "For what it's worth, Trina likes him."

Mom chuckled. "That's because Peter has mastered the art of the teenage girl. He doesn't ask her anything personal, always brings her a coffee—I swear she's developed Frankie's taste in expensive coffee with whip cream on top."

I laughed. "There are worse habits to have. How's she doing? For real? Senior year is coming, she's got to be trying to make everything she wants to do covered."

"She's fine. Having a car has made life easier for her. Interestingly enough, she's been volunteering at the animal shelter. It kills her because she wants to bring every single one of them home."

I could imagine. "You're trying not to break down and let her get a dog or a cat before she leaves for college, aren't you?"

"I'm a terrible mother." But the laughter in her voice made me smile.

"It's gonna be fine, Mom."

She sighed. "I should be the one telling you that."

"Okay. I'm waiting."

Another laugh and I grinned. "It's going to be fine, Coop. It's going to be better than fine. I'm very proud of you, baby. Happy Birthday."

"Thanks, Mom."

"All right, go do something crazy with Frankie."

I chuckled. "I'll tell her you gave us permission."

She was still laughing when we got off the phone. Peter. I stared at my phone for a minute and blew out a breath. Well, if she brought him, that meant I'd have backup when I checked him out and made sure he was good enough.

I could practically *hear* Frankie's scolding look even as she tried not to laugh at me. She was so good about indulging me, but this was my mom and she deserved the best. Frankie got that.

A buzz from my phone reminded me I'd been on the way somewhere. Right, I fired off a quick text to Frankie.

Laughter swelled up within me.

That wasn't what she meant, but didn't mean I wasn't thinking about it. Her answer was a laughing emoji followed by a kiss face and heart.

Yeah, I loved her too.

A happy sigh escaped me as I shoved my phone into my pocket and picked up my pace. Rachel asked me to meet her at the deli a couple of blocks down on West 3rd. She was standing outside of it, jacket on, foot tapping with a large bag and a pair of drinks in a carrier.

"I'm not that late," I said by way of greeting and the scorching look she gave me would have pissed me off in high school. But over the last few years, I'd gotten to know Rachel. Those dismissive, cutting looks were a way she maintained control.

"It's crowded in there," she said by way of explanation as I took the drinks off her hands. "I thought we could walk over to Washington Park."

It was right around the corner, so I didn't see why not. "Want me to carry that?" I nodded to the food bag. She passed it over then took our drinks out of the drink tray so I could toss it in the bin. Then once I had my drink, we were on our way.

Rachel didn't say anything as we walked. Not that I expected her to, even if she'd been the one to ask me to meet her. No, she needed to build up to it. Opening up was not something that came easily to her. The few months she'd lived at the brownstone had seen her grow more comfortable with all of us.

While I used to think of her as the snarky bitch, later Frankie's friend, she was definitely my friend now and I was hers. So I could afford to let her get to the opening up on her own.

Besides, maybe she just wanted to buy me lunch for my birthday. Despite all of her little romantic and thoughtful missives to Frankie once upon a time, Rachel was not the most—poetic of people, I supposed was the nicest way of putting it. Then again, I enjoyed her direct bluntness. Even when she used it to deflect.

The gray skies and damp ground didn't seem to discourage folks from setting up in and around the square. It wasn't uncommon to spot street artists or musicians out here. There'd been a "statue" a few weeks back that I swore Frankie stared at way too long trying to see if he'd break character.

Shaking my head at the memory, I slowed when Rachel motioned to a bench a pair of students had just abandoned. We grabbed it before someone else could slide in and make themselves comfortable. It was damp, but she just stripped her jacket off and set it down for us to sit on.

It wasn't until we'd separated the food and I was chewing on the oversized hot club sandwich she'd gotten for me, and she munched on her chips, that she said anything at all, "Happy birthday, by the way."

"Thanks," I said, lifting my chin. "Appreciate it."

"Yep."

Then silence. Her gaze wasn't on me, but on the others in the park. I just hung there, waiting. Sooner or later she would get around to what she wanted to discuss. Later proved to be after I'd finished my sandwich, the pickle, and all the chips, and thrown away the refuse.

"Did Frankie tell you about the program I applied to?"

"The foreign study? Yeah. She mentioned it." Worried about it too. The idea of Rachel jetting off so far away, where Frankie wouldn't be just a short drive away, bugged her a lot more than she wanted to admit. But Frankie's idea of friendship was to support even the ideas that scared her.

Maybe because they scared her. Taking risks was never something she did casually. Challenge herself? Absolutely. Push herself? Definitely. But taking risks took consideration, and I didn't mind that. It was healthy for her to look at all her options and much better for my own sanity that she took care with herself.

That said, we'd support her every step of the way and Frankie would do no less for us. Had done way more at times.

"Cool." Rachel nodded, then took a drink of her lemonade. Unlike me, she hadn't eaten her sandwich yet. I didn't think she'd even finished the chips.

Leaning back, I stretched out my legs and studied her profile.

"Take a picture," she grumped. "It'll last longer."

"You're the photographer," I reminded her. "But take your time. Normally, I'd tell you I had all day, but I have a date tonight. So, I have four or five hours."

The corner of her mouth kicked up and she gave a little shake like she fought laughing. I hid my own grin and took a drink as she snorted. "Ass."

"Sometimes," I agreed with her.

"But fine, I wouldn't want to make you late for your date."

"Don't worry," I assured her. "Wild horses couldn't keep me from it." My birthday and Frankie? Yeah, love you Rach, not happening. "I'll totally be available tomorrow for a couple of hours to sit here and stare off into space if you need it."

This time, she really did laugh. "You are such a jackass."

"Prick," I reminded her. "We're all pricks, but you're the whole fucking cactus." When she wiped at her eyes while laughing, I pretended not to notice.

"Thank you," she said, still chuckling. "I think I needed that reminder."

"Always at your service. How is Dick by the way?" The cactus we'd sent her for Christmas in senior year had appeared at the Brownstone while she lived there, then vanished back to her new place after she moved out. Little Dick she'd called him, though I'd pointed out there was nothing little about him.

"He's fine," she said with a smirk. "If I get into this program, I may have to leave him with Jeremy for a few months."

"I'm positive Jeremy will not mind. He already looks after Tiddles, Tabby, and Tory as well as Little Miss Abigail. I'm sure having a boy cactus to babysit will offer him a change of pace."

"We should find him a date."

"Probably, but now you're distracting and like I said, I only have a few hours."

"Dominic."

"Nope, I'm Coop."

That earned me a slug in the arm. Damn, she'd been working out. I chuckled at the dark look she sent me. "You know what I meant."

"I do, particularly since we're talking about dicks." At her glower, I raised my hands. "Right, shutting up. Please continue. Dominic…"

Rolling her eyes, Rachel said, "Why do I put up with you?"

"Because you have good taste and I'm easier to talk to. You don't care if you disappoint me in some way. You don't want to disappoint Frankie."

"I am not that shallow."

"It's not shallow at all," I pointed out. "It's the value you put on your relationship with Frankie. I get it. I always have." It was hard to put your own feelings on the backburner when the object of your affection didn't feel the same way.

I'd done it for years.

"I let that go a long time ago."

"I know," I assured her. "It's just not easy to turn off."

She groaned. "I wish it was, and not because of Frankie."

"Because of Dominic." Not even remotely close to a guess because this was where we were and why we were here.

"Yeah." Head tilted back, she stared up at the sky. "This isn't easy."

"If it was easy, you wouldn't be struggling." She was struggling, I had zero doubt about that.

"I probably shouldn't be dumping all this on you on your birthday, either."

"Friends don't dump, they vent and they ask for help. You don't need to worry about the date when you need that."

While I wasn't looking directly at her, I was aware of the way she stared at me. The war she waged with herself had been there for a long time. Rachel craved control, over herself, over her circumstances, over her interactions. She needed it and whatever her relationship with Dominic was, it did not give her even an ounce of control.

"I have no idea what to do about him. I tell him we're not seeing each other, I don't answer his calls, I don't respond to his emails—he still shows up, he still drops off gifts and then one minute I'm telling him he has to go and the next I'm ripping his clothes off." She sounded so damn disgusted with herself. "It's fucking ridiculous. He—makes me crazy. Even when he listens and doesn't come around or call, then we run into each other somewhere and one thing leads to another, even when I tell myself it won't. Sexually? Super compatible."

Okay, more information than I needed to know. But also, good it was one less reason to rip the guy's head off.

"But he's—not the guy for me. We don't agree on so many things and…"

She trailed off long enough, I had to ask. "Like?"

"It doesn't matter. The point is—he's a one-night stand. He was *supposed* to be a one-night stand. A fun little distraction and then I wouldn't see him again. But I can't even enjoy other people or other one-night stands since him. It's like I'm there until I'm not. It's making me crazy."

"Rach," I said, keeping my voice as gentle as I could. "You've known him for a couple of years now."

"You think I don't know that?" She glared at me, but it wasn't me she was pissed at.

"I think I want to know what has you so scared."

"Nothing. Just—he's not the guy for me. This isn't the plan I had. He isn't."

"Okay, plans can change."

She shook her head. "Not this much."

Right. Twisting on the bench, I leaned against the back and faced her even though she kept her gaze on the park. "Then why not him? Be specific. If you really want to end this with him, then tell me why."

"Why do I have to tell you?"

"Because then you're also telling yourself." If that wasn't enough, I added, "You're fighting yourself. You're not just fighting him. So, a part of you wants him. A part of you is rejecting wanting him. You've been seeing other people. Maybe he is too?"

"I've *tried* seeing other people. They're meaningless and half the time nothing happens."

"And the other half?"

She glared at me. "I don't know if he's seeing other people. He probably is. His secrets have secrets."

There we go. "And that's making you crazy?"

"It shouldn't matter to me at all. He's Frankie's attorney. Even if she offered to fire him and the law firm for me." Surprise colored her voice. She should know better, however, Frankie would always put her friends and family first. Dominic irritated me at times, but he had been honest and open with Frankie. And it was her call. "Last week…"

Yeah, we weren't going to just let that go. "Last week?"

"Last week, I was in Times Square, just—taking pictures. Slices of life. Motion. The split between the people heading in to see the shows on Broadway and the tourists, as well as the residents and the people that work there. I have this really great visual I'm building."

I waited.

"Then he was just there, you know, like he was waiting for me to notice him or something. He had this—indulgent expression on his face and his smile…" She sighed. "Right, so we ended up grabbing food and I spent the whole weekend with him."

"Did you talk?"

A shrug.

"You left him Sunday night or Monday morning?"

"Monday morning, right after he went to the gym. I grabbed my stuff and got out of his apartment and went home."

"Okay."

"And I found a note from him in my camera bag." She shook her head. "He said he knew I would likely be gone before he got back, but he would love to take me to dinner. The next move was mine."

She was running. Oh, Rach…

"You spent the whole weekend with him and you didn't talk?"

"We talked about ordering food. We talked about—you know some stuff but nothing…"

"Rach," I interrupted and it pulled her gaze to mine. "Do you talk to him at all like you talk to me? Or to Frankie? Or even to Jeremy?"

"No," she said finally. "We talk about some stuff, but talking about anything always seems to lead to clothes coming off. You'd think after two years I'd have gotten him out of my system."

"Not going to comment on that other than to tell you, I will never get Frankie out of my system and I don't want to." I held up a hand when she opened her mouth. "That said, I'm going to offer you a little hard truth. Not because I think you deserve it, but because I think you need it."

Her knuckles went a little white against the side of her cup. "I'm listening."

"Good. I'm not knocking sex or one-night stands. But if you are trying to start a relationship with someone, the first place you go isn't sex. It shouldn't be. An infatuation isn't love. But you fall into bed with someone and it leads to enhanced feelings of bonding and affection. Suddenly, you think you're more in love than you are."

"I didn't say I was in love with him."

"You're not saying you aren't, either." I met her flat stare without blinking and she grimaced. "When we have sex, or when we hug or snuggle or make out, dopamine is released, which is pleasure. But also oxytocin and vasopressin, which are bonding."

Her grimace deepened and she looked away.

I still had her attention though. "So, what ends up happening is when you get physically involved with someone, you not only experience pleasure, you feel bonded to them. This is why when you get into a dating relationship that is very physical very early on, we're in love with an idea of who we *think* they are."

I'd been lucky as hell with Frankie, we'd been stupid and damn near lost the best thing that ever happened to us. "Look, most of us want touch and commitment. Some are ace and aren't interested, but most of us want both sex and romance, so we kind of rush into those things and then retroactively try to build a relationship afterwards. And then what ends up happening is someone betrays us or they're not who we think they are, because we weren't in love with *them* but with who we thought they should be."

Her hard swallow tugged at my heart.

Our relationship with Frankie, our history, that saved us. "So, we fly in blind and then it backfires. Go to dinner. Talk about crap. Get to know each other. Don't fuck."

"That the best you got, Brennen?"

I shrugged. "If you had someone better to ask you wouldn't be talking to me—finally."

She sighed. "I hate my life."

"Well, hate it over a bottle of wine and a nice meal. Talk to the man and see if there's anything there. Just stop fucking him every time you see him."

"Easier said than done."

I laughed.

"It's not funny," she complained, hitting my biceps with the back of her hand, but she was smiling.

"Someday…" I promised her. "You'll look back and laugh too."

She flipped me off.

"Until then, I got your back. So does Frankie. All of us do. And if you need someone to kick his ass…"

Now she genuinely laughed. "I know, Frankie already promised Jake would be all in for that."

Yeah. He would.

So would I.

Her laughter faded. "Thanks, Coop."

"Anytime, Rach. Anytime."

"Except in about four hours…"

"You can totally leave me a message," I offered. "I promise to return it tomorrow."

This time when she laughed—it was real.

Chapter Nine

CELEBRATE GOOD TIMES

We'd had dinner together at home with Jeremy making all of Coop's favorites. The fact he enjoyed most meals made that part easy, but it was fun to have all five of us in one spot for longer than a quick meal. Still, we couldn't linger. I'd made reservations for both of us.

The guys were always *asking* me out on dates, but the rule of birthday boy got what the birthday boy wanted, also meant I could ask them out. Granted, I'd dipped into my experiences with the guys for this one. But I was rather proud of the plans I'd made.

I'd gotten dressed up for the occasion, one that earned me a lot of generous looks from the guys and more than one grumble that I was leaving.

"Too bad, so sad, my brother boyfriends," Coop declared with a cocky grin. "Tonight, it's my birthday and my date with our girl, you will just have to ask her to wear it again some other time. You know what they say…"

"Yeah," Jake retorted in a dry tone of voice. "The birthday boy gets what the birthday boy wants and right now he seems to want a fat lip and a black eye."

He and Ian knuckle bumped and I rolled my eyes before making a quick round of kisses. "Behave boys, there will be no fighting. Just make Coop go running with us this weekend."

Archie laughed and Coop let out a squawk. "Hey! That's mean."

I grinned at him. "You can run right behind me and watch my ass. You said that's very inspiring."

The guys laughed as I threaded my arm through Coop's. His frown turned into a smile. "Your ass is extremely inspiring. Night boys!" Outside, he glanced up at the sky and then down at me. I had on a light jacket but I wasn't really that cold. "Have I mentioned how much I love this outfit?"

"You did," I said as we walked down the steps. Once upon a time, I would have objected to wearing it. It showed off a lot more skin than I would have been comfortable with. After the tour and the photography sessions with Rachel, I'd actually enjoyed trying it on.

I enjoyed it even more when I'd come down for dinner. The guys' expressions ranged from mouth-open staring to wild grins. The last had definitely been Archie's and I could almost imagine the lingerie he'd be buying now, but that was fine. Coop's delight had been the one I'd been going for, not that I minded the attention they all gave me.

The outfit was close to the two-piece one Coop had picked out during that dress shopping trip in senior year. Only this top had long sleeves made out of lace, and the top and bottom were connected with a cutout around my belly button and lower back.

The green was perfect, and though the top and bottom were also lace, they were over full cover panels that meant my ass and breasts were not also on display. The peekaboo with my belly button and arms was fine. It also let me show off my belly button piercing.

When he caught my hand and raised his arm at the bottom of the steps, I did a little twirl.

"Where to next?" Coop asked. I hadn't actually revealed our plans for the evening. It was a surprise.

"Next…" Right on cue our car pulled up. "We take a ride!"

He laughed.

Thankfully, the ride wasn't a long one. I'd done my research to find something special and I was dying to show it to him. The fact they'd opened one in one of the midtown hotels made this even better. Coop didn't say anything when we got out at the hotel, hand-in-hand we walked inside.

The minute his gaze landed on the sign, his expression morphed from amusement to delight back to amusement, and then he grinned at me. "You love me."

"Yes, I do," I promised him. "Even when you're so busy, you forget to take your lunch with you or you aren't getting enough sleep and I have to worry and chase across town after you."

"Aww, I'm not the overachiever in the group either," he teased, then kissed the tip of my nose.

"Wouldn't matter, I'd go anywhere for you. Besides, I love that you love what you do." He was going to be so good at it. He had more study in front of him, a degree to finish, then clinical hours to put in. "I'm proud of you."

Eyes gentling, he turned to face me and cupped my cheeks. "Right back atcha, Beautiful."

The kiss was achingly sweet and brief. "To be continued," I whispered and I swore he smiled with his whole body as his eyes lit up.

"I'm looking forward to it."

Taking his hand again, we headed for the doorman in front of the elevators that would take us up to the top floor restaurant. You couldn't even get in without a reservation. I'd made it a couple of months earlier, with a little help from Jeremy.

"Brennen," I told him. "Party of two."

If it were possible, Coop's grin grew. The man checked his digital tablet, then nodded. Turning, he used a key then pressed a button and the elevator doors opened. "Bienvenue au puits d'amour. S'il vous plaît profitez de votre soirée."

"Merci," I said as the elevator doors closed and we began the smooth ride all the way to the top.

"You're going to order everything in French, aren't you?" Coop's smile said he didn't mind in the slightest.

"Absolument. Je sais combien tu aimes m'entendre parler français."

He was still laughing when the doors opened to the fancy French restaurant with one of the finest pâtissiers in the city, or so they claimed. That was only *part* of the reason we were here.

A hostess greeted us as soon as we stepped out into the dining room. It was very cozy up here, the lighting was set to low and romantic, the tables and chairs placed to provide privacy. Apparently, their system let them know who we were before we came up, which was great, because she just led us through this dining room to the second one that was located behind a huge oaken door. This one was a room made almost entirely out of glass that gave us an exceptional view of the city, and the tables here were even fewer and farther apart.

Coop moved to pull out my chair for me as I eased off my jacket, then he took the chair closest to mine. Our hostess murmured a quiet good evening and enjoy, before she withdrew.

"What are you up to?" Coop asked and I couldn't stop my own grin.

"Figured out I was up to something, have you?"

He snorted. "You've been up to mischief for as long as I've known you."

"Yeah well, you've been in that mischief with me for nearly as long."

"This is also true," he said, then a waiter approached with a tray bearing two large glass mugs of coffee, rimmed in chocolate—dark for me, milk for Coop—and a pair of shot glasses with Amaretto in them.

"Good evening," he said, his lack of a French accent making me smile. "Welcome to Puits D'Amour, thank you for choosing us this evening for your late-night rendezvous."

Since it wasn't even nine yet, it was hardly late, but Coop's grin was worth it.

"If the gentleman would be so kind as to show me his identification."

Coop pulled out his wallet before giving me an indulgent look. The waiter glanced at it then nodded.

"Thank you." He set the coffees in front of us and the scent was rich and indulgent. Then he set the shots of Amaretto down next to Coop. "This evening's rendezvous will begin and end with coffee, as per special request. I will give you a few minutes to enjoy your coffee before I bring out the first round?"

"Merci," I told him and he inclined his head.

"Okay, if the goal was to get me horny, we were there five seconds after you walked downstairs in this dress," Coop teased me before he glanced down at the coffee then at me.

"That wasn't the goal," I promised. "Just a lovely perk."

"Uh huh." He studied me. "Spill, Beautiful. I can see the excitement dancing in your eyes."

I laughed. "Okay, that's not fair, you guys surprise me all the time."

"We're good at it. You suck."

Mouth open, I gaped at him and he just laughed.

"Beautiful, you have the most expressive face and when you're excited, you don't hide it."

"Terrible man, why do I love you?"

"I used to ask myself that question, but I don't anymore." He picked up his coffee and raised it to me, so I lifted my own to clink the glasses together gently. "I love you and I love that you love me. That's all I have to know."

I waited a beat for him to take a sip before I did and the little orgasm in my mouth had me closing my eyes to savor. French roasted coffee, dark blend, with the dark chocolate all around the rim and a hint of cream in the coffee itself was like perfection. Giving into temptation, I ran my tongue around the rim before I took another drink.

At his faint sound of choking, I giggled.

"You are so bad," he accused me as he grinned and I lifted my shoulders.

"Guilty."

Still, the coffee was amazing. Coop added the Amaretto to his, but I shook my head at the offer. I did not want to fall asleep on him, not even if he thought it was funny.

Since we had already eaten dinner, this was a dessert date. The waiter returned with three large bowls, each one containing a different dessert. I'd picked them out on purpose.

After he set each bowl down along with the different sets of spoons, so we had a clean one for each dish, he glanced at our coffees.

"Not yet," Coop said, particularly since we hadn't finished these. Once he was gone, Coop looked at me expectantly and I chuckled.

"Oh, this is my favorite part."

"I think I can change your mind later."

"I'm pretty sure you can too," I teased. "However, partenaire parfait, Perfect Partner—this is a dish done with vanilla bean ice cream drizzled in white chocolate." At the next dish, the one with crumbly cake and crispy torte along with ice cream and drizzled in caramel with cinnamon. "Croustillant missionaire—Missionary Crisp."

That got him, he laughed and then lifted his chin toward the third dish that looked like death by chocolate. Man, what a way to go.

"That is called a *double farci,* Double Stuffed." His laughter deepened, but I used the spoon to tease some of those layers apart to get him a bite. "This has cheesecake ice cream, white chocolate, vanilla bean custard and brown sugar with a dark chocolate drizzle and sprinkle. It's supposed to taste like the fanciest chocolate creme cookie you've ever had."

When I held it up for him, he closed his lips around the spoon and sucked the bite right off of it. His eyes closed as he savored the bite. "Holy crap," he muttered as he opened his eyes.

"Good?"

"Yes." He reached forward and grabbed a spoon to get another bite but instead of eating it, he held the chocolate drenched bite out to me, no sooner did I take the bite then he caught me in a kiss and chased every bit of the chocolate with his tongue.

Right.

A shudder went through me as he lifted his head. "Just like I thought, that would be better."

Amusement and delight vied for top billing, but we took turns feeding each other bites then testing how they tasted on our tongues. He seemed especially fond of the Double Stuffed and we both liked the Perfect Partner. Poor Missionary Crisp though, we did make an effort at it.

I was practically vibrating from all the sugar. When it was time for our next round of coffee, I was happy that it was darker and far stronger than the first round. Even the dark chocolate seemed richer somehow.

"Happy birthday," I murmured for our coffee toast this time.

"Thank you, Beautiful."

We lingered for a little while longer, teasing each other, reminiscing about past birthdays. The guys tried not to linger on the topic too much, but I was determined to take back everything that had been pulled away. Maddy's choices may have created an issue on *one* of my birthdays, but she didn't get to ruin them all.

Bless him, Coop didn't bat an eyelash or bring up why he might be worried about it. Nope, we just laughed. When we were done, we took a separate elevator to go down to our room.

"Aha!" Coop threaded his arms around me and pulled me back against his chest after I pressed the button for another floor. "I knew you had more planned."

"Of course, I did." I held up my phone. "I even checked in on the phone and everything."

I loved the new system. I didn't have to pick up a key because the phone let me scan it as a key and it worked to open the door. I'd gotten us a suite. It wasn't huge, but we didn't need huge. It had a lovely view of Times Square and all the lights.

"You really went to a lot of trouble," he murmured once we were inside. I set my phone and purse down with my jacket.

Turning to face him, I looped my arms around his neck. "You're important to me… and I miss you."

He let out a little sigh, then rested his forehead against mine. "I'll work on my schedule—"

I pressed a finger to his lips even as I stroked my free hand through the hair at his nape. "This isn't me criticizing you or trying to get you to change anything. It's me valuing you every minute we get together. I've been very spoiled the last few years."

He nipped my finger and then raised his brows. "Yeah?"

"Oh, yeah. You see, my best friend lived three doors down from me for years. He was always right there whenever I needed him. I saw him every day. Sometimes, I saw him for hours in and out every day. Only twice did he leave for summer vacations where I didn't get to see him and he still called me all the time."

"Sounds like a good guy."

"The very best. Then when we started dating, he was more than just always there. He moved in, he shared my days, my nights, my weekends, my hopes, my dreams, my holidays—my love for others."

"Wow, this guy sounds a little too good to be true. What flaw does this paragon of virtue possess?"

I smacked his chest once and he grinned. "He's a brat," I pointed out.

"He also thinks he's a funny guy."

"Hysterical," Coop assured me as he began walking me backwards. "Class clown."

I snorted. "The point," I emphasized the last word. "I was trying to make is, that I was very spoiled with you always being there. This year—everyone is so busy. I don't want to drift apart."

He stopped in the doorway separating the sitting room from the bedroom. Lifting his head, he studied me. "Beautiful, are you really worried that we're going to think you—that *I* am going to think you love me less because I'm not seeing you as much because of competing schedules?"

"Well, when you say it like that…"

"Hey." He ran his hands up and down my arms. "This is important. I'm having an amazing time with the woman that I love because she wanted to make my birthday special. What you need to remember is that you make every day special. I know the new schedule is hard. I miss you when we're apart. I missed you when you and Bubba were doing the tour."

I bit my lip.

"But you knew I supported you on that, right?"

"Yes, I absolutely knew you did. You guys were amazing about that."

"And you're amazing about my schedule. You're just as busy as I am, you're juggling school, music, learning the business, and trying to be there to support all of us, and we're all going in different directions. But there's not a shadow of a doubt in my mind that you don't have my back. That I can't pick up the phone and call you or any of the guys. You'd be there. Just like we're there for them."

"Yes, exactly like that." So, I'd been worrying for nothing. "I just need you to know you're important to me and that you matter. I want to be there for you. I want you to succeed, even if it means we have to schedule time—like this."

"This isn't so bad," he told me and I smiled. "This is pretty damn great, but all I really need to know is that you're waiting for me when I come home or coming home to me. That's all I've ever really needed. We're navigating all the messy stuff and we're juggling schedules. There's gonna be hard times and easier ones. But I trust you to get through them with me. With us."

Wrapping my arms around his neck, I hugged him tightly and he scooped me up, picking me right off the floor to return the fierce embrace. "You were really worried about this, weren't you, Beautiful?"

"A little," I admitted, tucking my face against his throat. "It's stupid…"

"No, it's not. You're entitled to your feelings, but I'm really glad you told me." He pressed a kiss to my hair and carried me into the bedroom. "We don't talk about the future that much. We're always so busy dealing with today."

At the edge of the bed, he paused and I lifted my head to meet his gaze.

"Maybe we should make time to talk about it," I suggested. Because I wasn't the only one in this relationship. "I don't want you guys worrying about me."

"Eh, too late for that," he murmured as he set me on my feet. "We're always going to worry, but yes, we should make a point of checking in with each other and seeing where we are. You and Bubba talk to us about plans for Bound Hearts all the time, make sure we're all on the same page. I think it's a good idea for all of us."

"Yeah?"

"Yeah," he said, then traced his fingers up my neck to cup my nape. "You know what else I think is a good idea?"

"Getting me naked so you can have the rest of your present?"

"Wait," he said, pausing as he released me and stepped back. "You mean I get more?"

I laughed. "Smart ass."

"Yes, I am. But I'm good with sitting here and talking about whatever you need, Beautiful. This has been a damn good birthday as far as I'm concerned."

"Oh," I said slowly. "Well, if you don't want…"

I didn't even make it two steps before he caught my arm and tugged me back, we landed on the bed together with a bit of a bounce before his mouth closed over mine. The kiss held every bit of promise and affection, but it also held lust, laughter, and yes, chocolate.

"Truth or dare," he murmured in between kisses as he slid warm hands up my bare legs to find a second secret. Jerking upward, he stared down at me even as he teased a finger along the seam of my pussy. "Frankie, you went that whole evening, dinner, car ride, sex chocolate—and you had no panties on?"

I grinned. "Happy birthday, Coop. Dare me to do whatever you want."

His fist pump lasted all of a second before he claimed my mouth again.

The press of his lips on mine was both sensuous and silly. He grinned and I laughed. Then our teeth clacked and I cracked up harder, until he pushed two fingers into me and then I was groaning.

"Dare," he murmured, placing little nipping, biting kisses along my jaw to my throat as he skated his thumb over my clit. Okay, the challenge was to respond while he drove me crazy.

"That's what I said," I replied in a breathless voice as I carded my fingers through his hair. It was so damn soft under my hands. He pressed his lips to my pulse point and sucked against the skin. I squirmed at the pressure he added both there and with his thumb as he curled his fingers inside of me.

What was it with these guys and not even taking off their clothes before they had me coming? That thought fractured on the crest of the orgasm that shoved me over the edge. My little scream seemed to entertain him as he chuckled against my throat, before he traced his tongue over the hickey he had to have left.

"That sounded like I needed to work a little harder," he teased. My inner muscles were still spasming around his fingers as I fisted his hair. He lifted his head with a teasing grin. "Oh, right—dare."

I groaned because he was teasing my clit again and there was nowhere to go to escape the overstimulation.

"Aww, Beautiful, you don't have to whimper." His grin grew wicked.

The growl I released just made his grin grow even happier as he pressed a hard and fast kiss to my lips before sliding down half of the bed. He paused to press a kiss to my belly button and the piercing there. A whisper of his lips teasing the skin around it before he glanced up at me.

I pushed up on my elbows, but he gripped my bare legs and tugged me to the edge of the bed and my ass was barely balanced with my thighs over his shoulders.

"Remind me not to hurt this dress," Coop said as he eased his fingers out of me and then palmed my ass like he planned to massage it. "Since we came here for some French and dessert, I don't want to get too carried away."

Grinning, I pushed the hair out of my eyes so I could lock gazes with him. "And my dare?" Because my heart raced and the tease of his breath against my skin promised all kinds of distractions in a minute.

A slow smile spread across his face just before he licked his lips. The pressure of his hands against my thighs and his thumbs on my folds pressing me wider, was enough to almost make me inhale spit.

"I dare you," he said in a deep voice that had my belly bottoming out. I fisted the comforter on the bed because he was so close to my pussy that the next movement of his lips teased the soft flesh there. "To sing the French national anthem while I indulge myself in this dessert."

The… "*La Marseillaise*?" Shock rippled through me. "Are you se—" I choked as he licked me from entrance to clit before he thrust his tongue and added pressure to my clit with his thumbs.

My brain short-circuited at the rush of heat and tension coiling tightly within me. Coop alternated thrusting with his tongue, to sucking against my clit, to thrumming it with his thumbs. The swift changes shattered my focus, an effect he enhanced by chuckling, teasing my clit.

The vibrations sent little shocks that had me rolling my hips and I wasn't sure whether I was writhing to get away or to get closer. But the squeeze of his hands on my ass helped. I caught him staring up at me and I flushed as I tried to cobble together what the hell the lines of the song were, much less the tune.

It came out warbly at best. I made it through the first refrain before the orgasm crashed down on me. The last note came out on a scream and he lifted his head, the dampness shining on his chin and lips. The delight in his eyes was both reward and teasing enticement to continue.

Clenching my ass, I tugged him back toward me as I crossed my ankles behind his back. At his raised eyebrows, I began the second refrain. No lie, it came out on trembling notes as I fought for some semblance of breath control.

"Fuck, I love you," Coop said before he went to work devouring my pussy like it was his favorite sweet treat. Somehow, I made it through the whole damn thing, but I was a shaking, half-sobbing mess by the time I finished.

He looked so damned pleased with himself as he eased away from my shaking legs. After he wiped his face on the comforter, he half-picked me up and then helped me out of the dress.

"Totally naked under all that beautiful lace," he murmured as he stared down at me. "You know opening presents used to be my favorite thing."

"Not anymore?" I asked, still looking for a few unscrambled brain cells to put back together.

"Nope," he said, unbuttoning his shirt with purpose. I had the best view in the whole place as he stripped out of those nice clothes, his grin unwavering. "Playing with my present will always be my favorite thing."

His dick bounced against his belly, thick, proud, and reddened at the top. The gleam of silver there would never not make me catch my breath. A year, he'd had that piercing. A year since he'd revealed it to me on his *last* birthday.

"I love you," I whispered as he crawled over me and settled his hips between my legs even as he braced himself on his elbows.

"Yeah?"

"Oh yeah" Still shaking or not, I reached down to wrap my hand around him. I swore he pulsed against my palm and he gave a full body shudder. "I love all of you from the top of your head to the tips of your toes to this beautiful pierced dick."

"I like the sound of that," he whispered as I caressed his length in firm, slow motions, and took my time tracing the tip. "You did beautifully with the anthem by the way."

I giggled. "Truth or dare?"

"Truth, Beautiful, I don't know if you can handle any more dares. You already sound a little hoarse."

"Well, I guess we should stop…" I let out a little forlorn sigh. "I hate to think we've gotten so out of practice."

I let my lashes dip down, hiding my eyes.

"You did not just…" Coop fought a smile despite the scandalized tone.

"Well, we'll just have to work our way back up to it."

His little growl was just delightful. "Dare, Beautiful. Dare me. I dare you."

"That's not how this works," I said with a chortle as I angled him against my pussy, and began to tease the tip along my slit. "I do the daring, you just tell me whether you'll take a truth or a dare."

His gray-green eyes darkened with both humor and lust. "Dare."

"It would serve you right if I said you had to sing the French anthem all the way through while not losing your rhythm or finishing before you finished the song…"

"Challenge," he began as he thrust forward. The first long push was always breathtaking as it pushed the air out of my lungs. The stretch to accommodate him bordered right on the edge of pain but I always craved it. The piercing just added to the rush of pleasure.

Still, I managed to press a finger to his lips before he finished accepting the dare. "That's not my dare," I said on what little air I managed to suck back in.

He bit the tip of my finger and the look on his face said get to the point, even if he continued to fight his smile.

"I dare you to get us to twenty-one orgasms for twenty-one years—between us."

Shock registered briefly before his whole expression turned positively jubilant. "Do the three I already got out of you count?"

I considered it. "Yes."

He gave a little rocking motion and I swore the angle was perfect because it struck sparks across my already sensitive nerves.

"So, three down," he whispered, before narrowing the distance until his lips brushed mine with each word. "Eighteen to go."

"Uh huh."

"I hope you don't have plans tomorrow, Beautiful," he murmured before he nipped my lower lip. "Because I don't think either of us is going to be walking."

Wrapping my arms around him, I arched upward to meet his lips for a real kiss, whispering, "Challenge accepted."

Chapter Ten
PLAYING ALL THE OLD FAVORITES

Archie

I glared at my watch. Dammit, I was late. Again. Not that staring at the digital face did a damn thing to change the time on it. The smartwatch also indicated missed messages on my phone. I tilted my head back and turned my stare on the ceiling of the subway.

There were any number of ways for me to get back from Brooklyn. I could have called a car. I could have driven one of the three cars I had parked there currently. Hell, I could have taken a damn cab. No, I'd walked the half-mile to the nearest subway entrance and then endured the two train switches to get home.

Why?

Fuck if I knew. I raked a hand over my face. Then shifted my weight as we reached the stop closest to home. My phone buzzed in my back pocket.

Fuck.

Fuck.

Fuck.

I was either pissing her off or worrying her. I pulled the phone out as I headed for the exit stairs. It was a busy time of day, so I kept a solid half of my attention on my surroundings so I didn't crash into someone.

The messages on the screen were not from Frankie. Well—one of them was. But not all of them.

Bubba

C'mon, Arch, pick up the phone and let her know you're fine.

Coop

Dude, not cool. You were supposed to be home an hour ago.

Jake

You're a lucky asshole that she loves you. Stop pushing it.

Well, that boded well.

The last message stopped me dead at the top of the stairs and I took the hit against my shoulder as someone ran into me. I muttered sorry but they were already moving away. One hand automatically going to check my wallet was still where it should be—my front pocket right now—I stared at the message.

Edward

If my presence is a problem, I'll go. Frankie invited me, but I don't want to be an issue between the two of you.

Right. I was an asshole.

Me

Stay. I'm almost there. I just need to change and we can go

Next, I skipped the guys' messages and went straight to hers. I damn near laughed at the message waiting for me.

I did not deserve her.

It took me seven. He must have been watching for me because Jeremy opened the door before I even reached the steps. Braced for his disapproval, I climbed up to where he and not so little Miss Abigail waited. She thumped her tail, but sat patiently beside him.

"I'm late," I told him. "I know. I'd say I lost track of time but…"

"I understand. Miss Frankie has made all the arrangements and I pulled out a suit for this evening and set it out for you. The car is due here in an hour."

Oh.

"You have time to shower," he continued and that didn't sound like a suggestion but an order. "Then come down and join the others for drinks and cake before you all leave."

"Sounds like a plan." I reached out to give Miss Abigail some ear scritches as Jeremy let me in. "Thanks, Jere."

"You're more than welcome, Mr. Archie. Might I also recommend a shave?"

"You got it."

Conversation drifted from somewhere near the backyard. They might be out in the garden, allowing me time to come in and get changed without running into anyone.

"Happy birthday, Mr. Archie."

I paused on the steps heading upstairs. "Thank you, Jeremy. For everything."

He held my gaze for a moment, then nodded firmly. Some of the tension in my gut relaxed. It wasn't disapproval or even disappointment in his eyes, but concern. Turning, I hurried up and threw myself through a shower. I made quick work of shaving and scrubbed until I couldn't smell the oil on my skin anymore.

Fifteen minutes later, I knotted the tie properly. It was brand new, red and gold, and matched the pocket square. There were new cufflinks too. Someone had been shopping.

After giving myself the once over, I turned and found Frankie standing in the doorway. All the breath knocked out of me. She wore a strapless cocktail dress, in the exact same deep burgundy red of my tie, and the charm bracelet and necklace I'd given her. She wore the class ring Jake had given her. The only other jewelry was a pair of simple red earrings that I'd given her for Christmas.

"How much trouble am I in, Babe? Because you look like fifty million bucks."

Pushing away from the door, she strolled toward me with a gentle smile. "You're not in trouble at all." Okay, that actually made me feel worse. She smoothed her hands over the front of my suit jacket. "Stop beating yourself up. I planned for you to be running a bit later because you've been losing yourself in your work."

I sighed, covering her hands with mine. "Babe, you shouldn't have to make considerations…"

At the arch of her brows, I snapped my mouth closed. Yeah, I knew that look. She nodded and then reached up to kiss me lightly. The sweet jasmine and vanilla lingered on her. Oh, the perfume I gave her for her birthday because it reminded me of her.

She blamed it on the name of "Red."

Still, I loved it.

Loved her more. Capturing her for a lingering kiss, I sighed before resting my forehead to hers. The green of her eyes always captivated me, more so now than even when we were younger. There was a kindness in her eyes—even when she was angry with us. With me. The kindness was always there.

"I'm sorry I'm a mess, Babe."

"You're not a mess and if you are, you're my mess, and I'm here, you're here and it's going to be okay."

She'd said that before. "You sure about that?"

"Absolutely."

This time my smile didn't need to be forced. "I adore you."

"I know, you show me a hundred different ways. Now… I invited Eddie…" Yeah that was weird that she called him that, and kind of sweet in a way too. Like, she took that name back from that mad bitch of a mother she'd been stuck with. "He wasn't certain about coming because he didn't want to intrude."

"He's not and thank you for asking him. I probably should have, but I didn't think about it." Probably wouldn't have. I was so used to his absences. Numbed myself to the disappointment they'd once generated. "I'm glad he's here." Weirdly, I meant it. "And I love the plans you've made."

She grinned. "Well, everything is up to you. I mean, we can go down, have drinks and then come back up and get naked. I'll even let you sit down before I wrap my lips around your cock and suck you off until you're dizzy."

Fuck.

Me.

All the blood in my body flooded south and I closed my eyes, just savoring that image with the cheerful twinkle in her eyes overlaying it.

"That said," she continued, the amusement in her voice promising me that my reaction had not escaped her notice. "We can also have drinks, go out for dinner and some dancing, then escape over to the Glen, where I promise that sucking you off is still on the menu."

Laughing softly, I met her playful gaze with a grin. "So, what I hear you saying is that I'm going to get to fuck that beautiful mouth no matter where we end up tonight?"

"Pretty much." And look at that, she'd managed to deliver that alluring promise and provocative image with only the faintest of blushes.

"Okay, one drink, one appetizer, light meal, and plenty of water in and around three dances. Hydration is important. Then I want to eat strawberries and chocolates with some whipped cream off your skin for dessert."

Her tongue stroked over her lower lip and her breath quickened at my description. "That sounds positively decadent."

Yeah, it did.

"Then I think we better get downstairs and have drinks before I figure out whether I can fuck your mouth right now…"

When she opened her mouth, I stole another kiss. She practically purred at the contact and I chuckled.

"You're killing me, Babe."

"Good thing I know mouth to mouth."

I smacked her ass and she let out a half-gasp, but I rubbed her through the skirt dress and then froze. It was on the tip of my tongue to ask if she was wearing panties or not. Coop's story had given all of us pause and her wicked little smile had definitely left a mark.

Yeah, better I wait to find out.

"Let's go," I said, grinning despite the abruptness. "I suddenly find myself in a hurry to get through all the social bits of this celebration."

Her laughter wreathed us as I half-propelled her out of the room before I gave into every single dirty impulse I had. The thought of my cum dripping down her thighs during dinner had a certain appeal—to me. Pretty sure she wouldn't enjoy it as much.

My dick gave a protest, but I ignored it as we descended the stairs. The doors to the back garden stood open. Edward stood there listening to Jake as he discussed his latest flying lesson. I should have taken that flying class with him. Maybe I'd do that in the spring. I loved the idea of taking up our own planes.

Bubba caught sight of us and he already had a cold beer in hand to offer me as Frankie and I walked out. Coop lounged in a chair, feet up and his head back. He had Tory on his lap, though the other two cats were not in evidence, and Miss Abigail sprawled at his feet.

The cats had grown more accustomed to Miss Abigail over the last few months, but they didn't always want to hang out with her. Tory was different. Then again, Tory had a thing for Coop and she pretty much liked hanging out with him.

"Edward," I said as I grasped the hand he offered. "Eddie, I guess, if you prefer."

Frankie gave me a secretive little smile as she slipped around us and took the glass of wine Jake held out to her. She leaned up and murmured something to him and the semi-glare he'd been giving me vanished.

He nodded, then gave her a light kiss and shot me an apologetic look. I lifted my chin. We were fine. He had a reason to kick my ass for being late, no arguments here.

"Edward or Eddie is fine," Edward said with ease. "I'd like to earn my way back to Dad, if that's at all possible."

Shock rippled through me and for the first time in a long while, I was speechless.

"But I'll earn it," he continued. "Thank you for letting me come to your birthday."

You know what… "Thank you for wanting to come, Eddie." Yeah, that was going to take some getting used to. Then again, I'd begun to reserve calling him "Edward" for more disdainful times. Of which, we'd had— almost none in a long, long time. "But we should both thank Frankie, she's the brains behind this outfit."

Eddie actually chuckled. "Well then…" He turned and raised his glass toward her. "To Frankie, the loveliest hostess and very much the best decision my son has ever made."

"Yeah, but what's her excuse?" Coop drawled with a grin. Everyone laughed, even me, but Frankie smacked his arm.

The drinks in the garden proved very nice, Frankie perched on Bubba's knee rather than sitting on the chairs. It was cooler out here, but Jeremy had turned on the heat lamps. He also brought out some hors d'oeuvres, including my favorite meatballs and Frankie's preferred stuffed mushrooms. There were also meat and cheese skewers.

From the looks of it, we had plenty to eat if we elected to stay. Frankie finished her wine though and declined a second glass and I polished off my beer. Still, we lingered. Jake brought me up to speed on the discussion he'd been having with Eddie regarding the engine design we were working on and the tests.

Eventually though, Frankie said it was time to go. In agreement, I led the way inside with Eddie while she lingered to say good night to the guys. We wouldn't be back tonight. If anything, I loved that she'd made arrangements, but then left the final call to my decision.

I collected a coat for Frankie after pulling on mine, then glanced to where Eddie gazed toward the doors to the garden. He frowned briefly then glanced at me and I raised my brows, waiting.

"I'm not judging," he told me solemnly, almost too solemnly. So, I let out a breath and let go of the instant need to go to war with him before he'd even said anything.

"Okay," I said, accepting the answer for what it was. "But is something else bothering you?"

"No," he said. "Impressing me. Surprising me. Maybe even making me a bit envious."

Okay, now he really had my attention.

"She's an exceptional young woman," Eddie continued. "But all four of you are exceptional young men. This family you've built. It impressed Dad. It impresses the hell out of me."

The mention of Grandpa robbed any remaining heat of rebellion from me. "Thank you," I said slowly. "We work really hard at this." Which was true, but it wasn't always hard work. "She's worth it." Then because it was important to make this clear. "So are they. Brother boyfriends, as Sara calls it."

To his credit, Eddie didn't laugh in my face but he did look amused. I was saved by whatever comment he had been thinking about as Frankie joined us and I held up her coat for her.

"Sorry," she said, flushed and grinning. "Jake and Coop decided to settle a bet and chose right now to do it."

Yeah, I'll just *bet* they had. "It's fine, Babe. Eddie and I can actually manage conversations all on our own these days." I pressed a kiss to her cheek as I hugged her from behind and then glanced at Eddie. "He's impressed with our romantic geometry."

"Our…" She made a snorting sound and I got swatted. It was perfect. Right on time, Eddie's phone buzzed and it saved me from a second swat. "You're lucky the car is here."

"Yes," I told her, pulling her to me for a kiss. "I am very lucky." For way more than the car's arrival.

Dinner was at a familiar favorite called La Vite e Cenare. I hadn't thought about this place in *years*. At my expression, Frankie bit her lip. Eddie moved ahead of us, giving us some privacy. I could read the worry waiting for me and I kissed her gently.

"Babe, thank you."

"Are you sure? I second-guessed this a dozen times after Eddie told me about it, but Jeremy said you loved this place when you were younger."

"I did," I said, nodding. "Grandpa and Nana used to bring me here whenever they brought me to the city. They make the best manicotti and ravioli. I mean—it's—" I did a chef's kiss.

Sadness struck along with nostalgia and maybe a bit of melancholy.

"I'd half-forgotten about this…" And that would have been a damn tragedy. "So yes, thank you, Babe. I love it."

I pressed another kiss to her lips and she smiled. "I want the ravioli," she told me and I grinned.

"Excellent choice."

Dinner was every bit as good as I remembered. Eddie proved to have a few memories of this place himself. They were great. Including a couple of birthdays celebrated here. Which should have been my warning that we would get serenaded by the staff.

The ravioli was amazing. The company was fantastic—even having Eddie there. When he would have excused himself after the meal, I insisted that he stay for dessert. The tiramisu was to die for, and we ordered espressos to drink.

Not that I needed anything to keep me awake. After the meal, we walked out to two different cars, but Eddie pulled me aside not too far because we both glanced to where Frankie waited by the doors. She was giving us a bit of privacy.

"Thank you, again, for letting me come." Eddie reached into his jacket and pulled out an envelope. "And don't look at me like that, of course I did something for your birthday."

Right. New leaf and all that. "Sorry, please, continue."

He nodded. "This was a small investment I made the day you were born. It was for some stock that a lot of people thought wouldn't go anywhere, but I liked the sound of it. I decided that if it went well, then it was yours and if it didn't—well, it was my gamble after all."

"I'm guessing it went well?"

"You could say that." He handed me the envelope. Since he was waiting, I went ahead and slit it open. Inside was a financial statement. The investment had been in a little startup online service.

One that wasn't so little or even remotely a startup anymore. It was a global giant.

"I bought a hundred shares that day. With maturation and stock splits, it's about seventy-five thousand shares today. Not enough to be a threat to their board, but worth about twelve point six million dollars in standard trading at today's share price."

That was… "A hell of a gamble."

Eddie nodded. "You were the more valuable gamble. Hopefully, I'm doing better with it now than I did then."

He held out his hand and I took it. On impulse, I gave him a half hug, one that caught him off guard if his sudden stiffening was any indication. Though, it was only a brief hesitation before he returned the hug.

"You know," I said as we took a step back. "You didn't have to give this to me."

"Someday," he said. "You'll have kids of your own, at least I hope you will, and I know the kind of investment you'll put into them. Save that for them if you want. Or give it away. It's not worth anything near as much as you are."

He cleared his throat and I had to swallow back a lump.

"And as much as it pains me to say," he continued. "You should probably call your mother."

"Not tonight."

"Agreed."

"But—yeah, I'll give her a call."

Eddie nodded, then glanced over at Frankie before he looked back at me. "Dinner after Halloween? Maybe before Thanksgiving? I'd like to talk to you kids about some other things."

"I'd like that."

Another handshake, then he moved over to give Frankie a kiss on the cheek and another brief hug before he headed for his car. Frankie took my hand and looked at me with those kind eyes and I shook my head.

"You really do make my world better," I told her. "But would you mind terribly if we skipped the dancing tonight?"

"Want to get me naked and see how many ways I can make you scream?" The absolute nonchalance in that offer…

"Hell, yes," I told her. Then pressed a hard kiss to her lips. "Don't mind me if I go for more screams from you."

"I wouldn't dream of it."

The envelope I tucked into my jacket pocket for later, then I took Frankie to the car. Tonight was about us. About her. Because she'd made this about me and did something I hadn't really expected to be able to ever do.

She'd made it possible for me to look forward to seeing my father.

Miracles and Frankie.

"Happy birthday," she said as we settled into the backseat and the driver pulled away.

"You know," I whispered, pressing my cheek to the top of her head. "It really is."

Chapter Eleven

MISERY LOVES COMPANY, IN THEORY

Frankie

Jeremy indulged me in dressing up Miss Abigail for Halloween. The holiday fell midweek and while we'd actually been invited to a few parties, none of us had really wanted to go to any of them. By mutual consent, we decided to give out candy and watch not-horror movies.

I dressed up for fun, so Miss Abigail and I wore matching costumes. The guys hadn't stopped chuckling since I made our grand appearance. Then again, I thought I made an adorable Starbuck's barista while Miss Abigail was the perfect oversized latte. She even put up with the hat for the pictures, though she shook it off after that.

Coop, Jake, Ian, and Archie took turns with me answering the door. We had a whole host of goblins, ghouls, superheroes, and cartoon characters that I flat out just didn't recognize.

When we would ask and they gave us a name, Jake or Archie would take the time to look it up. Miss Abigail, though, was a *huge* hit with the kids. The guys made a concession for Halloween in a series of shirts that were definitely entertaining.

Coop wore his *Professional Ghost Friend* like a champ and Jake's *Gym Ghost* cracked me up. Ian wore one that said *Ghost Writer* and Archie's *Oh Sheet!* suited them all so well. By nine though, we had run out of candy—something I thought would be impossible since Jeremy must have purchased fifteen or twenty bags of it—and our visitors had slowed from a trickle to nothing.

The constant stream of visitors for the past four hours had been both entertaining and exhausting.

Jake was dragging on a jacket and so was Archie. At my questioning look, Jake said, "We're taking Miss Abigail for a walk, Baby Girl."

"Oh." I stood up, but both of them gave me frowns when I coughed. "That's nothing." I had a dry throat from the colder air tonight. Halloween in New York didn't always mean freezing temperatures, but it definitely didn't mean warm ones either.

"We got it, Babe," Archie said firmly. "You've been up and down all night. Go get changed into something comfy. Maybe Jeremy will let us bribe him into hot cocoa and you can pick out the movie."

"Great plan," Coop announced, wrapping an arm around me. "We'll stay here all nice and cozy while they freeze their balls off."

Jeremy cleared his throat.

"While they freeze their butts off," Coop corrected without missing a beat and the guys laughed. Ian gave me a measured look and I didn't roll my eyes, but I also didn't argue. My throat was scratchy, it wasn't a big deal. We were all tired, it'd been nonstop the last few weeks, though the birthdays had been totally worth any missed sleep.

We'd also wrapped up midterms this week, which was part of the reason none of us wanted to hit a party tonight. Though, Ian and I had done a TikTok live thing earlier in the day at the behest of Andrea. Our social media manager despaired we'd never grow more active, but the hour-long live had made her happy. It also kept Bound Hearts out there, which was her goal.

Ian had given me the sheet music for the two songs he'd been working on per the request of the other producers. They were good. Really good. He almost had the lyrics down and I couldn't wait to hear them when they were done.

"Fine," I agreed because this was just not worth the argument. Thankfully, Jake and Archie were already out the door before I yawned on my way up the stairs.

"I heard that," Coop said from behind me and I flipped him off over my shoulder. His laughter followed me up the stairs. Ian caught up to me when I got all the way up to my room and I glanced back at him as I headed into the bathroom.

"I'm fine," I told him, but he just nodded.

"I know."

"You're still worried." I managed to not cough and filled a cup with water and took a drink. That would help.

"There's a cold going around at school," he said. "Not impossible for you to have caught it."

"Blegh," I said, making a face. "I don't want a cold."

His soft chuckle made me grin. "No one wants one, but maybe take it easy for the next couple of days?"

"I'd love to," I told him as I washed my face. "I'm supposed to go up to Hank and Kelly's this weekend. Midterms are done, but I have lunch with Eddie on Friday before Jake and I catch the train." I did a quick brush of my teeth, more because I'd eaten a ton of chocolate than anything else.

The guys didn't *always* go up with me, but Jake and I planned on him accompanying me because Alec asked for his help on his science project. Archie hadn't even objected, which had been kind of weird, but then again, we'd all been busy.

"I thought you guys didn't have your next mentor meeting until next week," Ian moved out of the doorway as I stripped off my shirt and headed for my closet. Coop flopped on the bed with Tory and Tabby.

"We don't, but I've got a project due in my project management class and he's bringing me some examples and reports that I can use as supporting materials."

"Uh huh," Coop said as he studied me.

"Don't start." I pointed a finger at him. "I coughed. Everyone does it."

They didn't say anything, but while I wasn't looking at them, it wasn't hard to picture them glancing at each other. I stripped out of the barista outfit and dug out some sleep shorts and then a t-shirt.

I pulled out a dark blue one that had to be Ian's, I thought. Maybe it was Jake's. They were always leaving clothes up here, which just made it easier for me to steal.

After I pulled it on, I wasn't surprised to find Ian standing right behind me. He cupped my cheek with his palm and I sighed as I leaned into it. It was hard to dismiss the worry this close up or the fact that Coop wore that little frown he got whenever he was concerned.

"I really don't feel that bad," I promised both of them. "It was a cough."

"You're also beat," Coop supplied helpfully. "You've been shorting your sleep and you got up early twice this week *before* they went running to finish an assignment before you went out running too."

Sighing, I dragged my gaze back to Ian's worried blue eyes. "I promise. I don't feel bad."

"Okay," he murmured. Pressing his lips to my forehead, he kissed me gently. "Keep an eye on it?"

"Absolutely." When he would have dipped his head to give me another kiss, I pressed two fingers to his lips. "If we're keeping an eye on it and I'm sick, we wouldn't want me to get you guys sick."

He tilted his head at my playful rejection, the twinkle in his eyes promising me I'd pay for that. Oh, I couldn't wait. As it was, he gave my ass a pinch before he dragged me closer and nuzzled a kiss to my lips. "If you aren't feeling bad, then I'm not worried about it."

Grinning, I wrinkled my nose at him. "Now I don't know whether I want to get spanked for getting you sick or for telling you not to kiss me in case I get you sick… hmmm…"

"Does it really matter as long as you get spanked?" Coop asked, humor decorating every single syllable.

I mean—I couldn't argue with that. Ian scooped me up and carried me over to the bed where he tossed me down onto the pillows. I landed with a bounce. The cats evacuated at speed after giving us all dirty looks.

"I thought we were gonna watch a movie—"

"We are," Coop said as he snagged me and dragged me over to him. "We're all gonna watch it up here. The guys will bring up the hot cocoa and the popcorn. Until then…" He rolled over and pinned me to bed. "Trick or treat?"

"Let me guess—we kiss and the treat is you get the kiss but the trick is you get a cold with the kiss…"

"But you don't feel bad," he teased. "Besides, any cold you have I'm going to get anyway so—give it to me…" But he wasn't kissing me, the asshole started tickling me and I squealed. Even trying to wiggle away from him, I ended up against Ian, who grinned.

"You two are awful!"

"Why are they awful, Baby Girl?" Jake asked as he swung into the room, bringing the rich scent of hot chocolate with him and popcorn wasn't far behind.

"Cause!" I declared, stealing another kiss from Ian before he shifted me over so I was sandwiched between him and Coop. They piled up the pillows and pulled the blankets over my legs.

Silly *and* adorable.

"Good to know." Jake set the tray with the drinks down on my desk. "Need me to beat up the boyfriends?"

"Bring it," Ian said easily.

"Yeah," Coop declared. "You take on Bubba, and I'll keep Frankie warm."

Archie just snorted. Asses. All of them. Ian pulled off his shirt, and at some point, he'd pulled on pajama bottoms. Coop had also gotten ready for bed. The guys passed me my hot cocoa and Coop turned on the television.

"What are we watching?"

"Halloween movie with no horror," Jake called from the bathroom. He emerged again in sleep shorts and a tank top, scratching his beard. I loved the sprawl of his colorful tattoo visible from beneath the edges of the shirt.

They all looked at me and I was like. "I dunno—Scooby Doo?" The snorts that earned me made me chuckle, but then I let out another cough and tried to cover with a sip of hot cocoa. Archie cut a look at me and I stuck my tongue out at him.

"Shaun of the Dead?" Coop smirked at me.

"Keep it up, Brennen and you can sleep in your own room."

He clasped his hands over his heart. "This is my room."

Jake chuckled. "Hocus Pocus or Beetlejuice?"

Oh, I brightened up at that. "Beetlejuice!"

"Sold," Archie said, then stuck out a fist, so did Jake, then Coop, and even though he rolled his eyes, Ian did as well. "One. Two. Three."

"Fuck," Coop grunted as they played a round of Rochambeau. He got rock, with two pieces of paper from Jake and Ian, but Archie only laughed at him.

He'd done a rock too. "Let's go, and let Jake have your spot."

"Yeah, yeah." Despite his protests, he shifted easily enough and Jake slid in next to me. With Archie and Coop sprawling on the sides and facing the foot of the bed, they fired up the movie and turned off the lights.

I loved Beetlejuice.

I loved being curled up with my guys even more

Two days after Halloween, I woke up with more than a sore throat and Jake propped his head up on his hand as he gazed down at me. Bless him, he didn't say anything until I said, "I think I'm sick."

It came out so hoarse and rough, he smiled gently and pressed his lips to my forehead. "We know. You've been flush for two days, Baby Girl."

I groaned, closing my eyes and putting a hand up to my face. My head hurt, my throat hurt. Even my muscles hurt. When I tried to sit up, Jake wrapped an arm around me and tugged me up against the pillows.

He nodded over to the nightstand next to the bed and I could have cried. Cold meds sat there with a tumbler on the warming plate. I'd bet anything there was hot tea in there.

"Ian or Coop?"

"Both of them, but Coop was up here earlier and he noticed how hot you were running." There wasn't an ounce of reproach in his voice. I cradled the tumbler and then took a sip of the tea. "Archie sounded a little rough this morning, so Jeremy banished him to his own room for a few hours."

I grimaced.

"Bubba's got a stuffed nose but otherwise he seems fine, and Coop's got the constitution of an ox, so he'll be swapping out with me after he gets back from work later."

"Jake," I protested, but he just shook his head at me.

"Nope. You've got a cold and a fever. You're the worst off. It's not our first rodeo."

"And if you get sick?" Misery might love company but I didn't want them sick. I told them I wasn't and then they were all sleeping in here anyway.

"Then we get sick. I've never been afraid of your cooties."

That just made me giggle. Unfortunately, that giggle turned into a cough. I covered my mouth and grimaced. Reaching past me, Jake got the meds out and held them over to me. I took them. The tea was amazing, but my throat felt like I'd swallowed crushed glass and I swore my pulse thumped in my head.

"You hungry at all?"

I shook my head, I kind of just wanted to go back to sleep. "I have to call my dad."

"I'll do it if you want."

"And I have to call Eddie."

"I can do that too."

Sniffling, I took another swallow of the tea and then put it back on the warming plate before I turned to snuggle into Jake. He chuckled, stroking my hair.

"Hot," I grumbled.

"Yes, you are, in more ways than one." He nuzzled a kiss to my head. "Go to sleep, Baby Girl. I'm going to get a damp cloth. Hopefully the meds will work and we'll get that fever down."

I hated being sick.

He slipped out of the bed, but came back with the cold wash cloth, after he tucked it around my neck and let me cuddle right up to him, I was out.

The next time I woke up, Jake was still there. He had a book open on the Kindle and he was reading. He scooted out to go grab food for me and more hot tea while I went to the bathroom. I stood under a tepid shower when he came back up, but I was already swaying from the headache before I was totally done.

Skipping clothes altogether, I just crawled back into bed. There was soup, meds, more tea and water and then a Jake to snuggle before I went back to sleep.

The whole weekend passed with only brief moments of being awake enough to take meds and eat. My fever finally broke sometime on Sunday morning. Ian was there and he picked me up and carried my nasty, sweaty self right into the shower.

Thankfully, he was an old hand at washing my hair. They all were. Jake was waiting when we were done and they toweled me off and combed out the tangles before I got to be in fresh pajamas.

They'd even changed out the bedsheets. Jake also looked a little flushed and Ian told him to get in the bed and handed him the same meds I was taking. Archie definitely had the cold so he came up to join us, leaving Coop and Ian to run all over the place, but I could actually help.

What a shitty weekend.

Well, not so shitty I guessed because by Monday, I was mostly better except for feeling like a snot factory. Coop had finally taken a turn and he was definitely rough. Archie was already bouncing back, and Jake's fever broke.

So far, Ian was the only one who'd escaped unscathed, but we skipped classes to look after everyone else. Thankfully, none of us managed to get Jeremy sick. Which was definitely a win.

"Hey," Coop said in a raspy voice. He was the last of us still sick. Jake, like me, had a mild cough and a stuffy nose but he'd felt a hell of a lot better after the fever passed. Archie seemed to have dodged all of that.

Coop, though, he got all the cooties. "Hey," I greeted him, his forehead was definitely damp and his hair sticky. "How are you doing?"

"I feel like ass," he complained and I chuckled.

"I recognize that feeling."

"Your cooties had some kick." The half-echo of my earlier thought made me smile even more. He shoved himself up and I twisted to get him water. If he had to drink tea, he would, but he wasn't a fan.

"Well, maybe next time, we skip making out while I'm sick."

He gave it a beat like he was considering it, then shook his head. "Nah. Totally worth it."

"You're terrible."

"But you love me."

Not even a question. I leaned in and when he lowered the water bottle, I nuzzled a kiss to his stubbly cheek. "I love you even when you're gross," I promised him.

"Good." He made a face. "Cause I'm pretty sure I'm offending myself."

"Stay there," I told him and slid out of bed. Once I got the shower going, I came back for him. He had listened so well because he was seated on the edge of the bed.

I showered with him and when I was soaping over his stomach he braced a hand on the wall and said, "What are the chances of me talking you into a little play?"

"Not even," I chastised him and had to bite back a laugh at his pout. "Don't start. You're pale, trembling, and you've been sick for four days. I can't remember the last time you were sick for even two."

He grunted. "Yeah well, based on this experience, I have no desire to repeat it. Especially if it doesn't come with blowjobs or even a little hand one."

Laughter escaped me and I pinched his ass, but he grinned despite the shadows of fatigue. After the shower, I got him into fresh pajamas and moved him over to a chair so I could strip the bed. I owed Jeremy big time for all the times we'd had to change the sheets the last few days.

Later, with the bed remade and after I'd come back up with lunch, Coop and I just hung out and caught up on some shows. It had been a while for both of us. The guys had all checked in throughout the day and I'd head in for my classes the next day.

Until all of them were better though, I would no sooner leave them than they'd leave me.

"What's wrong?"

I glanced at him. "Why do you think something is wrong?"

"You're frowning and thinking real hard."

I made a face. "I've missed five days of classes."

He laughed. "You're already caught up on the reading, aren't you?"

My face heated.

"Right, you're gonna be fine, Beautiful. I promise. If you need anything, just let us know."

I pinched his side and he wrapped an arm around me and snuggled me close.

"You know, I get why you want to cuddle when you feel bad," he mused. "Besides the fact you smell nice."

"Yeah?" I rubbed my cheek against his shirt. "You smell nice too."

"Thank you," he answered without missing a beat. "You do it cause it's comforting and safe. Also, we'll do just about anything to make you feel better and you know it."

I smiled. "Yes, I do know that." Tilting my head back, I glanced up at him. "I'll do just about anything to make you feel better too."

"Blowjob still not on the table?"

I rolled my eyes. "Keep your fever gone for twenty-four hours and I'll totally give you a blowjob."

A whistle cut through the room and I glanced over at Jake who grinned. "My fever's been gone for twenty-four hours. Give me one and he can watch."

"You're an asshole," Coop said as I laughed and Jake grinned.

"Yes, but you'd still watch."

"I would, in fact, watch." It wasn't long before he was laughing too, and while I was more than willing to give Jake the aforementioned blowjob, he just climbed in to cuddle with us and we went back to watching—whatever the hell it was Coop had put on.

"What is this again?"

Chapter Twelve
TURBULENCE

"Ease up on the throttle." Brick's relaxed tone translated cleanly over the headsets. The private single engine plane we were using today was lighter than the twin engine we normally took up. The wind velocity had also increased. While we hadn't had a full-on snow yet, the forecasters were all predicting it by Thanksgiving. We had three days until the big event. Our families had all begun arriving, with Kelly and Hank coming down early the previous Friday to set up at the house on Long Island.

The house in the Hamptons belonged to Archie's grandfather. When his dad proposed they use it for Thanksgiving, Frankie had been the one to turn and tell Archie we absolutely did not have to use his grandfather's house. To her surprise, and maybe mine, but definitely Coop's, Archie just shrugged it off.

"Jake." The gentle reprimand in the older pilot's voice snapped my attention back to where I was. "Head in the cockpit or we're going back."

"I'm here," I promised. "Sorry. Have a lot of family arriving over the next day or two." In fact, *mine* was due today. I was both excited and more than a little worried. I kept trying to tell myself that I didn't need to worry. Klara was family. Dad was family. Mom was family. They were all dating.

That was great, right?

I liked it and at the same time, a part of me braced. Braced for something to go wrong. For disappointment that would hit the girls, Mom, Klara, and Hell, even the disappointment for Dad. There was nothing I could do for them.

"Well, that's the holidays, kid." Brick chuckled. "Never changes. Whether it's the wife's family or mine, there's always gonna be drama. Just accept that part and you don't spend all the time worrying about it."

"Sounds like you're speaking from experience."

"I'm an only child. My wife has five siblings. You can imagine which holidays are quiet and which ones aren't."

I laughed. "I have three younger sisters."

"So, you get it."

Yeah. Yeah, I did. "Right. Okay. Let's focus on what we're doing up here today."

"Well today, Mr. Benton, you're cruising on a sightseeing tour that's angling us up the coast. We're going to make a full circuit, probably swing over Vermont before we angle back to Long Island. This is your…" He checked his board. "Twenty-fifth hour. So, you're doing good. You're going to need to start the solo hours come spring."

I grinned. I needed sixty hours to qualify for a full license. But at least fifteen of those hours had to be solo.

"Solo doesn't mean bring your girl and show off."

I snorted. "Man, I'm not bringing Frankie anywhere until I'm one hundred percent sure it's safe."

He snorted. "One hundred percent might be pushing it, but you're doing good kid. You're doing good."

I appreciated it. From the first, Brick and I hit it off. He was a great flying instructor. Patient, direct, and absolutely zero tolerance for bullshit. The man had no sense of fear as far as I could tell. He was so calm from my first time on the stick. Then again, I had spent a lot of time pouring over manuals, the engine itself, and the various workings of the planes.

The only thing Brick hadn't let me do was take it apart and put it back together. I could respect that. I wanted to know the engine. I needed to know how it felt, the power, the lift, when it struggled and when it soared. It was one thing to understand the theory and to see the guts of it at all and it was something else to experience it firsthand.

"Still debating taking her skydiving," I admitted. The fact her eyes had lit up at the offhand remark was part of the reason it was still on my mind. Brick had joked about it when I said I needed to be perfect. Frankie's safety was important to me. Risking me?

No problem.

Risking her?

Not an option.

"Yeah? I know a couple of good instructors if you're serious."

That might actually make a really cool Christmas present to do when it warmed up again.

Ninety minutes later, we were touching down at the airport. Brick didn't talk me through it, but he was ready to take over if I asked. As it was, I kept the wings even, watched the altimeter, landing gear was ready, nose was slightly up as we came in and the first bounce knocked my teeth together.

But the second was much smoother as I throttled down on the engines and slowed us. Three bounces. Much better than my last landing.

"Don't forget what I said," Brick reminded me after I checked in with the Tower and taxied toward the flight hanger.

I snorted. "Any landing I can walk away from is a good landing. You know, that's not as comforting as you think it is."

The older man laughed. "Not meant to be comforting at all."

The private airport was laid out a lot differently than commercial and international ones. We didn't have a gate per se. In fact, I tended to park at the hanger when I came out for lessons. We'd pulled a couple of the cars out of parking when we'd headed out to the big house.

Miss Abigail came with us, the cats, however, stayed in the city. Frankie debated bringing them but with so many people, they'd probably just hide anyway. So, we would head back in a couple of times to check on them and in the meanwhile, Archie set up cameras pretty much everywhere so she could see them whenever she wanted.

"There's your girl." He pointed to where Frankie stood next to her car, she'd driven out for the lesson today and, despite all my protests, said she planned to wait. Then as soon as I spotted the Kindle in her bag, headphones, and her digital tablet, I realized she was getting a couple of hours to herself.

My girl wanted to keep me company, but she also wanted to escape the insanity back at the house. I got that. That reminded me, I needed to text Coop. Bubba would be all right, I was pretty sure. But Archie and Frankie were not used to insane, oversized family gatherings and this might be a lot more than they were prepped for.

We needed to keep that in mind.

Brick waited as I ran through the post-flight check, then signed off on everything. "Go on, kid. Have a good Thanksgiving. We'll book some flight hours next month, but probably scale back some until the new year."

"Sounds good," I told him, shaking his hand before I crossed to where Frankie waited. It wasn't until I was almost there that I spotted the hot coffee in her hands. "Somebody loves me," I greeted her and laughed when she drew the coffee back to herself and struck a puzzled expression.

"Why would you say that?"

I just eyed the coffee and she grinned.

"Oh this," she said it with a careless ease, like she hadn't driven twenty minutes away to get my favorite coffee, timing it so she was back with it when I arrived. "Well, yes, I do love you, but the coffee was for me." She couldn't even hold onto the straight face. Not that I cared.

The thrill her declaration always sent through me added to the adrenaline already buzzing in my system. Flying both exhilarated and relaxed me, it was hard to explain. Bubba and Archie got it because they both liked to let go on their motorcycle and sports car, respectively. But it wasn't *quite* the same thing.

Closing the distance, I cupped her cold cheeks in my palms and her mouth opened in anticipation of mine. Years of practice made kissing her a dance, but one that I never grew tired of, and I swore there were new facets to be explored with each one. I put a hand out to take the coffee, then she wrapped her arms around my neck as she sucked on my tongue.

Falling into her would always be better than flying. A nip. A bite. A scrape of teeth over my lip and the soft huff of her laughter as she fisted my hair. I soaked in every bit of the contact. She tasted of sweetness, a little sugar, coffee, peppermint, and someone had definitely been eating apple fritters. The barest suggestion of the fruit was right there on her lips, like a sugary glaze.

"Fuck, I love you," I whispered against her lips before backing her right up to the car. Her laughter in no way deterred the hunger in my kiss. My dick had already been at attention from the moment I spotted her waiting, but now he practically beat against my zipper wanting out and the icy air was the only thing slowing me down.

The softness of her groan had me dragging my head upward. The pink flush to her cheeks had been exacerbated by my beard. I brushed my fingers along the curve of her jaw.

"Hey, Baby Girl," I murmured and her smile grew.

"Hi."

"Thank you for waiting for me."

"And for your coffee."

"You can totally drink it if you want," I offered. "I'll just kiss it off you. Better than hits of caffeine anyway."

Her snort was adorable. "I'm more than happy to share my coffee, my kisses, and anything else that you might be interested in."

"Oh, offer accepted." Sliding my hand around her nape, I massaged the muscles there and loved how she leaned back into my touch. "When do we have to be back?"

"I might have said you had a three hour flight today."

I closed my eyes, savoring her clever, clever mind.

"Well, then, would you like to take the stick?"

The absolute silence to my inquiry had me cracking an eye open. Mischief and laughter vied for dominance in the playful green of her eyes. "Did you really just?"

"Oh yeah." Then I looked at her car. "Archie mentioned christening all the furniture with you—how did he put it? Screaming around his cock."

The flush on her cheeks deepened, but it was the way her glistening lips spread into a smile that held me captivated. "So, what I hear you saying, Jake… is you want me to christen my car, screaming around your cock?"

All my blood pounded south. "Yes, please." Then a delightful thought occurred to me. "I even know where I wanna park if you'll let me fuck any part of you in the car."

Head tilted back, she spread her fingers against my chest as though she really had to think about it. Then she cut a glance at me that was every bit as wanton as I felt. "How far away is it?"

The drive took us past the Standish place by about a mile. Frankie didn't question my directions. I savored the trip, resting one hand on her thigh while she drove and I sipped my coffee. The buzz of excitement under my skin had me grinning.

"I know this place," she murmured as we followed a public road to the part where it cut off and became private. There was a chain across the road with a warning against trespassing. "Jake…" She admonished me, but I was already out of the car.

After I unhooked the chain, I waved her through. The wind was a lot brisker this close to the ocean. Soon as she was clear, I reattached the chain and jogged back to the passenger side. Inside, I rubbed my hands together. That was a bracing damn cold.

Catching Frankie's scandalized look, I locked eyes with her. "Trust me?"

Almost immediately, her expression softened. It was like a sucker punch to the gut. The weight of her love wrapped around me like the heat on a hot Texas day. Her trust was a precious gift I would never squander. Nope, I'd learned that lesson the hard way.

"Thank you," I murmured as I settled my hand on her thigh, she covered my hand with hers and then continued up the road. "It's not that far, just follow the fork to the right instead of the left."

The right took us over to the cliffs. It was one of the few places where I preferred the north shore on Long Island to the south. Not that they were "true" cliffs, but they did give us an excellent view and it was private, since the whole property was private. Frankie leaned forward a little as she pulled right up to where I directed her and then, once in park, she stared at the view and then back at me.

In winter, it was almost sad desolation out there. The vegetation had gone a dead yellow or paler, like all the color had leached out of it. Against the sand and rocks, it all kind of blended together. The gray clouds added a stormy cast to the ocean. It was like being a million miles away and in our own backyard, well after a fashion.

"This place is Brick's wife's family's summer place. They never use it in winter." She hadn't asked me for any kind of explanation, but I figured she'd be a lot more comfortable if she understood that we really did have privacy out here.

"I thought half the thrill was the idea we might get caught," she teased me as she tilted her head to watch me. I unbuckled my seatbelt, then hers, before I reached down and pushed both of our seats all the way back. Her amusement reflected in both her eyes and the way her lips twitched into a smile.

"Maybe when we were in high school, Baby Girl. But let's be blunt, anyone who walked in and got an eyeful of you would have gotten a really brutal beatdown. Probably not fair, but then—I never claimed to be fair where you're concerned.

"This is true," she admitted without an ounce of admonition, if anything, she looked almost—happy about it.

"Do you mean to tell me that after all this time, I'm not going to get in trouble for telling you about all the guys I beat up for you?"

Her lips compressed. Fuck.

"Too soon?" I dared, but she only clucked her tongue as she wiggled out of her jacket and toed off her shoes.

"Do I need to call the guys or send them a message?"

"Nope," I said, motioning to my phone that was already silenced. "I told them we were gonna take a couple of hours. Maybe more."

"Good." Then she climbed over and settled on my lap. I stared up at her. "Let's be clear about one thing, Jacob Benton."

Oh shit. She pulled out the big guns. "Ma'am?" I eyed her.

"You beat up those poor boys for you. Not for me."

I considered that statement. "I can see why you'd think that," I finally admitted. When she raised her eyebrows and sat up, hips rolling so that her denim covered pussy could rub against my rapidly growing erection, I said fuck it. This was not the hill I was getting blue balls on. "Actually, you're right. I totally beat the shit out of them for me. I'm man enough to admit it."

Frankie tossed her head back and laughed. So open, carefree, and sexy as fuck that I drank in the sight of her as I rested my hands on her hips. "I know you'd beat up anyone I asked you to."

"Yes, ma'am." Not even a question.

She curled her fingers under the hem of her shirt and tugged it up and over to reveal the dark blue bra she was wearing. Oh, someone had been filling her lingerie drawer again. Thank you, Archie. "I know you know I can kick an ass or two myself."

"Abso-fucking-lutely. And look fucking gorgeous while doing it." The guy she put down at the club in the Bahamas sprang to mind and my dick went to stone. Yeah. "I accept all of that, still gonna crack a head or three if they look at you the wrong way."

"I know," she said and there it was again, that warmth and adoration in her eyes. "I love that you want to keep me safe."

Damn straight I did. "And if I enjoy doing it, all the better, right?"

Yes, living dangerously was my new middle name.

Thank fuck, she started laughing even as she flicked the buttons on my jeans and then began to push up my t-shirt. Right. Less talking, more stripping. I had the jacket and shirt off, then my shoes and lifted my knees to bump her forward and caught her as she fell toward me.

Mouths fused together, I made quick work of the hooks on her bra. The lacy things were too fucking sexy to rip up the first time. Once everyone got to enjoy them *then* we could play shred her panties. Then again, she had worn them today. There was a chance…

As if reading my mind, she chuckled. "Ian still hasn't seen this set."

"Thank you," I muttered, then nipped her lower lip. "Save this set for me. I have visions of tearing out the crotch with my teeth."

The sudden inhale from her made me grin. "Yes, sir."

I chuckled. "You don't have to sir me, Baby Girl. You save that for Bubba."

"Yeah?" she shifted against me as she got my jeans open and her hand under my boxers and wrapped around my cock. The pump into her hand was reflexive, but she was already kissing me as her hair draped my skin. The caress of it as sweet as she was.

"Yeah," I said in between breaths as I began to peel her jeans down.

"I'm going to have to move."

"Nah." I objected to that because with her bra off, her breasts were rubbing against my skin and those peaked tips were definitely inciting me. That and her hair. She wasn't going anywhere. "Wiggle that ass."

I gave her a little swat for good measure and her throaty chuckle went straight to my dick as she gave me a caressing squeeze. But then she began to roll against me, doing exactly what I wanted and I peeled the jeans and panties down as she moved up my body.

Now, it meant she had to let go of my cock, but her breasts were suddenly at my mouth and I sucked one nipple in hungrily. Her gasp broke off into a moan and then we had her jeans off and her bare legs were on either side of me. But I refused to let go of her breast. I'd missed these breasts the last few nights. The craziness of family being everywhere, and the fact her little sister was practically her clone *and* her shadow, made any play we got in, a quick and hurried affair.

Hell, I'd been balls deep inside of her in the closet the last time Chloe just wandered into our room calling her name. Damn funny, but definitely needed to educate the kids on some boundaries. Then again…

Laughter escaped me and I had to let go of her breast as she leaned back and looked at me. Flushed, with her lips kiss swollen, and my beard marks all over her breast—yeah, she was a goddess. My girl. "Care to share?"

"Oh, I share you all the time." The quip slipped out easily and it earned me another husky laugh. She peeled my jeans back then fisted my cock again and it was my turn to exhale harshly. With one stroke from base to tip, she had my full attention. "Right, I was just thinking I haven't seen your breasts in a while."

"Chloe."

I nodded and she shook her head with an affectionate smile. "I'll talk to her."

"Or we'll get creative," I told her. "It worked Saturday morning."

She laughed and before I could really enjoy it, she shifted forward and then sank down on me taking me in one long thrust that had my hips pushing up from the seat as I clamped my hands on her hips. Oh, she wanted to play that way. I could fuck her from this angle just as easily.

"I like when you get creative, Jake," she promised me as she leaned down and then our lips and tongues tangled. She kissed me like she needed me for air, fuck knew I needed her. We didn't need any more conversation. I set the rhythm, a punishing pace that hit right with every thrust. Her nails dug into my shoulder and when she threw her head back with that first orgasm, I kissed her pulse point then angled her forward so I could play with her breasts.

"Hmm," I groaned as she spasmed around my cock, that first one had been a little fast. I wanted to take my time. "Hello girls, miss me?"

Frankie laughed as she moved with me, and I teased one nipple then the other and then gripped her nape to pull her down for another kiss. One of us must have hit the dash because music came on, but I barely registered it as I surged up into her silky hot body and drank in her sighs and moans. When she came the next time, I followed her in a hot rush.

Our teeth clacked once as she kissed me while still laughing and shuddering. "Car christened?" she panted.

I gave it some thought. The air in here had gone humid and her skin was damp and slick against mine. Even the windows had fogged up. Then the sexy thumping beat of the song registered. Oh, that was Frankie singing.

Yeah, I could go for round two.

"Let's make sure," I told her. "Crawl up here and sit on my face."

"Um," she glanced around the car and then back at me.

"You can do it, Baby Girl, plenty of room and don't worry about any mess, I'm going to take care of that too."

Yeah, eating myself out of her was a kink I enjoyed, largely cause then I'd fuck back into her and fill her up again. But bless her, she didn't argue and when that gorgeous pink pussy of hers was in my face, I sank my fingers into her ass and went to town.

We were there for a lot longer than a couple of hours.

Round two turned into three. Then we were laughing and hydrating. By the time she slid down into the well and sucked me off, I was in heaven. It was snowing in heaven too. The fat white flakes were falling steadily.

Yeah.

Me. My girl. Her car.

Definitely got the job done.

Chapter Thirteen

TALKING TURKEYS

Frankie

Thanksgiving week had turned out to be an "event." Ian and Jake left early to fetch their families from the airport. They were the last to arrive because of work and schedules. Still, plenty of time, since it was the day before. Coop burrowed deeper into the blankets, refusing to move or consider the world. Then again, it had been after one when I went to sleep, and Coop was still up talking to his mom.

After I showered, I went in search of Archie and coffee. Not necessarily in that order. The house in the Hamptons was huge. It definitely qualified for "mansion" status. Then again, it was only a bit larger than the Standish house in Texas.

I'd been worried about Archie since we drove out here. The last time we'd been here had been the weekend before my car accident. Ice shivered up my spine at both the memory of the accident and the loss of his Ferrari. I hated that it had been so brutally totaled.

Then again, I hated most of the memories conjured by that particular weekend. We'd spent it with my grandparents, unaware that Maddy was socked away somewhere in this house. Ted hadn't known she was here. None of us had.

Shoving the debris of all those broken memories back into the bin in the back of my mind, I followed my nose downstairs. Jeremy had set up residence in the kitchen. He had coffee brewing and the beginnings of breakfast already on the grill.

Little Miss Abigail sat like a queen on her dog bed in the corner of the kitchen. It kept her out from underfoot, but let her keep an eye on Jeremy. It also allowed Jeremy to keep Alec, Chloe, and Craig from driving her nuts. The kids' high energy was contagious and there had already been one broken vase from them riling her up.

Or vice versa, really.

Either way, it was safer for the dog and the kids alike. "Good morning, Jeremy," I said to him as I headed for the coffee, pausing only long enough to give Miss Abigail a good scritching. "Good morning, Abby baby."

She gave me a doggy grin as Jeremy chuckled. "Good morning, Miss Frankie. Miss Kelly has gone for a run this morning along with Mr. Hank. Though your father did not seem as thrilled with the prospect. Mr. Alec is up and watching movies in the entertainment room. Miss Chloe and Mr. Craig are both still asleep. Mr. Bubba and Mr. Jake have gone to fetch their families."

I glanced at him as I filled up my coffee cup and raised my brows.

"Mr. Edward is in the sunroom with his coffee and paper. Mr. Archie *was* with him." Worry colored every syllable. Hopefully this didn't mean Eddie and Archie had a fight or a disagreement.

"Do you know where he went?" I had a couple of ideas.

Jeremy shook his head. "Unfortunately, no."

"I'll find him." I fixed a second cup of coffee and put it into one of the capped tumblers we'd brought with us. The twenty-ounce tumblers were a vital necessity some mornings.

"Thank you, Miss Frankie. I'll keep the children occupied should they come looking."

I pressed a kiss to Jeremy's cheek. "You're the best."

Then I set out into the house. There were a few rooms that had been closed and locked for the visit. His grandfather's suite. His office. The library.

The library had been locked more for us than to keep the family out, but it was also one of Grandpa Ted's favorite rooms. They were all in the south wing. It had the best view of the beach there. I didn't expect to find Archie in any of those rooms, but I climbed the stairs in the south wing and then followed it to the sunroom at the end of the hall.

Archie and I had escaped up here a couple of times during that long weekend. If he wanted to hide out from the others, he might have slipped out here. With care for the coffee, I nudged the pocket sliding door open. Sprawled on one of the chairs, Archie glanced at the door and me.

The distance in his eyes faded as he focused and then he was up. "Babe, you didn't have to bring me coffee."

"Fine, I'll drink it," I told him lightly as I put his tumbler behind my back.

Amusement curved his lips, and he dipped his head to press a soft kiss to my mouth. He tasted like toothpaste and coffee. "Thank you," he murmured. "Morning."

"Morning," I exhaled the word then stole another kiss before I gave him the coffee. He glanced down the hall as he reached for the door. "Coop is still asleep," I told him. "Jake and Ian aren't back yet."

"The last part I knew," he said as he slid the door closed. "They texted about a half hour ago that traffic on the parkway is a bear."

I grimaced.

"They'll be fine," he assured me. "They planned for the traffic. I offered to get a helicopter."

A laugh escaped me. "I don't see either of them being that comfortable…"

"No," he said, his grin real if brief. "But it was too fun to make the offer to not do it."

Shaking my head, I moved over to the love seat lounger and settled down on it. Then patted the seat next to me. Archie didn't disappoint, he wrapped an arm around my shoulders after he sat down. Pressing a kiss to my temple, he sighed. "How much trouble am I in?"

"Why would you be in trouble?" I challenged.

"Because you have 'we need to talk' face on."

We need to talk face? I leaned back and eyed him. "Explain."

"You get this adorable little crinkle right here," he said, stroking his index finger down the space between my brows. "Your nose scrunches just a little." With care, he tapped the tip of my nose before he pressed a kiss to it. "You look at me with the most soulful eyes and a hint of a smile. It's like you can't decide whether to laugh or to yell. Maybe both. That's usually the early warning signs of 'we need to talk' and I need to talk fast if I want to get out of whatever hot water I landed in."

Disbelief and amusement twined through me. "You're terrible."

"And you love it."

"Hmm." I squinted at him, then smiled. "I love you."

"That counts."

"And I would like to talk, but we don't *have* to."

He dropped his chin, his shoulders drooping. "I'm not hiding."

That confession about fucking broke my heart. "Archie…"

"I'm not," he said. "Edward and I were talking this morning and it got—a little heated. Rather than fight, I walked away. I'm not hiding, I'm just cooling off."

Setting my coffee and his aside, I moved to straddle his lap and cup his face. I didn't want him hiding his eyes from me, or anything else. When he opened his mouth, I pressed a finger to his lips. "First, I'm not in any way, shape, or form upset with you."

His mouth closed with a little click of his teeth.

"Second, you and Eddie have a lot of history and baggage to sort through. It's not all going to be roses and orchestras. I'm never going to judge you for taking the high road *or* the low one. You do you."

His eyes softened.

"Third, what I want to talk to you about is something I've debated on and off all year, but—I think now it's time."

He frowned.

"It's not bad, so kick that thought right to the curb, Mister."

That got me a smile. He wrapped a hand around my nape and dragged me in for a kiss. As much as this was a deflect and distract technique, it was also a demand and a need. One I was more than happy to answer.

Eventually, he let me up for air. Cocky smirk adorably in place, he said, "Please, continue."

I snorted and his smirk turned into a real smile. Archie made it impossible to stay angry with him when I *was* angry with him. When all I wanted to do was cherish the smile on his face, I swore he turned me into a puddle. "Stop smiling at me like that or I'll forget everything and just stare dreamily into your eyes."

"You say that like it's a bad thing." He pursed his lips. "Should I be offended?"

"Never," I promised. "And I'll stare dreamily at you any time you want, but right now…"

"Yeah, yeah. You want to talk to me about something." He huffed out a mock sigh. "Are you sure I can't distract you? Maybe if you got naked and sat on my dick, keeping it all warm and snug, that would help."

"Right. Remind me to thank Rachel for bringing up dick warming a couple of weeks ago."

"To be fair to her," Archie admitted. "I had heard of it before, but the idea of your pussy wrapped around my cock doesn't make me think let's just sit still."

I giggled. "Good to know. We may have to work up to it."

"I could be persuaded. Though I feel like this will be a lot of pass and fail tests."

"More on failing?"

"Depends on how you define failing."

I couldn't really respond to that because—"Well, you're not wrong."

"That's my girl," he said with a grin.

Another kiss and then I climbed off his lap and handed him back his coffee. His pout didn't persuade me and I twisted to sit sideways so I could face him.

"You know, I'm still seeing my therapist." Every other week, we had a standing appointment for a sixty-minute session. Except for when I'd been sick and when we'd gone on our June trip, I hadn't missed a single one.

A small frown filtered through the humor in Archie's expression. "Yeah, you're okay, right?"

His first concern was always me. Always. It was enough to knot me up inside. "I'm okay. I promise."

"You'd tell us if you weren't, right?"

"Yes. I struggled a lot last year. Both with the tour, with Maddy's death, with all of it. And I should have said something sooner." But when something had cracked inside of me, Ian had been right there to catch me. "I'm working on that and I have been."

Nodding slowly, Archie studied me like he could read my thoughts and test each statement. Finally, he said, "I worry about you. We all do."

"I worry about you," I murmured, taking the opening. "We all do." Because I'd seen the concern in Coop's eyes and Jake's. Ian and I had talked about it. More than once, I'd caught Jeremy's worried stares and concerned looks.

"I'm fine." Of course, he just brushed it all to the side.

"You are," I agreed with him softly. "Sometimes. Other times, you're not. That's okay, because I miss Grandpa Ted too."

The storm and shadow colliding in his eyes all but shuttered away the light and he looked down at his coffee.

"Losing him hurt," I admitted. "He wasn't my grandfather, but he was an amazing man. He loved you so much. It hurts me to see you hurting. It was a different kind of grief. That was when my therapist recommended a grief and loss group that meets off campus every month."

"What?"

"The Thursdays I sometimes spend at the library?"

"You're going to a group for grief?"

I nodded. "Everyone processes grief differently. It's weird on some levels to grieve for Maddy." I raised my hand before he could say anything. "And I know it's okay, that I'm grieving for her and that processing that loss is going to be something I make my peace with. I'm getting there. Losing Ted was different, part of my grief is, I'm mourning your loss—what you lost in losing him."

He sighed. "Babe…"

"I'm not telling you all this to make you feel bad or to get you to fix it for me. I know you would in a heartbeat. You love fixing things for me and making my life easier. You make my life so much better, just by being in it."

His smile lifted some of the shadows. "I do miss him," he said in a soft voice. "I'll be fine some days and others… I'll go to send him a message or call him and it hits me all over again."

Yeah. I got that. "It hurts. There's a kind of gasping sensation." It wasn't even a stretch for me to describe it. Archie nodded then drained his coffee like he was taking a shot.

He sighed. "And I thought it was great to come here but being here, I keep—thinking about him."

"Same. That's why I wanted to tell you that—that going to the group meetings with me *is* an option."

Incredulity slid across his face. "Babe… I love that therapy works for you. Not sure I'm the poster child for it."

Snorting, I thwapped his hand lightly. "No one is the poster child. The first two meetings I went to, I didn't say a word. I just listened. I didn't know how going to those meetings would help me. But it did and I can't even tell you—how. Just…at the third meeting, it was a week before my birthday…" The anniversary of Maddy's death. Bitch. "It was the first time I said anything. It wasn't much, but I remember exactly what I said and it was like I finally started putting myself back together."

"Can I ask?" He stroked his fingers down my cheek.

"I said, 'In five days, I'm going to turn twenty and my mother will have been dead a year exactly. I don't want her death to spoil my birthday. I guess, I'm selfish like that.'" Archie scowled, but he didn't say anything when I shook my head. "Then, I lifted my shoulders and said, 'But since she tried to kill me on my birthday, I guess not giving her the satisfaction is my right?'"

His eyebrows lifted.

"They just accepted it, didn't ask any questions or anything. And I was able to talk about it a little more at the next meeting and with my therapist. I just—I'm angry. I'm sad. I'm a lot of complicated emotions. There are no easy answers, but every little bit helps. I wanted you to know the help was there for you too. I could go and hold your hand, or we can find you one where you can have privacy…whatever you need."

Blowing out a breath, I blinked to keep back the tears that had begun to burn in my eyes. Archie lifted me up from my spot and pulled me into his lap. I sighed. This hadn't been about me seeking comfort. Still, with care for my coffee, I wrapped an arm around his neck as he hugged me tight.

When he buried his face against my throat, some of the tension bled out of me. Sometimes, to take care of them, I had to let them take care of me. How could I fault that? I needed to take care of them every bit as much sometimes. They just didn't always need me like this.

"Thank you for telling me," he said after a long moment where I just stroked his hair. "I don't know if it's something I can do."

"Okay."

No more pushing. I'd opened the door. If he wanted to go through it, then I'd go with him, if not, we could hang out right here. Bit by bit, he relaxed as I continued to run my fingers over his scalp. Voices rose in the distance. One of the kids shouted. A door slammed. They were all so far away.

Archie let out a little huff of sound and tightened his arm around my waist. The soft little puffs of his breathing tickled my throat. I shifted only a little and stole a sip of my coffee. His laughter threaded through my veins, far more potent than my beloved caffeine.

Another shout followed by a similarly argumentative one approached. Chloe and Craig from the sounds of it. They were up and arguing.

It was their favorite pastime. Archie groaned. "Not ready to share you, yet."

"They aren't supposed to come up here," I reminded him. Though when I was a kid that probably would have made me want to go even more. His somewhat derisive snort suggested he agreed with me. "I thought you liked them." The gentle tease earned me another laugh and he finally leaned back but kept me firmly on his lap.

"I do like them. They're smart, funny, adore their big sister, and are full of mischief."

"But…?" I gave voice to the unspoken syllable hanging off the end of that sentence. He rolled his eyes.

"But they *never* stop."

"They're kids."

Archie crossed his eyes and I giggled. His sudden grin extinguished any worries that the twins really were making him crazy. "No, they're supernatural beings of infinite power and drive. They have discovered the secret to attaining all they want in the world and they are not remotely ashamed to abuse that power." The firm nod he delivered at the end of that sentence had me smothering laughter all over again.

"The secret to attaining all they want, do tell."

"I don't know," he admitted. "It's a dangerous power. You seem only under its sway about half the time. If I tell you, what if it makes you susceptible to the rest?"

It was a damn fight to keep a straight face at his oh so dry and sober question. "I have you to watch my back."

"I'm fucking useless. All Chloe has to do is turn those eyes on me and give me that little hopeful smile and I'm a goner."

My heart melted.

"Don't look at me like that," Archie said, with a sniff. "It's embarrassing."

"It's adorable."

"She's so sure of herself," Archie continued. "Sure of her charm, and she's got heart. Maybe not quite as big as her sister's, but it's there and it's all pure and undamaged, no one has abused it and no one fucking will either."

The growl that punctuated the end of the sentence made me bite my lip. "I'll protect you from Chloe," I promised. He snorted, but it wasn't a derisive sound. More, one that said it wouldn't be enough and my sister was determined enough for three armies, so he might be right.

My sister.

A little thrill went through me at that. "What about my brothers?" Yes, I was just the tiniest bit possessive. The guys were my family, my chosen family. My first family. But Hank, Kelly, and their kids were *also* my family, and a family I wanted, even if they overwhelmed me more often than not.

"Alec's all right," Archie admitted grudgingly. "Good head on his shoulders. Smart like his sister. Likes all the right things. Thinks you walk on air. He keeps reminding us he might be smaller but he's cunning enough to think of ways to get us if we hurt you."

My jaw fell open. "He what?"

With one finger, Archie pushed my chin up so my mouth closed. "He's a good little brother and very protective of you. Jake and Coop are giving him lessons in how to do it and offered to back him up if he's got to pound one of us."

Head tilted, I shook my head. "And you and Ian?"

"Oh, Ian's got his side covered and I've got all the fun tools for building stuff. We'll sort it out. Craig's the one we all have to watch out for." He made wide eyes. "I swear, that kid is stealthy and silent when he wants to be. For someone so loud, he can sneak in places he's not supposed to be and get all the dirty details."

I winced.

Archie laughed. "None of those, no we learned that lesson over the summer, thank you. I'm getting keys made for the bedroom so we can lock the door here."

It was my turn to hide my face.

"They are strictly forbidden from the kitchen, though," Archie reminded me. "And don't worry, Jeremy took care of that, so we don't have to explain to Kelly or Hank what happened to the stove."

I busted out laughing all over again. Despite his comical contortions to contain his own laughter, Archie joined me.

"In my defense," he said, still grinning. "I didn't know the kids would take me seriously when I dared them to do it better."

Biting my lip, I grinned. "They do take some getting used to and they can be very literal when they choose to be."

"Well, I figure with Coop's and Jake's sisters being here, we'll sic them on the kids and let them play entertainment."

"It's gonna be so many people." I'd realized it was a lot from the beginning, but this was like a lot, a lot. We locked eyes. My own concerns reflected in his eyes. The noise level in the house was already high. The fact we could hear Chloe and Craig's voices, if not the content, was a testament to that.

"I can get us a helicopter and we can be out of here in twenty minutes, extraction point on the south lawn."

I would have laughed, but Archie was serious. "You know—that kind of helps."

His expression gentled. "Good. I want you to have a good holiday. You deserve the best."

I pinched him. "So do you. Our fathers have been conspiring."

"Yeah," he said slowly, capturing my hand and lifting it to his lips so he could kiss my palm. "Not sure whether to be worried or impressed."

"Probably both," I admitted. "And at the same time, it's kind of cute."

"Cute?"

"Well, yeah. I mean—I like that Hank reached out to him and that Eddie is attempting to build a friendship. Or maybe they already have. It's easier than if they disliked each other, you know?"

Rubbing a slow circle against my back, Archie nodded. "Yeah, I get it. We've already been down the despise route."

We had.

"Babe?"

"Hmm?"

"Thank you for being you."

I smiled. "My pleasure."

"Not this exact moment," Archie said. "But it will most certainly be later. We have a plan."

"Should I worry about this plan?"

"Not in the slightest. It's Operation Distract the Family, at least two of us will be on duty at all times so two of us can steal away with you."

A shiver of pleasure fluttered right up my spine. "I think I like this plan."

"You think?" He pinched my ass and I laughed, before I cupped his cheek, then nuzzled his lips with a kiss.

"Trust me," I murmured. "Later, I'll know and so will you."

Another shout, this time much closer and clearer. "I'll find them before you will!"

Chloe.

"We're about to be busted," Archie said, but he didn't sound upset about the fact. Resting my cheek to his, we watched the door. It took Chloe a few minutes to knock on each door in the hallway.

Bless her, she didn't open a single one. Then she got to the door to the sunroom. The soft patter of her knocks increased in volume when it was on our door.

"Who's there?" Archie called, pitching his voice deep.

Chloe squealed and I damn near ruined the effect by laughing.

"Chloe!" she yelled back.

"Chloe who?" Archie roared. Tears escaped the corners of my eyes as I held my breath to keep the laughter smothered.

"Chloe Jackson, Archie. You know that." There was that little stamp of a foot to punctuate it. "I would like my sister, please. So does Mom. We're going to do a turkey trot today."

"A what?" I mouthed and looked at Archie but he shook his head. "Sorry," he said in his "beast" voice. "No turkeys here."

Silence was her only answer. No way she gave up. Then came another knock. Raising his brows, Archie looked at me. Taking a page from his book, I growled out, "Who's there?"

"Your father," came the dry response. "And I'm opening the door in five seconds so everyone should be dressed and appropriate for innocent eyes, I have no wish to be scarred for life."

Chloe burst out laughing and so did I. Archie's arms tightened around me and we were still grinning when Hank opened the door. Chloe flew across to us. Archie barely rescued my coffee before we got our good morning hugs.

Whew.

Lots of people.

Lots of hugs.

But it was kind of fun, too.

"Turkey trot?" I asked and Hank chuckled.

"Trust us. You'll have fun."

Sure. Why not?

Chapter Fourteen

TURKEY TROT

Frankie

"Running," I said slowly and slanted a look at Hank who seemed to be failing at his attempt to not laugh. "A turkey trot is running?"

"It's a race for fun," Kelly corrected with an easy smile. They were wearing matching t-shirts with giant turkeys on them and Hank even sported a feathered hat. The kids were all wearing the same thing and they had shirts for us.

Shirts that Archie, the traitor, and Eddie were already wearing. Even Little Miss Abigail had one on. I didn't say a word about Jeremy not wearing one, and I wouldn't have, except then *he* walked into the kitchen not two minutes later wearing one himself.

"We go, we burn some calories, we take pictures, we have a few laughs…" Kelly continued, explaining this in the most soothing voice I'd ever heard out of her.

The shirts even had our names printed on the back. No way this was a spontaneous thing. It had taken planning. Eddie had shown up in his, so it was probably more of the budding bro-dadmance they had going on.

Coop wandered into the kitchen, eyes half-closed, his hair damp like he'd just showered and his feet dragging as he made his way across to the coffee maker. Chloe stared up at me imploringly as I looked at the shirt in my hand.

Coffee mug acquired, Coop turned just as his mom and Trina walked in. Oh fuck me, they were wearing the shirts too. From the corner of my eye, I caught Archie holding up a hand, counting down from five fingers, as soon as he hit one, Coop took a long drink and then seemed to register we were all there.

"Oh, hell no," he grunted, then dropped a kiss on my lips before he made as if to escape.

"Cooper Brennen," Carly said and he shook his head.

"Lalalalalala," he chanted as he dodged all of them and escaped. I chuckled, shaking my head as I glanced at the shirt in my hands again.

That would not work for me, I'd already been cornered. "Fine," I said and just pulled it on over the shirt I was wearing. I'd yanked on a sports bra earlier. So go me. Alec did a fist pump and grinned at me before he held up his hand and I high-fived him. "I'm not wearing the hat," I told Kelly firmly when she offered one to me.

"Awww." Despite the teasing sentiment echoed by the kids and *Archie*—him I flipped off, much to his delight—I stood my ground. Though when he and Eddie both donned the feathered hats, I totally took that picture and sent it right off to Ian and Jake.

Too bad they were missing out on the fun. Jake's response came swiftly.

Jake

Thanks for the warning, Baby Girl,
we'll take the long way back.

Why did I love these assholes?

"I'll be on your team, Frankie," Trina announced as she came to stand next to me. "Girls against the guys?"

"Oh!" Chloe bounced. "Me too! Ooh! That means we get Miss Abigail too!"

"That's sexist," Alec announced with a narrow-eyed look at Chloe. "Frankie is not sexist. She also prefers boys. She lives with four of them."

"That's not sexist," Craig said patiently and no matter how much I hoped they wouldn't go there, he added, "That's just sex."

Yep. They went there.

Alec thumped his brother. Chloe scowled, balling up her fists and charged Alec. Trina damn near peed herself as she collapsed back toward the counter laughing.

"Alec!" Hank said.

"Craig!" Kelly snapped.

I hooked Chloe before she could wade in and Archie stared at me before he went for Alec. Trina was still laughing. Then a whistle cut through the chaos, halting Craig long enough for Hank to catch his shoulders.

Jeremy gave us all a firm look. "This is a kitchen. Not the backyard. There will be no hooliganism in here, is that clear young Masters Jackson and Miss Jackson?"

"Ut oh," Chloe whispered into the silence. "He's using my last name."

Yep. He was. Jeremy had not once *ever* called me Miss Curtis, but he'd nailed *all* of the guys more than once. Trina's eyes were positively dancing as she shot me an unrestrained grin and Carly shook her head.

"Right," Eddie said, clapping his hands together. "Gloves, hats, and jackets for those who need them."

Alec scowled at Craig and Chloe, then up at Archie before his expression faded. Whatever Archie said to him mollified his temper. Thankfully, it didn't take us long to do all of that. I glanced at Eddie when he held up my jacket for me.

"No offense, I blame you for all of this," I told him with a grin and he chuckled.

"Hey!" Hank protested but Eddie just smiled.

"I blame me too."

Miss Abigail had already gone to Jeremy, Chloe and Alec stuck with me, so did Trina. Craig planted himself at Hank's side *after* Kelly gave him a scolding. Carly vanished back into the house for a minute, probably to see if she could get Coop to come along, but she was alone when she met us out at the cars.

So many C-names. It was cute and funny.

"You know," Archie said as he pressed up behind me. Eddie and Hank were wrangling over what cars for everyone, before Jeremy just took over and split us up by group size. "I should get extra boyfriend points for this."

Head tilted back, I grinned up at him. "You get all the points."

"Gross," Trina said with a grin as she took a picture of us with her phone. I kissed Archie and he winked before he headed over to the other car. Apparently, I didn't get to ride with my only boyfriend on the trip. Nope, Archie was with Eddie and I was with Hank and Kelly. Carly diverted to their car, but Trina decided to stay with me when Chloe and Alec raced after Archie.

Man, thrown over for him. Then again, if I'd been given the option... Trina's phone made a whooping noise and she grinned even wider.

"What did you do?" I asked as Craig climbed into the third seat with Miss Abigail. Jeremy was driving, so Kelly went back there with Craig, leaving Hank in the passenger seat and Trina and I in the middle.

"You'll see," she told me, her grin growing ever more devilish.

A split-second later, the door opened and Coop came stomping out— in his shirt—with a hat over his hair and gloves on. He pinched his sister, climbing in to sit in the middle and half-squashed her against the far side.

I laughed before climbing in after him. Trina leaned around him and said, "You're welcome."

Crazy. Crazy people.

As it turned out, the Turkey Trot was a hell of a lot bigger than I expected. There were bounce houses, games, food, and drinks. It was almost like a carnival. Coop's grumbling turned into full on teasing of his sister, but Trina's smile never flagged.

The pair had missed each other, for all their bitching and complaining. It was sweet. I'd missed her too and it never failed to amaze me how grown-up she seemed. We were a long way from the adolescent who launched into me for dating the other guys.

After we parked, Eddie and Hank diverted from all of us to pick up our race tags. "It's an *actual* race?"

Cause, no way I was winning.

"We'll do the walk part," Coop volunteered and then grunted when Trina elbowed him.

"I think someone's regretting their junior fifteen being added to their freshman fifteen," Trina ragged on him and I rolled my eyes. Coop leapt on that bait and then they were off, bickering.

Carly wore such a look of affection as she stared at her kids, that I couldn't even fault Trina for giving Coop shit. Not that he had a damn thing to worry about. Alec and Archie were plotting some mischief and Chloe had already picked her team—not mine as it turned out, but Miss Abigail's.

Jeremy was giving her instructions, because Miss Abigail's training was absolute and there would be no running around like the wild women of Borneo.

Yeah, I left that one alone.

"You're not really upset," Kelly said gently when I glanced at her. "Are you?"

"About this?" I glanced around to the hordes of people. It was early, but noisy and we were hardly the only family decked out in matching shirts. I'd pulled off the jacket, because the long-sleeved shirt I had on was thick and between that, the gloves and the knit cap, I was warm enough. "No. Not upset at all. Weirded out? A little stunned? Maybe a little."

"I can't believe you kids have never done a Turkey Trot," she admitted. "When that came up in conversation, I'm afraid I insisted. One, it's a great way to blow some calories before we stuff our faces tomorrow. Two, it's good to take the edge off and there's a lot of people tripping over each other, even in that huge house."

She frowned again.

"True," I said, when she didn't continue. I liked Kelly, I really did, and I couldn't quite figure out why I didn't relax around her as easily as I did the others. She was genuinely kind and she always seemed to go out of her way for me. "I wish Jake and Ian were back."

"Don't worry," Kelly told me with a bright smile. "We left them their shirts and stuff. Even if they don't make it all the way out here, we can do a big family photo when we're all back at the house."

A big family photo. My stomach did that sinking feeling again.

"Here we go," Hank said as he and Eddie returned. They split up and started passing out our numbers.

"Wait," Coop said, intervening as he snagged one set of tags from Eddie and then pinned me with a number before he pinned one on himself and Archie laughed as he took his.

Hank gave us a bland look and then I snickered. They'd firmly put me in the number right in between the two of theirs.

"Subtle," he commented, but Kelly just gave him a gentle elbow. Despite the chaos, the debate over how to break up or compete together took on an energy all its own. Archie and Eddie were both up for the actual eight-mile run. Kelly seemed to relish the idea even though she and Hank had *already* gone for a run. The woman was crazy. Nice, but crazy.

I volunteered to stick with the kids and so did Coop, but eventually everyone circled around to doing the five kilometer walk or run. It was a little longer for the kids, shorter for the runners, and perfect for Miss Abigail.

If the runners wanted to, they could go ahead and the rest of us could get our stroll on.

As it was, we ended up speed walking, though Jeremy dropped back with Chloe and Craig when they flagged. I would have joined him, but he waved me onward.

"They're fine," Coop said, catching my hand. Trina had moved up to join Carly, probably to stay safe since Coop threatened to dump her in the mud that had formed along the "course," thanks to the constant drizzle that finally begun to turn to snow.

"You're more awake," I said, bumping him. "You know, I wouldn't have blamed you if you'd skipped entirely."

"Nah," he said. "I should have taken you with me on my way out of the kitchen. I blame the lack of caffeine for making me slow on the comprehension."

"Everything good with Carly?"

"Yep. Actually, it's pretty great. She didn't bring Peter."

"No, really?" I shot him a look and he hip bumped me. "I didn't notice."

"Yeah, yeah. But she said it was a lot to do the 'meet the family' over the holidays and she wasn't quite ready for that."

"Fair. You weren't ready for it either."

Coop wrinkled his nose. "I would have handled it."

"Absolutely, and like a champion. But you don't have to, so this is good, you know?"

"Yeah. Mom wanted to know about our future plans," he admitted. "That was a little weird."

"She knows what you're studying." Clearly it couldn't be that weird.

"Um," Coop's cheeks went a little ruddy, flushing deeper and it was from more than the snow. We picked up our pace because it was definitely getting colder out here. "Not my future career plans, that's pretty locked. She meant future as in—you, me, and the guys."

"Oh."

I made a face and he nodded. "Exactly."

Um. Huh.

"Hey," Archie said as he fell back and joined us. "What's with the faces?"

"Carly was asking Coop about our future last night."

"She knows what he's studying…" His answer was so close to mine, I had to laugh. Coop shook his head.

"Our future, bonehead. All of us and Frankie."

It was Archie's turn to make a face. "Oh."

"Yep." Coop said. "That."

I hooked my arm through Archie's, and Coop kept hold of my gloved hand, at least until we all made the call to run the last few yards. The cold weather front they'd been promising had truly moved in and the snow, while beautiful, was only adding to the chill.

A surprise waited for us back at the square with the tents, the games, and the food. Jake's whistle cut across the crowd and I let them go before I jogged ahead.

Ian was a couple of steps behind him. I got a hug and a kiss from both, and that was about it before Jake's sisters swarmed me. They were all so much taller, especially Louisa, damn, she was gonna end up as tall as Jake at the rate she was going.

Alicia was there and Klara. Jake's dad had actually gone back to the house with Jeremy and the kids, as well as Miss Abigail. In deference to the kids' shorter legs, Jeremy led them on a shorter route. Sara was in one of the tents looking at crafts. I went with Alicia and Klara to Sara while everyone else got hot apple cider and hot cocoa.

"There she is," Sara said as soon as she saw me. The fierceness of the hugs I got from all of them didn't even weird me out anymore. "You look fantastic." She gave me a once over. "Maybe a bit skinny."

"Don't start," Klara advised. "Frankie looks fantastic. She's fit and trim. Our boys probably give her all the cardio she could need."

Alicia groaned and then swatted Klara, making the laughing woman smile even wider. The warmth and familiarity around them chased away even a little bit of chill. Klara's hair had grown out and she, like Alicia, wore soft looking turtlenecks in a similar blue, dark jeans and knee-high boots.

While they didn't have on the family "Turkey Trot" shirts, they were coordinated beautifully. A light tug on my arm pulled my attention to Sara and she nodded to one of the other tables. At least inside the tent some of the wind cut out. Or maybe this wasn't a tent, there were wooden beams and structures—maybe a transformed gazebo or something?

I didn't know. "I thought we'd give them a moment," Sara said as she hooked her arm through mine. "I know you're all cold and we should head back to the house, but how about we linger in here for a few while those two enjoy their reunion?"

"That sounds like fun. I forget sometimes that they aren't living together full time yet."

"No, but they're close. There's been a lot of travel," Sara said. "A lot of decisions to be made. A lot of fences to be mended." She glanced back once. "I've got my fingers crossed."

"Me too," I admitted. "I know Jake's been worried."

"So has Ian," Sara confided. "He doesn't want Jake to be disappointed again. It took a long time for Jake's anger at his father to calm down."

She didn't have to tell me.

"But Joe thinks they're in a good place and from what I've seen, I think they are too. Might even be a summer wedding or Christmas." She looked thoughtful. "We should probably put some feelers out about this week."

"About a potential wedding?" Pretty sure that was none of our business. At least until they invited us or something.

"Oh yes, we don't warnt there to be any conflicts."

Conflicts?

"Speaking of conflicts," Sara transitioned so smoothly I almost didn't see the trap before it closed. "How are you and the brother boyfriends doing? Ian's been circumspect when we ask him about the future."

Oh boy.

"She asked about the future?" Ian clarified as I toweled my hair off. The showers at the house were great, but they weren't quite as large as the one at home. So, we couldn't share more than two at a time.

"Yep," I told him. I'd needed the shower to fully chase away the chill.

"Great," Coop said. "That's at least two of them then." He walked out of the bathroom with a towel around his hips. "Mom was asking me last night."

Ian sighed. "I'll talk to her." He turned from where he leaned against the door when there was a knock. Cracking it open, he checked before he pulled it wider.

Jake and Archie came in, the conquering heroes, with huge cups of hot cocoa. "Oh, definitely my favorites," I said as I tossed my towel at Coop.

"Hey!"

But it wasn't like he protested much. It was just the five of us and Ian had cranked up the heat in the room, so I wasn't too worried about being naked, especially after the heat from the shower.

"All yours, Baby Girl," Jake said, holding out the largest mug with the biggest pile of whip cream.

Cradling the mug to myself, I sighed happily.

"And who are we talking to about what?" Archie asked as he turned the lock on the door and passed Ian his hot cocoa.

"My mother," Ian said dryly. "Apparently, she brought up weddings and cornered Frankie about the future."

"Well, to be fair," I corrected. "She was talking about Alicia and Klara and Jake's dad, and not having any conflicting plans."

"Oh, I did not hear that," Jake said from behind me. "I do not want to think about that right now. The girls are all crazy about the idea, but I want to just pretend they are all celibate and dating platonically."

I wasn't the only one who turned to give Jake a look and he shrugged without an ounce of apology.

"Name me one person in this room who wants to think about their parents having sex."

Dead silence greeted that comment.

"Point made," he said and I saluted him with my hot cocoa.

"Okay," Coop announced as he headed for the closet. "New plan."

"Yep," Archie agreed and Ian sighed.

"I think we can handle them," I reminded all of them. "It's about to be pure bedlam with all the food and the football."

"Angel, you don't have to sound so disgusted about the games."

I grinned. "I'll be in a food coma and napping. My point is, there are so many here, that I think we can handle the various parental units."

"Sure," Archie said. "It's no big deal if Eddie and Hank are already debating how to split up future holidays."

I stared.

"Or that my mom is really interested in how we decide where we're all going to settle down and what, if any conflicts, may arise from future job prospects."

"Shouldn't worry us that my parents are looking to summer in New England going forward."

We all glanced at Jake.

"Team Deny Deny Deny," he said firmly. "Also, Baby Girl, as much as I hate to say it, please put on clothes. You're far too tempting and I'd be just as content hiding in here for the next four days, but apparently, we're going to have to deal with all the questions instead."

I sighed. "Okay. New plan."

Archie dropped a kiss on my nose as I passed him and Ian tugged me in for a quick hug and a chocolatey kiss. Coop waited until I was in the closet to yank the door closed. Their curses damn near drowned out my laughter.

Thankfully, he didn't spill any of my hot cocoa as he pinned me to the wall for a thorough and breathless kiss. Not to mention the orgasm he wrangled out of me on his fingers.

Fuck me.

Panting, I said, "Part of the new plan?"

"Nope," he grinned unrepentant. "Scoring back the boyfriend points Trina said I lost this morning."

Confusion filtered through me followed by laughter. "Mission accomplished."

He nodded, then kissed me before he freed the closet door to our amused audience. "Damn straight."

Right.

Get dressed.

Make a new plan.

I wasn't quite sure what the old plan was, but hey, if it involved orgasms of any kind, I was totally in.

Chapter Fifteen

FAMILY, FATHERS, FISHING, FORMALITIES, AND THE FUTURE

Ian

"I just asked about future plans," Mom chided me as she poured hot water over the tea bag in her cup. It was still early, pitch dark outside and the snow from the day before had dropped a good several inches, but I didn't think it would linger for too long.

Arms folded, I eyed my mother. We didn't have a lot of time before others would rouse. I was surprised Dad wasn't already down here, but then he'd been up late with Jake's dad. We'd ended up playing billiards pretty late and they were still catching up when I finally called it.

"Don't you give me that look, Ian Joseph," she said in a stiff tone. "I love Frankie, I love the boys, and I love you. That means I have a right to worry, to be invested, and most of all, to be *curious.*"

"Curious would be fine." I kept my tone calm and even. "But you're *all* here and you're *all* asking."

She frowned, tea cup paused, as she considered me. "I hadn't thought about that."

Letting out a breath, I relaxed my posture and dropped my arms. Turning to the coffee pot, I got it going. I was still in pajama bottoms and a t-shirt. We had a fancy espresso machine as well, but I'd let Archie pull Frankie the perfect cup. Regular coffee would do it.

"Everyone is asking?" Mom finally said with a real wince in her tone.

"Pretty much," I told her over my shoulder. "And we get it. All of us, we really do. But it's not a conversation we're ready to have with all of you yet."

The first hiss of the water brought with it the aromatic blend of coffee. I debated pulling out food to get started on breakfast, but Jeremy had his rules about kitchens. With this many people, he'd be cross. Then again, he shouldn't have to cook for all of us.

To which he would respond with a flinty stare and I'd back the fuck off because there were some areas one didn't cross Jeremy in. This was one of them. Might as well just save myself the trip to the dog house. I checked my watch, then looked out the windows again. It was too dark to see if it was still snowing.

"But you have had the conversation."

Of course, she'd zero in on that. Squaring my shoulders, I blew out a breath. Fine. Let's do this. Pivoting, I faced her again. The faint smile at the corners of her lips didn't fool me in the slightest.

"We have had several conversations," I informed her. "Beginning with wanting to date Frankie as far back as seventh grade and then discovering she actually was interested in us in senior year. We've had discussions about the practicalities of balancing a relationship between five people and managing personal feelings and jealousy. We've had discussions about school, about careers, and about working together to make those things happen."

I ticked each item off and I swore her eyes narrowed.

"We've had some very colorful discussions. So yes, Mom, we *talk.*

When we're ready to invite you into the discussion, I—" Fuck me, I'd say it. "And the rest of the brother boyfriends will let you know. Until then…"

"What our son is trying to tell you, my love," Dad said as he made his way into the kitchen, "is to butt out and leave them alone."

More or less.

"But he is far too polite," he continued, then gave me a firm look. "And *respectful* to put it so plainly or use a tone."

Message sent.

I nodded.

Message received.

"I appreciate that you both care," I told them, and I meant it. "I know you love Frankie. I know you love me. I know this all comes from a good place, but it's pressure. We're in our junior year and the last couple of years have been brutal enough."

Mom set her teacup aside and I accepted her hug, moving to meet her before she even took a couple of steps. "I worry about you all," she admitted. "I can't help it."

"I know." And I really did know. I worried about Frankie all the time, it was part of wanting to protect and take care of her. I'd accepted it was just part of who I was. Part of all of us really. "We all do. I promise, when we're ready to have the conversation—whatever the conversation looks like—we will involve you. We're going to be all right, Mom. I promise."

She squeezed me and then gave a little sigh as she leaned back. "You know, I remember when you were shorter than me."

I chuckled.

She patted my chest. "And needed *me* to tell *you* that everything was going to be all right."

"He still needs you to do that, sweetheart," Dad said, slipping an arm around her and then pressing a kiss to the top of her head. "Just not right now."

Since she was swiping tears from her eyes, I lifted my gaze to Dad's and mouthed 'thank you.' He nodded.

"So," Dad said, just picking up the dropped conversation. "What are the plans for today?"

Miss Abigail came trotting out, tail wagging with Jeremy behind her. He was already dressed for the day, his button down shirt pressed and a tie in place. The fact he wasn't wearing his suit jacket was his only deference to the early hour.

"Good morning, Jeremy," I said as I dropped to greet Miss Abigail. She sat immediately and preened as I stroked and scritched her. "If you'll give me five minutes, I'll run up and throw some clothes on and take her for a light run."

Jeremy nodded. "I would appreciate that Mr. Bubba. I can get breakfast started. Her snow boots are by the door."

"On it." I glanced at Mom and Dad but Mom smiled.

"Go on, we'll see if Jeremy will let us help or if we get banished."

Right. Not my circus, so I just grinned. "Be right back."

Jake was pulling on a sweatshirt when I let myself back in the room. Frankie was buried in the middle of the bed, the only sign of her was the blonde hair spilling over Coop's arm. I swore he treated her like his favorite teddy bear.

Then again, who was I to talk.

"Run?" I mouthed more than gave voice to the word.

He smothered a yawn then nodded before glancing at the bed. Then crossed over and gave Archie a light jab between the shoulder blades.

Cracking his eyes open, Archie glared at us then groaned before he looked around. Yep, checking on where Frankie was. We all did it. He eyed Coop and I could read his mind.

Jake shot me a look and I eased onto the bed and extracted a mumbling Frankie with care. Archie rolled off the other side and then Jake leaned past me and we both shoved Coop right out of the bed.

His squawk of indignation didn't even stir Frankie, and I tucked her in more securely. It took me a little longer than five minutes, but we were all out of the room and downstairs.

We still needed the rest of *our* plan.

Coop

The guys *sucked.* I could be in bed with Frankie, celebrating the holiday early. Instead, not only was I not in bed with her, I was out running with this band of sadists.

"Stop bitching," Jake said with a light shove at my shoulder. I didn't even complain that I hadn't said anything, I just flipped him off.

Miss Abigail was in her element jogging along with us. She hadn't liked the snowy rain from the day before, but today's light snowfall and the crunchy snow under her little boots seemed to entertain her.

We were a mile out before Archie groaned. "Someone go first, I'm not the one to tackle this. Eddie's not gonna say shit, he's way too concerned about alienating one or both of us."

Which, while on the one hand made it easier to avoid the "future" conversations, it wasn't ideal. "He'll get there," I told him. "You both will. Look at how far Hank's come in the last couple of years."

"I hate to break this to you," Bubba said over his shoulder with a half-grin. "Hank's been one hundred percent invested as her dad since he found out about her. He's been testing those boundaries every chance he gets."

He wasn't wrong.

"I'll go first." Jake passed Abigail's leash over to Archie as he slowed our pace. I, for one, was fine with walking, except jogging was what kept us warm. "Mom, Klara, and Dad are talking marriage."

"Congrats?" I checked.

He gave me a wry grin. "Yeah, thanks."

"Excellent," Bubba said as he clapped him on the shoulder. "I know that's got to be a bit weird, but I really like the idea of your mom being happy."

No argument from me. Jake's smile grew. "Yeah, same. The flip side is they are going to ask us all to be a part of the wedding."

"Not a big deal, though I need some guidance on what to give them for the gift," Archie commented. "I don't even know what you give a first-time bride and groom, much less a reunited family." Then he paused…

"Not a house," Bubba and Jake said in one breath and Archie scowled.

Yeah, he was that predictable.

And generous.

"We'll worry about presents later," I suggested. "Us participating in the wedding is fine, just it means everyone then turns their eyes in our direction."

Jake tipped his head back with a groan and Archie shook his head.

"This is one area where the disenfranchised has the advantage," he pointed out and I flipped him off, as did Jake. "Seriously," he continued, ignoring us. "You guys are worried about what your parents are going to say and or do or ask.. and I wouldn't care except…"

"They're all going to ask Frankie at some point, try to feel it out from her if they can't get it out of us," I reminded him. "My mom is going to leave it alone and so is Trina."

"How'd you pull that off?" Jake asked me.

"That was what Mom and I were up talking about the other night. I let her tell me all her concerns, offer her advice, and then asked her to let me handle the rest. I don't want her scaring Frankie off or applying pressure where none needs to be. The last thing we need is for her to decide a year in Europe without any of us, or our families, is ideal."

Bubba snorted. I didn't disagree. Frankie wasn't leaving us. That said, Mom and Trina didn't have the faith in her that we did. So, rather than rock the boat, I asked them to be supportive—*quietly.*

"Mom and Dad are going to leave it alone now as well," Bubba said as he stretched his arms up. "I had a talk with her a little while ago and I get it, she's worried about all of us. Wants to make sure we're still thinking things through."

"She does know we're still in college, right?" Archie's tone was dry as he paused while Miss Abigail scouted a spot. Another reason for us to slow from the run. "Who brought the poop bags?"

"Got it," Bubba told him as she walked in circles. "And yes, she does know, but Mom is a planner. She doesn't want any of us to get hurt. That means caution and application of care."

I chuckled and rolled my head around. "Your mom is like you and overthinking things, and you don't want her to word it badly."

"Pretty much," he said. Silence draped us as Miss Abigail finished her business and Bubba walked over to deal with that. There were cans ahead where we could make a deposit. "I'll tell you guys what I told her. We're talking. We talk all the time. We make decisions together, we figure out how to balance our relationships and support our goals and dreams. We're not in a rush. We don't have to be."

He had a point.

"No, we pretty much have what we want right now." I made it easily a half-dozen steps before I realized they weren't following. Pivoting, I had to swallow a laugh at the varying degrees of surprise and shock on their faces.

Even Archie looked stunned. Of all the times to not have my phone. I'd kill to take a picture of this just to show it to Frankie in thirty or forty years.

"You guys do have what you want, right? I know I'm not the only one happy." I raised my brows. "We have the girl we've always wanted. We have her in our corner, she's still our best friend and supporter. She's an incredible lover. She keeps our egos in check. She lets us take care of her. We can protect her all the time. We know where we are this year and next. And we'll handle the year after that when it gets here, like we have everything else. Together."

The silence lingered for another moment, then Archie scowled. "You do not get to be the reasonable one *all* the time."

"Yes, he does," Jake said. "He absolutely does." He thumped Archie on the shoulder with a light fist. "You talk your way out of any trouble with her, I tease her until she can't not smile, Bubba wraps her up in a safe haven and Coop..."

He looked at me and I waited for it.

"Coop is her best friend when she needs it. He keeps his head even when the rest of us can't." Bubba gave me a wry look and I lifted my shoulders.

"Hey, someone's gotta make you assholes look good."

Yep, I got a run after that. Fortunately, I was still fast. They didn't nail me with snowballs until I was almost back to the house.

Jake

Back at the house, we found nearly everyone up. The moms were in the kitchen with Jeremy supervising. Klara was sitting in the living room with the girls and Frankie. The parade was going to be starting soon. I gripped the back of the sofa and dipped my head to give her a kiss.

She grinned up at me. "You guys were out early."

I translated that easily. "You're welcome for letting you sleep in."

"You guys live together, can you possibly *stop* staring at her like a giant dork?" Blake asked and I picked up a pillow and nailed her without looking.

"Of course not," Becca said melodramatically. "They're in love."

Frankie's eyes twinkled. "Becca has a boyfriend."

I snapped my head toward my little sister and she gritted her teeth, her expression every shade of "oh shit." "Why would you tell him that?"

"So, it's true? You're dating?" She was barely sixteen. Who the hell was she dating?

"Maybe next time don't give your brother a hard time," Klara suggested. From the corner of my eye, I caught Frankie fist bumping Klara. Yeah, I liked that they liked each other.

Becca wilted under my stare though. "Look, I've known Carter since freshman year and we're not *dating* dating. If you want to ask someone about dating, Louisa's got a thing for a *senior*."

"Bitch," Louisa said without looking up and I spared my youngest sister a look and she flipped me off. "I'm not having sex with him, he's never even kissed me and he thinks of me as a baby sister. He's also fucking terrified of you. Blake, however, is thinking about going all the way."

"Oh my god," Blake shouted and rounded on Louisa. "*Why* would you tell him that?"

"So you won't get knocked up," Louisa said bluntly, and I had to admit there were times when Louisa was my favorite. I folded my arms and stared at them.

Groaning, Becca said, "She *was* not thinking about going all the way, not anymore."

"Becca!" Blake was flushed a deep shade of pink. "Shut up. All of you. The only person in this room I'll discuss my sex life with is Frankie, thank you very much. The rest of you can just fu—oh, hi Dad."

All three girls cringed and Klara just laughed. "Don't let him stop you. Trust me, your father knows all about sex."

I groaned, along with the girls, and Frankie glanced up at me with a grin. "Troublemaker," I murmured.

"I love you," she mouthed and my heart did a little fist pump.

"Children," Dad said "Let's go, everyone gets a job. There's a table to be set, dishes to be put out, and rooms to straighten."

"But Dad, the parade is about to start…" Louisa didn't glance up from her phone when she issued that complaint.

"True, Frankie and Klara want to watch and not listen to you three bicker about sex, boys, and all the things you're *not* doing."

Trina sank down a little lower in her chair. Apparently, she didn't want to get noticed.

Blake scowled at me. Right, cause this was my fault. No, I hadn't forgotten that Becca had a boyfriend. We'd talk later. I did like that Louisa's guy was scared of me. Probably been a freshman when we were in school.

That gave me some possibilities.

"Let them watch," I suggested to Dad. "As long as they leave Frankie alone."

"Of course," Blake told me in that irritating fuck off tone she liked, that was just this side of too polite. "We weren't picking on *her*. Though maybe we should question her taste."

I rolled my eyes, but Frankie just grinned. "Ignore them," I said. "I'm begging you."

"Frankie!" The charge of the twins arrived and Chloe all but leapt the sofa to land on the cushion next to Frankie. Craig was a heartbeat behind her.

"Dammit!" He stomped his foot then turned red when Frankie glanced at him. "Crap."

I did not laugh.

"Sorry, I mean," he said and I put a hand on the kid's shoulder, because he was about as tomato red as the girls had been a minute ago.

"Just let it go, kid, we get it." I winked at him and he exhaled a sigh.

"Jake!" Alec yelled from somewhere outside of the living room. "Can you help me with this drone?"

Drone? I stared at Frankie and she shook her head.

"He's trying to build a drone," Chloe informed me. "It's not going well and he brought *all* the parts with him."

"Cool. You good, Baby Girl?"

"I'm fine," she said as she accepted Chloe's brush and hair ties. "You better go before I draft you into helping me do hair!"

"Oh, yay!" Louisa suddenly dragged her attention from her phone. "Will you do mine next?"

"Kid's name is Austin," Dad murmured. Yeah, I'd caught that too. The only Austin I remembered had been a pimply-faced little punk. Huh. I'd have to look into that.

"Jake?"

"Yeah, Alec," I called. "I'm coming. Gimme five." Then I glanced at Dad. "Did you guys actually need help?"

He gave me a look like I'd sprouted a second head. Right. We'd stay out of the kitchen. He clapped my arm and I bent to give Frankie another kiss on her adorable mouth before I gave Klara a kiss on the cheek.

"Be back in a bit. Behave, girls."

I didn't even have to look back to know I'd gotten one set of rolled eyes, one flip off, and one blown raspberry. Insolent brats. It was good to have them here.

Archie

Jake and I spent two hours disassembling, sorting, then helping Alec lay out the drone. He'd apparently found the remains of one and had been trying to put it back together ever since. With a little web searching, we figured out what parts we needed to replace and repair.

Despite Alec's frustration, he accepted that we would have to make arrangements to finish the assembly *after* we got the parts in. I didn't have enough here to even begin machining some replacements. That said, he'd done a damn good job.

We washed up when Frankie came to warn us dinner was ready. The television in the main living room had been tuned to movies after the parade. Football was in the game room with the pool table. It took a few minutes to wrangle everyone into the formal dining room.

I hadn't even thought about the fact we would be using the main dining area because of so many people. It was like a sock in the gut to walk into the huge room with its enormous table easily capable of seating twenty to twenty-five people. There were two other tables set up-for the kids probably.

Nearly everyone was in the room and they'd all begun to take seats. The guys were there and Frankie was getting her siblings settled. The room was brightly lit, there were decorations on the table, and huge platters of food. A dog bed had also been brought in and Miss Abigail sat like a queen.

I'd be damned, Jeremy was going to be joining us. That—that was excellent. Hank was talking to Jake's dad. Bubba's dad carried another platter out, with Sara a step behind him carrying wine. Klara and Alicia had their heads together as they talked sweetly to each other.

Jake watched them with a small smile on his face, even as he flicked his sister's hand just before she could pinch him. Coop appeared with his mother and sister, they were all hauling something from the kitchen.

I should probably go help, but that was when my gaze landed on the seat at the head of the table and all the air left my lungs. A picture of Grandpa Ted sat there and the seat had his favorite jacket hung over the back of it.

"They all insisted," Eddie said as he came to stand next to me, his voice low. "When I thought to offer the house for everyone, part of me did it because he would have loved this. This would have been his element."

Yeah. He would have.

Grief was a hard fist, refusing to let me catch a breath.

"He was really proud of you. Proud of what all of you were building. And he really liked Frankie."

Just the thought of her had me tracking my gaze to where she stood. Her eyes were on me, the warmth in them enough to melt the frozen cell keeping me prisoner. I sucked in air and when she lifted her brows.

Was I all right?

I nodded slowly. "I know, he did. He tested her the first night he met her."

"I bet he did," Eddie said softly. "She passed with flying colors."

"And then some. Not that it mattered." I didn't have to explain that. He got it. "I miss him."

Saying it aloud actually seemed to leave bloody score marks in my soul.

"So do I," Eddie said, then he settled a hand on my shoulder. "So do I."

The moment couldn't have been more than a few seconds, but the world steadied beneath my feet as my father offered me comfort and across the room, my heart gazed back at me offering me shelter.

I had a lot to be thankful for, so much. One more squeeze, then Eddie moved into the room and gave me a moment. I glanced from Frankie back to Grandpa's picture and I nodded. I missed him.

But I was damn grateful for every moment I'd had with him. Whispering a quiet thanks to him, I shook off the melancholy and thrust myself into the fray.

We were going to celebrate today with noisy family, arguments, siblings yelling at each other, parents being exasperated and one gorgeous, green-eyed babe who helped color in all the parts of my world.

Yeah, I was thankful for all of it.

Jake gave me a gentle shove as he cut past me to steal a kiss from Frankie and I laughed.

I was even grateful for the assholes.

Chapter Sixteen

COME AND KISS ME

Ian

The last week of November and the first week of December raced past us. Filled with work, school, deadlines, a couple of parties, and at least one Christmas tree hunting trip, we were all constantly on the go. Despite our best attempts, we'd only managed a couple of meals with all of us home at the same time.

Fortunately, this was the kind of busy that made all of us thrive, even with Frankie's tendency to overcommit, shorten her sleep, and habit of abandoning her own self-care. Right, a habit that drove me to distraction because I didn't want her hurting herself. At the same time, our awareness meant we all adapted, even making a point of tagging off if one of us noticed something the others didn't.

"Some days," the love of my life commented from where she perched on the foot of my bed. "I genuinely wonder why you all put up with me."

I paused from where I'd been threading my belt through the loops on my slacks.

"And before you say it," she continued, shooting me an exasperated smile, like she could already hear my scolding. Good. "I know it's not about putting up with anyone. It's about supporting each other and *loving* each other."

Good girl. I nodded.

"That said," she continued as I finished buckling my belt after checking the shirt was tucked in. "I feel like I'm literally trying to go from zero to one twenty, then throttle back down to thirty or forty, all the while I want people to just get the fuck out of our way."

With far more drama than she usually exhibited, she flung herself backwards on the bed. The dress she wore wasn't in any danger of wrinkling. The bodice hugged her chest, the back was bare except for a single silver chain that connected the sides. The fabric dipped right over the soft swell of her ass before it flared into a skirt.

The deep, rich blue of the dress was almost as vivid as the skies over the ski slopes in Colorado. Her hair created a halo around her as she stared up at the ceiling. Shoes for the evening rested next to her on the bed. Crossing over to the bed, I caught one of her legs and lifted until her foot rested against my knee.

With care, I slid her pair of low heels first onto one foot then the other. She watched me from beneath hooded lashes. The shoes were only to wear inside and while we observed. When it was time to play, the shoes and the dress would go.

But she wore them for me, and I could admire just how beautiful she looked in these colors. It also gave me a playful excuse to run a hand up her leg. When my fingers encountered nothing but bare skin, not even a hint of lace when I reached the juncture of her thighs, I smiled.

Her lips twitched upward, tilting into a playful grin that threatened all my carefully constructed plans as my chest and cock both swelled. "Someone told me not to wear anything that might inhibit contact."

I had, hadn't I? I rubbed her thigh gently, drawing lazy circles. "Good girl," I murmured and her cheeks flushed pink. "Now." I studied her, my gaze fixed on her expressions as she lifted herself up on her elbows. All the while, I enjoyed the sensation of goosebumps dimpling her skin as I rubbed a path from the inside of her thigh to the outside and back. "Tell me truthfully, Angel. Are you up for a scene tonight or do you just want to go and watch? We can always play when we get back."

Scenes at the club were always carefully negotiated. Frankie wasn't an exhibitionist by nature, but she enjoyed my pleasure in showing her off. At the same time, I savored the gifts she gave me, the trust. At the club, she gave me everything in a beautiful surrender that entrusted me with her protection and safety.

The absolute lack of self-consciousness or inhibitions when it came to our scenes demonstrated the depth of her faith in me. I would never allow anything to abuse her or her trust.

"You asked for the playdate tonight," she commented. "You specifically mentioned a scene."

"I did," I agreed. I needed tonight. It wasn't until the day before that I recognized my agitation levels had begun to increase. Some of it, I could acknowledge, were my own concerns over the music I was currently writing.

The rest of it though? It was feeding off the low-level anxiety humming around Frankie. Between school, mentorship, worrying about Archie, her counseling sessions, and our families? She was on edge. More each day.

I needed to shut that down for her, even for a few hours. Needed to give her a reprieve and shower her in sensation, endorphin release, and pleasure. I needed for her to let go and trust that I would catch her.

So yes, I had asked for tonight. Rather than dismiss her comment, I turned it over in my head as I caressed her legs, without giving into the urge to trace up to her pussy and plunging my fingers into her. She'd be slick, warm, and ready. But that wasn't what we needed.

Not yet anyway.

We'd get there.

"I do need tonight," I admitted. "I need to take care of you. I also want you comfortable for it and you're tired. We can shift the plan to stay here, run a tub of water and let you soak before I give you a massage."

Her deep green eyes darkened at the confession. The fact she savored the care I could give her even as she treasured my openness in admitting it, made the openness not only desirable, but something to be truly treasured.

I needed to care for her. My friend. My love. My angel. My sub.

She was only my sub for this, but that in and of itself, was a gift. An unrestrained trust flourishing between us that let her relax and shrug off the worries of the world. In the same breath, as I took on that burden it settled me in a way I could never describe.

"A real scene would do more for both of us," she told me after a long moment's contemplation. We never made impulsive decisions when it came to our play. Whether it was learning a new knot, a new suspension technique, or working with another rope Dom who could give us the kind of instruction I wanted, to make things safe as aces for my angel, we never rushed or made demands.

We thought about it, giving it all the right consideration. Frankie loved to make me happy and fuck knew, I'd cut off a damn arm for her. Neither of us rushed anything though. It truly helped to establish, though, that when we asked for something—we were serious.

Easing her legs down, I held out my hands to her and she clasped mine. Pulling her up, I slid an arm under her ass and lifted her all the way until we were on eye level with each other.

"What do you need, Angel?"

She smiled without reservation or artifice. "You."

Dipping my head, I rested my forehead to hers. "I'm always yours."

Her answering sigh only made my smile grow. "Do you still need me?"

"Always," I promised. This time I gave her a kiss, then gave her ass a firm squeeze before I set her on her feet. She lifted her arms to wrap around my neck and I obediently sank into the kiss she offered when her lips parted beneath mine.

The slow massage of her mouth against me, and the teasing licks of her tongue, settled what little agitation remained in my system. Worrying about her was as natural as breathing. She accepted all of me, even the parts that longed to wrap her up in the thickest, softest cotton and protect her forever.

I would never deny her a single experience in life, even if I wanted to make sure life never got another chance to take a crack at her. She'd paid for her success and her happiness in blood, sweat, tears, and rejection.

Never again.

The soft stroke of her finger on my cheek had me breaking from intimacy of breathing each other in and I lifted my head. "Warm coat," I reminded her. "Gloves."

"Yes, sir."

Tease. Another kiss and another gentle squeeze to her ass. I could already see the design the knots would make against her skin later. But first, we had to get there.

The car dropped us off right in front of the club and I made arrangements for him to pick us up closer to midnight. It was barely seven now. Five hours would be more than enough time for our evening at the club.

Where the club we'd frequented back in Texas had been located in a building in an industrial area. New York actually boasted several different types of sex clubs and BDSM dungeons. The Box was our favorite if we wanted to play outside the house. Located in Chelsea, and occupying the upper floor of a renovated factory—it was a haven in the midst of Manhattan.

Membership cost. Everyone applied to become a member and they actually did a rigorous background check. Frankie and I applied together, a Dom and my submissive. Part of the reason we'd applied as a couple had been to establish Frankie wasn't there to play with anyone else and neither was I.

We also applied as a couple because there were some rooms open to established couples that were not available to other patrons. I didn't begrudge anyone their fetish or kink. But I didn't want to create a problem we would later have to deal with if anyone considered Frankie open game as a sub.

Just not happening.

While reservations were available for non-members and other tourists of the lifestyle, membership did offer us privileges—like privacy and security to play without worry of encountering someone unaware of the rules.

Also, the public areas of the club offered a bar. But the private areas were restricted. Rules required zero inebriation from the guests who would be playing. Three of the seven luxurious rooms were clearly marked as demo rooms. What happened inside them was visible to anyone who cared to make their way to a room and watch.

The other four were designed specifically for personal privacy. They also required reservations. We had my favorite room reserved for three hours, beginning at nine.

The goal of The Box was to provide a safe and healthy environment where couples, independents, and others exploring their own natures, could foster trust. The bite in the air, along with the twinkle of lights on the door to the pub that made up the lower level of the Box, reminded me that Christmas was right around the corner.

In fact, finals for the semester were the next week. Another reason to steal away here for a few hours. The man at the door greeted us as he held it open to let us in. We flashed the hammered metal necklaces we wore. Their faux coin charm that proved us members of the Box granting us entry via the door leading upstairs rather than into the pub proper.

The place made great food, but we'd had dinner earlier. With a hand at Frankie's lower back, I followed her up the stairs, just one step behind her. At the top, we paused in the coat room where we could check our coats and gloves. I'd also brought my own bag with me.

The hostess accepted the bag to place it in our reserved room. After, she passed a small "menu" that included the evening's exhibitions and I trailed my fingers up Frankie's bare back while she reviewed our options. When I reached her throat, I threaded a black, silk, choker around her neck and then fastened it.

Not a proper collar, but we'd yet to find one we both liked. So, the black silk worked. Another sign making it clear she wasn't available to anyone else. As soon as I smoothed the collar into place, she tilted her head back to look up at me. Yes, this was exactly what we both needed.

I could drown in those gorgeous eyes. As it was, I let them settle me as the tension beneath my skin relaxed. The calm that enfolded me in these moments offered a kind of peace that only Frankie could provide.

"Ready, Angel?"

"Yes, sir," she answered in a voice that was pure decadence and erotic obedience. Wrapping my arm around her, I pressed a kiss to her temple.

"Have you chosen what you want to watch?"

"Yes, sir."

The game just made me smile.

"What do you want to watch?"

She touched a finger to one description on the menu and I read the information. It was a forty-five minute scene. The couple was familiar. The description of the scene surprised me, but one look at the blown-wide pupils in Frankie's eyes and the wordless part of her lips decided me.

Glancing to the hostess waiting to show us inside, I said, "The St. Andrew's Cross."

"A lovely choice. Gemma and Rush are a delight to watch."

I agreed. We'd seen a couple of their scenes over the last few months. Frankie enjoyed Rush's tutoring—he was a master with ropes and I'd been getting some instruction from him on and off this year. It started with a demo class and we followed it up over the last couple of months with a private session, where Frankie came to enjoy the fruits of my labor.

Rush was also the only other man outside of the guys I'd allowed to see Frankie sink into subspace. When she went, she was so gorgeously drifting into that world that I wanted to protect the space for her, even from being viewed.

However, one of the things I liked about Rush, he was a big believer in catering to his sub. No two subs were alike and treating them like they were interchangeable was anathema to him. That I respected most of all.

The hostess opened the door to the main body of the public rooms of The Box. The bar was right there near the entrance. Featuring an array of comfortable lounging areas like booths, tables, and high tops, spread out so that the guests could enjoy socialization or not as their preference.

Frankie settled against me, tucked under my arm as we made our way through the bar and to the first resting room. The lights were low, it was filled with couches, soft music, and a couple of lovely fish tanks. Only one of the sofas was occupied and a man cradled a woman against him and she looked very much asleep.

Aftercare was also something emphasized at The Box, with spaces provided both public and private where you could cradle them and let your sub recover in peace and quiet.

The St. Andrew's Cross was available in the Scarlett Room. The running joke of not calling any room red amused me. Not half as much as it did Frankie, but then she'd read those books. I kept my opinion to myself.

We weren't the first or last to arrive to the lounge set up just outside of the Scarlett Room. I chose one of the loveseats near the front but not quite on top of the glass. Settling on it, I tugged Frankie down to sit in my lap.

She relaxed into the curve of my body, tucking her head against my shoulder. Like me, she was riveted on the glass. Well, more precisely on what was happening behind the glass.

The lights lowered around us until only the yellow gleam along the floor provided the directions for how to leave the room if you needed the help. Rush led Gemma into the room. A blindfold covered her eyes and she wore black and red lingerie. It was practically see-through. The netting over her breasts actually seemed to be choking her nipples and I had to wonder if Rush had chosen the outfit with the idea of adding a little nipple torture to the experience.

Rush, despite his name, took his time guiding her over to the pillows at the base of the cross. He murmured in her ears, rubbed his hands over her arms and legs. The lingerie hid very little, from Rush or anyone else. While I couldn't hear what he was saying, I could imagine the praise or the dirty talk.

Gemma relaxed more and more, her body seemingly flowing against the pillows and leaning into Rush the more he talked and moved his hands over her. Eventually, heated kisses turned to nipple punishment, then a light spanking and while the sound had been off before, the first slap of his hand against her bare ass sent the sound rippling through our room.

Frankie's ass clenched against my leg. I slid a hand up under her dress and along her thigh. Good girl kept her focus on the couple in front of us, even as I ran my fingers along her soaking wet slit. The fact her glutes clenched on my thigh made me smile.

The soft moans and sharp cries from the sub played like a little symphony. In the dark, all I could make out was Frankie's profile as I stroked small circles around her clit. More than once, her hips would lift to meet my fingers. Each time she did, I halted the motion until she settled.

Her breathing deepened as Rush moved his sub over to the cross and the moment she was lashed to it, I could read the relaxation in the lines of her muscles. Yeah, if she hadn't already sunk into subspace during the prep, she'd vanished into it there.

Next came out a leather flogger. The light slaps across the sub's thighs and buttocks interested Frankie. She shifted in her seat. When she settled and her breathing deepened again, I began to massage her clit. This time, she didn't arch her hips or push against my fingers. No, she kept her legs open even as her thighs tensed and let me tease and caress at my leisure.

With the leather flogger, Rush pushed his sub and the first animalistic moan mingling with the explosive groan as she began to pump her hips at the air was all the encouragement I needed—Rush too it would seem. He traded out the flogger for a bullet vibrator and when he began to massage her clit, sinking his fingers into her, I increased the pressure on Frankie's.

The first hint of her orgasm came with a sudden hungry suck in of air. I clamped my lips over hers, swallowing the sound as I pushed my fingers into her slick channel, and curled them. Her body obeyed the command even as I increased the pressure of my thumb. She came apart in my arms, soaking her dress and part of my leg.

Gemma's lusty cries of release filled the room and hers weren't the only ones. More than one sub came for their dom. Releasing her from the cross, he carried her over to the bed and the screen darkened as the inner lights came up. Whatever personal aftercare they indulged in, or sex, it wasn't for our consumption.

And fine by me, the only care I was interested in right now was for the beautiful blonde panting against my shoulder while her pussy clenched and spasmed around my fingers. Loosening my grip on her lips, I lifted my head to find her staring up at me with a sleepy, dazed expression.

Not quite subspace. No. That was good. I wanted time to bring her there completely.

"Snack?" I murmured, as I eased my fingers out of her. Even with the lights up, it was still intimately dim in here. I licked my fingers of her sweetness one at a time. Her breathing deepened again and I didn't resist the imploring look as I dipped my fingers to her lips and she sucked one of them tightly into her mouth before she ran her tongue all over it.

My cock gave a little jerk. Yes, I loved the hungry feel of her mouth wrapped around me. Even more, I loved those delightful little licks of her tongue as she cleaned herself from my fingers. It was both an erotic invitation and a sweet promise of care.

"Water," she suggested only after she released my finger. "Otherwise, I'm happy right here with you."

Agreed. I asked a hostess for water and we enjoyed the quiet of the St. Andrew's Observation room as only one or two couples lingered in the room after others moved on. Eventually, our hostess came to find us and it was time to take Frankie to our private room.

I'd reserved the French Kiss room for us. It was a beautiful room featuring 18th century decor and the most intricate system of hooks and eyelets and pulleys. My bag awaited us, the hostess lingered only to make sure we didn't need anything else. Then she closed the door and I locked it.

Frankie turned to face me. She flowed as she moved, a dream taking form. Everything about her seemed to focus on me. Devotion flooded my system. Devotion and need.

Crossing to where she stood, I did a twirl of my finger and she turned away obediently. I unhooked the chain on her dress and it fell forward, pooling at her waist and then I eased it down over her hips, until she stood there completely nude, wearing only her heels.

At her feet, I held up my hand. She accepted the offer and I balanced her as she stepped out of the dress. Not losing my grip on her hand, I pressed a kiss to her thighs, then ran my nose along the smooth skin at the juncture of her thighs. She'd taken more and more to the waxing and while I'd never asked for it, I had to admit I did enjoy the effect.

After one last kiss to her abdomen, I rose. This time I brushed my lips to hers. "Kneel," I murmured. "Relax for a bit, I need to get things ready for you, Are you warm enough?"

Her nipples were tight and peaked. The pebbled shape of them suggested either deep desire or a chill. One was acceptable, the other was not.

"Yes," she promised. "Very warm." As if to prove the point, a flush spread across her chest and I smiled. Obediently, she moved to her knees while I continued to balance her. She settled right onto the pillow waiting for her.

Letting go of her hand, I stroked mine over her hair. For a moment, we held there, just suspended in the moment. Frankie's breathing was deep. The flush on her chest spread up to her throat and it turned her breasts a lovely shade of pink. The gleam in her eyes shimmered with affection and so many promises.

It was the dilation of her eyes though that tugged at me. The peace of this moment filled in all those restless places, soothing the anxiety left behind by the pressure of deadlines and musical notes. Music that just seemed too intimate to share and at the same time—

With care and deliberate attention, I put those thoughts to the side. I emptied my mind of anything that wasn't Frankie, the scene, and the knots I wanted to do. That act brought me into a sharp kind of clarity, where every nuance of her reactions filtered through me.

It took me almost a half hour to get her into position where the first knots had her right arm tucked across her chest and holding her own shoulder as her legs lifted. I wanted to give her the sensation of falling into an embrace, but the safety of knowing the landing would ever be gentle and pleasurable.

Every caress of the silk ropes over her skin took me deeper. I checked with Frankie regularly, but she drifted. Floating in subspace while I stretched the royal blue ropes over her skin, tying them and twisting, until the pattern created something beautiful on the exquisite flesh.

When I slid the last knot over her left ankle and then eased her into the suspension, Frankie let out a little orgasmic sigh that had my zipper leaving imprints on my aching cock. The trickle of dampness on her thighs was a reward all its own.

"Still with me, Angel?" I murmured close to her ear and she let out a lusty sigh, but didn't give me words. My precious girl, I slid a hand up her thigh and then landed a solid smack against her bare ass, canted at the perfect angle for me to massage or grip.

A gasp escaped her. "Yes, sir. Always."

"Much better," I murmured, then nibbled a kiss along the shell of her ear. "Green light?"

"So. Very. Green." The husky dip in her words locked around me like a fist on my cock. It pumped me from tip to base and back again. Oh, we would get there. But I needed her to come again.

Maybe a few times.

"Hold on, Angel," I warned and then delivered another firm slap to her other butt cheek before I cupped my palm over it and rubbed the heat in.

We had hours of pleasure ahead of us.

Chapter Seventeen

HOLD ON, ANGEL

Frankie

Three words. Three simple words, but they were the prelude to pleasure when Ian put his mind to it and today, his mind was definitely engaged. From the first brush of his fingers against my pussy to when he kissed the orgasm from my lips while we watched the scene play out in the St. Andrews Cross room, my body had been humming.

Our arrival in the reserved suite had left me tingling from head to toe. When it came to reservations and scene plans, Ian often took care of every single one. He would, from time to time, plan a possible scene with me if it involved something new to try.

Honestly, those discussions were as heady and provocative as they were educational and stimulating. More than once, I'd been on fire just thinking about what Ian would choose to do. Today proved to be no different.

When he directed me to kneel, a shudder of delicious anticipation rolled over me. I was so ready for tonight, for him, for this. When Ian asked because he needed this, it had echoed a need I hadn't realized I'd been suppressing.

Maybe it was all the craziness of Thanksgiving combined with the dash to the end of the semester. Maybe it was the group for grief counseling I'd been going to had seemed so much more poignant the last couple of months. Or maybe that was just my worry about Archie. At least one thing had been made abundantly clear over that holiday week in the Hamptons—Archie and his father were on the path to mending fences.

I loved that so damn much. For Archie far more than for Eddie, but I didn't want to be cruel. I was happy for Eddie too. When Ian began to lace the ropes over my skin, all the thoughts crowding into my brain trickled away.

With the kind of care and gentleness I'd come to associate with him, Ian stroked the silken ropes over my skin before he worked them into rope shackles that then decorated my arm and over my chest. He knew just how to tease me until I trembled, edging me without once running his fingers along my pussy.

The dampness on my thighs would tell him how much I enjoyed this. A part of me wanted to tell him, to just make a list out loud of all the pieces of this I enjoyed. At the same time, the words didn't even form on my lips. They were too relaxed as I savored the way he massaged my arms, my legs, my back, and even my breasts.

Every now and then, he would pause to nuzzle one of my nipples. The hard sucking sensation. The scrape of his teeth. The lave of his tongue. Then he'd release them from the heat of his mouth to blow a chilly breath over them that just made me want to squirm.

Squirming though, didn't earn me any points with Ian. Squirming or restless movements when he told me to be still, or worked on me in any way, would only mean he would relax his work on me, ease back until I settled. Then, and only then, would he begin his work again.

Aching for release or not, I refused to buck against him or try to chase his touch, no matter how much I longed for it. I missed when he finished the last knot. I was too busy floating. The solid slap of his hand against my ass sent a jolt of heat and pleasure to fuse in my core.

I moaned at the end of the first sharp gasp. He massaged the heat into my flesh, then delivered another swat. Alternating from one ass cheek to the other, he delivered a spanking I couldn't track or count no matter how I tried. He varied the speed, the force, and then spent longer and longer on massaging the heat into my ass.

My pussy contracted and spasmed with each strike toward the end. My heart raced as exultation spread through me. I wanted to push back against his hand or grind forward. But there was literally nothing to get any friction against.

The ropes twined all over my body held me suspended, in a perfect cocoon of hedonistic delight. I didn't need to think, only feel. Ian controlled the present, the pressure, and the pleasure. He controlled me, massaging the reactions from my body he wanted, and I surrendered to every delicious one.

Tears gathered in my eyes and drifted down my cheeks when he paused to press a gentle kiss against my still stinging ass. It probably had a rosy glow to it and the fact it was tilted upward, baring my pussy to his inspection, only added to my joy.

Soft murmurs of praise escaped him. The words were there, right at the tips of my fingers. Honestly, all I could feel—all I could hear—was the warmth dripping from his honeyed voice as he kissed his way along me. Then his lips pressed against mine and I opened to him.

Lashes fluttering upward, I met the deep blue of his eyes as he locked gazes with me. The fact his tongue stroked mine, teasing gently to get me to open to him more, all the while he held my gaze captive pulled me into the most intimate of embraces.

As easily as it would be to lose myself in him, I would never be lost. Ian would never let me float away. He would never lose me. For all that I drifted in a sea of ecstasy, those orgasms right there lapping against my skin like the waves of silken water, Ian was there to act as my anchor. He lashed me to the earth, and to him, as sure as he had to the suspension in this room.

Featherlight brushes of his fingers on my cheek kept me focused on him. "Green?" A soft inquiry, a necessary check-in, a desire to always make sure I was still with him.

As if I would be anywhere else. "Green," I whispered, my lips so dry that I found it even hard to get the word out. It came out more of a croak than something sexy.

The soft slash of his mouth turned into a smile populated with sunshine and heat. Ian would always bring that with him. The realization danced through me, a fanciful thought. Something of it must have shown on my expression, because he cradled my cheeks in his hands. The stroke of his thumbs chased away my tears.

"One more time," he said, his tone firm and demanding obedience even as it glided over me like the gentlest of pets. "Green?"

"Very green. Green like summer and sunshine and you playing with me in the swimming pool." Because that was the safety he offered me. The warmth he encased me in. The kind of care he showered over me. At the same time, it was all the playfulness of those days splashing in the water that helped get us to where we were today.

Concern morphed into puzzlement which in turn became adoration. "Angel… you amaze me."

I grinned, leaning my cheek into his palm. Floating in mid-air, my body spun in cotton candy and pleasure, I sighed as I stared into his eyes. "I love you."

They really were the only words I could come up with in response. He pressed his lips to mine, the sweetness as captivating now as it had been during that first kiss in the pool. For all that I floated, those memories threaded through me.

Different moments, strung together on a network of fairy lights like some animated film montage. Another kiss, this one far more biting in its intensity, the grip of his hand sliding up to tangle in my hair tugging at my scalp, and a huff of sound pulled me back from the mental safari to the past.

"I want you here," he said in that firm, loving voice that brooked zero arguments. "Right here and with me."

"Yes," I promised. "Sir." The last bit was only a teasing hint of afterthought. I hadn't forgotten. The tenderness in his eyes didn't hide the humor.

"I adore you," he murmured with one last caress before he moved away from my face and I floated with a little grin.

"I know." Not even the soft brush of leather over my bound legs could diminish the smugness in my tone. The first lash of the soft leather stroking over my skin and in between the knots of rope sent a surge of electricity through my system.

Flogging was so new to us, but the rush of heat pulsing in my core turned almost molten as he alternated between light strikes and teasing strokes. More than once, he trailed those soft leather strands over my ass, my back and then down over my chest. But he flogged only my arms and legs with the gentle strikes.

Each light sting from the strikes added another layer of heat to the fire burning inside of me. Even the tease of my nipples didn't give me the kind of friction I craved and at the same time, it lit me up.

Tears streamed down my face as I laughed and sobbed. The barest brush of that leather threading between my legs caught my clit and the orgasm unraveled with a breathless force that had me crying out. No matter how still I tried to stay, my muscles locked and my ass clenched as the pleasure just detonated within me.

"That's my beautiful angel," Ian praised. "My sweet, so good girl." The words were just an added caress, a bombardment to my already overwhelmed system. Nothing prepared me for the first thrust of his cock filling my clenched pussy.

It took some effort to push in against the spasming walls. The world just began to shred apart as I lost the ability to focus on anything. My skin was so alive, the air on it left me tingling. The hot pulse of his cock stretching me as he pushed inside, expanded that bubble of tension to new heights.

The weight of his hands on my hips, guiding me as I flowed back and forth, riding him as he thrust forward to fill me. The next cry that burst out of me was a ragged call of his name. This only seemed to spur him on.

The slap of skin increased and his hands slid over the ropes, tugging and adjusting before he cupped my breasts. The profound relief as he massaged the nipples even as he slammed into me over and over split me wide open. This time, the pleasure fountaining within me was endless.

My vision whited out, my body vibrated and there was the sense of flying even as heat pulsed within me, and then nothing. Nothing except a cloud of pleasure, lifting me up in my cocoon of safety. The steady thump of his heart filled my ear and the gentle massage of his hands roaming over skin roused me.

"Shh," he murmured when I lifted my head. The ropes were gone, my skin was hot and flush against Ian's. He cradled me on his lap and against his chest. The softest blanket had been wrapped around me. "We have plenty of time," he soothed and it wasn't until those words registered that I heard my own little whimpers.

The sound faded away as I snuggled him. He adjusted the blanket again and it hit me why I'd been whimpering. After freeing me, he'd been rubbing my arms and legs, but I must have started shivering.

Little bits of data floated back out as I processed them. I didn't need to know. Right now, in this place and in this moment, Ian would take care of everything. The motion to get the blanket around me would have taken him away and right now, he was the gravity keeping me on earth.

I didn't want to lose him.

"You can't lose me, Angel," he promised in the sweetest tone. "One, I'd find you. Two, you'd find me."

Absolute confidence in those words. "You believe that." Not a question.

"I do." He pressed a kiss to the top of my head. "You're not gonna lose me, Angel. Besides… even if I did slip away, the guys would hunt me down and beat me silly."

I giggled. Even if it wasn't funny, but the way he said it was. "I know, I trust you."

"That means the world to me." He rubbed my back slowly and my eyes were drifting closed. "A little water, Angel, then you can sleep."

I would have protested cause my eyes were so heavy, but my throat was a little sore. The press of the bottle to my lips had me sighing before I took the first swallow of the glorious cool liquid. I drank half the bottle before I dozed again.

Twice more I woke to Ian's soft murmurs. It took him promising me food and coffee to get me to fully rouse, and his soft chuckle at my hopeful, "Coffee?" made me smile.

Once I was up though, we took our time. I was sore, but not in a debilitating way. The marks of the silks on my skin were faint, even the welts left by the flogger had faded to faint pink lines.

In the shower, he massaged my scalp as he washed my hair, then my back as he soaped away the dried sweat on my skin. Then it was my turn and I reveled in washing him. When we played, the act of touching him was something of a reward, and I savored these moments when he let me take care of him.

After we'd toweled off and redressed, we still had a little time left on our reservation. The minute Ian took a seat on the long, comfortable sofa in the room and patted his lap, I curled right back against him.

"Do you feel better?" The soft question was one I should have asked, but there was a kind of serenity to him that washed over me as I settled against him.

"I do," I said after a moment's self-reflection. "Honestly, I feel—new?

Different? Relaxed?" I couldn't quite put my finger on it.

"Are you asking me or telling me?"

Giggling, I tipped my head back and met his similarly amused gaze. "Both?"

To my absolute delight, he laughed. The sound vibrated in his chest and it only set me off on a fresh wave of giggles. His smile turned indulgent and I leaned up to press a kiss, while still laughing, to the corner of that smile.

"You feel better too." It wasn't a question.

"I do," he admitted. "I needed this even more than I realized."

"Do you need to talk about it?" Granted, I was loose-limbed, and boneless from our play, but my mind was rousing and my heart would always make time to listen to him.

"Not sure it's a talking thing, Angel, it's more about the music I've been working on."

I nodded, tipping my head so I could keep watching him.

A soft sigh escaped him. "I think I'm making it a much larger deal than it needs to be."

"Ian."

He focused on me.

"Don't dismiss your feelings."

The corner of his mouth kicked a little higher. "Yes, ma'am."

Cupping his cheek with my palm, I nipped at his jaw. "Tell me?"

Tightening his arms around me, he took his time and I waited him out. "I already said this seemed odd because the music is so personal."

"Yes." He had said exactly that to me. "I remember."

"I've written four or five songs so far." For a moment, he pursed his lips like he didn't want to say more and then his gaze fell back to meet mine. "They all feel personal. They all feel like they're about you."

"And you don't want anyone else to sing them."

"Hell no," he admitted, the ferociousness in his tone kindling a fresh wave of heat inside. "You're mine, not theirs."

"How can I help?" It was my turn to soothe him. I rubbed small circles against the center of his chest. "I know I haven't been working on them as much with you. Maybe we sit down this week, you can play them for me?"

"You've been slammed, Angel."

I lifted my shoulders. "We're always going to be busy. I will make the time. I should have—"

He silenced me with two fingers to my lips. "If you finish that sentence with any variant on letting me down, I will be very cross with you."

Wrinkling my nose, I nipped his fingertips. "It's right up there with putting up with me."

"Yes," he said firmly. "It is."

"But you see," I countered. "Looking after you *is* important to me. If you don't want to part with those songs, then you don't have to. But I want to help. I *love* your music."

His expression softened all over again. "You've always been my number one fan."

"And the only panties thrown at you that you can keep."

That had him laughing all over again. "What happens when you have no panties to throw?"

"I figure I'll just throw myself. You're pretty good at catching."

"Every time," he promised. Then he cradled me to him and I tucked my head to his shoulder. "Yes, I would like to play them for you. Maybe that's what I need to do in order to let them go. I just don't know what I tell them if that doesn't work…"

"We'll write one together," I suggested. Not that I was all good at those lyrics. "Then it's one we write about someone else."

He huffed.

"Little Miss Abigail for example."

That got me a laugh.

"I'd suggest the cats, but not sure how much arrogance you want to inject into the song."

"Could write one about Archie," he mused. "What do you think?"

I grinned. "He did love the song you helped me write for him when it was his birthday."

"Fair point. We'll write it about Coop," Ian said.

I half sat up and met his gaze. "Can I call it Player Three Is In the Game?"

Another laugh broke free from him, but more, the worry that had begun to tense his brow vanished. "You realize, we may end up with another album after all?"

"Sounds like a win to me."

He tucked a strand of my hair behind an ear then gave me a long, studious look. "You're the win."

"I'd say compliments will get you nowhere, but we both know I melt when you praise me."

"Good girl."

The shiver raced right up my spine and it was my turn to laugh again. We were still smiling when we slipped out of the club and into the waiting car. Granted, I floated all the way home.

Hold on, Angel.

That was my plan.

Every single day.

Chapter Eighteen
RETAIL THERAPY

Frankie

"What about this one?" Kelly held up another shirt, this one in a caramel shade. The cut was nice, but… "And don't look at me that way, I know it seems weird to get dress shirts for the holidays, but Hank—he's not a shopping fan."

"Really?" I had no idea how I hadn't just laughed out loud. Considering a week earlier, I'd been in *this* same store with Hank picking out something pretty for Kelly for Christmas. He'd told me she wasn't a shopping fan either.

The look on her face was equal parts exasperation and affection. "No. He's just interested in so much more than appearances. Granted, he looks like the hot professor you just want to…"

At my grimace, she trailed off and shot me an apologetic look.

"Sorry."

"You are not," I teased and then tapped the shirt. "I like this one and it will look great on him. But that mint green is way too cool a color for him."

"Cool colors?" Oh, now I had her attention. "Have you been holding out on me?"

I flat out snorted. "Not even. I'd bet that I hate shopping more than Hank does, but that said—I have been ruthlessly educated on color palettes, seasons, and all that other crap, so I pick out the right colors to compliment my own looks."

Kelly's grin grew. "The distaste in your voice entertains me." But she'd added the caramel-colored shirt to the purchase stack and returned the green one. "What about this one?"

The purple was a little on the bright side. "Maybe if we go for a darker grape shade and maybe pair it with fun ties."

"Fun ties it is!" This was one of the first times in quite a while that it was just Kelly and me. The fact she'd managed to sneak down to the city for the day without the kids made it a no brainer to make time for the visit.

In all fairness, most of our interactions had often included the buffer of the kids, especially Chloe, who had the most amazing relationship with her mom. If not the kids, then Hank was there or one of the guys.

I really couldn't think of a single time that it had been *us*. That was more on me than on her. We were going through the different ties. I'd picked out a couple for Christmas presents already, but only one of those had been a "fun" one and I didn't think it would pair well with the ones Kelly picked out.

"Okay," Kelly said while flicking through the ties. "Tell me truthfully, if I get all four of the boys the same set of ties and suspenders or some other matching gift, is that gonna be weird?"

I laughed. "Not as weird as you might think." I picked out the Egyptian motif tie. It had hieroglyphics on it and it was done in a flattering gold and gleaming browns. "What about this one?"

"Sold," she said with a grin as I passed the tie over to her. "How not weird? The boys are always gracious with the kids, even after everything that happened over the summer."

Fresh laughter escaped me. "Kelly, they were fine with the kids coming down for a week in July. We had a lot of fun and you and Hank deserved some vacation time for you. It also gives me time with them, since I'm such a late arrival in their lives."

"First," Kelly said, pausing as she faced me. "You are their sister and they adore you. Late arrival or not, there is more than enough room in this family for you and we'd have made room regardless."

That declaration carried not one whit of anything disingenuous. If anything, it was so firm and forceful, I didn't dare debate it.

"Second, Alec came clean about Craig blowing up the experiment *in* the oven."

I bit down on the inside of my cheek. I needed to not laugh nor try to dismiss the concern.

"We'll discuss you covering for them later—"

"Actually," I interrupted and held up a palm. "That week they were my responsibility. They also had to pay for the mistake and for disobeying the rules. Trust me, when Jeremy was done, they were masters at cleaning sticky stuff out of grout."

I tried not to picture the beautiful cake they'd legit "exploded" when they combined some version of microwave technology with the pan they'd put the cake into the oven with.

Eyes narrowed, she assessed me for a beat. "Please tell me the pudding in the center was just because they hadn't been able to cook it all the way through."

"Nope, that pudding had been frozen though for pudding pops we'd been experimenting on the day before, and they layered the cake over it, and thought if they wrapped the wooden handles with foil it would help cook it faster."

Abject horror crept across Kelly's face.

"And to be fair, it might have worked." If they hadn't found old plans of Archie's and hadn't doubled up on foil and metal everywhere so they could really get the heat going, or that they'd added a Sterno to the center, thinking the heat would do the final trick. "I mean as a hypothesis goes, working with the information they had at the time, it was possible to see where they were coming from."

"How much *actual* damage did they do?"

I mimed zipping my lips. "They scared themselves and the cats mostly. It wasn't the first time we've had to replace the stove and they had to clean it all up, with Jeremy supervising."

Leaning back against the table, Kelly folded her arms but kept one hand pressed to her mouth.

"Seriously, it's fine," I reassured her. "Archie was impressed with their ingenuity." Before Kelly could respond to that, I held up a hand. "He didn't tell *them* that. He told me later, after he went over everything they did so he could figure out what they did wrong."

"I shudder to ask," Kelly said, hiding behind her hand as she stared at me through her spread fingers.

"I don't know what they did wrong, but Archie was also forbidden from repeating it *in* the house." If I had my way, he wouldn't try to create an explosion anywhere else, but I knew better. Archie would test it until he figured out not only how to make it work, but also how to make it safe for the kids.

"I feel so bad that you all had to deal with that."

Shrugging, I shook my head. "Honestly, I think outside of a bit startling—" Like legit making me jump out of my skin and screaming, not that I would bring that up. "It wasn't the worst thing, I've ever seen. Like I said, we had to replace the stove before. I was just glad they were okay and seemed to have scared themselves from doing more unsupervised 'experiments' for the time being."

I should have seen it coming, but honest surprise flared through me when Kelly pushed away from the table and wrapped her arms around me.

The woman knew how to hug. Weirder than me not noticing Kelly going into hug mode, was the fact I found myself hugging her back.

"Hey," I managed to say with a bit of a laugh. "No flinching or pulling away. I feel like I've maxed out on a new achievement."

Her laughter added to the warmth of the embrace. "I wasn't going to say anything," she admitted as she eased back. "You always look like I'm about to take you to task rather than hug you."

"I've just never…"

"I know," she confirmed, soothing tone in place as she rubbed my upper arms. "That's why Chloe and I have been working on you. It's all a part of our cunning plan."

Right. "It's not that subtle."

"Or that cunning," she admitted, hooking our arms together as she tugged the cart we'd been filling steadily. "I'm not going to lie though. I love that you're beginning to trust me."

Guilt twisted in my gut. "Kelly…"

"Nope, no apologies needed. Nor, for that matter, do I need explanations." Kelly slanted a look at me. "Have we reached that time when I can just be blunt and honest with you and not scare you off?"

"Okay, the fact that you're asking that makes me want to apologize for being so difficult."

"You're not difficult at all," Kelly retorted. "You're valuable. You're precious. You're a member of my family. You also endured far too many years of emotional abuse and neglect. I wouldn't trust this crazy woman who wants to hug me all the time. I wouldn't be able to help but question her motives too."

I grimaced.

"See, I understand that," she continued as we made our way through the store toward the registers. Oh, if we were done, I would cheer. I could definitely use a cup of coffee. "I've understood it since the day Hank got that first call from your mother wanting him to do the test. We talked about it for a long time. I was also there when she told him he wasn't the father."

A sigh escaped me. Some days, it seemed like I'd never escape the shadow of Maddy's bitch-umbrella and how far it drifted over my life.

"My point," she said, giving me a squeeze before pausing a few feet before the counter with the sales lady waiting to check us out to turn and look at me. "You're Hank's daughter. But you're also one of my kids. Before you try to tell me I don't have to do that, I know that I don't have to. I knew from the moment Hank heard you were his that you would also be mine."

Heat rushed to my cheeks, but I made myself listen to the whole thing.

"You are. You're *family* young lady. You always will be. So, please understand that I am very well aware that I am *not* your mother. I will never try to take her place or assume that you need me to step in and mother you."

"Thanks?" Honestly, no one needed to take Maddy's place.

Her huffed little sigh of impatience made me grin. Kelly rolled with everything, she always seemed to put a positive spin on things and for all that she could crowd in on me with her affection, it was also kind of nice that I'd never had to prove anything to her.

Not once.

"Thank you," I said, meaning it. "I really do like you and I know I'm a little squirrely about all the affection but… it's growing on me."

"Best news I've had all day. Now, let's pay for this and then I'm treating you to a lovely high tea at one of my favorite spots in midtown. It's not something I've gotten to share with Chloe yet, but I'd like to do it with you. My mom used to bring me into the city a couple of times a year and we'd do that."

"I'd like that," I admitted. "I'd really like that." I checked the time. "I'm going to send Eddie a message…"

"Oh, am I interrupting your plans?"

"Yes and no." Honest was better. "Eddie and I try to have lunch a couple of times a month to go over where I am in my classes. He has taken mentoring very seriously, and this afternoon I have meetings to observe at

Standish. But things come up and I'd like to go and have tea with you. I'll ask him if we can skip the lunch until next week and I can just take a car to meet him this afternoon."

Kelly studied me for a long moment, then she grinned. "Well, in that case, want to call the car to pick us up here?" The almost playful look in her eyes had me grinning.

"On it." I also pretended not to notice that as I walked away to make the call both to Eddie and to the car, she shifted something out from under the shirts. A little present she probably didn't want me to notice, so I would be a good girl and *not* notice it.

While I could have texted, lunch dates were a little more personal, and another demonstration of Eddie's efforts in how he tackled projects both at home and in business. It was a line he'd never really straddled before and while I might have had a hard time believing we'd be in this place even a year and a half ago, we were there now.

"Hello, Frankie," Eddie greeted me as he answered the call. "I was just about to step into a meeting."

"Sorry," I said. "I could have left a message."

"Nothing to be sorry about. They can wait a few moments. What's up?"

"I'm going to have to ask for a raincheck for our lunch date, but I can be down to corporate by two if that still works for you."

"Absolutely," he agreed easily enough. "Anything wrong? Is there something I can do to help?"

"No, absolutely nothing wrong. Kelly's in the city to do some shopping and she asked about going to get tea together before she leaves. I know it's rather last minute…"

"I will happily collect my raincheck next week for lunch. You'll be almost done with finals, right?"

I exhaled. "Yeah, I'm ready for the break. I also have my full prospectus and detailed project plan broken down for you to review."

"I'm looking forward to it. Enjoy your tea, if it runs long, just let me know. Though I may steal you for dinner if we're here too late this evening."

I laughed. "How about, I text Archie and let him know I may be late and see if he wants to come and have dinner with us?"

The momentary pause worried me. Had I overstepped? "Frankie," Eddie said slowly. "You don't have to do that."

"You want to know something fun?" I grinned, because when it came to Archie and his dad, there were things I *could* do. "I would love to have dinner with both of you. It's fun and entertaining. I also like getting Archie's perspective on the business concepts."

All true.

Chuckling, Eddie said, "I am reminded of something my father told me."

"That was?"

"Never argue with a beautiful or determined woman. If she's both, just get out of her way."

I snorted.

"I would enjoy having dinner with both of you as well, but we'll call those plans tentative."

"That would be great, now, I'll let you go to your meeting and I promise to let you know if I'm going to be later than two."

"Thank you, Frankie."

The weight in those first words were for a lot more than just me checking in.

"Any time," I promised. Then after that, I sent a message to our car service and asked for the pickup. Then messaged Archie. He could be in class or he could be studying. It depended on whether his professor was one who allowed them to do in class reviews or just let them take the class time as study time.

Turning, I caught sight of Kelly heading in my direction with her bags. Archie's message vibrated my phone and then popped up on the screen.

I snorted out loud.

He ended it with a set of heart eyes and then a blown kiss emoji.

"That look right there just eliminates so many of my concerns," Kelly announced when she reached me and at my quizzical look, she just grinned. "There's a dewy-eyed thing you have going on whenever you talk to one of your boys. It lights you up and relaxes you. I like it. I think it looks amazing on you."

The heat suffusing my face meant there was no way of hiding my blush.

"I'm pretty fond of it—and them—myself."

Offering me her arm again when I took one of the two bags so I could help her carry things, Kelly said, "What are my chances of getting the story of how all of you met and came to this part of the relationship out of you?"

I considered it, not answering right away. "Depends, I suppose…"

"On?"

"Is running involved in getting tea?"

It took her a moment, but her sudden laughter just made me grin. "You, young lady, are a smart ass."

"You know," I said, letting go of her arm so I could open the outer door to let us both out into the cold. Thankfully, the car was right there so it didn't matter that I hadn't gotten my coat buttoned up. "I hear that a lot."

We were both laughing as we got into the car.

Chapter Nineteen

HAPPY FUCKING BIRTHDAY TO ME

Jake

As birthdays went, my twenty-first stealthed in like a soldier on a mission. I woke up to Frankie curled around me. Our last exams had been two days prior and we were done with classes until the second week of January. In the meantime, with Christmas in full swing, the house decorated, and a lot of plans made for the five of us, I'd elected for a quiet birthday.

Funnily enough, or maybe I should say predictably, it was Archie who offered to get us a room or a suite at a hotel so I could have Frankie all to myself. Not that I wouldn't normally leap to that idea, I kind of wanted our family around both of us.

Threading my fingers through the blonde strands of her hair, I combed it back away from her face. We'd gone out to dinner after the game last night. Frankie hung out with my whole team and their various partners. The win, the party, and then home for some naked calisthenics. A soft chuckle broke out of me at the description. Naked play with Frankie was definitely one of my favorite activities.

She was plastered up against me. Even as I stroked the hair away from her face, I smiled at the blue butterfly just behind her ear. She'd added a pair of them now. I had a feeling she'd be adding another soon. The butterflies were just for Frankie and I loved that my baby girl was putting herself out there, putting herself first in some areas, and going after what she wanted.

If I had to guess, the butterflies were for her literally and figuratively trusting herself and her own wings. Maybe I should incorporate one into a new tattoo. Food for thought. Frankie loved my dragons, maybe a variation on that.

The sheets rustled as her breathing shifted. Sleeping still, but she'd already started to wake up. Hmm… I had a better idea for waking her up. I checked my breath against my palm. Not too bad. Then I scratched at my beard. Not bristly.

The secret was to keep it brushed and oiled as necessary to moisturize it. Don't let it get too long or too short. Then rubbing my cheeks on her thighs drove Frankie wild.

Definitely a win in my book. Easing Frankie over, I did it in stages. Another sweet trick to our girl, she was a cuddler but also a deep sleeper. At least around us. The measure of trust she'd shown us so quickly had settled something deep inside of me a long time ago.

It settled my own irritation at sharing her. Looking back at it now? It hadn't even been true irritation. A part of me had kind of always known I'd end up sharing her. I'd shared her with Coop from the day I met her. A fact that had annoyed my soon to become best friend more than he'd ever wanted to admit.

At least then.

Later on, we talked about it. After Bubba showed up and set his sights on her, and definitely after Archie. The sheet tracked downward, leaving all that bare skin for me to admire and I smiled at the assortment of little hickeys littering the curve of one breast. Only two of those were mine.

The others, though only a little older, served as yet another reminder of our family. As tempting as it was to retrace that path with another set of heated, biting kisses to leave new marks—I resisted the impulse. I had a plan.

One that involved blazing a fresh path this morning. I kissed each breast, barely doing more than teasing my beard against her nipples. They tightened, almost reflexively. Smiling, I pressed another kiss beneath them then to her sternum and down her center to the gem twinkling at me from her belly button.

This piercing was one of her best ideas. I'd never imagined her with this gleaming gem hidden away from public view where only *we* got to enjoy it. Now? I couldn't imagine her without it. I loved the sweet little diamond that currently twinkled there. We'd added a sapphire and ruby over the last year that she could trade out and there was an emerald under the tree to go with the other pieces that we'd accumulated.

The closer I came to her pussy, the more the sweet scent of her arousal began to tickle my nostrils. There were so many amazing things about this particular situation.

Frankie being naked, for example.

That was amazing.

I stroked my hands over her thighs and she shifted, a restless motion that had me stealing a look upward. Her lashes fluttered, but her eyes didn't open. Yet, anyway.

Licking my lips, I leaned in to slide my hands under her ass and I'd just begun to lick a stripe from her entrance to her clit when my phone rang.

Fuck. My. World.

The swift inhalation and irritated little mew that followed it echoed my own thoughts. I glanced up to find Frankie staring at me, her cheeks already flushed and then my phone rang again.

"Ignore it," I decided. It was my birthday.

After two more rings, it finally went to voicemail. Excellent.

"Jake…"

"Morning, Baby Girl," I mumbled before burying my face in her pussy again, humming the birthday song. Laughter escaped her along with a gasp, but I'd barely gotten in a solid tongue thrust when my phone rang again.

Cutting my gaze toward the nightstand, I swirled my tongue around her clit and Frankie's hips lifted. I gripped her ass, then pinned one of her hips as I studiously ignored the phone.

I'd almost edged her toward an orgasm when it rang the third time.

"For fuck's sake," I snarled, pressing a kiss to her inner thigh and then crawling over to grab the phone. Hitting answer, I barely registered the name on the screen. "This better be really fucking important, because your timing sucks."

"Good morning to you too," Dad said in a deep tone so populated by enough smugness and laughter, there was no way he didn't know he was interrupting. "Happy birthday."

I groaned, flopping onto my back as I glanced over at Frankie. She blew a tendril of hair out of her flushed face as she tracked my movements. Her nipples just beckoned to be nipped and sucked. More, I'd only gotten the first few licks in and it took more than a couple to get to the center of Frankie's—yeah, okay. I nipped that thought in the bud.

One, I'd laugh. And two, I'd want to say it while she was orgasming. Three, I liked my nuts where they were. Especially when she stroked her hand over them and then up my chest.

"Thanks, Dad," I said with more of a sigh than I wanted to let loose. "It's got to be afternoon there…" I pulled the phone away to look at the time. Germany was what? Seven? Eight hours ahead? I couldn't fucking remember.

"No." Now he sounded even more amused and I rubbed a hand against my eyes.

If I complained, he'd grow even more vague and drag this call out for all he was worth. Dad could be a real dick when he wanted to be. Most of the time, I'd find it funny, except right now both my mouth and dick wanted to be somewhere else.

"It's actually early here," he was saying, though I didn't quite track it as Frankie pressed a kiss to one of my dragons. I lifted my hand to watch her. Those green eyes seemed to gleam in the half-light of the room. It was very gray, like the skies outside were leaden.

She traced her tongue around one of my nipples. I raised my brows and a smile quirked her lips as she sat up, half-straddling my thighs. Then she cupped her own breasts, and my dick went from half-hard to stone in a split-second.

"Your mom and I were talking this morning," Dad continued. "About the day you were born. The fact I was on station, she couldn't settle all night…"

Frankie rolled her own nipples while she watched me and I licked my lips. Coop might be the voyeur but this was kind of hot.

Who was I kidding? Watching her knead and massage her breasts, in between rolling and pinching her nipples, had me wanting to sit forward and take over. Then she abandoned her nipples to drop her hands to my chest. I covered one of her hands against my pec and then tugged it up to my lips.

Gazes locked, I sucked her finger against my tongue and began to tease the tip like it was her clit. The message must have gone straight through because the pink flush on her face suffused her chest and gave her a warm glow.

"She didn't want to go to the hospital without me…"

Right, hospital, took all night and most of the day before Mom gave up on Dad making it back in time. Klara got there, took her to the hospital and all night, Mom paced and they measured and I took my sweet ass time arriving…

I'd heard this story before and Frankie slid the fingers I'd just licked between her legs where she spread her pink pussy wide enough for me to see it at this angle. Fuck me, I wanted off the phone.

Then she toyed with herself until her breath came in little pants and her skin flushed an even rosier color. When she held those glistening fingers out to me, I sucked on them hungrily.

"…I made it, barely, you were already crowning by the time I got into the room." Yeah yeah, Klara was already in the prime position, so Dad moved up to hold Mom's hand.

The treat of licking her sweetness clean from her fingers wasn't enough. Frankie's pupils were fat and tempting as they tried to drown out the green.

"…They didn't even do an epidural and your mom was a trooper…"

I mouthed, "Two minutes," to my baby girl as I motioned to the phone. The smile curving her lips should have been my first warning.

Should have been.

To be fair though, Frankie's next move shocked me to a delighted level. No lie. With her hair trailing over my chest, she kissed the wing of the dragon, then my nipple, then followed the dragon's wings down to my abdomen.

"…stubborn as hell, right from the beginning. From your first cry…"

My dick twitched at the first brush of her hair over it. Fuck me. My skin and my balls tingled in anticipation as her lips glided over the hard tip of my dick. I half sat up, but she put a hand on my stomach and stared up at me.

Oh, fuck.

The look on her face warned me. Frankie wouldn't be deterred and this was my birthday, I wanted to eat her out first. I had no way to communicate that without putting Dad on mute and since he hadn't fucking *shut up* about the day I was born, I hesitated.

Pressing a finger to her lips, Frankie glanced at my phone then at me. Then she dropped her gaze to my dick.

Fuck.

Fuck.

Please?

Blowing out a breath, I spread my legs a little further as she adjusted to lay down between my thighs. This was going to kill me.

In all the right ways.

Falling back against the pillows, I shifted enough so I could watch her. She wrapped her hand around the base of my dick and I swore it was both the cool and warm welcome. Hot and silken. Maybe icy hot, the first stroke from base to tip made me pump my hips up and she put her free hand on my hip.

The not so gentle shove reminded me to behave. Oh, Baby Girl, you and me…

"…Jacob, are you even listening to me?"

"Sure I am, have you gotten to the part where Klara punched you in the nose for Mom because you said something stupid about me getting all my stubbornness from her?"

Distracted? Absolutely, because Frankie dropped down to wrap her lips around my dick again. I was torn between keeping my gaze on hers and watching the way my dick disappeared into her mouth.

The hot, wet clamp of her lips around me was a piece of heaven. The fact she kept stroking me with her tongue and hollowing out her cheeks as she sucked me deep was like the most delicious form of torture.

Dad snorted. "I believe she socked me in the nose because I said it was better you put your mother through it than Klara, because stubborn and hot headed was better than stubborn and cunning."

Right. "Too bad for you…" I should win a fucking prize for acting because my voice didn't crack or strain once. Not even when Frankie swallowed me all the way into her throat. Wrapping my fist into her hair, I followed every move she made.

Frankie set the pace and I arched my hips to thrust against her throat. At the first sound of gagging, I almost swore and tried to pull back.

Speaking of stubborn, she chased my cock and my pleasure with the kind of relentless obsession that I was finding it harder and harder to hold back as my balls tightened.

"…I got hot headed from Mom, cunning from Klara, and pure pig-headed stubborn from you." Right, taking my life in my hands here but Frankie had my dick so that was covered.

Increasing her pace, she seemed intent on driving me mad. All I could feel was the heated sheath of her mouth swallowing around me. The rough ridge at the back of her throat as my dick hit it and then the shudder that went up my cock to my spine and skittered all the way up to stab pleasure into my brain.

She was going to suck the soul right out of me and I was so fucking here for that.

"…what the hell are you doing?" Klara's voice came over the line clear and intent. "Why are you torturing Jake on his birthday?"

"Kick his ass, Klara!" My money was on her.

"I'm sorry, Jakey-boy, I'll deal with your father." At her crisp delivery, Mom laughed somewhere in the background.

Wait. Mom. Dad. Klara. All on the phone. My brain scrabbled for that thought even as Frankie fisted the base of my cock, the tightness was going to keep me from coming.

Hopefully, the look I tossed her was more gratitude than distressed. Not that it slowed her from shifting the play over my dick. Light grazes of her teeth that sent shivers through me. Hard suction that threatened to part me from my soul. Then those devilish little licks like I was her favorite fucking treat.

Sweat dampened my brow and my voice might betray me, but I just managed a, "Yeah…" That was all I could squeeze out.

"Jake, darling, we're hanging up the phone." Mom. "Happy birthday and our apologies to Frankie."

"No prob." Firing the words out in single syllables helped. "Dad. Want. Ed. To. Give. Me. Shit."

"Yes," Mom said with so much exasperation, I laughed. Even if it came out a bit strangled. "And because he and Klara both proposed last night…"

"Awe. Some."

I was so fucking close to coming, that I tugged at Frankie's hair gently. A warning, but she merely lifted her head, grinned like a cat, licked her lips, and then swallowed me down.

Yep.

I was gonna come.

"Great. Grats. I'll. Beat. Dad. Up. Later."

There was a huff of real laughter exploding like he'd been holding it in. The slap of a hand against him didn't stop his laughter.

"Dad's a dick," I muttered.

That only made him laugh harder but they hung up. The moment of perfect silence was all I needed as my spine went molten, my balls dragged up tight, and I came so fucking hard, I saw stars.

Frankie elongated the release, sucking down every drop and stroking my cock with tongue. It was almost too much and I swore a second burst of cum left me at her torture.

Spent, exhausted, and panting, I collapsed with my phone still in my hand. "Fuck. Me."

The only two words I could squeeze out.

"I intend to," Frankie informed me as she crawled up the bed—crawled up me, really. Then she pulled the phone from my hand and straddled my face.

"Hello there," I whispered to that soaking wet pussy right over my lips. "Where were we?"

I didn't wait for Frankie's answer. She was already the best birthday present a guy could want for the rest of his life. This literally was the icing on my cake that I could have and eat too.

Laughing at my own thought, I went to work teasing that swollen nub of her clit where it peaked out from its hood.

Five minutes and she was screaming.

Five more minutes and she came again, her cries almost hoarse.

Five minutes after that, my dick was back on board and we were sliding into the slick channel of her pussy and I had her lips fused to mine as we writhed together.

Maybe this would be where we spent the rest of the day.

That was a damn good plan.

Happy fucking birthday to me.

Chapter Twenty

HOLIDAY BLUES

Frankie

Christmas together, a tradition we'd pretty much cemented in our senior year of high school, proved both exhausting and rejuvenating. Exhausting, because a stupid stomach flu got into the house. It hit Jeremy first, of all of us, and I'd never seen him so miserable.

It started just two days after Christmas. I'd woken up early and went down to get coffee and Little Miss Abigail. A little achy and crampy, I needed to get on the move before I gave into the soreness and burrowed in bed for the day.

I'd even bundled up for the effort. Only, Jeremy hadn't been in the kitchen. In fact, it didn't look like he'd been in the kitchen in a while. Dishes in the sink were left over from the night before. We'd gone out to see a double-feature of movies, came in late, had a snack and then we'd all gone up—while trying to be quiet and not wake Jeremy.

But not once in all the time since we moved to Manhattan—honestly, not even a time once in the four years I'd known him via Archie before we moved—had he ever taken a day off. Even when the flu-cold-thing-from-hell hit the house back in October. Had it been October?

The dates felt fuzzy at this point. Still, I made my way down the hall on the other side of the sitting room. While Jeremy pretty much ruled the first floor, including the kitchen and sitting room, he also had his own suite.

I'd only been down this hall once and that was to sneak a present to hang on his door. It just didn't seem appropriate to invade his privacy when he spent so much time on all of us. Still, it was silent in the hall. When I knocked, I tried to keep it light. Little Miss Abigail wouldn't go off barking but she would bark twice—to alert—and I grimaced at her first bark.

A shuffle of step on the far side alerted me to his arrival and then the door opened slowly.

"Jeremy," I exhaled his name. "You look…"

"Forgive me, Miss Frankie," he said in a voice so thick and stuffy, it would have given him away if his pallor, hint of morning stubble, and bloodshot eyes hadn't already. "I'll…"

"Get right back in that bed, Mister." I straightened up. "What do you need?" I could smell the faint odor of sour sickness, but I wouldn't shove myself inside past him without invitation.

Especially when he felt so bad.

"I should get the breakfast started at least…"

Right. "No, you shouldn't do anything more than look after you. So, first thing's first, back into bed. Unless you need me to change the bedding. Then, I'll walk Miss Abigail. We'll be back and the coffee can brew while I'm out. I'll tackle breakfast after that."

His grimace was the only warning before he turned sharply and vanished into his bathroom.

The sound of vomiting made me grimace, but I focused on Miss Abigail's worried look from where she lay—*on Jeremy's bed.* Right, no comments about the rules not applying in here. If Jeremy needed a snuggle buddy, I wasn't saying a word.

In fact, I waited until the water came on, the sound of the toilet flushed, and then Jeremy said in a voice that sounded a great deal wearier. "Forgive me, Miss Frankie. I may have overestimated my energy."

"I got you, Jeremy," I told him as I went the rest of the way in. I found Jeremy sitting on the closed lid of his toilet, looking rather out of sorts. "Can you sit there for a minute? Fresh sheets always help, then I can clean out a bucket to bring in here for you too."

"Miss Frankie…" It wasn't an argument, but the sigh of weariness held me in place. "Thank you."

"Glad to help."

It took me ten minutes to square him away. I would have bundled up the sheets right into the washing, but Jeremy insisted I call the service. Right. Laundry service.

We didn't use it all the time, but we did send out all the bedding in the house semi-regularly. Bless Jeremy for that, cause I didn't ever want to picture him washing our bedsheets again.

Right. No.

"Can you change on your own or do you need me to get one of the guys?" I'd offer to help myself, but everyone had their personal hard limits. I didn't imagine Jeremy wanted my help.

"I'll manage."

Good to his word, he did so while I kept my back firmly to him. I was there if he needed me, but otherwise I gave him his privacy. Once I had him back in bed, I called Miss Abigail. She hesitated once, the look of concern on her face for Jeremy plain as day.

"It's all right," I promised her. "We're going to be quick. But you need a walk, little lady."

She trotted behind me. Good as gold, she waited for me to get the laundry bag set by the door. Then I washed my hands before starting the coffee. I also put the electric kettle on. There were any number of teas in Jeremy's pantry and at least two were good for nausea.

After that, I pulled on my jacket and hat before firing text up to the boys for when they woke up. Phone in my pocket, Miss Abigail's snow boots on and my gloves in place, we headed out. Good to my word, I gave her a brisk walk to and from the park.

Granted, she probably would have enjoyed a longer walk, but she was done with her business five minutes into it. Our girl was ready to be home as soon as I was. Once there, she kept me company as I got the kitchen organized, the tea made and drank a huge tumbler of coffee.

With tea, water, crackers, and Jeremy's favorite toast loaded on a tray, we made our way down to Jeremy's room. He was sitting up, but not looking much happier when I let us in at his call of acknowledgement.

Miss Abigail went straight to the bed and right up on it. Neither Jeremy nor I commented as she settled herself with her head in his lap. As bad as Jeremy felt, he did seem quite pleased with the tea and the toast. I made sure he had his cell phone handy and did my absolute best not to laugh when I told him to text me if he needed anything and I hadn't been back.

Then came the toughest battle of all, a list of what needed to be taken care of. I swore, Jeremy dug his heels in stubbornly, insisting he'd be right as rain in twenty-four hours. It could all keep.

Twelve hours later, he relented—particularly after Archie went down next. My poor sweetheart looked worse than he had after his first hangover. Like Jeremy, he woke up throwing up and it apparently went downhill from there.

I split my time between both Jeremy and Archie. Jake and Coop were helping, but there was no mistaking the fact they were circling the same drain.

Ian made it to the next morning, and after I'd stripped and remade all the beds before he vanished into his bathroom.

"How long?" Exhaustion crept through me and my stomach wasn't any more thrilled with this than they were. But so far, I'd only had some cramps and one of us needed to stay on our feet.

"Last night," he admitted with a wince from where he leaned against the wall. I spared him a look and he raised his hands. "I know, Angel. But I was managing it and there's a lot to do with *all* of us sick."

"I know, and I'm going to do it. You all take care of me when I get sick, I'm damn well taking care of you." At his smile, I shook my head. "Shower, get out of those clothes, let's get you into something looser."

It was a testament to how bad he felt that he didn't argue another word. For the next two days, I divided my time between farming laundry out to the service, and getting the new bed covers on. For the boys, we'd worked out a rotation, it let me get them out of one bed and into another, so at least one bed *always* had clean sheets.

Jeremy insisted I reach out to a service to help me. Right, the only two I was feeding with any kind of regularity was Abigail and myself. It could wait. The guys alternated between being starving and unable to keep anything down.

"Have I ever mentioned how much I love you?" Jake asked from where he sat on the floor a foot from the toilet. Today had been the worst for him and after he barely made it in here the last time, he refused to leave until his stomach cut it the fuck out.

Totally got that.

"You have," I promised him, before wiping a cold cloth over his face. He looked so rough, despite the fact that he'd showered the day before. The fever came and went. "You've even apologized about fourteen times for throwing up on me."

Head hanging, Jake made a little moaning sound. "That is so not sexy."

"Thankfully, I love you even when you're a big ass ol' dork."

"That's Coop."

I snorted at the pouty note in his voice. "That's both of you."

"Okay, I can live with that."

Day four of Jeremy being sick dawned with him sleeping right through his normal wake-up time. I let myself into his room and moved around quietly. There was far less mess. Okay, Jeremy was feeling better. Grabbing his dishes, I clicked my tongue softly to call Abby.

Equally as quiet, Miss Abigail trotted out after me as I took Jeremy's tray to the kitchen. I made short work of scrubbing everything up. I'd taken to essentially dividing up a set up of dishes for each of the guys. Then I sanitized everything in between to be on the safe side.

I wasn't taking any chances. A buzz to my phone alerted me that the service I'd requested would be here that afternoon. They would take the bulk of the main house and clean it from top to bottom. Not the bedrooms though.

I'd handle those when they were done.

Leaning against the counter, I stared down at Miss Abigail. "You up for a longer walk today, little miss? I feel like you've been getting the short end of the stick this week."

Also, my cramps could fuck off. I needed to pick up some Midol or something. One upside to the implant, my periods tended to be short. Even better, the cramps and stuff weren't anywhere near as bad.

Downside, when they showed up, they still sucked. I filled a thermos with coffee. Set up the electric kettle, then checked the list on the fridge. Groceries today. We needed some basics, nothing fancy. No one had really eaten all that much this week.

I checked the calendar. New Year's Eve was the following day. We were staying in this year. It would also be the one-year anniversary of Grandpa Ted's death.

Right.

I swallowed back that swell of feeling. "Let's go," I told Miss Abigail. We just had to be there for Archie. Despite my best intentions, we only made it about half the planned miles I wanted to do for her. She wasn't rushed, but she kept bumping my leg and looking up at me. "Yeah," I said, clapping a hand over my side. "Maybe today is my day to just curl up with the heating pad."

Miss Abigail gave me a positively mournful look. Yeah, right there with you girl. I did make a stop at one of the little groceries about a mile from the house, picked up the Midol I wanted and some candy. Fortunately, Al who ran the place knew us *and* Miss Abigail. When I stuck my head in the door, he grabbed what I needed and then just charged our account.

"You're the best, Al!" I called.

"Shall I send you down some of those chocolate croissants when the bakery brings them tonight?"

"You know the secret to getting to my heart."

He laughed. "Yeah, I think those boyfriends of yours might have something to say about that."

I giggled. "Our secret."

"Safer for me that way," he called before waving us off. I was almost sweating by the time we paused at the coffee shop. Man, if I got sick now it would *suck* but at least everyone else was mostly better.

I got their largest mocha and added an extra shot of dark chocolate and espresso. They provided Miss Abigail with a lovely cup of whip cream that she sucked down like there was no tomorrow. The cold air whipping through the streets was hardly a deterrent for others in the neighborhood.

The stitch in my side grew persistently worse on my way home. I managed only a couple of swallows of the coffee. It actually made my stomach revolt. Yeah, that shit could fuck right off to fucksville. Archie surprised me by opening the door when Miss Abigail and I arrived.

He took care of her snow boots while I set my coffee and bag aside to strip out of my boots and coat. "You're flushed," he commented.

"You look hot too," I told him with a teasing smile and a flash of a grin appeared on his face before it vanished behind worry again.

"Babe, you've been doing everything."

"I know, don't yell at me. Jeremy already complained. How are you feeling?"

"Better." He paused when I tried to take another sip of my coffee and yeah, that did not go well. Fuck, that tasted awful. Three steps later, I shot into the water closet guest toilet on the first floor and threw up.

Fuck.

Me.

It wasn't even waves of nausea. It was like my body flat out rejected the coffee. Ugh.

"Bed," Archie ordered.

"What's going on?" Coop sounded like Hell. But he was up. That was more than he'd managed in four days. Poor guy had been suffering.

"Frankie's sick. Get her upstairs, I'll clean this up."

Right, I didn't argue, just said, "Feed Miss Abigail. Ann Bradshaw and her crew are coming from the service today."

The service didn't come unless Miss Bradshaw, who *owned* the service, came with them. She was a sweet lady, brisk and to the point. She also had coffee or tea with Jeremy every other week. As much as he enjoyed seeing her, I hoped he preferred that I'd waited until he felt better.

By afternoon, Jeremy had emerged from his room to supervise the cleaning staff. The cats *and* Miss Abigail hid out together in my room. I tried to sleep but wasn't comfortable enough. The vomiting didn't linger—thankfully. I was exhausted though, and coffee as much as I loved it was not sitting well.

Bland didn't help much and the cramps just seemed to get worse. Seriously, days of this and my period hadn't shown up. Was it trying to make up for the last five months of being reasonable all at once?

Archie and Coop took turns hanging out with me. I tried to sleep. I tried to get comfortable. I tried to watch something to distract me. Nothing worked. If anything, the agitation just got worse and I swore everything hurt. Even my breasts.

Rachel checked in late in the day, she'd gone to Ohio for the holidays, but something happened that made her ditch out early. She'd gone back to

Texas, but was due back in the city the following week. We also had a lunch date to discuss her plans for senior year of college.

I was so fucking excited for her but selfishly, I hated the idea of her going. Thankfully, Archie's family had an airline and access to private planes. Not that I couldn't afford a ticket to go and visit her.

It wasn't even like we spent all the time together anymore, we were both so busy and we talked more via phone and text than anything else. What did it matter if she was in Europe and I was here?

The minute the tears started though, I couldn't seem to shake off that cloud of misery. The words on the screen wavered as I sent her a soppy message.

Then my phone was ringing and it was a video call. Wiping at my eyes, I answered it with a weepy smile. "Sorry, I'm not trying to be all emotional and shit."

"You're not," Rachel said, her brow crinkling as she studied me. "You're actually being all over the place and I'm worried. What's wrong? I mean, besides everyone being sick and you having to look after them?"

"They're better, well—getting there. Jake and Ian are still rough, but Jeremy is up. Coop and Archie are too but they're napping right now." I hoped anyway. I needed to feel better soon. I didn't want Archie alone tonight or tomorrow.

"Uh huh. And you're PMSing?" Something about the way she asked that question made me frown.

"Don't judge. I am occasionally known for being a bit of a drama queen when I'm this crampy."

"Uh huh."

I frowned. "What?"

"You have any home tests?"

Home tests? "For what?"

"For the fact that it's been almost two months since your last period. I know you had it the first week of November. Remember? We had to stop for coffee…”

I didn’t hear the rest of it past the rushing in my ears. Beginning of November.

She was right.

I’d been glad it meant I wouldn’t have to worry about it over Thanksgiving then…

Surely, I’d had it the first week of December. Sometimes it didn’t do more than a little trickle and some discomfort. It was really stressful here. But then we’d gone to the club and that helped. A lot. More than I even realized. No bloat. No discomfort.

No cramps.

“That can’t be right.”

“Uh huh, it can be.” Rachel fixed me with a look. “We’re not sync’d or anything, but we’ve been pretty close this year and my period is right on schedule.”

It was the first week of January. Almost. “Mine is too…”

“Right. Frankie-babe? Look at me.”

I fixed my gaze on the screen.

“Do me a solid. Get a test. Take it. Fifteen minutes and we’ll know.”

Fifteen minutes.

Oh, I was gonna be sick. My heart plummeted about fifteen feet and my skin went icy hot. The sweat seemed to make itself known as it slid down the back of my neck.

“Rach…”

“Get the test,” she repeated, all confidence and calm. “Take it. Then we tackle what comes next.”

“Okay.”

“Go, call me as soon as you’re done.”

Right.

The call ended but I didn’t move. A shuffle step at the door captured my attention.

Coop studied me, concern and affection rolling off him in waves. "What do you need, Beautiful?"

To not freak out. But those words wouldn't unglue themselves from my tongue.

Don't freak, I repeated internally.

"A pregnancy test."

The silence between us swelling like an overinflated balloon, before he exhaled a long breath. "Is there a particular kind?"

I gave him a blank look.

"I'll ask Rach," he promised then crossed the room and planted a hard kiss on my lips. It tasted like peppermint and hints of butter. Someone had just brushed their teeth. "It's going to be alright."

"Coop?"

"I promise," he reminded me as I clasped his hand and he fisted mine tightly. "One thing at a time."

That was what Rachel said.

"I have…"

"I know," he said, not even needing me to finish saying I had birth control. I took care. I had regular checkups. But the truth was, we had a lot of sex.

A lot of it.

"It's going to be okay, Beautiful."

"What's wrong?" Archie asked from the door. Panic scrambled through me, but Coop kept my hand in his with a gentle squeeze.

"I'm running to the store for Frankie," Coop said. "Come sit with her and look after her so she doesn't panic."

Another kiss and he let me go to cross the room. He paused for a beat, murmuring something to Archie.

The pregnancy test. Yeah, we could hardly keep this a secret.

His eyes widened a fraction, then laser focused on me. Archie's expression turned fierce. "We got this, Babe. It's going to be fine." All at once, the exhaustion and illness of the last few days fled. "Go, Coop. I'll take care of our girl."

Another shaky breath escaped me. I could not wrap my head around this.

"It's going to be okay," Archie repeated Coop's earlier assurance as he slid onto the bed and wrapped an arm around me. Miss Abigail hadn't moved from her spot with her head on my lap. Tiddles sauntered away, but only to the other side of her where he lay down with his back to hers.

It was almost sweet.

Pregnant.

Archie said something else, but I swore my brain remained stuck in that gear.

No way, right?

Chapter Twenty-One

TWO PINK LINES

Frankie

"Breathe," the command from Ian helped so much. Particularly because I hadn't even realized I'd held my breath while we waited for the first of the five different box tests that Coop bought to finish.

"It's going to be fine," Coop reminded me, wrapping a hand around my ankle. Miss Abigail had gone down to have tea with Jeremy. The cleaning service was not due for another couple of hours. I could barely keep anything down, but that was nerves.

Absolutely one hundred thousand percent nerves.

Ian sat with me in his lap, my back to his chest. He was still feeling like crap and should be in bed, but considering the look he'd given me promised my ass would pay for that later, I let it go. Well, that and the fact and I really needed him here right now. Jake and Archie were both waiting, arms folded in almost mirror positions bracketing either side of the entrance to the bathroom.

All the kits were lined up in there, one after another.

Also, I wasn't going to think about how much pee that required. At the first beep of the alarm, Archie was in the bathroom a split-second ahead of Jake.

Absolute silence filtered back at us. The tension in my shoulders must have ramped even higher, because Ian began rubbing his cheek against the top of my head even as he stroked my arm. Coop echoed the motion, rubbing my calf as I closed my eyes and waited.

Another long minute passed, then Coop said, "For fuck's sake, you're killing us. What the Hell do they say?"

Ian squeezed me. "Everyone take a fucking breath." There was zero chance of mistaking the command in his voice for anything else. I dragged my eyes open. Following Coop's gaze, I glanced to where Jake and Archie stood.

"All four of them say the same thing." Jake let out a breath. "Positive."

Not that I needed him to say it cause the looks on their faces said everything I was feeling.

Holy. Shit.

"What about the fifth one?" Coop asked. Right. There had been five.

"Yeah, not sure what the fuck this means." Jake retrieved it then carried it over. There were two pink lines. That was clear enough. Only there were two more behind it. So maybe a bad test?

"Four out of five." Those were literally the only words I could come up with, and even then.

I was *not* ready for this. Leaning back against Ian, I closed my eyes again. The stitch in my side that had been plaguing me for days, along with the cramps, seemed to intensify. Maybe I just needed to relax.

How the hell I was supposed to do that, I had zero idea.

"Then our next step is to get you to a doctor," Ian said into the quiet and I tilted my head back to look at him. Like Jake, he was still pale. To be honest, all of them were, though I had a feeling this was every bit as much to do with getting over their stomach flu as it did the test results.

"It's New Year's Eve," I pointed out. "I doubt a lot of doctor offices are open, much less able to see patients at the last minute."

"That's where knowing people and having money definitely comes in handy," Archie announced. "I'll make a couple of calls. Get dressed, Babe."

I didn't even get to say anything before he was out of the room, a seething ball of electricity fired from a cannon.

Coop glanced at me then the guys. "I'm going to keep an eye on him. You two need to relax too."

Once it was just me, Ian, and Jake, I tried to cobble together enough thoughts to even say anything.

"I'll get clothes out for you," Jake offered. "If you want. Bubba can help you get dressed—or do you want something to drink? Fuck—crackers maybe? You haven't really been throwing up that much, right?"

Right. "I can get my clothes." That wasn't entirely what I meant to say, but it was so much better than drooling and releasing a series of nonsense syllables. Considering how close to that I was, I didn't plan on examining it too closely.

Today's plans had been to look after the boys, make them take it easy, keep an eye on Jeremy, and maybe curl up with a book or a movie.

Right. That wasn't currently happening.

It wasn't until I pulled out a new shirt and pants that I glanced down at myself.

"I'm already dressed."

Right.

I put the clothes away and diverted into the bathroom. The tests waited on the counter like a jury of my peers staring at me dispassionately. False positives happened, right?

Even—four false positives? Or was that pushing it?

"Baby Girl," Jake said softly from the doorway and I lifted my gaze to meet his in the mirror. "Coop's right. It's going to be all right."

"Uh huh." Not that I was discounting any of them. "My gut, my heart, and my brain are all in the midst of a great debate over this, and currently, I think I'm losing."

Putting some toothpaste on the brush, I concentrated on brushing my teeth. Maybe they didn't need it. I had brushed them that morning, right? I literally could not remember right now. Took Abigail for a walk. Did some dishes. Started the coffeemaker.

Oh right, bought stuff for my period. That was funny.

And coffee.

After I finished brushing my teeth and rinsing my mouth, Jake threaded his arms around me and pulled me back to his chest. I met his gaze and a beat later, Ian appeared in the mirror with us. They both wore the exact same expression.

"It's scary," Jake said. "No lie. I'd probably take being kicked in the balls as a better shock right now. Not that I'm eager to test that theory."

Ian chuckled.

"But the point stands," Jake continued, holding my attention. "We'll figure it out. One step at a time. But the most important part is to know you're okay."

"Agreed." Ian reached over to trail a finger down my cheek and I turned my head to meet his gaze. "You. Your health. Then we talk about what you want to do."

"What I want to do? Shouldn't this be an all of us conversation?" Considering there was literally zero way of saying which of them…yeah, no long breaks from anyone the last few months. We'd been very locked together.

"Yes," he agreed. "But it starts with what you want to do. It's your body. We'll figure it out. Together. All of us."

Even as my stomach bottomed out and I shuddered, Jake tightened his arms and Ian caught one of my hands. "Together," I managed to eek out in the most pathetic voice ever. Yeah, no. I squared my shoulders and lifted my chin. "Together," I said more forcefully.

"That's my girl," Jake told me, then pressed a kiss to the top of my head. As soon as Jake released me, Ian opened his arms and I slid right into them. When Jake closed the circle against my back, I just closed my eyes and let them serve as buffers against the whole world.

It was going to be okay.

"We never talked about this," I said, hoping they understood me, even if my face against Ian's sweatshirt muffled the words.

"No," Jake said softly. "Not really, but it's also not something we've ignored."

No, we hadn't.

From condoms to the implant… fuck the implant.

Four years.

They were good for up to four years.

I'd gotten mine, what? Right before Christmas…senior year. Three years earlier.

So, it should still be good, right?

"Hey Babe," Archie said as he came into the bathroom. He'd changed and shaved. Today was not the day for a crisis. "We've got a car on the way to get us. I got an appointment with Doctor Stephens. She's in her office working on paperwork today, but said she'd make time to see you."

"When?"

"As soon as we get there." He tucked a finger under my chin as Ian let me go. "You okay to go now?"

"Probably not that much of a choice," I reminded him.

"All the choice in the world, Beautiful. We can wait until after the New Year."

No, we really couldn't. I didn't think I'd be able to think of anything else and the guys would worry.

"Rachel will be back by then too," Coop offered. "She also said you aren't answering your phone but figured out why. When you're ready, call her."

Fuck, I'd forgotten about Rachel. "I will. But—let's go see the doctor first." My side still hurt and I was still feeling a bit queasy if I thought about coffee.

That was fucking evil.

"All right, shoes and coats everyone," Coop said with a clap of his hands and he got everyone moving. Fifteen minutes later, sandwiched between Coop and Jake, I had my hand wrapped up tight in Coop's. Doctor Stephens had become our general practitioner since we moved to the city. The guys liked her and so did I.

Made appointments easier too. Also, maybe a little weird, but we lived together. Why would having the same doctor be weird?

The closer we got to her office, the more the dread hit. We had the tests at home. But this was making it super real. Jake wrapped his hand around my free one. The fact I was trembling finally registered.

Ian kept one eye on me, like Coop and Jake, he was just right there. All I had to do was reach out to him. Archie was the same. They were all keeping it together so much better than me.

All too soon, we were there and the doc was right there to check us in. She had one nurse with her. I drew an absolute blank on her name at the moment, but I let her shepherd me back to a room and get changed.

I also got to pee in a cup. Good times.

Those tests also confirmed it. Next was the blood test. It was more for confirmation, but the urine test was ninety-nine percent accurate.

This was not making me feel better.

Two little pink lines. "Hey Frankie," the doctor greeted me when she came into the room. "Big day," she said. "I've asked the boys to wait a bit so we can talk."

"Is something wrong?"

"Well, that's what we're going to figure out," she told me in an even, kind voice. "We're also going over your records and your history."

That didn't bode well.

"One of the things I'd like to do is a quick ultrasound to take a look. Then we're going to go over everything, see where you are. Sound good?"

See where I was…

I was about three seconds from freaking the fuck out, but sure, that sounded good. I laid back on the bed when she motioned to me. "You'd think you do this every day."

"I know," she said, flashing me a warm smile. "Irritating, isn't it?"

A laugh escaped me. A real one. "A little."

"Well, if it's only a little. I need to work harder."

That made me snort for real.

"Right," she moved to my side and tested pressing on my stomach. More than once I flinched. "Tell me about the last few days…"

So, I told her about the stomach flu going through the house. The fact I hadn't really gotten sick. Though I'd had cramps. I thought it was my period.

I confirmed that no, I hadn't had one since November, then again it wasn't *that* unusual to miss a period now and then. They'd always been kind of awful, but the implant helped.

She nodded as I spoke. We discussed whether I had alcohol—yes— not ideal. Also about smoking. Nope. Edibles? Now and then, but I'd been avoiding them with the workload I had.

They did help with stress.

That brought up my visits to the grief counseling group I went to and my own regular appointments. She had warmed up the ultrasound jelly before she put it on my stomach.

Cold sweat dotted my skin all over again. I'd almost managed to shove some of the why out of my head. Maybe the guys should be here. Then again, she wanted to do all of this before we sat down and talked as a group.

"I'm going to hazard a guess that you don't know which of the guys it might be?" There was zero judgment in the question. She also wasn't looking at me, but focused on the screen. It was a lot of blue-gray blur that didn't seem all that translatable into something solid.

"No," I said. "I suppose that's something we're going to need to know."

"Well, only if there's a major medical issue in any of their backgrounds. Or issue with Rh factors, but we can tackle all of that in a bit. Since this is a surprise for you, I'm going to also assume this wasn't planned."

"Nope."

"Is it unwelcome?"

"I don't know."

That was probably the hardest question to answer.

"Good answer."

I blinked and glanced at her and she grinned.

"Everyone thinks they know, even when it's the goal, they think they'll know. Then it happens and there's no predicting how you feel."

That… helped.

"Now," she said as she glanced at the screen, her expression sober. "I need to show you a couple of things…"

Chapter Twenty-Two
CAT'S IN THE CRADLE

Archie

The moment the door closed behind her, I turned to the guys. "I don't like her being back there without us." The only reason I hadn't made a stink sooner was the fact Frankie hadn't complained when the nurse took her back alone *first*.

I turned the word first over in my head again and again. A mantra against just charging through the door to go and find her.

"Breathe," Coop said for like the eighteen hundredth time. As irritating as that might be, I still sucked in a breath at the warning. Unlike me and Bubba, Jake and Coop were both sitting.

To be fair, Jake still felt a bit like shit. So, I left him alone. Coop though? "How the fuck are you so relaxed?"

"Because no matter how much we freak out, it can't change what is. We're all adults. We all knew the risks." He rubbed his face. "Did I ever tell

273

you guys that I slipped once. Like we almost went there without a condom *before* the implant?"

Bubba frowned at him. "Seriously?"

"I said it was a slip," Coop said, his expression mild. "We caught it and backed off…but it could have happened then."

One by one, he met Bubba's gaze then Jake's. The lack of surprise on Jake's face suggested he already knew this. Didn't really shock me. Finally, Coop met my gaze again.

"We're in this together," he said like I needed the reminder. Maybe I did. "We'll face this like we have every other fucking thing that's come down the road. At least this one isn't a horror story."

"Like Maddy," Jake said.

Yeah, the nightmare of her standing there pointing a gun at Frankie because Frankie wouldn't move would never totally erase from my mind.

"Mitch." Bubba shook his head, and I swore the muscles in his arms flexed as he ground out the name.

"Sharon," I said. "All those fucking girls." But Sharon had been the worst.

"Cheryl," Coop reminded us, and it was my turn to scrub a hand over my face.

"The tour," Bubba brought up.

"Meeting her dad," Jake offered and we all split a look. Yeah, meeting her dad had been intense.

"Especially after the sibling bombshell." It was the one time when the urge to beat my father to a pulp had hit me. The idea that Frankie might somehow be my sibling.

"Exactly," Coop said, pulling me back from that hate-fueled nightmare. "We talked about this then, remember?"

I frowned. A huff of laughter escaped. "Fuck, we did talk about it then."

"Yep," Jake stretched out his legs. "Doesn't matter which of us is the dad."

"We're all the dads," Bubba said a heartbeat before I could. But I didn't disagree and Coop spread his hands as if to say, "see?"

Right.

This was all of us.

Folding my arms, I blew out another breath. "Then time for the tough questions."

"I'm in," Jake said. "Whatever she needs or wants. Timing isn't ideal, but there are five of us and we can make this work."

"Right, didn't think anyone was bailing." In fact, that wasn't even a blip on my radar.

"Agreed," Bubba and Coop said in unison.

"Look," Bubba continued, raising a hand. "We all know we're in. We all know we're committed to her. Do we need to make any other decisions right now?"

"You can't fix this for her," I told him because there was a muscle ticking in his jaw. "I know, it's making me crazy that I can't."

He dropped his chin and then groaned as he paced away. Yeah, I felt it. What a fucking way to end the year.

Then again, better than last year, and that was food for thought.

Jake

Fake it until you make it. That was what I told myself when Coop left to get the tests. While we stood around and waited for them to finish. Sitting here in the waiting room though, not an ounce of this was faking it.

"You ever wonder what your kids will look like?" Okay, to be fair, I was thinking that but the look on Archie's face when I asked that question made me want to laugh aloud.

"No," he said briefly but I wasn't sure who he meant to lie to, us or himself.

Probably himself.

"Nah," Coop said. "I mean, really, Frankie and I would make the most beautiful babies. Probably wouldn't be fair to the rest of you."

I didn't laugh. But I did flip him off and Coop grinned.

"Don't hate, you would only be as lucky to be as beautiful as me."

Bubba flat out snorted, but Archie laughed.

"Fine," I challenged. "You'd have a blond, green-eyed beauty of a little girl. I'll do you a solid and make sure she knows how to kick anyone's ass she wants to."

Coop's grin grew. "You think she won't have the diplomatic skills to defuse most situations?"

"Sure, I'll bet she can even counsel them on how to not be an asshole while she kicks their ass."

He looked thoughtful for a minute then pointed his thumb and forefinger at me. "Deal."

"Your daughter with Frankie would just be drop dead gorgeous, have excellent dramatic timing, and a heart way too big for the world." Bubba looked at Archie. "You're gonna have to hire a bodyguard or Jake will never sleep."

I really saw no lies there.

"Totally doable. Your daughter with Frankie would also be a blonde bombshell, probably have control and achievement issues. We'll have to make sure Coop is on hand when she decides to overcommit."

That got a genuine chuckle out of Bubba. They looked at me and I raised my hands. "Boys. I need to make boys. If y'all are all firing X chromosomes, we need some Ys to balance it out."

"And to help you kick the asses of anyone looking at their sisters," Coop retorted drily.

"Like you have a problem with that," I countered.

"Point," Archie said.

Silence draped us as we all looked at the door. Waiting for *someone* to come and get us.

"Question," Bubba said thoughtfully. "How many kids are we discussing?"

"One at a time," Coop said. "One at a time."

Probably better to think of it that way.

"But I kind of like outnumbering any amount of kids, so four sounds like a good number," Coop continued.

Shifting on the sofa, I pinned him with a look. "Four?"

"What, were you thinking, eight?"

"Woah," Archie said, but before anyone else could lodge a protest, the door opened and I hit my feet before the nurse appeared.

"Gentlemen, if you'll follow me…"

Ian

Considering how restless we'd all been behaving, the calm swirling over us right now seemed completely out of place. We made our way down the hall toward a room that was going to feel more than a little crowded.

Frankie sat on the little bed, ankles crossed and hands white knuckled and locked together. I circled the bed to the other side, getting out of Coop's way. It didn't remotely surprise me when he slid a hand over hers. She transferred that grip on herself to him.

Ignoring the doctor for a minute, I studied Frankie. Worry coated her. Worry, discomfort, and right beneath all of that, was fear. All joking aside, whatever the doctor had told her wasn't good news.

"Frankie wanted all of you here for this, so to be clear, what I am sharing with you is only because she has authorized you to receive her medical information."

I nodded, folding my arms before I reached over to pluck her off that bed and get the fuck out of here. She didn't need me doing an end run. When her gaze found mine, I summoned a smiled and her breathing settled a little. Archie took the spot next to me and Jake was on the other side of Coop. We formed a half-circle, facing the doctor.

"I explained this to Frankie, but I'm taking this from the top." She glanced at Frankie for confirmation, who nodded.

"Doctor," Archie said. "Not to be rude, but can we get to it. You're elongating the torture at the moment. Is Frankie okay?"

Not quite how I would have approached it, but it was exactly what I wanted to know. Frankie brushed a hand down my arm then reached a hand over to Archie. I shifted so I could slide an arm around her shoulders and Archie latched onto her hand nearly as tightly as she'd been holding Coop's.

"I'm going to be okay," she spoke in such a solemn, sober tone, every internal alarm I possessed went off. "I am pregnant."

I locked my attention onto her.

"But it's not viable."

All of us were looking at her.

She swallowed and I tightened my arm.

"I did an ultrasound to confirm, based on her symptoms and medical history," the doctor picked up the thread of the conversation. "Implants are generally safe, but when a pregnancy does happen while you have one, they are almost always ectopic."

"It's implanted in her fallopian tube?" Coop shot his gaze from Frankie to the doctor. I'd heard about that before, but Coop's sudden switch from relaxed and calm to furious intensity had every hair on my body standing up.

"It's in a fallopian tube and I think we've caught it in enough time that we can avoid surgery." The doctor focused on Frankie again. "I can give you an injection of methotrexate, you'll feel rough for a couple of days, but it will stop the growth and help dissolve the cells."

Fuck.

"One thing to understand, we may have to do a second injection. We're also going to have to monitor your progress. If we don't get a reaction in the next few days, I will recommend a surgery to go in and remove it before it damages the tube."

Frankie wasn't moving, her attention was on the doctor.

"What are the risks?" Archie asked.

"Well, if we do nothing, the risks are considerable. But we're not going to do nothing, and we've caught it early. The shot does have some minor side effects drowsiness, headache, swollen gums, decreased appetite. Most, if not all, will pass as your body adapts."

The doctor explained every step, including needing to check Frankie's HCG levels in two days. Two to four was the usual time frame, but she wanted to be proactive. Particularly if a second shot was needed.

"The good news," she said in the kindest of tones, her attention on Frankie. "We caught this early enough that it shouldn't do any lasting damage to your fallopian tube. Future pregnancy is still an option. Though we may want to address your choice of birth control going forward."

Condoms for a while.

Fine.

Whatever it took.

"Now, I'm going to leave the five of you to talk, while I get the injection ready?" The last was a question, but Frankie only nodded.

Once she and the nurse were out of the room, Coop crushed Frankie to him and I dragged Archie over as I folded into the hug. Jake was there, bracing a hand on my shoulder.

"It's going to be okay," Coop said softly.

A little sob tore from her and broke my fucking heart. "He's right," I assured her. "It really will be okay."

"This is stupid," she muttered, tearful and Jake pinched her as we pulled back. "Ow."

"You don't get to call yourself names," he said steadily and she thumped him. It was such a classic move that we were all laughing. But I wasn't the only one wiping at my eyes. "I'm sorry, Baby Girl. I know—you know, I don't. What do you need?"

Good fucking question.

"I don't know," she admitted. "This wasn't even something I thought about really hard, until like a few hours ago and now…"

Now, it was already gone.

She sniffled. "Maybe we should talk about—the future and all of this."

"When you're ready," Archie said in a firm tone. The helplessness shredding me earlier was back in full force. "When we're all ready and on our schedule, no one else's."

With a watery smile, she leaned into Coop. "Sorry to be such a drama queen."

I rolled my eyes and held up a finger. "Yeah, that's one."

A very real smile curved the corners of her mouth, even as more tears slipped down her cheeks. "Bet I can get to five before we get home."

"I know you can," I said. "But first, are you ready to do this?"

"No," she said with a kind of blunt honesty. "But I don't have much choice. For all that this scared the fuck out of me, I do want to be able to have kids someday. Maybe. Like in—five or six or—seven years?"

"Sounds good to me," Jake said. "Though I think we need to start a new bet."

I shot him a look. Really?

"Yeah, the one who gives her the most orgasms gets to shoot their shot first. Gives us years to figure this out."

Dead silence blanketed the room.

"You know," Archie said. "That's not a bad idea."

The whispery, sobbing laughter that escaped Frankie was perfect though. I couldn't even figure out how I felt right now. The idea of a kid hadn't been more than a passing thought before today. Now, it was gone before any of us could even reconcile with what it meant.

"I'm not saying yes to the bet," I added when Frankie wiped away her tears. "But I'm also not saying no."

She snorted and I cupped her cheek, thumbing away another tear streak as she leaned into the contact.

"When we're done… can we go home and just marathon movies with all the crap food we can stomach to eat?"

My own gut lurched and Jake grimaced.

"Okay, very bland stuff," Frankie added and I pressed a kiss to her forehead.

"We'll figure it out," Coop said and I nodded.

We would absolutely figure it out.

A half-hour later, armed with all the things to watch for and another appointment, we left. We were all fighting to be cheerful, to say something that would make the others laugh. But there was also a poignant, almost painful, silence that would occasionally wrap around us.

It was all going to be okay. We'd damn well make sure it was.

But one thing today highlighted that we needed to address sooner rather than later?

We did need to talk about the future. All of us.

Chapter Twenty-Three
GOODBYE YELLOW BRICK ROAD

Frankie

"So, what did they say?" Five days into the New Year and while I still felt a little rough, and my period flat out sucked, I was doing better propped up in bed with a heating pad on my stomach while splitting several different containers of Chinese with Ian. He'd gone over to the place on Broadway to grab my favorites.

Dim sum. Lion's head meatballs. Gu-Lu Pork with Pineapple. Fat rice noodles were tasty too. I'd started out picking at the dim sum, but it was the best tasting food I'd had in days.

For the first time since before the New Year, I was actively hungry. Ian's flash of a smile as I snagged another dim sum with my chopsticks reminded me that it really had been a while since I'd willingly ate. Maybe the meds had done their job. I hadn't needed a second shot.

The nagging sense of off in my system could fuck off. Rachel came home the day before and crawled into bed with me so we could watch weepy movies together. The stupid need to cry had been rather satisfied by that. Still…

I stole a glance at Ian as I picked up the container of rice noodles. He hadn't answered, if anything, his attention seemed very focused on his food. "Ian?"

He flicked a look up to me, one corner of his mouth curving up. "Sorry, Angel. Lost in thought there."

"Don't worry, I don't mind tracking you down."

A real grin danced in his eyes as he saluted me with a small meatball before he finished the bite. "You're very determined like that."

Shoulders up, I spread my hands. "Someone has to keep you in line, Sir Ian."

That earned me a light clap against my ankle that ended in a squeeze. "No one better at it."

Flushing, I nudged him with my foot. "Now, talk to me. I'm not going to break."

"It's been a hell of a week, Angel."

"Yeah," I sighed the syllable out, just elongating it as I stared across the room at the new images Rachel had left pinned to one of my cork boards.

She was always sneaking photographs in here. Sometimes, they were from high school. Some from her summer in Europe. More from the last couple of years here in the city.

"I know." Focusing on him again, I added, "But I'm okay. I feel a little weird. Probably a little emotional, but I already called my therapist and I told her what was going on. We're going to talk more about it next week."

He nodded slowly. "I'm glad you ask for help when you need it now."

"I'm still learning, I mean—it is easier most days." I could tell them anything and it didn't matter which of them I went to, they were always willing to listen or to cheer me up. Sometimes, I just wanted a hug and they gave me those too. "I know you're there. I know all of you are. But I'm here too. Let me help if I can."

"You help every day just by being you." When he plucked another dim sum out of the box with his chopsticks to feed me, I opened my mouth easily. "Taking care of you helps too."

Yeah, I knew that part. Ian needed to take care of me on a level that was different from the others, but no less valuable and loving. Understanding that need, and experiencing it, were two different things.

I adored him though. Adored him for how he adored me. "Then feed me and tell me what's going through that mind of yours."

With care, he plucked another bite from my container of rice noodles, wrapping it up before he added a bit of meatball and then fed me all of that.

"Tell me what you thought about the songs," he said, his tone more that of giving an order rather than making a request. Some of the tension humming in my system settled. The liquid warmth of his voice combined with the determination and command just wrapped me up in the fiercest of hugs.

Not answering immediately, I considered the songs he'd played for me the day before. "The lyrics to Keys and Kisses kind of broke my heart."

With a gentle hand he squeezed my ankle.

"I loved the music portion, but I think it could be more melancholy. We promise hope at the end, but I don't think it's totally earned with the lyrics as you've written them. I think that we should drag out that sense of gloom, then press toward the end. Having the drive to not give up in the face of hopelessness is far more powerful than only having hope when it's offered."

"Maybe drop it into a minor key, instead of the major at the end." He took another bite, then stood up. Crossing the room, he pulled my guitar off the wall and glanced at me. When I wasn't using the red guitar they'd gotten me, I liked having it in here. "This okay, Angel?"

"Of course." To my absolute delight, he carried the guitar back to the bed and began to work his way through the notes for Keys and Kisses.

Sticking my chopsticks into the container, I set it down on the tray before reaching for the lyric sheets on the nightstand.

I set Keys and Kisses on the top and then glanced at Ian when he took it from the top. He dropped the opening refrain into a minor chord. The third note down on the fretboard. It added a particular kind of sorrow and loneliness to the words.

On his next pass, I began to sing the lyrics. Letting his music guide me, I really felt the song. It was a moment of having to choose the pain we faced or choose ourselves. The song was about the day I broke up with him. When I broke my own heart, but it was the choice I needed to make.

As we wound through the song, it followed the journey we'd faced. Together, but apart. Saving our friendship might have cost us both our hearts. Determination to hold on, to recover, it was there. At the same time, it made me weepy as the song moved us ever closer to homecoming.

When we reached the end, waking in the hospital, hurt and angry, the wound one to the soul left me wanting to cry, especially the last line.

"But your kisses are the keys I need right now. I chose me, but I also chose you. Choose me again. Choose me and we can make this work. Love… in the darkness chases away the loneliness and the pain. Let me be with you. Be with me."

Each line followed a descending scale and my voice so thick on the last line, that I finished sniffling. The pain was right there, so personal, and yet I had the distance to experience it without crippling me.

It was always the not knowing of what Mitch had done. Knowing there were several minutes just erased from my memory. I'd never get that time back, but I didn't have to give him a damn thing more.

Balancing the guitar with just one hand, he stretched the other out to me. "I love that," he murmured. "Are you okay with it?"

I sniffed and lifted my shoulders as I tangled our fingers together. "Not sure anyone else would understand why it's so dark and yet there is still light twining through there."

"They don't have to," he said. "It's for us."

"So you don't want to sell that one." It wasn't even a question. Licking my lips, I swiped away another tear as I squeezed his hand. "Show me your other favorites, let's see which ones we want to keep."

"Second album?"

"Rules and Roses is doing really well." Even though we hadn't toured since the previous autumn. We'd discussed doing some shows over the coming summer, but Coop's work tied him here and I didn't want to be away for weeks and weeks at a time.

Andrea was currently working on a plan to feature our "works in progress" on TikTok and teasing our followers as we got each song ready.

"It is and there is interest in us doing a second album."

I licked my lips. "Will we have to tour, you think?"

"What if we broke it up? Do four weeks in the late summer, then another two weeks over the holidays. Then a couple of weeks here and there, never too long. We have senior year, but we can plan ahead."

"And maybe when we're not on tour, we could do a virtual concert?"

Ian considered me for a minute while tapping a hand against the guitar. Casting his head down, he seemed lost in thought. There was a lot to think about. The songs they were interested in commissioning, and the songs he didn't want to share.

"I won't tour without you," he said finally. "But I like the idea of the virtual concert."

"I like the shorter dates. At least then the guys have a better chance of going with and if they can't…"

"We'll be back here to see them." Another slow nod. "I like this plan."

"But?" Because I swore one hung unspoken in the air between us.

"But I don't want any more pressure on you. So, we do this at our pace and our time. If it takes us a year, it takes us a year."

"I like that plan." I didn't take the surprise flickering over his face as an insult. "I want to enjoy this with you," I continued. "I love watching you create and I adore getting to do it with you."

A true smile softened his lips. "Tell me how you are. For real?"

"Sad." I lifted my shoulders. "Just—sad. But not like I can't see my way out or like it's drowning me." It was hard to verbalize my feelings. I'd struggled at my therapy session the day before. Excellent timing.

"Have you thought about kids?" The question came out cautious and wary.

Tucking my toes beneath his thigh, I met his curious stare. "A lot more this week than I have in the past." Although… "That might not be entirely true. I have thought about kids. Thought about whether I'd be a good mother or not. I had the poster child for how to not parent."

Leaning back against the pillows, I adjusted the heating pad and turned it up a little.

"Then I remember there were some good times with Maddy. The memories I clung to when everything seemed to turn to shit. Memories that warmed me up at night when I didn't have a real mother there to support me." The words came out easier now. Discussing the loss and the rejection.

I could distance myself from it, see the good and the bad. Maddy had been a disturbed woman. She'd probably been disturbed her whole life. The idea of having Eddie and then losing him again was not something she could tolerate.

Instead of walking away, she'd fought for him. Fought for him in a really whacked out manner, but…

"All of that aside, there are other issues than my abandonment and emotional abuse. What if her mental issues are heritable? So, that's something to think about."

Ian watched me with the kindest of eyes, the light in them a port in any storm. Allowing me the long pauses, he listened to each word and didn't rush to fill in the gaps.

"Having kids? Yeah, I want to. I think. Some day. Just—not right now, while we're all building and chasing dreams. Sometimes, I wonder if it will work out with all of us, but the last few days tells me it will."

"I can speak for all of us," Ian said in a gentle tone. "We're all going to be the fathers. It won't matter whose sperm survived the quest…"

A giggle escaped me. "Now you sound like you guys are the Fellowship trying to get the sperm to Mordor."

His grimace set me off laughing more. But as much as he scowled and shook his head, humor shone in his expression. "That's at least two more."

The delicious shiver that went through me contrasted with the soreness. "Another thing to look forward to."

Sex was off the table for a bit and then condoms were back in play until we got the birth control settled. A hormonal IUD was in my future, and then we would be more vigilant.

"I want to work on this music with you. I want to keep talking about our future with everyone. I don't want to lose you guys. I know after school it might get tougher. But I think staying together is better than any alternative."

"Sounds good to me, Angel."

"And Ian?"

"Hmm."

"Have you thought about kids?"

He flashed a grin at me. "She'll be a stunning blonde with your eyes and impish sense of humor. She'll be beautiful and drive us all to distraction because the world will be her oyster whether she knows it or not."

"That's extremely specific."

"Yes, but then I've seen my future in your eyes for so long, I can't imagine it being anywhere else. Kids. A home. More dogs someday. Maybe another cat."

I laughed.

"Wherever you are, that's where I want to be."

"I love you," I whispered. He took my extended hand and leaned forward to brush his lips lightly against mine.

"That's the best part of all of this."

"Me loving you?"

"Yep." Another light caress of his hand down my cheek. "That's my treasure and my future. Everything else is just icing."

I sighed.

"Now," he said, scooting back. "Let's divide out these songs, Angel. Then we can figure out which ones we want to sell."

We.

Always us.

"I think we should write one called 'The Future in Your Eyes'. Cause you know, that sounds like something I'd listen to."

"Write me the words Angel, we'll put it to music."

The last few days had been a reality check, a moment that transformed our fairy tale to the real world. "You know what I learned this week?" I smiled when he glanced at me. "You guys are princes no matter what world I'm in."

Chapter Twenty-Four

NOW WE'RE IN IT

Frankie

I popped home to change after classes. Today, I'd had a meeting with my academic advisor as well as the proposal pitch to my marketing instructor. Both had me sweating under the office clothes I'd elected to wear. That reminded me, I owed Eddie a lunch and a day at the office. The new schedule had been shifted a little because they'd combined two classes and eliminated a third. And all of that happened *before* classes started.

The new schedule had me on campus four days a week. That left me one day for interning at Standish and the weekends for homework and the guys. Not the best schedule, but they were doing the same things I was and by some miracle, with the exception of a handful of practices for Jake, we'd all managed to isolate Saturdays as our coordinated off day.

Three weeks into January, the wind outside had turned bitter. I was still a little achy and sore. The spotting would stop soon—thank fuck. We

293

were going to discuss removing the implant and putting the IUD in, in a month.

But condoms were back in the house. I'd already seen them. Not that we'd done anything more than cuddle and curl up together. The guys were great, no pressure, no pushing, and all the kisses a girl could want.

Hell, I could get drunk off those kisses.

Still…

"Hey, Babe," Archie said as I came out of my closet. I swore my pulse rabbited and my heart sped off for orbit. He shot me an apologetic look at the little squeak I made. "Sorry, I thought you saw me."

"It's fine." I laughed. "Lost in my own head." I'd changed into tight black leggings, one of Jake's oversized sweatshirts over a tank top underneath and a pair of Uggs on my feet. I liked comfy clothes when I went to the group grief therapy.

This month would be…different.

"Today is the day, right?" Archie asked. Like me, he'd gone for casual. Dressed in jeans, a t-shirt that was barely visible under the pullover sweater, he looked *good*.

"You got a haircut," I murmured as I closed the distance to him. He had taken some of the length off. It didn't curl against the back of his neck anymore. In fact, he'd shaved it a little close to the tops of his ears, but left the rest of it thick.

"I did," he answered in a quiet voice, then ducked his head as I ran my fingers through the thickness. It was so damn soft and he looked at me with quiet, fathomless eyes. But those dark brown eyes of his weren't fathomless, they housed all that wit, charm, and determination. "Thought it was time. Healing has to start somewhere."

Yes, it did. Sliding my hand to his nape, I rose up on my tip toes to kiss him. It was just the barest brush of my lips to his and then Archie's arms stole around me, crushing me to him. Even if all the air whooshed out of me, I hugged him with equal force.

"Yes, it does," I whispered. "And I love it. You look good enough to eat."

His dry smile and soft huff at the comment, made me smile in return.

"What were you asking about today?" I kept my arms wrapped around his neck as he pressed his forehead to mine. It also let me stroke my fingers through his hair. Archie's whole body seemed to melt into mine as I caressed his scalp.

When he was too stressed to relax, I'd discovered he had a weakness for this and it would help to let him settle enough to sleep.

"Today's the day you go to your grief counseling?" It was such a soft question, I almost missed the wording. Leaning back, I glanced up at him. There was the faintest hint of red on his cheeks.

"Yes, it starts in about an hour."

He nodded, pressing his head back into my fingers until I started stroking his scalp again. I waited him out, because he'd come to find me. Finally, he focused on me again.

"Would you like some company?"

"I always like your company," I told him and his smile flickered. "But yes, I would love for you to come with me."

Catching my hands, he pulled them down to hold them. "Then I want to go with you. I don't know if I'll say anything…"

"You don't have to." The sadness I'd told Ian about was still there, ever present, but each day passing seemed to blunt it a little. Who knew how I'd feel in a few months. "It's really a process. You can just sit and listen."

"It helps you?" The curiosity was there, the gleam in his eyes as he studied me. He wanted to understand the therapy, to take it apart like one of his machines and rebuild it from the ground up.

That was how Archie fixed things. Because he could break them down to their components.

"It does," I promised him.

He nodded, then lifted my hands to kiss. "You have any plans after?"

"Nope."

"Can I take you to dinner?"

"Are you trying to butter me up, Standish?"

"You know it, Babe." He gave it a beat and his smile turned to mischief. "Is it working?"

"I probably shouldn't tell you this. It will inflate your ego."

"No help for that now. It's always hard when you're around."

I groaned and he grinned but he kissed my hands again before he released me to go in my closet. He came out a minute later with my knee length soft brown coat with a warm scarf I could wrap around my ears and face if the breeze got too cutting.

"You never have to butter me up," I told him as he helped me into the coat. "I'm always gonna be a sure thing for you." Then before he could scold me, I pivoted and tapped his nose with my finger. "But I do love when you do."

That drew a genuine, deep smile from him and he dropped another kiss on my lips. Descending the stairs, I paused abruptly on the second level's small landing. Jeremy stood at the front door with Ann Bradshaw. I hadn't even realized she was here.

They spoke in quiet tones and she pressed a kiss to his cheek before he opened the door and let her out. Behind me, Archie was as still as stone. Neither of us said a word. No quips. No teasing. Nothing.

Closing the door, Jeremy turned and glanced up at us. "Mr. Archie. Miss Frankie."

"Hey Jere-Bear," Archie said easily as we resumed our descent. "We're off for a few hours. Probably going to have dinner out."

He nodded as he gave me a fully assessing gaze. "Are you feeling up for an evening out, Miss Frankie?"

I didn't assume Jeremy didn't know. It hadn't been a topic of discussion between us, but he could just as easily have been filled in by the guys. No matter what he knew, he would not be the one to say anything. Discretion was his middle name.

"I do," I told him. "I'm looking forward to it. And Archie will whisk me straight home if I'm even a little tired."

"This is true," Archie said with an easy smile. "So, if you have any plans, go for it." He patted Jeremy's arm. "No worries here."

"Hmm." There was a lot of weight in that singular syllable. "Thank you for the thought. Have a good evening. Do not keep her out too late."

Archie's smile turned positively wicked, but I pinched him before he could make whatever smart-ass remark danced over his tongue. He shot me an "awww" look but behaved himself.

Outside, I pulled on my gloves. The sun hadn't set yet, but it was still brittle and cold. A car swung in for us and Archie opened the back door rather than wait for the driver.

We slid in and I gave him the address then we were off. Archie didn't say much on the way to the group session. It took place in a community room in the mental health center. Located on the fourth floor, the best part of the meeting's location was the coffee shop on the first floor.

The beauty of my guys knowing me so well, he didn't ask before he opened the door to the shop and we picked up large coffees. Archie's silence had grown heavier as we got in the elevator and took it up. Once we reached the room, I greeted Stanley, the man was a genuine gift. He was also the counselor who hosted the group sessions and kept us going, smoothing over the rougher jagged parts when someone lost it.

He could always bring us back to the topic at hand. He was a phenomenal listener, truly seeming to focus on everything you said. If I didn't already like my therapist, he would be the guy I might consider seeing.

"Welcome, Archie," Stanley said with a grin. The fact he wore a #TeamStanley button with a plant on it just made me laugh. "I'm glad you could join us. Has Frankie told you the rules for our group?"

"Only to be respectful, I don't have to talk, but I do have to listen. There's no pressure to involve myself."

"Precisely. This is a safe space. No one discusses group outside of group. What you share here, stays here. Even if you see each other outside of group sessions, we ask for you to maintain respectful emotional distance. Can you do that?"

Archie slid a look at me and I grinned. "Stanley is amazing," I assured him. "He's gotten me through some pretty rough times here."

"You've gotten yourself through them," Stanley reminded me with a firm look. "I'm just the cruise director, you still have to steer the boat."

More people were coming in.

"If you want to grab your seats, we'll get this kicked off in five minutes."

"Thanks, Stanley!"

Holding Archie's hand, I let him choose where we sat. The group's chairs were set in a circle. It afforded some intimacy when we talked. Some people stood. Others sat. There was less pressure to interact before sessions began.

As more people filtered in, they began to fill in the circle. Most kept a buffer chair between themselves and the others already seated until there were few spaces left. The last ones in before Stanley shut the door had to choose which gaps to fill in.

Stanley kicked us off as normal. Introducing himself and then asking if we had any newcomers. Archie raised his hand, albeit reluctantly, as did a few others. While a couple were willing to introduce themselves, Archie wasn't one of those.

Not that I could blame him.

I hadn't said anything in my first meeting either. After the introductions, Stanley opened the floor to let those who wanted to talk, talk.

A mom who lost a child to cancer.

A brother who lost his sibling to drugs.

A husband mourning a wife.

There were so many stories in this room. All of them soaked in tears and misery. Yet, the burden of carrying them seemed to be lighter after ripping yourself open to share.

It wasn't always an evisceration. Sometimes, it was just lancing an old wound to let it flush out the poison. There were times though, that even when I talked about what held me back or why it would spring up out of nowhere and for no reason, that I couldn't explain it. A holiday dinner where Ted should be at the table? Mother's Day or her birthday, days when I couldn't help but think about Maddy.

Stupid moments, inconsequential ones that wouldn't mean anything to anyone who wasn't me. Those were the ones that would make me miss a step while I hurried to a lunch date or away from a class. A turn of phrase, or a voice from a stranger while standing in the store and you can't see them. A momentary reflection of a mother and child doing something as innocuous as holding hands that threw me back.

Those incidents were what made me crazy. They were also the ones Stanley called landmines. Hidden emotional ordinance that triggered a sharp rush of adrenaline in an effort to dodge the phantom bullets. But more often, they were laden with shrapnel and it only took one piece to pierce something vital.

We couldn't see the landmines, so the chances of realizing we were on a minefield were slim if at all, before we found one of those devices buried in some innocuous location.

I didn't doubt if Archie had similar experiences. I'd seen his face after a meal at a familiar restaurant or when we were at the house in the Hamptons. It had been there in the middle of the night when I'd wake up to see him staring into the darkness. Sometimes, he hid away at the shop so he could drown out those thoughts with something else.

Fingers linked with mine, Archie shifted so he faced me more than the group. I squeezed his hand and leaned into him when he settled his cheek against my hair.

One of the newcomers began to speak. My heart squeezed for the stutter in his voice. His mother passed away the week after Christmas. She'd been killed in a car accident. The sudden loss coupled with a fight they'd had over the holiday left him a mess.

When he couldn't get through the whole thing without a choked sob, Stanley rose to put an arm around his shoulders. The young man glanced at him as he scrubbed at his face. Poor guy. Like me, he was an ugly crier.

"Sorry," he tried to apologize around hiccups. But Stanley reassured him and then pulled him away from the group for a little after telling us to take a break. A good chunk of the people rose. Some went to the restrooms. Others left for a refreshment.

You could tell the guarded from the not so guarded, I didn't move away from Archie, leaning into him to offer him the comfort he seemed to be craving. Fifteen minutes later, we resumed.

The young man, Jerry, had stepped out to take a breath. In all likelihood, he would talk to Stanley later. The last half of the session let those who wanted to talk about their grief, or the positive things they'd done since our last meeting. They talked about how they remembered the people they had lost.

Listening to the tales, the big gains and the little ones, I wanted to participate. The next time Stanley asked who else wanted to talk, I raised my hand.

"Frankie," Stanley said in that warm welcoming tone of his. "Thank you for coming today. What do you want to tell us about the last month?"

Blowing out a breath, I really didn't know what I was going to say before the words flowed out. Like I'd said earlier, sometimes you had to lance a wound and drain off the infection.

"Right before New Year's, I found out I was pregnant." The room went quiet and Archie's fingers flexed around mine. "It was the day before the one-year anniversary marking the loss of Grandpa Ted. We'd all been sick, we'd had a good Christmas, but stomach flu ripped through the whole house. I thought I was doing great and then I wasn't. But the best part was,

I was never alone for any of it. The guys were with me every single step. When we found out it was ectopic, it—it was so weird, I didn't know what I felt."

I paused because I was kind of rambling and I wanted to focus on the positives of it.

"Even before I found out that I was pregnant, it was already a case that it wasn't viable. That we had to do something. The doctor had great medical suggestions and I was uncomfortable for a few days, physically. The guys all looked after me."

I tapped my chest with my free hand. "I wasn't always sure of what I felt during all of it. Like—I was sad. Relieved. Then exhausted and weirdly, guilty at times."

With every single syllable, some of the weight on my chest moved.

"It's not like we planned to be pregnant," I explained. "I felt kind of dumb when I didn't even realize it might be an issue. Then it wasn't, and I almost hated that I was relieved." I bit my lower lip as I turned my next words over in my head. "My feelings are—all over the place. I can't even define them for myself."

Stanley nodded. "How are you feeling today?"

"Better." It wasn't a question, I did feel better. The sadness was there. The loss for both Ted and Maddy were there. "I know this is another chip out of the tree, but it will keep growing and eventually that scar in the bark will be character and I'll be stronger."

"What things have you done to help you cope?"

"Taken care of my family and let them take care of me. I haven't tried to hide from the pain even when I don't know what to do with it. I've talked some—but I don't always have the words to explain what is going on with me."

"You're amazing," Archie murmured. I didn't think his voice carried, so I just shifted so I could glance up at him.

"Helping others—helping my family—it helps me too."

Would Archie understand? The faint smile on his lips still held a ghost of sadness. But there was more than that there too. "Sometimes you have to let others help you so you're not alone. We don't have to figure it out immediately. We have time."

Exactly.

If Stanley or anyone else said anything more, I didn't hear them, too lost in Archie's eyes to focus on anything else.

Then the meeting was over. As with the earlier break, some people gathered together to talk. Some just made a beeline for the door—that had been me the first three or four times I came. Some just sat, alone with their thoughts, maybe trying to put it into perspective.

Stanley finished saying farewell to one girl, Amanda, she was struggling with the loss of a younger brother who'd overdosed. She was in one of my statistics classes. We never talked about group when we were in class, and we didn't talk about class here.

She sent me a smile and a small wave as she left. Turning to us, Stanley held his hand out to me. I had to let go of Archie to shake Stanley's hand, but he covered my hand in his with his free hand and gave me a very intense look.

"I am sorry for your loss," he told me. "I don't know if you've processed it that far. I am sorry for it and I am so proud of you for sharing it today, for showing others your strength and vulnerability." While he didn't glance at Archie, the weight of his observation remained present. "Thank you for trusting us."

"Thank you for having this group. I really didn't know if it would do me any good but..."

"It's helped her a lot," Archie said and I glanced at him. He'd slid his hands into his pockets. I caught the swift look he'd given to where Stanley held my hand in his, but there was no rancor or jealousy in his gaze. "I'd like to come again, if you both don't mind?"

"I will never mind having your company," I told him firmly.

"And I look forward to getting to know you, Mr. Standish—"

"Archie." No one else used formal names here but then we'd all made the concerted effort to learn those names. Archie was still wary, but at least, he was also interested.

"Archie." Releasing me, Stanley shook his hand. "We have meetings each week, though this is also the monthly one for those who need to talk but don't have the time to devote to a weekly schedule. Also, if you want to talk to a private counselor and need some recommendations, I'll hook you up."

"Thank you."

We lingered for only a few more minutes, then Archie and I bid our farewells. He was quiet all the way to the car, then the restaurant and it wasn't until he'd ordered wine and poured a glass for me—thank fuck no one carded me—that he said, "I didn't see it."

"Didn't see what?"

"How talking about the shitty things that happened could possibly make it better."

I waited.

"But it's not just the bad things," he continued swirling the wine in his own glass. "It's talking about the light in the darkness. The moments that make the pain something you want to feel—because it means they were there, that you loved and were loved."

When he focused all that intensity on me, I nodded. "You just have to be open to it. It took me a while. But—I feel better when I'm done. The loss is a little duller, the sadness a little less, and the pain? I think it's always going to be there, but it's that sharpness that makes me appreciate what we have so much."

"Thank you," he said, raising his glass finally and I clinked mine to his.

"Am I fishing for compliments if I ask for what?"

He chuckled. "Fish away, Babe, I will happily sink my teeth into your bait anytime."

That sent a delicious shiver through me.

"And I was saying thank you for giving me time to decide, for just being patient with me—for telling me how you felt after what happened with the ectopic pregnancy. A part of me wishes it hadn't been that and a part of me is glad it's not a decision we have to make now."

I understood that.

"But Grandpa Ted has been really vocal with me," he admitted and at my raised eyebrows, he grinned. "I can hear him in my head, heard him the day we got the tests. 'That girl, Sprout, she's the one you love and you support, and you be there for. If you do that, the challenges won't matter because you'll be together.'"

Tears gathered in my eyes.

"I miss him so fucking much," he admitted. "I hate even saying it aloud, but I miss him. I miss his stories. I miss talking to him. I hate thinking about him and hurting."

After a swallow of the wine, I reached over to take his hand.

"I got to talk about him, think about him, just a little today. At the meeting, when you talked about what happened. I could feel him right there, hand on my shoulder and chuckling. Life, is what happens when you make plans. I want plans. I want life. I want you."

Licking my lips, I swallowed around the lump of grief in my throat. "I'm not going anywhere."

"You're going everywhere," he promised, his eyes almost aglow. "But I'm going to be there too. We're all going to be there."

"Because no matter what the challenges are," I said slowly. "We'll face them."

"Damn straight. Together." Then he moved from the seat across from me to shift onto the booth next to me. One arm around my shoulders, he pulled me in and then he pulled out his phone. "Tell the boys how much you love me."

This time the coil of tension wrapping around me, teased my soul and

I tilted my head back to meet the kiss he had waiting. Even the little rapid snapping of images only enhanced the moment as his lips massaged mine.

Yes. We were still hurting. We were still fumbling. But we were doing it together. When he let me up for air, he showed me the phone.

The middle fingers from Jake and Coop made me laugh. Ian's, "Need to work on your tongue action, man," left me near tears again for a whole different reason.

Cupping Archie's face, I kissed him again, fierce and demanding. Bless him, he sent those photos too and somewhere in my back pocket my phone began to buzz.

Chuckling, he kissed me again and then our appetizers were there. The stones of grief and loss on my chest had been dislodged, the pressure eased, and for the first time in months, the smile in Archie's eyes wasn't marred by a dark cloud.

But rain or not, I wasn't going anywhere.

We were in it. All of us. For the long haul.

Chapter Twenty-Five
THE LIVING YEARS

Archie

For four weeks, I went to every single weekly meeting of the grief group. Even when she had to change her schedule or cut out of a class a little early, Frankie always met me there. Four weeks. Four of the weekly sessions. Then it was time for the monthly meeting. Frankie had a doctor's appointment beforehand.

The guys volunteered to go with us, but Frankie told them we had a date after. That's what those meetings had been. Dates.

Until that night.

When Frankie headed up to change, I came clean with the guys. "Honestly," I told them. "I don't even know why I decided to not say anything. I don't think I was intentionally holding back."

"You don't have to explain," Bubba said. "Thanks for telling us and seriously, if I can do anything…"

Jake clapped me on the shoulder. "It's been good for you. I didn't know what you were doing, but you seem—lighter."

I chuckled. "That's just all the running." I'd always enjoyed running, but last year I'd doubled down on it. Run enough, work out enough, and sometimes, I could sleep without any trouble. Run enough. Fuck Frankie enough. Play at the workshop enough. I loved all of these things, her especially, but I kept trying to fill that well with her and that wasn't fair to Frankie.

"Man, seeing you tell us you're being all proactive with the self-care and really giving yourself a chance to experience your feelings—" Coop put a hand over his heart. "Does a guy proud."

"Then you bring up the running." Chuckling, Bubba unscrewed the cap on his water bottle.

"Yeah, sadly that makes me question all of your sanities." Coop nodded, but his gaze wasn't on us but the stairs.

"We're still on for the weekend," Jake said in a low voice.

"Yep."

We had plans for a game on Sunday, but since Frankie and Rachel were meeting to discuss Europe, it would give the four of us time to make the plan we'd been debating the last few weeks.

A plan that after one grief meeting had solidified from nebulous anxiety to foregone conclusion. Coop was right, we'd always known what we wanted. We'd been building it all this time. Facing it was not only the easiest thing on the planet, but also the most desirable.

"What's this weekend?" Frankie asked as she descended the stairs. The black yoga pants she wore hugged her hips and the silky soft cashmere pull over sweater seemed to have wrapped her in a cloud. The fact she wore Uggs every chance she got was adorable.

Grief counseling didn't mean dressing up. Group was a lot more comfortable when we were. I got that more and more. "We're gonna catch a game or two. Maybe get a run in," I told her as she settled under my arm and

I brushed a kiss to the top of her head.

"Boys need sports time," Coop announced. "We need to be manly, thump our chests, and in my case, let the other guys think their dicks are bigger. But then, we know the truth."

The last was delivered with just the right amount of smarm. He dodged the pillow Jake flung at him and stole a kiss from Frankie.

"Be good tonight, you two. Don't do anything I wouldn't."

I laughed. "I'll do anything she wants, experimentation is half the fun."

That got a deep red flush and a real laugh out of Frankie. I loved it. Loved her. "Right, behave yourself," Frankie said crisply, slipping away to give Bubba and Jake kisses goodbye. "I'm gonna be with Rachel all day on Sunday, unless that plan changes."

"It'll be great," I assured her. "Dad and I had the attorneys go over that paperwork you asked for and then we sent it to Dominic."

Frankie's grin was worth every moment of having to deal with that arrogant dick. The grant Frankie planned to provide via one of our satellite foundations that she would take over funding, would provide Rachel with the capital and the access to spend her senior year abroad, studying photography, art, culture, and anything else she wanted.

It would also get her away from Dominic and let her have a life again. The idea this guy had her so turned around irked me. I liked our Rachel feisty, dangerous, dark, and cutting. This guy made her cry, that just left me violent.

But we were supposed to stay out of it. Right.

Jake cracked his knuckles. It would have been hard to miss the vicious little grin on his face. He liked Dominic less than I did. The only thing keeping me from breaking his legs was Frankie's request for us to stay out of it.

We'd agreed.

For now.

If he did one more damn thing to upset Rachel, which in turn upset Frankie, I wouldn't favor his chances.

"C'mon, Babe," I caught her hand. "I'm looking forward to our date and after-date. Don't wait up boys, I'm planning to spoil our girl tonight."

Laughter followed us, but I caught Bubba's measured look and nodded my head. Sex wasn't on the table yet. We'd all been taking our time, easing back into those waters. Frankie had a new IUD and though we'd fooled around and used condoms, none of us wanted to push her yet.

Particularly when she was still *sad*. That one syllable word had gutted me when she used it. Sad was not a description I liked for her. Frankie was too vivacious, too warm, and full of life. She brightened the world around her.

She definitely brightened my world. The last thing I wanted was for her to be sad. It took me back to that summer between junior and senior years when her sadness had been caused by *us*. Not something I could forgive myself for.

Not easily.

Our future? All of ours? It depended on that openness and that vulnerability. Frankie wasn't hiding her pain from us, we might not be able to fix it—and fuck if I didn't hate that more than anything else—but we could be there for her.

That strength and determination as she fought to find the balance and the happiness she wanted, inspired me. That was why I was going to the grief meetings, and because on some levels, it was helping.

A little.

Missing Grandpa was an ache I didn't think would ever go away. I still missed Nana. A sigh escaped me as we settled in the car. Our driver was one of the regulars and he already knew where we were going.

"You okay?" Frankie asked.

I smiled at her. "Yeah, I think I am." The words came out slow and thoughtful. "I just realized that I do miss Grandpa. It's right there. Just like I always missed Nana. But I don't miss Nana as much as I did then and… is it weird that it helps me to think they're together?"

Tucking her head against my shoulder and winding her arm through mine, Frankie smiled. "Not weird at all. I wish I'd gotten to meet her—your nana. Grandpa Ted told some great stories about her."

"She would have loved you." No doubt existed within me. They'd never laid eyes on each other. Well, not exactly. But Nana would have adored Frankie. They were a lot alike. They both made the world around them better.

"I know I would have loved her," she confirmed. "Cause you adore her and I see that love in your eyes."

Another kiss to the top of her head. "We should ask Eddie out to dinner."

I didn't say anything today. I thought about it. Even debated whether I could stand up and give voice to my thoughts. While today wasn't that day, I focused on the next meeting.

Honestly, going to grief counseling—fuck, going to any counseling—was not something I could see myself doing. Not really. It seemed so off the wall. Too much really. But Frankie was right, sitting there week after week for the last four weeks, the fissure inside of me had gradually shifted.

It didn't quite feel like a gaping wound anymore. It wasn't better. And I was definitely still "sad," but the loss wasn't swallowing me. Not anymore. The fact Frankie was right there every step of the way reminded me that I wasn't alone. I didn't want to be a burden, but the one time I mentioned it—she'd pinched me hard enough to leave a mark.

Duly noted.

We called Eddie on the way to group counseling. Instead of meeting us somewhere, he invited us over to his place after. For the first time in years, honestly, I couldn't even pin down the number, I found myself looking forward to a meal with him.

The private elevator took us up to his penthouse. The scent of grilling onions, roasted garlic, and what I was pretty sure were mushrooms filled the air as the doors opened.

"Hey kids," Eddie greeted us, sticking his head out of the kitchen. "Come on in. I've got a bottle of wine open to breathe and chilling. But Archie can also fix drinks."

"That I can," I said with some amusement as I helped Frankie out of her coat. "What do you want, Babe?"

"Um," Frankie said as she pushed up the sleeves on her sweater. "Actually, Amaretto Sour with the orange slices?"

"Got any oranges in there, Eddie?" I called after I hung her coat, followed by mine.

"Heads up," my father said and I turned in time to catch the orange he tossed at me. "Make me one too?"

"Sounds like I'll be making three."

"I'll go help, Eddie," Frankie murmured, giving me a kiss and I paused for a minute as she headed into the kitchen. Eddie's warm greeting and Frankie's laughter had me tossing the orange up into the air briefly and then down again.

More laughter filtered out of the kitchen.

"I'm perfectly capable of preparing the meal," Eddie said in a teasing tone I really hadn't heard in years. The man in that kitchen was not the remote, distant, and oftentimes uncaring father I'd come to know and despise.

Gone was the remote attitude. He let us see him—me and Frankie. The day he'd thought Frankie was his kid, I could see why he wanted her so badly. It hurt, on some levels, that Frankie was the kid he wanted to make up to. But the thing was, Frankie had become the bridge that let us get to know each other—for real.

Moving over to the bar, I went to work fixing the drinks. Amaretto, a little sweet and sour, Sprite, ice, and the orange slices. The whole time I prepared them, I listened to Frankie teasing Eddie and his laughter as he ribbed her right back.

In some ways, he got Frankie as a daughter after all. As much as I'd resented the way he'd damn near imploded the life I'd been building with her, he'd also made it up to her. To me.

To all of us.

Drinks finished, I set them on a tray to carry them into the kitchen and had to pause because a picture sat on the media console combined with a distressed wood sideboard.

The picture held me captive for a minute and I left the drinks to walk over to it. It was me. A very *young* me, but I was all dressed up in my suit, standing next to Eddie and Grandpa. They were dressed similarly.

But what struck me more than anything else was how we were *all* standing. I had one hand in the pocket of my slacks, so did Eddie, and Grandpa, had both of his hands tucked in like he had all the time in the world. We each wore the same expression, but where they were just amused, I was flat out fucking delighted.

I also had no memory of this shot—at all.

Picking it up, I stared at it. Eddie didn't have a lot of personal items in the place, though he had added a couple of pieces of art. Both seemed familiar, but only one did I truly recognize.

It had been Grandpa's. Before that, it had been Nana's. Something he picked up for her during one of their trips to Europe. It was a street in Warsaw, maybe. A street artist had captured it during a festival. There was so much life, joy, and *people*, just living their lives in the painting. It was something Nana loved.

She used to tell me stories about the people in the painting. They were all real to her, captured for this brief moment in time through an artist's eye and their open happiness just dragged everyone along with them.

A smile curved my lips as I glanced from the photo of us to the painting again.

"Mom loved that painting," Eddie said from right behind me. "It was hung up in the living room in Connecticut. We had dinner drinks in front of it every evening. If we had company, Mom would secret me into the living room early and tell me stories about the people in the painting before I had to go up and have my supper."

"The best bedtime stories ever," I admitted. "I haven't thought about this painting in years."

"I hate to admit it," Eddie said as he came to stand next to me. From the corner of my eye, he seemed more focused on the painting than on me. "I forgot all about it until I was at Dad's and cleaning out the apartment. He hadn't really had a lot of time to settle there. I sent most of the things out to the house in the Hamptons. But this…this was hanging up in his bedroom."

That made sense.

"He still talked to Nana," I said with a kind of bittersweet regret. "He would talk about her like she was still here, make comments now and again, like he needed to remember to tell her something."

"He loved Mom." Real regret colored his voice. "I used to be so envious of how he loved her. How she would look at him. I wanted that. When I thought I found it, I was so damn selfish, I didn't understand—" He broke off and shook his head. "It doesn't matter now. I threw away, gave away, and sometimes just walked away, because I thought I was the one losing out."

"Dad," I said, twisting to face him. "Don't get me wrong. Maddy was a stone cold bitch, twisted and cruel. I know she probably had to have some redeeming qualities, somewhere. She somehow managed to produce Frankie. But—you deserved more than her. More than—what Grandpa and Nana did."

"They meant well," Eddie said, leaping to their defense. "I shouldn't have been so damn stubborn. Maybe if I'd just stood up to them, maybe if

I'd taken a really hard look at how toxic we were together…" All at once his gaze was thousand miles away. "But when I looked at her, all I saw was my future, my hope, my plans, and my dreams. I saw a kind of wild freedom that I didn't understand and she was just intoxicating."

As much as that admission might have made me grimace before, it didn't this time. There was such an epic amount of longing in his voice, decorated with regret and loss that I couldn't mock him for loving a woman I hated.

He'd had to kill the woman he loved.

What the hell did that do to a man?

"Grandpa have this too?" I held up the picture to show him and Eddie grinned. A genuine smile.

"Yeah. We were going to some event, there had been all this planning and new suits. You insisted on joining us to be measured for a suit. Dad said every young man needed to learn to look smart from the beginning."

"So, he just had a suit made for me?" And why didn't I remember this day?

"Yep. Then when it was time for us to go out, you refused to stay with the nanny or the sitter. So, Mom said you'd be her escort, then she could duck out at the boring parts and take you home."

I laughed. How could I not? "Nana loved going to events."

"No," Eddie said, slanting a grin at me. "She loved Dad. She loved making him happy and supporting him. But if she had her way, she'd have been content at home, in her garden, and looking after her family. I swore that for the longest time, I half-thought she was just gonna steal you away to raise you."

His smile faded a little.

"You know I asked her that once," I admitted. "Why couldn't I just live with them all the time?"

No surprise reflected in his face. I'd probably made it pretty clear who my preference was for. Even then. "What did she say?"

"That she would always be my nana, I would always have a home with her. But I also had parents and maybe my parents needed time to adjust, but I shouldn't ever give up on you." Then, because maybe he needed to hear it, I added, "She never did, you know. I know things were tense between the two of you. But she never gave up on you."

Dropping his chin, Eddie stared down at the photo of the three of us. "Mom—" he sighed and the flicker of pain on his face lingered before he shut it away. "I was an ass. I owed her a lot better than I gave."

"Yeah." Hard to disagree with that. "But she was right about you."

That got his attention and he snapped his gaze up to me. For a moment, I could see all of my own pain reflected in his eyes.

"She told me not to give up." I pursed my lips. "I know I did. I gave up on you."

Fuck, that was harder to admit than I thought it would be.

"It was easier, when I was angry with you. When—I just shut you out because I hated what you and Muriel did to each other. I hated being in the middle of it. The fact I felt like I had to choose." I shook my head. "I never wanted to choose between you, so I chose neither of you. If you couldn't choose me, why the hell should I choose you?"

"Not an unfair statement," Eddie said slowly. "I wasted too many good years bemoaning what I didn't have and ignoring what I did. I know apologies will never make up for—"

"You don't have to apologize. For anything. When push came to shove, you saved me. You saved *Frankie*. I can't—I never want to imagine what that had to feel like for you. But—I can never thank you enough for saving her. For—everything, the last year especially."

Since Grandpa died and the months before that.

"Archie…"

"It's okay, Dad." Wow, now *that* tasted fucking weird. "Really, it is. We have the rest of our lives. Maybe we won't have the most orthodox father and son relationship—but we're Standishes. Who says we can't just do whatever the hell we want?"

I met his gaze evenly and I didn't ignore the gleam of tears in his eyes. "You mean that?"

"I do."

Dad—yep, way not used to that—set the picture down on the sideboard again then took a deep breath. "I want to be there. For you. For her. For all of you. Brother boyfriends and all that."

I groaned and he chuckled.

"You know, Frankie took me to a grief counseling group. I've been going for the last month. I don't know if you'd like it or not, but maybe you can come with me? With us? See if it does anything for you?"

"I'd like that."

A sound from the kitchen pulled us both around and Dad swore.

"Dammit, I need to switch the heat around on the—"

"Don't worry," Frankie called, the beautiful beam of fucking sunshine that she was. "I've got it. I even snuck out and stole my drink. You two keep bonding. I'll happily finish cooking dinner."

I had to bite back a laugh, but Dad glanced at me. "Never let her go."

"Wasn't planning on it. Drink?"

Chapter Twenty-Six

SHAKE IT OUT

Frankie

Winter segued into spring so smoothly it was hard to believe that we didn't get buried in some huge winter storm *again*. Spring Break had us heading back out to the Hamptons. The definitive shift in Archie and Eddie's relationship had a kind of domino effect on the rest of us.

I still went to grief counseling, with Archie most of the time. Occasionally, Eddie joined us. He was even less comfortable than Archie had been. A couple of times, Archie had gone to meet Eddie for another grief group, so his dad didn't go alone.

The trip to the Hamptons for Spring Break was prompted by a request from Eddie. Little Miss Abigail came with us, the cats were fine at the brownstone and Jeremy had gone on vacation. It had taken a bit of arm twisting on my part and a little finessing on Archie's, but we convinced him to join Ann Bradshaw for a cruise she'd been discussing.

We bought their tickets—well, upgraded hers—and made sure Jeremy was set. He would be gone for exactly one week. We would be in the Hamptons and fingers crossed, he and Miss Bradshaw would have a good time.

They'd definitely hit it off the last few months. She'd been a regular— near weekly—visitor for lunch most days, twice for supper. Then Jeremy took her out for an evening meal and a show.

We were all twelve, we waited up to see how late he would get in and the guys were disappointed that he didn't bring her home with him, but Archie just shrugged.

"Jeremy's *way* too classy for that. He's not the guy who brings a girl home to seduce her."

"No?" I'd asked, planting a bare foot against his chest when he tried to get out of bed. "You did."

"I was seventeen," he pointed out. "And my house was the best place I had at the time where you felt comfortable."

I turned that over in my head. "I'll grant you that. I kind of miss your bed sometimes."

That earned me a speculative look from Jake. "Only *his* bed, Baby Girl?"

I wrinkled my nose then stuck my tongue out at Jake. "It was a really nice bed. You guys tended to prefer my bed."

"Still do," he retorted, but he caught my ankle and danced his fingers up my instep. I squealed with laughter, but there was nowhere to go, I had Ian on one side and Coop on the other and they were very intent on tickling the shit out of me too.

"Right! I miss all your beds," I declared, panting with laughter. Heat rushed to my face as Ian cupped my throat and then tilted my head back for a kiss.

"You can miss Archie's bed, Angel, we're not always in a competition."

Three derisive snorts greeted that comment and I giggled. Miss Abigail barked from where she stood at the foot of the oversized bed in our suite—well the suite we'd pretty much claimed at Thanksgiving. There'd been a few alterations—they had Archie written all over it—including a much larger bed that fit all five of us, plenty of lounging chairs and sofas, and what I was pretty sure was a sex swing in the corner.

"Right," Coop said. "Let's go Jake, we're walking the dog."

"Why are *we* walking the dog?" Jake asked even as he bent down and pressed a hard kiss to my lips. "Stay in this bed, hopefully naked and very well-fucked, but in the bed until we get back."

"Okay," I said, sprawling back against Ian. "If you insist."

He grinned then he was gone, leaving me with Archie and Ian. Moving up to take the spot Coop had abandoned, Archie propped himself up on his elbow and studied me. I didn't have to look over my shoulder to know Ian studied me too.

"What's wrong?" I asked.

"Nothing wrong, Angel," Ian said as he stroked my hair back off my face. "Just this week, we're all going to be lazy, relax…"

"…fool around in bed," Archie teased. "Unless you need me to get my bed up here from Texas."

I grinned. "Are you trying to ask if I'm up for more carnal invitations?" As much as I missed their dicks at times, to be honest, they'd all been a thousand percent more cuddly and we'd all been making a concerted effort at more time together, no matter how crazy the schedule.

"Yes," Archie answered simply. "And no."

No?

Surprise flickered through me. "Explain."

Wickedness danced in Archie's eyes as he grinned. "Well, we're actually going to take this week and rest, relax, rejuvenate because we've all been running."

"This is true, and we're going to celebrate a few things," Ian picked up the thread. "We're going to celebrate that Coop got that job offer."

That offer was fucking amazing for him. We'd have to cut our summer sojourn a little short, but I didn't mind and neither had the guys. Three weeks instead of the whole month was hardly a sacrifice.

"I fucking love that they asked him to work full time at the community center. He'll be able to start logging hours too." Hours toward a Master's he already had planned. "We just have to make sure he doesn't over do it."

"We'll take care of him, Babe." Archie tangled our fingers together. "Jake's gonna have his license by the end of the summer too. Staying closer to New York this year might actually work out better for all of us."

"Yeah?"

He flattened our hands together. "Yep," he said, a grin curling the corners of his mouth. "A little birdie mentioned you two want to record a second album. But neither of you want to be all the way out in California for weeks at a time."

"No," I said. "I don't. I don't want to leave any of you for months and months again. A week here or there, two at the most. We can make that work, but months away?"

I shook my head.

His smile was all charm and sweetness. "Bubba told us, and since he feels the same way, I've talked to Dad about doing a few more renovations here. We're keeping the Hamptons house."

A decision he and Eddie had made together. "Did I tell you I was a little excited about that?"

"Like the house?"

Actually… "I kind of do and I like making memories here. With all of you."

Ian pressed a kiss to the side of my throat. It was kind of fun to be just sitting there, curled against him while he ran his hands over my hip and back up again, nuzzling kisses and the whole time, Archie never let go of my gaze.

"Good. We're adding a recording studio for the both of you. We're going to renovate the basement in the other wing. We don't use it for anything, good sound proofing, better equipment and we can call that music engineer you liked…"

"Lauren?" I tried to sit up a little, but Ian and I were too tangled together and Archie slid his leg over mine, trapping me between them.

"Sure, if that was her name," he said, still grinning. "You guys can work on recording out here as necessary. We can even spend part of the summer out here. We're a little far for Coop to commute during the week, but he can come out on weekends and…"

I didn't need to hear the rest of it. I lunged upward to kiss him. His laughter greeted me before he began to devour my mouth. Ian's hot hands slid up under my top and the pair of them moved with almost perfect synchronicity.

My sleep shorts, panties, and top vanished. Ian glided his fingers right along the seam of my pussy. There wasn't even a hint of pretense that I wasn't as hungry for their touch as they were for mine. I tugged at Archie's shirt and he broke from kissing me to pull it off.

All at once, I was half-twisted and Ian captured my lips. Archie's hot mouth locked on a nipple and I bucked against the sensation. They were all demanding touches and sweeping caresses.

Ian lapped at my tongue as he slid two fingers into me. He cupped my free breast with his other hand and then Archie was there, spearing his fingers into me alongside Ian's.

Fuck, the stretch of their fingers had me writhing. I dug my nails in and ran my hands over everything I could touch. Then we were twisting. Archie was on his back on the bed and I hovered over him. Ian and Archie used their hands to guide me into place and then I sank down on Archie's sweet, curved dick and groaned.

Had it really been almost two months? All that time just melted away as he thrust upward and I began to rock on him. Some part of my mind cataloged Ian's motion behind me. He was stripping. Thankfully, Archie was already gloriously naked.

A shudder rolled through me as I sank down and Archie thrust up. Leaning down, I pressed my lips to his again. It was like getting the first real gulp of air after being denied for too long.

Ian stroked his hands down my back to ass. He urged me to tilt it out a little further and then massaged one cheek. I could almost feel it coming and I sank down into the kiss a second before the hot strike of Ian's hand collided with my ass. My whole body clenched at the heat and I shuddered as he massaged it out.

"Fuck," Archie groaned against my mouth. The second strike of Ian's palm was so much louder against the sound of our ragged breaths. The sharp edge of pain shoved me right into an orgasm I hadn't expected.

I clamped down on Archie's dick as he and Ian both massaged the heat into my ass.

"Jesus," Archie groaned. "She's gonna fucking make me come."

"Yeah?" Ian's voice sounded positively dark. "How about this?"

The series of spanks came in rapid succession, I couldn't track them. Light. Sharp. Light. Light. Sharp. I swore I spasmed with every smack. My body lit up inside and out.

The motion rocked me against Archie, and the second orgasm swept me right under as he let out a shout. I floated there, happily soaking in Ian's soft praise and Archie's gasping sounds as liquid heat filled me.

"Think I can return the favor?" Archie asked in a droll, tone and Ian just chuckled.

"Come ride my dick, Angel," Ian said. "Let Archie play with your ass."

Oh.

Yes.

Please.

They worked together to shift me over onto Ian's dick this time. He was so fucking hard, and I was still shaking from the earlier orgasms.

"I forgot how sweet and hot you are when I'm inside of you," Ian told me. "So fucking sweet for us."

"She really is," Archie commented, kissing my tattoo as he trailed his fingers down the seam of my ass. I expected lube. Then he landed a hollow palmed slap against my still stinging ass.

"Fuck," I swore as I arched this time.

"A little more force," Ian said as he cupped my nape, then dragged me in for a kiss. "She loves the sting and the heat."

Tears shocked into my eyes at the next strike and I swore my body went liquid. Yes, I loved the sting. The heat. The way hard fingers spread the pain over my muscles and then everything just loosened within me.

"Got it," Archie said, massaging my ass. "You ready for this, Babe?"

I opened my eyes to meet Ian's. "Green."

"She's ready. Be careful," he commanded even as he gripped my hips and began to fuck into me hard and fast from below. I followed the command and rocked down to meet him. "Watch the redness, watch for welts. When in doubt, go softer."

"Got it."

The next spanking was so damn intense, I barely recognized the orgasm when it hit, because it rolled over me swifter than a late afternoon thunderstorm. He alternated strikes with pressing his fingers against my ass.

Lube.

There it was.

Fuck, I couldn't breathe and right when I thought I'd come again, they both stopped, the room quieting except for the rapid breaths we were all releasing.

Then Archie put his dick where his fingers had been and he pushed into me, stretching that ring of muscle until I was being splintered apart. Impaled on both of them, I let out a little sob. Someone needed to move.

"Do you like this, Angel?" Ian asked and I managed to open my eyes to meet his.

"Yes, sir," I whispered. "I've missed you."

He grinned. "Then hold on Angel, this week, we're all about planning, reunions, and play."

Archie bit down on my throat as he pumped into me. It took them a minute to find their rhythm and I rocked between them. This time, I was ready for my orgasm and I let out a cry as they kept rocking into me, pushing me harder until I came apart sobbing.

The rush of their release was like setting my body on fire. Pure, molten lava fountaining inside of me. I floated there, a perfect merger between our play and our intimacy. Safe and sound with two of the four people I loved most in the world.

"Well-fucked," Archie commented in a lazy, voice as he eased away from me and patted my ass. "As requested."

A giggle escaped and then fresh warmth was against my back. "Did you miss me, Baby Girl?"

Ian huffed a laugh, but didn't protest when Jake rolled away with me and I was looking up at Coop who gazed down at me with a kind of naked longing that turned me inside out.

I didn't have the words, I just held out my hands and he came right to me. The guys were all there, sharing, loving, *being* with me. Being together— fuck. Coop thrust into me, fucking me hard and swift as I sprawled on Jake's chest. He kept kissing my neck and my arms. He moved me when Coop needed it and when Coop and I came together, I lay there shuddering as Jake petted me through the orgasm.

Archie reappeared with water and he told me to drink. Then I had Jake's mouth on mine, the kiss as full of passion as it was love. My pussy throbbed from the ferociousness of my earlier couplings, but Jake took his time, every move gentle and slow until he calmed me down, then and only then, did he push me.

And when he thrust into my pussy, I wrapped my lips around Ian's already stiffening cock. Spit-roasted, as the description went, and this was my favorite place to be—between my guys.

I lost track of time to be honest. We came again and collapsed into a shuddering pile of naked and sweaty limbs. Coop rescued me and pulled me into a shower. Archie joined us and this time, it was Archie's dick I sucked while Coop rocked and twisted his hips, so I felt every inch of his cock and piercing.

Mostly clean, and barely able to move, we wandered back out into the bedroom where food and the guys waited.

We even took a nap.

But I woke up to Jake's bearded face in my pussy and Coop's cock brushing my lips.

When the guys said we were spending our whole spring break in bed, they hadn't been kidding.

We fucked. Made love. Laughed. Talked. Figured out senior year plans. New album plans. Ian announced he'd sold all four of the songs we'd chosen to submit. Even better, one of the songs was picked out by one of his favorite bands. I loved this for him so fucking much.

We even played video games. And Archie proved his dominance, managing to win one race with me warming his cock. The other guys all got distracted.

Yeah, sorry, not sorry. I was just a little too tired to flex around his dick for that game. I was pretty sure they'd managed to pull my vagina during our near week-long orgy.

Worth it.

It was the weirdest, best, sweetest, and most amazing spring break in a while.

Between my new IUD land taking the time to make sure it was working, I rediscovered something about my guys. We didn't need sex to enjoy each other. We always had—yes, I was the blind one, I knew.

At the same time—having them. Feeling them as they filled me over and over? Being able to watch them fall apart as they came inside of me?

It was the fucking best. We didn't *have* to have sex.

But it was fun as hell when we did.

Our last day in the Hamptons, I slipped out of the house early to walk Miss Abigail. The sun was just rising as we headed down toward the beach. I could take her off her leash and let her run and play with the water if she desired.

She was such a good girl and stayed close.

The air was cool, but the days were getting longer. The sadness that had been a constant companion had shrunk. The future was right there in front of me and, if I glanced back at the house, it was behind me too.

My past and future were already my present.

"Hey," Coop called and I swung around again to find him descending the steps toward the sand. "Running away?"

I grinned.

"Never."

Chapter Twenty-Seven
RACHEL IN PARIS?

Frankie

"So, what's made the top of our list?" Flopping back against the pillows, I sat cross-legged on her bed while she packed her things. I'd totally be helping, but Rachel's type A plan was for me to get out of her way while she did everything.

"You mean *my* list?"

I sniffed and eyed her over the top of my digital tablet. Her grin was infectious though so I just rolled my eyes. "How about *the* list?"

"Deal." Hair pulled back into a ponytail and face bare of cosmetics, Rachel still looked like a million bucks. She was pulling out each item from her closet, holding it up and examining it. Each article of clothing earned an assessing look before it was sorted into one of four piles.

Europe.

Storage at the brownstone.

Donation.

My closet, but for returning later.

The last only had two items in it, but they were my favorite of her shirts and she knew it.

"Right, so," I continued. "The list begins with an internship with Rene Dubois, lead photographer for Paris Daily. He agreed to sponsor you for the program admission as well. You'll have a full semester at the Sorbonne studying with Mischa Condre, Alia Gagnon, and a possible feature in an end of the year show for student photographers and artists."

A half-smile curved her lips. "Please, take note, that I am not going to ask how you pulled all that off."

"Hashtag humblebrag," I teased her. "You know damn well you got into the Sorbonne *and* you got this internship on your own merits."

Holding up a dark, forest green dress to herself, it was strapless and would hug the body, and the rouching would do amazing things for her figure, not that she needed the help.

"I *am* kind of awesome," she admitted, her grin growing. "If I could legally marry myself, I would."

Laughter rushed through me and I shook my head. "So, your first semester will be primarily in Paris, though there is opportunity to travel with Rene on various assignments."

"Ooh, run and fetch girl," Rachel mocked playfully as she settled the green dress into the pile to go to Europe. Good girl.

"You need the heels that match that and the lingerie."

She flicked me a middle finger and I cackled. "Right, so what else is on this list of yours?"

"Christmas is something we do here at home, I thought, if you wanted, I could fly you back to spend the week after Christmas with us? If you didn't want to go to your family or spend it in Paris."

A flush of pleasure lit up her face. "You really don't have to do that for me, I know how much that holiday with your guys means to you."

"It does and I wouldn't have asked if we weren't all in agreement." Ian had suggested it when I'd been particularly melancholy about Rachel leaving. But she didn't need to know that. "You don't have to decide now, we can check in around Thanksgiving."

"Fair enough," she said after a moment's consideration. "Second semester?"

"You'll still be attending the Sorbonne in the spring, but your courses are all a form of independent study that will take you to Austria, Switzerland, Poland, Italy, and possibly Spain, but that is marked with asterisks that say it depends on who your assigned advisor is for the spring."

"That makes sense. Rene DuBois had a very busy career in Paris, so I'll likely be paired with another instructor or professional, quite possibly a group of us."

She paused for a moment, hugging a Torched sweatshirt to her chest. The locked arm motion and the deep shudder worried me.

"You're going to be amazing," I told her softly. "I'm kind of jealous of you, and at the same time, I have no idea if I could do what you're doing."

Flicking her eyes open, she stared at me. "You can do anything you want."

"Maybe," I said. "But being that far away from everyone I know? Tearing up the world and making my mark? You are such a fucking bad ass."

Her snort only made my grin wider. "Right, you push the boundaries on your comfort zones all the time."

"Yeah, but I'm also secure in the fact that I have all of you to catch me."

"And what?" She raised both her brows. "Y'all won't catch me?"

I snorted. "One," I said, holding up a finger. "You'll catch yourself long before I even realize you've started to fall. Two, if you are falling, you'll probably yank the asshole pushing you too far with you, so they can break your fall."

The first made her smile. The second made her grin.

"Third, if after all of that, you were still to hypothetically need me, don't worry, Team Frankie and the F-Men will be right there to fuck shit up."

"The F-Men?" The quirky comment did exactly what I hoped, Rachel fell onto the bed next to me laughing. "I fucking love you, blondie. Don't you ever fucking change."

Grinning, I glanced from the screen of the tablet to look down at her. "Well, I'll do my best. But from my experience, adulting sucks, and it ages all of us."

Shoving me over a little, she climbed up to sit next to me. "What are these dates?"

I had a few highlighted on the calendar. "Ian and I are going to plan some appearances, spread out a little so we're not gone for months at a time. Those dates are ones we already have tentatively said yes to."

"This one is in Germany."

Smugness filled me. "I know."

"Germany in September?"

I shot her an innocent look. "Well, it's Octoberfest."

"Uh huh."

"Jake and his dad have both told some funny stories about it."

She continued to eye me.

"We're only there for a week, well ten days, but we padded it with a couple of days on each side so we could sightsee."

"Sightsee."

"Did you know that Paris is only a six-hour train ride from Munich, you know give or take? Like, we can take the night train and sleep, then get to Paris and spend the day. If we have to go back, the night train takes us right back to Munich. If we want…"

Curling her arm around my neck, Rachel dragged me closer to press a kiss to the top of my head. "We should both swear off boys and run away together. I know you like dick and all, but the right strap-on can do wonders."

I snorted, leaning into her hug. "I'm very high maintenance. I would drive you crazy."

She appeared to consider that for a long moment. "Man, it might be worth the crash and burn."

"Nope," I informed her. "It wouldn't. Because I'm needy and if you dumped me, I would have to become a stalker and follow you everywhere just to make sure you were okay."

The corners of her lips twitched. "You make that sound like a bad thing."

It was my turn to roll my eyes. "Okay, let's talk summer and the following year. You should have all the academic credits you need by the end of the second semester to graduate in the States."

"But I'd need at least one more semester there to qualify for their graduation."

"Yep." After she'd let me go, I leaned my head against the wall and studied her. "Or you could have already scored some lucrative job pursuing hot fashion models…"

Rachel made a face. "High fashion models are like a size 0. I prefer to have something to hold onto if I'm going to pursue anyone."

I bit my lip and her eyes narrowed. "I meant pursuing them for your portfolio."

"Uh huh, sure you did." She made a face then stared at her closet and the stacks of clothes. "Why am I doing this again?"

"Because you wanted to go minimalist. Kind of focus on where you are rather than anything else. You also didn't want to take more than two suitcases and your camera 'bags.'"

"Right." She groaned and pushed up from the bed. "Solid plan."

"I'm happy to help."

"You are helping," she said as she walked over to her closet again. "You're gonna keep Little Dick for me, and store my things, underwriting my European vacation—well studi-cation." She glanced over her shoulder. "Thank you, for that. I know that you're the reason I got that grant, but I appreciated how sneakily you did that."

"Couldn't have been that sneaky if you figured it out so quickly."

"Well, you signed your name to it and Archie's and his dad's I think." The look she wore said, "what, was I supposed to not notice that?"

"I solemnly swear, I didn't interfere or influence anything else."

"Just the grant that will cover all my living and travel expenses while abroad and supplement my education fees and visa fees for what my scholarships don't. Oh—and provide me with living accommodations."

"Pretty much."

"You really are spending too much time with Archie."

"Not possible. Besides, according to all of you, my heart is way too big and I give far too much. So, I didn't add like anything for a car or driver service—but I can, if it will be helpful."

I caught the shirt she flung at me. "Oh," I said as I shook it out. "I like this one. Where did you get it?" It was a little big for her, but I loved the band on the front and the shirt itself was super soft.

"It's Dominic's. Keep it. Toss it. Give it to the boys."

I grimaced.

"Nope," she said firmly. "None of that. It used to be his, he didn't get all his shit when I told him to. You like it. Keep it. Otherwise, I'm just donating it."

Now was not the time to bring that up and, to be honest, I didn't want to put her on the spot about him again. Rachel had made her decision. I would respect it.

"I'll keep it." I eyed the pile for donation. The internal argument didn't need voicing aloud. But I could go through all that stuff for Dominic's things then put them aside in case Rachel wanted them later. Rachel never had to know. The worst that would happen is she would finally get over this thing and I'd get rid of the stuff later.

"Whatever you're thinking, don't," Rachel said and I caught her staring at me.

"Actually, what I was thinking was that I'd like you to do a couple of photoshoots with me and the guys before you go."

"Yeah?" She was rolling a few pairs of jeans and setting them in the pack pile. "What did you have in mind?"

"Photos of me, so I can do presents for them later. But I also need some of me and Ian for potential album covers. Then, I'd kind of like to do a day in the life with the guys. Slice of life pics." I grinned. "And if you weren't too objectionable to it, we could lure you into the photos too."

"Slice of life pics?" She eyed me. While, yes, I could be transparent. On this one, I'd practiced my innocent look. Besides, I really did want the pictures for the house. "Artistic? Collage? Poster? What are we going for?"

"Family."

Because we had a lot of little things all over the brownstone. Gifts, photos, and mementoes. After helping Eddie and Archie with Grandpa Ted's things and the numerous photo albums as well as digital displays of multiple pictures over the years.

They'd actually divided some of them up with Archie bringing a couple of albums home. Then he and Eddie began a project of scanning everything in. Not all the photos were even of people they knew, but there were a lot of photos of both Eddie and Archie as kids.

I wanted more memories like that. We snapped photos randomly, but I wanted pics of the guys that I could put up in my room and down on the walls. Family shots we could add to different places.

A flash of the images on the mantel at Hank's place danced through my head. Each time I'd gone up to visit, new photos had been added or had begun spreading out over the living room.

The kids. Me. The guys. Sometimes together, sometimes in singles. There was even one of Jeremy and Miss Abigail. I was pretty sure Chloe and Craig insisted on that one.

Rachel looked thoughtful. "I would love to do that for you, do you mind if I use some—with your approval of course—for my final portfolio for this semester?”

“Don’t you usually do the man on the street or strangers together?”

“Sometimes, this time it’s slice of life or even a day in the life of a person or an individual.” Then she tossed another shirt my way. This one was deep red, with spaghetti straps, and lace.

“Dominic’s?” I teased as I held it up.

The twitching corners of her mouth betrayed her before she began laughing. “Do you have any idea how tempting it would be to Photoshop that on him?”

“Don’t fight the temptation,” I said. “You deserve good memories too.”

That was why we abandoned the packing and spent the next forty minutes with Rachel teasing that red lace shirt and a pair of red lace tap bottoms that matched onto a really nice pic of Dominic. I didn’t ask when she’d gotten one of him in his underwear or in that pose.

She didn’t tell.

Still, by the time she was done, I had tears running down my face from laughing. At her questioning look, I managed to be almost sober in my careless shrug.

“Red’s not his color.”

A rich snort escaped her and she tapped her lower lip for a minute before she went to work again. The red cami and taps turned into a shade of rich chocolate. It looked damn good against his tanned skin.

“Better,” I said. “Guy’s got nice legs.”

“His eyes are up top,” Rachel reminded me with a laughing huff. “You also have enough dick to juggle. Trust me when I say, you don’t want to add him to your harem.”

“Even if I did, I wouldn’t go near him.”

That earned me the warmest of looks. “I love you, too.”

“Cool, love me enough to let me finish helping you sort out this mess before we go find food?” My stomach chose that moment to grumble rather loudly. "Or maybe order some in? I'm starving."

"Go ahead," she told me, waving me toward the closet. "Do your worst. I'll get the pizza ordered." Cell phone in hand, she headed to the door. "I'm also gonna get us some Cokes. Which one of the brother boyfriends is picking you up?"

"Jake," I told her. "He was working late at the aerodynamics lab so he said he'd come by to grab me when he was done."

"Right, adding an extra mushroom, onion, and pepperoni."

Turning to her closet, I grinned. This would go a lot faster if we were both doing it. And I hadn't missed some of the longing looks she'd given various articles of clothing.

Sometimes, memories were just a little too much. So, if I could help buffer that, I was all in. But ten minutes later when she came back into her dorm room with drinks in hand, she paused.

"What's wrong?"

I glanced at her and gave the tiniest of shrugs. "The tears thing is a leftover from the new year, but—I hate the idea of you being so far away. Selfishly, I never want you to leave me and at the same time, I can't wait to hear all about your adventures. Then to come and see you or have you steal away and see us."

Putting the drinks aside, Rachel crossed over to me and wrapped me up in a hug so tight, I shuddered with relief. It had been easier to think about when it had been months away.

Now, we were a matter of weeks and I'd be saying goodbye to my best friend for a year, possibly two. Who knew? If it went well, maybe she never came back.

"You're not getting rid of me," she scolded me. "Texts. Calls. Video calls. Me harassing those assholes you live with and of course, presents, and dirty pictures."

I burst out laughing and pulled back. "Who are the dirty pictures for?"

"Does it matter?" She grinned, a real one this time. One that lit up her eyes and transformed her whole expression. It was easy to forget just how beautiful she was when she was so damn strong and her personality dominated most people's opinions of her.

My girl left an impression.

"No, but I have a feeling if I'm looking at foreign dick pics, we should probably add some boob shots for the guys."

"Very democratic of you."

"Hey, the only underwear they get into is mine. But I'm not going to tell them they can't look."

"Right, they never take their eyes off you so no harm, no foul."

Well, since she put it that way… "Oh, did I tell you? Jeremy took Miss Bradshaw on an honest to god date."

"What?" Rachel swiveled and pinned me with a glare. "You did *not* tell me. Start talking and don't leave out any details." She thrust another shirt at me, male. This one still carried a scent of cologne. Right, into the box. "I can't believe you were holding out on me. You didn't even tell me when Jeremy and Ann went on that cruise."

"Okay, to be fair," I said, moving the shirt to the "take home with me" pile. "That was a gamble, they'd done a lot of talking and tea and visits. Their first official date—or at least the first one he clued us into didn't happen until *after* they got back."

"Accepted," she said after a moment's pause. "Now, tell me everything—oh and let's see if we can swing some of those photo sessions with those two around."

Grinning, I caught her eye and her own smile widened. "I love you."

"I know." She flung another shirt at me. "Damn man leaves his shit everywhere. Now—tell me everything."

Chapter Twenty-Eight
FROM CRADLE TO GRAVE

Coop

"I'm sorry," Frankie called as she jogged up the sidewalk. She'd already texted me four times to let me know she might be late, then she would be late. When a professor asked her to stay behind to go over a project sheet she'd turned in, it had turned into a long discussion on her goals and her work. So, it took her a while to get out of there.

"No worries," I reminded her as I pushed to my feet. I met her at the bottom step, relieving her of the backpack and dropping my lips to hers to steal a kiss. "We are not on a timetable tonight."

"No?"

"Nope." Holding up the backpack, I said, "You need anything in here?"

She laughed, even as she slid her phone into the back pocket of her jean shorts and pulled out a scrunchy from her pocket. "No," she said as she pulled her hair up into a ponytail. "I have my phone and my wallet. Do I need anything else?"

I grinned then shook my head. "Nope, we're keeping it low-key tonight."

Low-key date night. Right, we were all keeping it low-key and hadn't spent about four and a half months planning out the next four days. Totally low-key.

"Oh good," she said with a grin even if her relieved slump of her shoulders betrayed some of her tiredness. "This week has about kicked my ass."

As I set the bag inside, I caught Jake sitting on the stairs inside, leaning forward as though he were trying to catch every word. He mouthed good luck and I resisted the urge to flip him off.

My nerves had been just fine—until he looked at me with such worried eyes. Jackass. This would be fine. Perfectly fine. Completely and totally reasonable and fine.

Closing the door firmly behind me, I glanced down to where Frankie waited. Dressed in denim shorts and a t-shirt, her long legs were starting to get a hint of a tan, though nowhere near as much as we had at home.

She had on the class ring Jake had gotten her, Archie's charm bracelet, and the larimar ring I'd picked out for her on Martinique. They were such a part of her, I didn't always catalogue when she had them on.

Though, I did notice when they weren't there. Descending the steps, I held out a hand to her. She slotted her fingers through mine with the kind of ease and familiarity that reminded me of coming home.

"Telling me where we're going?"

"Nowhere special," I said as we headed toward to the park. "I just wanted some time to be you and me. To play, hang out, and pretend we're the only two people in the world. We used to be good at that."

Her laughter was its own reward. "I think we still are, when we want it."

Swinging our hands lightly, I chuckled. "Does it ever feel weird?"

"Want to vague that question up for me some more?" Her teasing loosened some of the knots in my gut. Right. This was Frankie.

My Frankie. The beautiful best friend who'd made my life better from the day she slugged a kid for me. "Yeah, I suppose that would help. I was thinking, does it ever feel weird that you know, we've been together since kindergarten. Now we're juniors in college, we're all legal—drinking age too."

That earned another laugh.

"We live in another city," I continued. "And for the first time, I just got a job that is not just for bills or dates, but doing what I want to do for the rest of my life." Even while I'd been volunteering at the community center, getting a job there had been kind of a low-level desire I hadn't even acknowledged—until they asked if I'd be interested.

"I think it's amazing," Frankie said, glancing up at me. "I love that you love working with kids. I think you've been the only one of us who has been really secure in who you are and who you want to be. It's impressive as hell."

Well, if that didn't puff me up, I didn't know what would. "You guys all knew, it was just a matter of figuring some things out."

"I've at various times wanted to be a teacher, a singer, a travel agent, a writer...I think I even flirted with lawyer once upon a time."

"You've never flirted with Dominic," I assured her. "He flirted with you but you didn't with him."

There was a downbeat, then an upbeat and she smacked me and I laughed. Sliding my arm around her, I sighed when she leaned into me. It didn't take us long to get to the park, we walked in half-silence for a while.

The occasional comment escaped.

"So, how are your mom and Peter?"

"He's not so bad," I admitted. The man had taken the initiative to reach out to me directly. Still wasn't wild about mom dating, but the guy seemed—all right.

"Wow, and you didn't even choke and die on those words."

"Yeah yeah, yuck it up." Not that it bothered me. "I'm still reserving the right to kick his ass."

"I know," she soothed me, before pressing a kiss to my jaw. "And I promise to help if he really needs it."

"See," I said, keeping our pace aimless even if I knew right where we were headed. "This is why you get me."

"Hey, I'm the girlfriend," she assured me. "But I'm also your best friend. And kicking asses for you is something I am very familiar with."

"Damn," I said with a shake of my head. "That should not be so damn hot."

"Well, I can try to be less hot, I suppose." The curve of her lips was so fucking bitable. I wanted to devour her. Fucking her right here in the middle of the park while the sun was still up probably wasn't the best plan.

Then again…

She laughed and it yanked my brain back up from my cock. Right. We were here for something special. It was late enough in the day that the playground wasn't as active. Sunset was in less than an hour. The weather had warmed up since Frankie's birthday, but not like Texas.

Right now, we'd be sweating if we were back there and we'd debated waiting for a visit home.

Debated it.

Then elected against it.

Our story started there, we'd begun a new chapter in Colorado, another in New York. We'd been turning the pages of this book for a while. I didn't want to go all the way back to Texas to kick off the next cliffhanger in our lives.

Okay, maybe cliffhanger was the wrong word. The anticipation hummed under my skin. "What did the professor say about your project?"

Probably better to change the subject a little. Though, Frankie read my mind and led us over to the swings. She sat in one and I moved behind her. She glanced over her shoulder as I gave her the first shove.

Laughter escaped her. "He loved the project. Thought it had merit."

Good. The guy needed to respect her talent. "And?"

"And… what? It's turned in now and it will be forty percent of my final grade."

"Frankie." It was a warning and a tease. No way that teacher kept her that long for a project that was being turned in and done.

"And," she said, letting the word drag out as I pushed her higher. "He." Each word was like a coin deposited into the slot as she came back. "Wanted. To. Recommend. It. For. Development."

Development.

I grabbed the swing on the last backward pass and held her and it to my chest. She let out a little oof, then grinned up at me. "It's a recommendation and nothing else. Eddie also loves the design of it and the scope. He's already indicated he'd like me to implement it at Standish."

"You really love working there now, don't you?"

"I'm learning," she admitted. "A lot. Eddie's—not a bad guy. I like that I can like him without all the other baggage. Even if the baggage is still out there. So yeah, I do like it."

I took advantage of our position to kiss her and then gave her another shove to get her swinging again. Moving around, I slid into the swing next to hers and got myself going. Then it was a race to see who could go higher.

My heart leapt into my throat when she jumped off at the highest arc, laughing and landed in the grass. A little tumble and back to her feet.

"Eh, you need to stick the landing."

"Beat it."

Oh well, never let it be said I couldn't rise to meet a challenge. I kicked myself higher, and higher. Then leapt. My knees objected to the landing, but I hit my feet and stayed on them.

"Yes!" She danced over to me and threw her arms around my neck.

With the last of the kids who'd been here having gone with their parents, I stole another kiss. This one long, lingering, and filled with the need to just feel her in my arms as she opened to the slow invasion of my tongue.

Lifting her up, I kept stealing little biting kisses as I walked us around the swing set. The slide was at the wrong angle, but it was the closest I could find.

With great reluctance, I set her on her feet and once I was sure she was steady, I backed off one step and then went to a knee.

Her breathless joy faded as surprise rippled over her face. I pressed a finger to my lips as she parted hers. Fuck me, if she didn't trust me and stay quiet.

"I came up with a lot of ways to do this. A lot of different ways to say it. All these plans and ideas—but the truth is… there was only ever one way to do it. The way I did it the first time."

Understanding kindled in her eyes. Pulling the ring out of my pocket, I held it out to her. It was a simple titanium band, adorned with two diamonds and one sapphire. It had cost about three months of the money I'd been socking away, and I would happily have paid a hell of a lot more.

"Beautiful, I love you. No ands, ifs, or buts. No beating around the bush. Will you marry me?" The words flowed right off my tongue.

I WILL ALWAYS FIND YOU

Jake

The night before had been Coop's night. The rest of us made ourselves scarce when they came home. They were out *late*. That had me a little worried. But only a little.

Frankie was ours. She'd been ours forever. I didn't think she needed the ring or the ceremony or even the ritual of it all. But I also thought she'd love it too.

Our girl.

Forever.

I was waiting for her outside of the last class she had before finals started. Who thought this was a good plan to do the week before finals?

Half-tempted to yell at the other assholes for this, I paused without pulling the phone out of my pocket. It had been my idea. Finals itself would be brutal, we had enough trouble making sure she had enough to eat and enough to sleep when she went into grinding for tests mode.

Right after finals, we had to put Rachel on a plane and less than a week later, we were all on the way to Texas for my parents' wedding.

This week? It was the best.

I spotted her before she saw me. She walked out of the lecture hall with a student on either side of her. Barely glancing at the guys as she spoke, she was juggling her books, notebooks and digital tablet to get it all repacked.

They hung on every single word she said. Irritation scraped through me like a match being struck. Those assholes had exactly three seconds to put some space between them and her or I'd take care of it for them.

Brutally.

Even as that annoyance crept up in me, Frankie glanced up. Not to look at the assholes. Nope. Her gaze shot right to mine. She said something else to her audience before she strode straight for me. The pair of panting idiots looked disappointed.

Or they did until they met my stare.

Go. Away. Now.

What do you know? They took off.

Good.

"Stop scowling at Dean and Sam."

Dean and…? "What?" I let out a laugh as I dropped my gaze to her and grinned when she rose up to kiss me. Yeah, there were never enough kisses in the world. "For real?"

"Yeah, they know and they get a lot of ribbing for it. But they are harmless and very much interested in the buxom brunette who is also in our class and doesn't even give them the time of day. I was giving them a couple of ideas for their final projects that are due this week. That's it."

I turned that over. "Hmmm."

"What?" She frowned at me.

I shrugged. "I've seen all the girls that come out of that class. None of them hold a candle to you, Baby Girl." I slid my hand down her back to give her ass a quick squeeze before I lifted the backpack away from her. "The best curves in the city, probably the East Coast. Maybe even the whole country."

To my delight, that got me a damn near frosty look. "Maybe?"

"Well…" I pretended to think about it. "You're here and not there so yeah, maybe the best in the whole country but trust me—wherever you are, the best curves are there."

"Nice save, number sixty-nine."

I waggled my brows. "I never need a save when we sixty-nine, Baby Girl."

Her laughter proved a delightful reward. Despite her earlier distraction, I wasn't getting a single read on her. No idea what she had going on in her head and she hadn't said a word earlier in the day.

Plan, I reminded myself. Stick to the plan.

"No lie, you are the best at that," she murmured before she gave me another kiss. Sure enough, my dick and my chest swelled at that compliment.

Slinging her backpack over one shoulder, I tucked her under my arm. "Ready for our date?"

I couldn't quite read the look she gave me. "You never told me where we were going."

"It's a surprise," I said, making a face at her. She crossed her eyes then stuck her tongue out. "Well," I murmured, sweeping my head down to kiss her. Her mouth softened under the slow invasion of mine and I coaxed that tongue into my mouth to suck on. When she wavered on her feet, I lifted my head with no small amount of smugness. "Don't stick that out at me unless you're prepared to use it."

"Is that a threat or a promise?" The husky note in her voice gave me all kinds of ideas. None of which we could take advantage of, right now.

"Both," I teased, then kissed her again before I turned us toward the doors. "C'mon, we're going to be late."

"Late?"

Despite my comment, I didn't explain it. A car waited for us near the circle. Once we were in, the driver took us up toward the park. Frankie leaned her head on my shoulder as I tangled our fingers together. There was no sign of a silvery colored band with two diamonds and a sapphire.

That was okay.

Even if my gut tensed. Coop hadn't been in a bad mood at all, but he'd just smiled when we asked how it went.

Shoving that thought aside, I focused on us.

At the library, I climbed out first and then held out a hand to Frankie. She gave me a bemused smile as she glanced up at the building then at me again.

"Trust me," I requested

"Always." Zero hesitation or doubt. The earlier smugness I experienced expanded like a warm balloon in my chest. Still balancing her backpack, I guided her inside and then up the stairs.

In the kid's section, there was a guest visiting the library tonight. Dr. James Sebastian. Frankie's eyes grew when she spotted him then she jerked her head to look at me before shooting their guest a look and then back to me.

"Yes, I know," I told her, a thousand percent more confident in choice for the evening. Dr. Sebastian was one of her favorite YouTube personalities. He was a historian and created a lot of programming for kids, but he also did the Pop Culture History Challenge, where he tackled what was and wasn't accurate in historical movies.

We'd seen all of his videos.

A few times over.

Because he was visiting the kids, we took a seat near the back, but Frankie was every bit as rapt as the other kids in the room. In fact, she leaned forward for most of it. Not that I wasn't. The man knew his shit.

When it was over, we lingered while the kids got their autographs and pictures. Finally, when it was our turn, Dr. Sebastian smiled when we introduced ourselves.

"Thank you for coming," he said. "Though I can't imagine this could have been all that entertaining."

"It was amazing," Frankie assured him. "We love all the stuff you do. History really is a favorite of both of ours."

"Well, not going to lie. I love it when adults can enjoy my work too." We lingered for just a few more minutes before letting the man go. Though Frankie got his card and his email address. Fortunately, the dude didn't flirt with her so I could continue to like him.

"That," Frankie informed me, "was amazing! Thank you for coming up with this."

"Wanna go take a look around upstairs? Maybe play in the stacks?"

The fact she wasn't remotely scandalized by the offer, but turned on, if the heat in her eyes said anything, had me skipping the next few steps.

Fuck it.

I slipped a titanium band from my pocket, this one had two diamonds and one pale blue topaz. Frankie went totally still. We were still standing in the kid's section of the library, but it had grown very quiet with everyone having left after the presentation.

Dropping down to one knee, because dammit, we were doing this right, I met her tremulous gaze and I smiled. All the anxiety and nervousness fled. This was my girl. The girl who promised she would always find me.

She always had.

"Baby Girl, the only thing I've ever wanted is you. Forever." I licked my lips before I added, "Will you marry me?"

Chapter Thirty

YOUR SONG

Ian

The ring in my pocket seemed to weigh everything, a leaden anchor that should be visible to everyone. At the same time, if I allowed myself even a moment's distraction, I found myself reaching to check that it was there.

I stood downstairs in the food court. I was half-tempted to take her out like Coop and Jake had done, but there weren't a lot of places that were special to us just because it was a place. Our memories had been made in the quiet moments when she'd listen to me play or offered to sing for me if I coaxed her.

Frankie had occupied a unique place in my heart from the first day I met her. Funny. Smart. Compassionate. Warm. Dedicated. Driven. Those were all the aspects about her that I'd noticed from the beginning. All of that fueled by an impossibly large heart that also hid a darker secret. The need to care for her grew hand in hand with my absolute affection for her.

The best damn friend a guy could have, Frankie had always been something of a dream. The unattainable. The love I held for her, seemingly doomed to be unrequited. Yet, here we were having survived so many mistakes, good intentions or not.

Survived school. Survived bitches who wanted to tear her down. Survived a mother who *did* tear her down. Found ways to work it out with three guys who owned as much of her soul as I did, and would gladly give up their own for her.

From the first time we decided to make this work, all of us committed to making it work—I didn't look back. Loving Frankie meant that I'd be sharing her with Coop, Jake, and Archie. My brother boyfriends well—at least until we became brother husbands.

That was another memory we'd made, thanks to my mom. So many memories.

They'd been made on the back of my motorcycle or in my parents' swimming pool. We had so many memories for so many things but there was one thing that I had done for her that no one else had done.

Something the guys helped me plan, and today was no different. A little coordination and Jake walked Frankie into the food court area before he made like he had to go. His soft kiss to her cheek before he darted out left her a little confused.

My sweet Angel. Two proposals and she'd been floored. The fact we could still surprise her just meant we had to do more work on reassuring her that she was the world for us. Today was my moment, so I gave her a minute to face the room again before I started playing the guitar.

Like a laser, she focused on me and the wonder in her expression, there it was. Like it had been that day in senior year when I played for her in the cafeteria to ask her to go to Homecoming with me. She'd been so red-faced and damn near in tears.

Today, the tears gleamed in her eyes as I crossed toward her slowly.

I'd spent the better part of two months writing this song and making sure she never got a hint of it. This was my surprise. My gift for her.

The gift to coax her into being mine forever.

The tables in the huge food court were almost all filled—students eating, studying, talking, and laughing. To my enormous pleasure, conversations tapered off as I sang to my girl.

Frankie stood frozen in her spot as I reached her. "Be mine," I sang. "Always and forever. Be mine."

A tear trickled down her cheek as her eyes shone brighter and brighter.

"This is my love song for you, Angel. Our song, to dance, make love, live, and share for the rest of our lives." Music was what I knew and sometimes, when words failed me—the notes in the song wouldn't. As the last note faded away, I slid the guitar on my back and then went down to one knee.

Even as awareness of the people around us swelled, movement as students stood. Some held camera phones, others were just straining to see. None of them mattered. None of them. They were just like us, working to get through their lives. But there was no one else here who could touch my focus. Not the way she did. Her soft inhale and teary eyes pulled at me.

"Will you marry me, Angel?" I asked, as I held out the ring in my palm. Like Coop and Jake, it was a titanium band with a pair of diamonds, though mine boasted an emerald. I wanted the green to match her eyes.

Chapter Thirty-One

I THINK I WANNA MARRY YOU

Archie

Three proposals down and one last one to go. Sliding my hands into my pockets, I turned the ring over in my hand, a titanium band with two diamonds and a ruby. The rings were designed to interlink. The diamonds would form an infinity symbol and the gems marked our promise and commitment to *her*.

Coop's and Jake's proposals seemed to have gone well. Bubba's too. Though they'd all asked her to not answer.

Yet.

Tonight?

Tonight was the night she could answer or she could make us wait. I was pretty philosophical about that, surprisingly enough. I'd waited years for her before. I could wait years again. Marrying her though?

That was something we all wanted to do. A commitment we were willing to make. The hows, whats, wheres, etc we would deal with later. A single message to my phone. I knew what it would say before I checked.

It's time.

Closing my eyes, I took a deep breath and squared my shoulders. We'd involved conspirators in this next step. One of whom all four of us had met with that morning. The other—well, she'd been on board with a surprising amount of amusement and affection.

Also, Rachel promised she would tear off and staple our balls and dicks—separately of course—to major landmarks around the world if we ever hurt her.

I could live with that.

The restaurant I'd chosen wasn't quite the Japanese Steakhouse or the fondue places, but it was really lovely. The Greek decor and columns appealed to Jake's love of history. The layout and bright colors had appealed to Coop's need for balance. The fact it had a stage and live music appealed to Bubba's need for theatre and another chance to sing for our girl.

Me?

I just knew she'd love this place. From the huge stone garden that made up the entrance and waiting room, to the fountain in the foyer and the tiles. There was seating upstairs and down. It was huge, while being cozy. Mysterious, while being available. Historical, yet wholly modern.

It was—like Frankie—perfect.

She appeared in the entrance to the foyer with accomplice number one and accomplice number two. The dads—yep, that shit would never not be weird—had swooped in to take her out to dinner. After everything the last three days, there was no way she didn't know I was going to propose.

I liked being her sure thing.

But she had no idea *how* I would propose. Glancing up and to my right, I caught the eyes of accomplice number three. Rachel rolled her eyes with a smirk and then gave a hand signal to someone on the far side of the dais.

The music started and a pair of "waitresses" slipped out from the back to start dancing. Bruno Mars' song was absolutely perfect. Over the top. Ridiculous. Too much.

Like all my catchphrases in one.

Sliding my hands in my pockets, I remained riveted as more dancers came out to join the sudden "flash mob." A soft cry and exclamation from Frankie told me the minute she began to "recognize" the performers.

KC. Yvette. And Aubrey. They'd flown across the country for the chance to do this. When we'd asked, we hadn't intended for them to have to shift their schedules so dramatically.

Right. They didn't care. Here they were.

So were Jake's sisters.

Trina.

Alec. Chloe. Craig.

Okay, maybe we had gone a bit over the top. The dads had backed off to let Frankie watch the whole show being done for her. The moment I moved though, her gaze skipped to me. I smiled as she grinned then covered her mouth with her hands to stare back at the group that kept getting larger.

People from classes. Friends from school. Even Jeremy and Miss Abigail were here, but Jeremy wasn't dancing, even if I did catch him tapping his foot. More and more, some were staff and backup dancers —damn the Torched girls were good—continued to join in.

Five steps from her, I caught her tear-filled eyes focusing on me. "It's going to be great, Babe," I promised. Dropping to one knee, I waited for that moment when the music paused

"From the day I met you—you were the one, Babe. The only one." I didn't have to pitch my voice to get it to carry. It was so quiet with the music off they could all hear me and I was just fucking fine with it. "I love you Francesca "Frankie" Curtis. I always have. I always will." Pulling the ring out, I held it out in my palm. "Will you marry me? Marry all of us?"

Two streams of tears flowed down her cheeks as she stared at the ring then at me. When she dipped her hand into her pocket and brought out the other three rings, I smiled.

With care, I formed them into the right order then slid all of them onto her finger.

"I…" she started but I kissed the rings on her finger and shook my head.

"One more thing…"

"More?"

Shock and delight.

Just like that for the rest of our lives, if I could, I wanted to shower her with shock and delight.

The music kicked off again and lighter than I'd been in a long time, I danced the three steps back to join the rest of them as Coop, Jake, and Bubba came to join us.

We danced, together, and for her, all the while lip syncing the words.

All we want to do is marry you.

Frankie and the boys will return for one final time in Farewells and Forever. To keep up with Heather and all her series as well as enjoy bonus scenes and other content join her reader's group on Facebook:

https://www.facebook.com/groups/HeathersPack/

\

Afterword

I'm not crying, you're crying.

Really, I'm not crying. I'm genuinely laughing. I chortled as I wrote the final words on this book. I said in the foreword that I truly enjoyed the experience of writing this book. I enjoyed seeing so many bits of story and seeds planted so long ago just flower beautifully.

I loved seeing *Frankie* flower beautifully. The lonely girl who began this series with her heart broken and missing all of her friends so terribly while she soldiered on, has grown into a beautiful, vivacious, and complex woman who is capable of enjoying life but also asking for help when she needs it.

The guys, have also grown. They are the brother boyfriends, the best friends, the family they have formed. They look after each other with the same kind of ferocious loyalty they look after Frankie. They rise and fall together.

They talk.

They support.

They plot.

They have fun.

Each of the guys had a semi-pivotal to truly pivotal moment, but the one that actually got me was the reconciliation between Archie and Eddie. I genuinely never thought I'd see this day happen.

Ever.

Yet, here we are.

Then there are all the other supporting characters. Too many to go into now, though I do want to make one note here in case you weren't sure what Coop was talking about when he mentioned that some people are "ace" to Rachel back in their chapter.

That refers to asexual individuals. So, if you didn't know, now you do.

Thank you again for reading, please, leave a review, join my reader group, and pre-order the final book in the Untouchable series.

Thanks for being the best.

xoxo

Heather

Farewells and Forever

Beautiful, I love you. No ands, ifs, or buts. No beating around the bush. Will you marry me?

From the first proposal on the playground when we were five to the one two weeks ago, Coop has always been there for me.

Baby Girl, the only thing I've ever wanted is you. Forever.

Protector. Best friend. Lover. Jake's a part of me in a way I can't define. Even when we were apart, I knew we would find each other.

This is my love song for you, Angel.

Music is Ian's love language. He doesn't just wrap me up to keep me safe from the world, he pulled me into his. He shared his love and the knots that bind our hearts are beyond anything I could have imagined.

From the day I met you—you were the one, Babe. The only one.

Archie's my hero in some ways, he pushes and he demands. At the same time, he savors and teases. He's a builder and a fixer. I had no idea that the day he arrived was the day the last piece missing in my world would lock into place.

Marry us.

My name is Frankie Curtis, the four men I love more than anything else in this world want me to marry them. They want forever.

They want *me*.

**Please note this is a reverse harem and the author suggests you always read the forward in her books. Contains some bullying elements, mature situations, violence, and is recommended for 17+. This is the twelfth and final book in the Untouchable series.*

About Heather Long

USA Today bestselling author, Heather Long, likes long walks in the park, science fiction, superheroes, Marines, and men who aren't douche bags. Her books are filled with heroes and heroines tangled in romance as hot as Texas summertime. From paranormal historical westerns to contemporary military romance, Heather might switch genres, but one thing is true in all of her stories—her characters drive the books. When she's not wrangling her menagerie of animals, she devotes her time to family and friends she considers family. She believes if you like your heroes so real you could lick the grit off their chest, and your heroines so likable, you're sure you've been friends with women just like them, you'll enjoy her worlds as much as she does.

Follow Heather & Sign up for her newsletter:
www.heatherlong.net
TikTok

Also by Heather Long

<u>82nd Street Vandals</u>

Savage Vandal

Vicious Rebel

Ruthless Traitor

Dirty Devil

<u>Always a Marine Series</u>

Once Her Man, Always Her Man

Retreat Hell! She Just Got Here

Tell It to the Marine

Proud to Serve Her

Her Marine

No Regrets, No Surrender

The Marine Cowboy

The Two and the Proud

A Marine and a Gentleman

Combat Barbie

Whiskey Tango Foxtrot

What Part of Marine Don't You Understand?

A Marine Affair

Marine Ever After

Marine in the Wind

Marine with Benefits

A Marine of Plenty

A Candle for a Marine

Marine under the Mistletoe

Have Yourself a Marine Christmas

Lest Old Marines Be Forgot

Her Marine Bodyguard

Smoke & Marines

<u>Bravo Team Wolf</u>

When Danger Bites

Bitten Under Fire

<u>Cardinal Sins</u>

Kill Song

First Chorus

<u>Chance Monroe</u>

Earth Witches Aren't Easy

Plan Witch from Out of Town

Bad Witch Rising

<u>Her Elite Assets</u>

Featuring:

Pure Copper

Target: Tungsten

Asset: Arsenic

Fevered Hearts

Marshal of Hel Dorado

Brave are the Lonely

Micah & Mrs. Miller

A Fistful of Dreams

Raising Kane

Wanted: Fevered or Alive

Wild and Fevered

The Quick & The Fevered

A Man Called Wyatt

Going Royal

Some Like It Royal

Some Like It Scandalous

Some Like It Deadly

Some Like it Secret

Some Like it Easy

Her Marine Prince

Blocked

Heart of the Nebula

Queenmaker

Deal Breaker

Throne Taker

Lone Star Leathernecks

Semper Fi Cowboy

As You Were, Cowboy

Magic & Mayhem

The Witch Singer

Bridget's Witch's Diary

The Witched Away Bride

Mongrels

Mongrels, Mischief & Mayhem

<u>Shackled Souls</u>

Succubus Chained

Succubus Unchained

Succubus Blessed

Shackled Souls (Omnibus)

<u>Space Cowboy</u>

Space Cowboy Survival Guide

<u>Untouchable</u>

Rules and Roses

Changes and Chocolates

Keys and Kisses

Whispers and Wishes

Hangovers and Holidays

Brazen and Breathless

Trials and Tiaras

Graduation and Gifts

Defiance and Dedication

Songs and Sweethearts

<u>Wolves of Willow Bend</u>

Wolf at Law

Wolf Bite

Caged Wolf

Wolf Claim

Wolf Next Door

Rogue Wolf

Bayou Wolf

Untamed Wolf

Wolf with Benefits

River Wolf

Single Wicked Wolf

Desert Wolf

Snow Wolf

Wolf on Board

Holly Jolly Wolf

Shadow Wolf

His Moonstruck Wolf

Thunder Wolf

Ghost Wolf

Outlaw Wolves

Wolf Unleashed